PRAISE FOR *THE DARKEST WEB*

"Taut, suspenseful courtroom scenes and strong, fascinating female characters made me unable to put the book down. A top-notch legal thriller."

—Victor Methos, Edgar Award nominee for *A Gambler's Jury* and 2020 winner of the Harper Lee Prize for *The Hallows*

"Sharp writing and clever storytelling, with two great lead characters. *The Darkest Web* is like a stick of dynamite that, once lit, races toward an explosive and satisfying climax. Kristin Wright is the real deal."

—Chad Zunker, Amazon Charts bestselling author of *An Equal Justice* and the Sam Callahan series

"This is one of those rare thrillers that combines a fast-paced plot that will keep you guessing, powerful characters you can't help but root for, and a richly beating heart that will capture you from the first chapter. Clear your schedule: *The Darkest Web* grabs hold of you and doesn't let go until the end."

—Amy Suiter Clarke, author of *Girl, 11*

"Wright has done it again in the addictive sequel to *The Darkest Flower*. *The Darkest Web* is as disturbing as it is captivating, and this female-driven legal thriller includes all the elements that made Wright's debut so successful, with twists and turns to make any reader consume it in one go, as I did. *The Darkest Web* will have you questioning the benefits of beauty and how well we truly know our colleagues."

—Elle Marr, Amazon Charts bestselling author of *The Missing Sister* and *Lies We Bury*

"*The Darkest Web* is a chilling, heart-gripping thriller that will grab you from the first page until the last. Not only is it a fast-paced legal drama, but it deals with very real trauma and delves into a world so horrifying you can't believe it's real. Kristin Wright is a master of getting into the twisted minds of evil people."

—Lyn Liao Butler, author of *The Tiger Mom's Tale*

"For fans of Liane Moriarty and John Grisham, *The Darkest Web* is an addictive story that hooks you from page one and keeps you riveted through every twist until the very last page. With skilled prose, Kristin Wright has written a sharp legal thriller with heart and complex characters readers will find themselves rooting for. In Allison Barton, Wright has created a strong, smart, relatable main character, and readers will want to devour every book in this masterful series."

—Elissa Grossell Dickey, author of *T he Speed of Light* and *Iris in the Dark*

"Kristin Wright cements herself as a top-notch writer of legal thrillers with *The Darkest Web*, an expertly woven tapestry of brutal murder and secret histories that ensnared me so completely I couldn't stop reading until every strand was unraveled."

—Ron Walters, author of *Deep Dive*

PRAISE FOR *THE DARKEST FLOWER*

"A female-forward courtroom drama."

—*Kirkus Reviews*

"In this enjoyable psychological thriller . . . the author, herself a lawyer in suburban Virginia, writes convincing courtroom scenes and presents the two very different women as fully realized characters. The whodunit remains tantalizingly unclear right up to the surprise ending. Those who like their legal dramas with a light touch will be satisfied."

—*Publishers Weekly*

"A fun—and funny—tale of PTA moms and the small-town lawyer mom whose quest for success leads to a moral dilemma. I found myself laughing out loud at the sociopathic PTA mom, Kira."

—Marcia Clark, bestselling author and iconic former LA prosecutor

"Impressive and intoxicating. The women inhabiting this story are bold, clever, complex, and deliciously thorny—quick to show you what they're capable of if you dare underestimate them. This book is a dark delight, and Kristin Wright is an author I'll be closely watching."

—Margarita Montimore, *USA Today* bestselling author of *Oona Out of Order*

"*The Darkest Flower* is juicy, suspenseful, and wickedly fun. With pitch-black humor, a fresh and engrossing voice, and one of the most fascinating characters I've come across, Kristin Wright explores the toxicity of privilege—and its ability to poison people from the inside out. From its attention-grabbing first line to the chilling revelations of its conclusion, this book is a stay-up-all-night read."

—Megan Collins, author of *The Winter Sister* and *Behind the Red Door*

"In *The Darkest Flower*, Kristin Wright takes the legal thriller to a new level when a PTA mom is poisoned (she survives!) and the main suspect is more venomous than the toxin used in the attempted murder. Dark. Twisty. Unforgettable female leads."

—Cara Reinard, author of *Sweet Water*

"*The Darkest Flower* is a fast-paced legal drama that pulls you in from the first page to the last. Like the best fiction, it is about so much more than the plight of its well-drawn characters and the jaw-dropping reveal, as it challenges you to reconsider your own beliefs about the things that matter most—family, friendship, and truth."

—Adam Mitzner, Amazon Charts bestselling author of *Dead Certain*

"*The Darkest Flower* is as much a riveting legal thriller as it is an exploration of modern-day motherhood and privilege. The story shows exactly what happens when the much-feared queen of the PTA gets accused of attempted murder. I couldn't stop reading."

—Kellye Garrett, author of the Detective by Day series and winner of the Anthony, Agatha, and Lefty Awards

"*The Darkest Flower* unfolds with the sinister beauty of a night-blooming poison. Wright has created a character so compelling in her deviousness that you find yourself reading just to find out what she says and does next. Relentlessly suspenseful, grimly humorous, and sneakily challenging, this twisty portrait of the extremes of motherly ambition will stay with you."

—Elly Blake, *New York Times* bestselling author of the Frostblood trilogy

"A twisty and darkly hilarious ride-along, Kristin Wright's timely thriller skewers the deadly sense of entitlement lurking below even the prettiest of facades."

—Mary Ann Marlowe, author of *Some Kind of Magic* and
Dating by the Book

"Wright's *The Darkest Flower* is a dark, visceral view into the lives of suburban PTA moms. The final twist thrills, leaving you wanting more."

—Roselle Lim, author of *Natalie Tan's Book of Luck and Fortune* and
Vanessa Yu's Magical Paris Tea Shop

"*The Darkest Flower* is a deliciously nasty drama about the dark side of motherhood, with an antiheroine you'll love to loathe and wicked wit dripping from every line. Clear your schedule, because you won't be able to put this one down until you reach the scandalous and oh-so-satisfying conclusion!"

—Layne Fargo, author of *Temper* and *They Never Learn*

"This is *Big Little Lies* if Cersei Lannister was heading the cast of malicious, impeccably groomed housewives. An addictive page-turner with a twist you won't see coming!"

—Michelle Hazen, author of *Breathe the Sky*

"PTA presidents and poison don't usually mix, but they're the perfect blend in Kristin Wright's fantastic thriller debut, *The Darkest Flower*. Wright has created a propulsive legal thriller with plenty of juicy secrets to uncover behind those perfect picket fences. *The Darkest Flower* is *Desperate Housewives* meets *Big Little Lies*, and you won't be able to turn the pages fast enough."

—Vanessa Lillie, Amazon bestselling author of
Little Voices and *For the Best*

THE
DARKEST
WEB

ALSO BY KRISTIN WRIGHT

The Darkest Flower

THE DARKEST WEB

KRISTIN WRIGHT

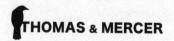

THOMAS & MERCER

Text copyright © 2022 by Kristin Wright
All rights reserved.

Published by Thomas & Mercer, Seattle

www.apub.com

Amazon, the Amazon logo, and Thomas & Mercer are trademarks of Amazon.com, Inc., or its affiliates.

ISBN-13: 9781542026352
ISBN-10: 1542026350

Cover design by Shasti O'Leary Soudant

Printed in the United States of America

To Frank, Austin, and Matthew
for your unwavering belief

Oh! what a tangled web we weave
When first we practice to deceive!

Sir Walter Scott, *Marmion: A Tale of Flodden Field*

PART ONE

BLACKWOOD

CHAPTER ONE

JANE

A police cruiser crawled close, watching as I dug for my key ring outside the office building. I froze, letting my sheet of hair hide my face. *Keep driving. Please.*

I didn't get my wish. The sound of the vehicle shifting to a stop at the curb behind me echoed in the early-morning stillness. His window whirred down. My blood chilled.

The ever-present question, the one that colored every interaction with a stranger: *Does he know who I am?* Adrenaline sped to my muscles for flight. Dampness began to gather in my armpits under my light suit coat. You'd think after all these years I'd be able to remain calm at times like these.

Yet it was always the same.

"Everything okay, ma'am?" asked the cop as I frantically mined the tone of his three words for clues. Did he know, or was he merely bored as his shift neared its end and his bed called his name? "Six is kind of early for work, isn't it?"

I fought the impulse to curl my body toward the door, to keep my face hidden, to ignore him, but he was a police officer, and I couldn't. I had to swallow before I could turn and give him the acknowledgment he would demand. "Yes, it's fine. I get here every day at this time. I'm a lawyer. This is my office." I held up the keys I'd found. "Would you like to see my ID?"

His friendly face—Latino, maybe, or Greek, tired, on the young side—gave no sign of recognition. No suspicion. Nothing but a widening smile as he took stock of me. "No, that's fine. You have a good day, now, all right?"

I waved, giving him a tight-lipped acknowledgment before turning away as quickly as I could. I juggled my travel coffee mug with my keys and got the door open, shutting it behind me and forcing my breathing to slow. *Start again, Jane.*

I had a ritual: before getting out of my car at work every morning, I always checked my pocketbook for my phone, the part of my hair for any problems, and the parking lot for watching eyes. Some people started their days focused on productivity or kindness: I focused on personal surveillance. Checking, first and foremost. Always checking.

The best chance of privacy came just after dawn. When every other lazybones was hitting "Snooze" or home squinting at the coffee measure, they couldn't be staring at me. It had always been worth getting up in the dark for that chunk of time to move through the city unmolested and unseen. My chest got looser when the light was thin and the breeze lifted scraps of refuse in the empty streets. I got so much more done in the mornings when I wasn't being looked at.

No one ever beat me to my desk at the law offices of Blackwood, Payne & Vivant. I dumped my bag in my drawer, slurped my coffee, woke up my computer to sort emails, took one more deep, calming breath, and went off to my boss's office to search for the deposition transcript he'd demanded I summarize for him.

Raymond V. Corrigan Jr. was unfamiliar with the concept of work-life balance. As bosses went, he had his good points—he needed us, he knew he needed us, he appreciated what we did, and he went to bat for us within the firm. He'd give us anything we wanted to keep us from leaving, except leisure time. Ray worked all the hours God sent—he'd told me to find the deposition in a midnight email—and he'd never comprehend anyone who didn't want to do the same.

The powers that be at Blackwood liked to think of themselves as a white-shoe law firm, but here in a branch office in Charlottesville, Virginia, they were a bit distant from both the big-time money and the big-time clients of your New Yorks or Chicagos. Our dusty-rose office chairs and chintz window valances would fit in on an eighties TV show. Our technology lagged about four years behind modern. Our pay hung steady several notches below what my law school classmates made.

I never minded any of that. No one would find me here, in the unmarked Honda Accord of law firms.

Somehow, Blackwood managed to equal the workload and brutality of the biggest of the big firms, but secretly, I was grateful. Hours and hours of work every day kept my mind from going places that would do me no good.

Ray's palatial lair was a floor above my tiny closet of an office. I rounded the corner to his hallway as soundlessly as a tiger stalking her prey—amazing what 1992's best cushioned wall-to-wall could do. Inside his open doorway, I stopped short. The office smelled funny. Off kilter, somehow. I had no idea what it normally smelled like—illicit bottom-drawer whiskey and Pledge, probably—but it had never smelled like this. This was . . . unsterile. A vaguely animal smell.

Against anything that would resemble good judgment, I kept walking, onto the Aubusson rug, past the faux leather armchairs intended for clients, around the desk big enough to double as a pool table.

A black wingtip-clad foot came into view.

The silence disappeared, replaced with a roaring in my ears. All the walls, the hiding places, the surveillance system I'd built so carefully—it was all gone, broken to shards at my feet. There'd be no staying invisible. Not now.

Ray Corrigan stretched out beneath his desk chair, faceup. A shaft of early-summer sun made his sightless brown eyes glitter amber. He had no visible wounds. His skin was still its normal tan from all his outdoor sports. He could have just opened his eyes from a late-night drunk.

Except that he was on the floor.

He wore the same blue tie as yesterday. His suit jacket was twisted, half scrunched under his back, half pulled across his midsection. His eyes didn't blink away the sunlight.

And then there was the blood on the plastic mat under the desk chair and the rug under my feet. One nude heel was already half an inch deep in saturated Aubusson pile.

I had two choices. One: walk out of here and let someone else find him, knowing it wouldn't be long before they'd discover I was the only living soul in the building. I'd be the primary suspect instantly.

Two: call the police and become the person who found him. I'd be the primary suspect, equally as instantly.

The choices were no choices at all. Everyone at this firm knew I got to work early. Everyone knew I fetched things from Ray's office before finishing my coffee nearly every day. My early-morning work habits had already made me the star of this show either way, even when no one yet knew he was dead.

I bit my lip and made myself touch his stubbly cheek—nothing. No movement. No life. Ray was dead and not from a heart attack. He'd been grinning and cursing at me last night from this very desk. He'd been a person.

I'd found him, and now my life would be under a microscope I'd do anything to avoid.

Despite the wreck on the floor in front of me, I gave myself a few seconds before running for the phone at the admin's desk in the hall. I let myself feel it.

Relief. It sang sweet through my veins.

Ray was dead.

Dead men can't spread secrets anymore.

CHAPTER TWO

ALLISON

The clerk spoke too close to the microphone, making me jump. *"Commonwealth versus Hubert Cobb."*

I glanced around. Other than the judge, the clerk, the bailiff, two prosecutors, and me, there was only one person left in the courtroom—a man in his midfifties with a pugnacious set to his mouth who was seated in the gallery. Nobody moved.

"Hubert Cobb?"

Nothing. The man crossed his arms over his chest and leaned back. The effect was vaguely threatening. Oh dear. Courtrooms were as much my workplace as my office, but nonlawyers would do almost anything to avoid them. And rightfully so. I would, too, if I weren't paid to be here.

Most, however, did at least stand up and face the music when their names were called, but unexpected things happened in court all the time.

Judge Turner exchanged glances with the prosecutor, then peered from atop the bench at the motionless man. "Mr. Hubert Cobb. Is that you, sir? We need you to come forward to be advised of your right to counsel. Come forward, sir."

"That's not my name," the man said, standing. "I'm *Herbert* Cobb. You done charged the wrong man."

"Move to amend, Your Honor." Emmett Amaro, the assistant commonwealth's attorney who'd been assigned the case, flipped through his file. "This is the correct defendant. Which he knows, because he answered the summons and showed up."

"No! It ain't me!"

With a sigh, Judge Turner glanced at the clock—close to a lunchtime he'd definitely be late for now. "Fine. Bailiff, would you mind conferring with this gentleman to explain that the commonwealth can correct a clerical error? Mr. Amaro, if you'd give us a second."

Judge Turner glanced at me, out in the gallery awaiting my turn. "Ms. Barton, do you have an order for me?"

"Yes, sir." I went up to the bench with the other prosecutor, Tiffany Ling. She'd agreed to allow one of my clients awaiting trial to leave the state to visit a dying family member. Judge Turner signed the paperwork, and I was on my way out the door.

"Ms. Barton, if you have a second." Emmett stopped me after glancing at the still-arguing bailiff and the idle judge.

"Yes?"

"Are we still doing Libby's piano lesson tonight?" he asked, with a carefully impersonal tone.

"If that works for you. She's looking forward to it."

"Great. See you then."

"All right, Mr. Amaro, bailiff. Mr. Cobb. Let's proceed," said the judge.

Near my hip, for only a second, Emmett's warm fingers slid over and into mine. One quick squeeze, palm to palm, and he was gone.

Outside the courthouse, still smiling, I turned my phone back on, giving myself a second to enjoy the lock screen photo taken several weeks before of my daughter, Libby, in her kindergarten graduation gear. I shouldn't have spent the money for those pictures, but if there was anything cuter than a six-year-old in a cap and gown, I didn't know what it was. My relentless practicality apparently could break, and had, to immortalize her messy hair, missing tooth, and huge, unrestrained grin. No regrets. The picture would give me joy for years.

With a sigh, I walked to my car and opened my email. Back to work, earning the money to pay for photos and all that food and shelter that came in so handy. The message at the top had an all-caps subject line: **MAY NEED CRIMINAL REPRESENTATION.**

And it was from Jane Knudsen.

Jane Knudsen. Good lord, I hadn't thought of her in at least five years. We'd lived together in Copeley as first-year law students at the University of Virginia, assigned as strangers to a suite of two bedrooms connected by a common area. We'd been roommates that one year, but never quite friends.

I'd struggled into law school after a year as a paralegal in a big Washington, DC, firm. I was twenty-two, wore glasses, and hadn't had sex or a decent haircut in three years. Jane walked into orientation dripping mystique all over the august hallways. She had ten pounds of shining raven hair piled high on her head, huge ice-blue eyes framed by dark lashes and perfect makeup, an upper lip so full it equaled both of mine put together, and a body that would make her the envy of any Victoria's Secret model. She wasn't pretty; she was beautiful in all caps.

She wasn't responsible for my already-low self-esteem or the bra-cup size that matched my college grades or the too-thick glasses; she merely made me aware of all those things, excruciatingly so, and constantly, simply by existing near me in a state of sensuality so great it was hard not to stare.

Neither of us knew anyone at law school when we arrived. When we oh-so-gingerly set up our rooms that first night, careful to avoid offense, I had the distinct impression she wished she had a single. Everything I said landed wrong. After that, the mere sight of Jane heated my cheeks with awkwardness, resentment, jealousy, and guilt that unlike my classmates, I hadn't made a lifelong friend of my new roommate. We were pleasant to each other, but that was all. I made other friends.

No one else felt that way about Jane, it seemed. Like many people who display no apparent desire for companionship, she had, almost from the first instant, a horde of classmates vying for the opportunity to get close to her nearly everywhere she went. Half the zip code panted after her: the other students, more than a few of the professors, the administrative staff, even the custodians. All the rest wanted whatever reflected glory they could get by being her friend, even at the arm's length she kept everyone, and those who never got close enough to join her parade spread vicious rumors and gossip. I never knew what to believe. She didn't share anything personal. She walked around as if totally unaware of other people.

Now she needed legal representation? And she'd contacted me. Why? I opened the email.

Allison—

I know it's been a while (ten years since we met, can you believe it?), but I've been with Blackwood, Payne & Vivant in the Charlottesville branch since the bar exam. I heard about your amazing sucess with that PTA client last year, and I'd like to set up a time to talk. I can come down to the Lynchburg area. Can you call me ASAP? My cell is 434-555-4398.
Thanks.

Jane Knudsen

I almost touched the underlined number in the email to call her right then but thought better of it while I was standing in the parking lot of a busy courthouse. Instead, I googled the name of her law firm. She must have mentioned it for a reason.

A local news article popped up. The details were sketchy, but EMS crews had responded to the downtown Charlottesville office of Blackwood, Payne & Vivant earlier this morning and pronounced a person dead on arrival. The victim's name would be released in later updates, after notification of next of kin.

Now my curiosity burned. Had Jane killed a coworker? She'd been so cool and unflappable it was almost impossible to imagine, but people could change.

Back at my office, I saluted my assistant, Maureen, with a wave of my phone. She waved back, the office landline at her ear. At the fridge, I pulled out my packed lunch and headed for my desk.

May need criminal representation, the email had said.

I googled Jane Knudsen while I ate. I'd last seen her in person at graduation, seven years before. If I'd known she'd stayed in Charlottesville after we left UVA Law, I'd forgotten, though a fair number of graduates did. She hadn't grown up there. She was from North Carolina.

Her face, with an oddly unflattering grin, cheekbones to die for, and heavy eyeshadow that made her look simultaneously a decade younger and a decade older than her thirty-two years, appeared next to her legal bio on her firm's webpage. Jane practiced insurance defense law at Blackwood. After seven years, she must be nearing partnership—the first few of my fellow classmates were beginning to announce that milestone on social media. Her name appeared on a couple of recent legal journal articles about insurance law and in a list of Race for the Cure participants a couple of times since graduation. Nothing else.

Odd. How was it even possible to have search results that sparse? Jane had gone to Duke for undergrad. Nobody got into Duke without awards or sports or something, but nothing about Jane Knudsen's high school achievements showed up.

Well. I'd lived with her for a whole year and had somehow managed not to know her at all. I shouldn't need Google. If I'd been a good roommate—even a decent one—I'd have gleaned her whole life history during late-night study sessions. My cluelessness was my own fault. Nothing left to do but call her.

When the last little bit of chicken pesto sandwich was gone, I balled up the plastic bag and tossed it away. I dialed Jane's number, weirdly nervous.

"Hello?"

"Jane?"

"This is Jane. Is this Allison?"

I'd forgotten her voice. Smoky, sexy, the kind a voice-over casting director would love. Somehow a cross between a businesslike Marilyn Monroe and a giggly Kathleen Turner. "It is. I got your email. What's going on?"

"This is privileged, right? All of it?"

"Yes, of course. Even if you don't retain me. You took the same ethics class I did," I said lightly, trying to put her at ease. There was a thread of something like panic in her voice.

"I'm in my car," Jane said. "I'm nearly to your office. I was hoping you'd have time to see me. My phone says I'll be there in ten minutes. Is that okay?"

"Um, sure," I said, glancing at the stacks of personal injury medical records I had to review. She'd already driven ninety minutes south from Charlottesville. "I'll let my assistant know you're coming."

"Great. See you soon."

I alerted Maureen, then took a detour to the bathroom to make sure I had no pesto in my teeth. Nothing like an imminent meeting with the most beautiful woman I'd ever seen in real life to make me more aware than usual of my chapped lips and lack of smoothing hair product.

When she walked through the doorway, glancing behind her, her profile nearly took my breath away. It occurred to me that she must regularly make people uncomfortable. Her eyebrows were bold and symmetrical, her lashes thick without additions, her full lips perfect in nude lipstick. How was it possible to have no flaws? I could feel my self-esteem going on vacation.

Two women who've been roommates should have gone naturally into a hug, but we didn't, awkward a thousand times over by seven years of radio silence and the fact that she'd already told me she needed criminal representation. We sat, me behind my desk and Jane in the client's chair. Jane glanced once at the door to make sure it was closed.

"Tell me what happened. I gather it's dire." I pulled out my yellow legal pad and gave her an encouraging smile.

"'Dire' is a good word," she said. With the same directness I remembered, she plunged right in. "I got to work early this morning. I do every morning, in fact. Today I found my senior partner dead on the floor of his office. Ray Corrigan is his name. Was, I mean. Oh my God, that's past tense." She swallowed. "No one else was around. He'd been shot."

"Did you shoot him?" I asked, doing her the courtesy of bluntness and watching her face.

She let out a brief, mirthless laugh. "No. I didn't." A pause. "I knew you'd ask that. I do remember that ethics class we had. Professor Muniz told us that most defendants will tell the same lie to their lawyers that they tell to law enforcement and everyone else. I can tell you I would never kill someone, that I didn't kill Ray, and you have no idea if I'm telling the truth." Despair flavored her words. It was the directness, more than her poker face, that set off the glimmer of relief: I believed her.

For now, anyway.

"No, I don't know," I agreed. "But that doesn't mean you're not entitled to a defense either way. How do you know he was shot? Did you see the blood?"

"When I found him, there was a pool of blood under him, but *he* looked fine otherwise. Dead, I mean, but with no obvious wound. I called for help, and when they loaded him on the stretcher, I saw . . ." She blanched. "There was a red spot here," she said, pointing at the bottom of her rib cage to the left side. "His suit coat must have covered it up before."

"Where was he when you found him?"

"In his office, partly on that plastic thing you use to roll a desk chair on so it doesn't damage the rug. Behind his desk. His desk chair was pushed back a good distance. The blood was mostly in the rug, but there was some on the plastic. His head was only a foot or two from the chair roller. I didn't see him from the doorway."

"Did you call 911?"

"Yes. And went to let them in, and showed them where he was."

"This was before the firm opened?"

"Yes. Around 6:15. This morning."

I remembered a girl who'd skipped Civil Procedure at least once a week because it started at eight. "Damn, Jane. Must be partnership time."

She flushed slightly. "Well, yes. It is. But I like the morning. Now, anyway. I always get to work around six. Like clockwork."

I needed to guard against thinking I knew her. This little change was a reminder that seven years was a long time. "Does everyone in your firm know that?"

"I'm famous for it. The cleaning crew goes through every night at around nine. Anyone who had access to that office after they're gone would know I'd be the first person to find him."

"Well, who else had access? How many in your firm?"

Her brow wrinkled. "There are seventeen lawyers. One is out on maternity leave. Then the support staff. They all have keys, too. And the cleaning staff, obviously. Possibly the building owners. Some security guards. A lot of the partners let their spouses have access to their keys. And before you ask—the keys are the old-fashioned metal kind. There's no electronic record of who used them. It's not exactly Fort Knox."

"Don't worry. I won't tell your clients."

She gave me a weary smile.

"Do you have reason to believe you'll be a suspect?"

She let out a sharp bark of laughter. "You mean besides the fact that being convicted of murder is the one piece of shit luck my life was missing to reach the pinnacle of horrific?"

The bitterness surprised me. I'd never seen any sign of it in law school. Reserve, yes. Bitterness, no. And since when had Jane had anything resembling a horrific life?

"Sorry," she said, collecting herself. "I don't practice criminal law, but I've watched enough TV to know the person who finds the body is always suspect. My shoe is literally covered in his blood from the carpet. And . . ."

"And?" I prompted, waiting for her.

"And he was my boss, and a well-known asshole."

"In what way?"

"In the law-firm-partner way. He supervised three associates. Our average billing last year was three thousand hours, each. Nearly sixty hours a week, fifty-two weeks a year. That doesn't include the non-billable hours we worked, and there were plenty of those. Besides being demanding, he was a dick. Unpleasant. Insulting. Occasionally drunk and insulting."

She bit her lip. I waited.

"He wasn't one hundred percent awful all the time. He was loyal to his associates. To me. He valued our work and didn't rat us out to the partnership for minor stuff. That said, his bonus was tied to the amount of money the group he supervised brought in, so keeping us working as many hours as possible, no matter what, directly increased his income."

"Would anyone else have a motive to kill him?"

Another bark. "Honestly, the list might be shorter if I told you who *wouldn't* have a motive to kill him. Let's see. I'd imagine the managing partner, who took home seven figures last year because of all those billable hours, probably liked him pretty well. Ray's got a daughter who just graduated from UVA Law and worked at the firm last summer. She still calls him Daddy, and I don't know of any reason she'd dislike him. Who else? Hmmm. Can't come up with any more possibilities, except maybe people on another continent who've never met him."

"Oooookay, then," I said, chuckling. "I get the idea. Did he have only the one child?"

"Yes. Brittany. She'll be leaving for her job in DC after she takes the bar exam in a couple months. She might know something, though. She was well liked when she worked here."

"Is he married? I notice you didn't have a wife on the list of people who wouldn't want to kill him."

"Felicity. I'm not sure which list to put her on. They've been married forever, and she's managed not to kill him in all that time, but they're not exactly . . . close. He bitches about her. She barks orders at him. She has some kind of interior design firm, I think. A year ago she redid his office." Jane's eyes went wide. "Maybe the firm will call her in again. That Aubusson rug she spent so much time picking out looks like the floor of a slaughterhouse now."

She clapped a hand over her mouth. The hysteria that made frequent appearances in witnesses to crimes bubbled out as a terrible giggling. "Oh God. I'm going to be convicted of this crime. I need to be muzzled."

"It's okay, Jane. You saw something awful today. Seeing someone who died violently can mess you up."

A single hiccup escaped before Jane got control of herself.

"Do his wife and daughter have keys?"

"I assume they'd have access. Or he could have let them in. He told me when I left work last night that he planned to work late."

"Did you go straight home?"

"Yes."

"Do you live with anyone?"

"No. Just me."

"Did you get online at home? See or call anyone? Order food? Anything we could use to demonstrate you were somewhere other than the office when Ray was killed?"

"No. I don't live far. I just went straight home to bed."

Probably no alibi, then. Somehow the fact that she lived alone surprised me, and didn't, at the same time. In law school, she'd always been so highly desired, yet clearly preferred to be by herself.

"When did you leave?"

"Around nine thirty or ten." She went quiet. Hair rose on the back of my neck.

"You said the cleaning crew comes through at about nine. Did you see them?"

Her perfect cheekbones darkened. "Y-yes. They came through. And then left."

"And you were still there after them? Were you the last person in the building other than Mr. Corrigan?"

"It's possible there was someone left on the second floor." From her expression, she knew better than that.

"But you don't know? Is there a chance you were the last person to see him alive?"

She sat back in her chair as if I'd hit her. "No. Absolutely no chance."

"How can you be sure?"

"Because when I came in this morning, he was dead. His killer was the last person to see him alive. And I didn't kill him."

CHAPTER THREE

JANE

In seven years, Allison hadn't changed in any noticeable way. Still the brown, utilitarian hairstyle. Still the slight figure that would never put on weight no matter how many sugar cookies she ate. Every time I passed through a grocery store bakery section, I thought of her. When we lived together, she used to buy sugar cookies from Kroger in fresh-baked packs of twelve a couple of times a week and eat them like calories weren't a thing. How I'd envied her metabolism. In law school, she'd looked like a high school student. Now she might pass for twenty-three, and she was the same age as I was.

Sugar cookies still tasted like judgment to me, though.

That sure hadn't changed. How she used to sit there in our shared common room, hunched at her desk with her casebooks, *looking* at me. Oh, she never said anything. She never criticized or tried to microman-age me. She tolerated me with a polite smile, like I was a visitor, even though we breathed together in the same suite in the dark going to sleep every night. I'd known she was judging me. After we weren't roommates anymore, she abandoned even the politeness.

She didn't believe I hadn't killed Ray. I could see it in her eyes—the judgment, just like before. I'd never told her any of the important things about myself, but I still woke in the middle of the night that whole first year, heart pounding with the certainty that the look in her eyes was worse than judgment: knowledge. Terrified that she'd plucked all my secrets out of my mind to watch like a movie at her leisure.

Terrified that she knew.

Allison Barton was an almost-famous criminal defense lawyer now, and given that I had enough of a connection to get in without an appointment today, she'd been the obvious choice. The only choice. She got that woman who poisoned her PTA friend off last year. The case had made CNN when it went to trial. The acquittal was in the *Washington Post* and all the state papers. Our alumni magazine had a nice write-up about her. She'd started her own firm and been named to some statewide "Best Lawyers Under 40" list.

I didn't need friends, and I could deal with suspicion and judgment. I'd felt them like a heat lamp on the back of my neck nearly all my life.

I tossed my hair over my shoulder. "I'd like to retain you. Hourly, for now. I'm sure we could negotiate a larger fee if I need you to defend me, but for now I'd feel more comfortable if you were with me when— and I do mean when—they call me in for questioning. I know insurance law backwards and forwards, but I know only enough about criminal law to be certain of all the ways I can be screwed over. Do you have a schedule of fees?"

"I do," she said, going into a drawer for a paper, then sliding it across her cluttered desk. A memory flashed of her messy half of the suite. Notes and papers everywhere. Some things never changed. I glanced at it and caught sight of her hourly rate, which was a lot lower than mine.

She waited for me to meet her eyes. "I'll represent you, and I'll need a five-thousand-dollar retainer to start off with. I'll take the hours out of that until it's gone, and then bill you. If you're charged with any crime and would like me to continue representing you, I'll need you to pay what is due plus whatever retainer on that schedule matches whatever crime you're looking at. Does that work?"

I scanned down the list to the bottom, where she had a very large dollar amount next to "Murder/Rape/Capital." I spared a half-hearted prayer to the God who'd deserted me that I would never need to write that check and pulled out my checkbook to write the smaller one.

We were in business.

꙲

Unsure where to go, I went where I always did—work. I was comfortable where I had tasks to distract me. By the time I got back to the office around four that afternoon, the managing partner had negotiated with the law enforcement people who'd swarmed the entire building earlier in the day and gotten most of the firm back to work. My lowly first-floor office was far enough away from the second-floor crime scene as to be unaffected. Several of the staff with workstations too close to Ray's office had been given temporary seats and laptops in the conference room next door to me.

Law firms never stop working. Time is income. In my first weeks of law school, one of my professors told a story about how he'd been working in a law firm in the World Trade Center on 9/11. He'd made it out of the building, hiked uptown in clouds of dust, and was billing clients again by that evening. I remembered sitting next to Allison that day and exchanging looks of mild terror.

After seven years of practice, that story was surprising only because it was hard to believe a lawyer would actually have quit billing long enough to escape.

Irene Robinson jumped up the second she saw me and planted herself in my extra office chair. She'd worked at Blackwood as an admin since she finished high school nearly twenty-five years before. As technology advanced, lawyers could do more and more work without an assistant. When she'd been hired, she'd worked only for Ray. Once the firm began expecting its lawyers to type for themselves, he'd had to share her with me and the other senior associate in our department, Josh. Like all other people, she might turn on me at a moment's notice. For now, though, she was as close to a best girlfriend as I'd had in years.

"What. The. Frack," said Irene, her brown eyes wide. No sign of grieving, but there wouldn't be. If Ray worked late, he expected Irene to work late, and often with no more than ten minutes' notice. Ray, at fifty-four, remembered a time when lawyers still dictated letters and their admins' lives. When they'd barked orders to "underlings," dumped absolutely as much as possible on their low-paid shoulders, and expected them to handle dry cleaning, lunch acquisition, airline tickets, difficult messages to wives, and even clothing changes when coffee got spilled. Irene had seen some shit.

I melted back in my seat and closed my eyes. "I'd give a lot of money to get a redo on this day. I'd call in sick."

She waved that away like so much nonsense. "Uh, no, ma'am. Then I'd have had to find him."

"I can't make the image of him on the floor go away. I keep thinking I might have to locate a liquor store tonight."

"Who did it, do you think?" she asked, a hand pushing her luxurious curls away from her eyes.

"For a second I wondered if he might have done it himself," I said.

"Nope," Irene said. "Don't most gun suicides shoot themselves in the head? They do in the movies. But nah. He was too mean to kill himself. He would have had to realize he'd be doing everyone a favor, and he would have hated that."

"Irene. Shhhh! Don't let them hear you saying that. God."

"You know everyone here is thinking it. Even Greg," she said, naming the managing partner. "Me, I feel like I just won a trip to Disney World."

"Irene!" I glanced at my doorway, wishing as always that the door were closed. "And what are you talking about? Greg loved Ray. Our group brought in millions in billing."

"Yeah, but Greg is no dummy. He knows it's you and Josh and Amir, not just Ray. Not even mostly Ray."

"Mostly you. You do all his work."

She didn't bother to deny it. "And Ray drove away associates. Hurt recruiting. There was that boy, couple years ago, you know. The one from Yale Law. They thought we'd be moving on up, with Yale on our bio page. Then Ray kept him here all night that time. Turned out he missed his brother's bachelor party. Remember? Kid took a job in DC right after."

"I remember."

"He got called on the carpet for that. They'd begged that one to take a chance on our firm." A comfortable silence fell.

I stretched out the tense place in my back. It was tense all the time, but usually I could ignore it. "So you're saying that the possible suspect pool includes Greg. Along with me, Josh, Amir, you, Ray's wife, the Yale Law guy who missed his brother's bachelor party, every associate, past and present, who's ever worked for him, all the partners, and basically anyone who's ever met him at all?"

"Yep, that about sums it up. You can go ahead and include C. J. on that list. He's told me a million times when I got home late he'd either divorce me or kill Ray. I guarantee he's been dumb enough to joke about that to someone else over the years."

I turned that over in my mind for a while, unable to imagine Irene's easygoing husband swatting a fly, let alone shooting her boss in his office in the middle of the night. "No. They're going to pin it on me. I found him."

"Or me," she said calmly. "I'm the long-suffering Black assistant who's heard one too many racist remarks."

My throat felt tight. For a second I wondered whether she was trying to get me to admit to killing Ray. Our casual work friendship would go straight under the bus if they came sniffing too close to her and her family. She had three kids in elementary school to protect and was the family breadwinner besides.

Irene had no idea whether I was innocent. No one who wasn't in the room when a bullet hole appeared in Ray Corrigan's stomach could be certain. She knew damn well I'd had the opportunity. The next silence wasn't so comfortable.

My phone dinged with an incoming email from our managing partner. Phones went off at all the temporary workstations in the next room as well. A mandatory staff meeting at five o'clock in the main conference room, no exceptions.

I should not have come back to work today.

When the time came, people got to their feet and herded into the opulent room. Someone had lined the walls with chairs as well—it was unusual for all staff to attend a single meeting, and the table didn't accommodate everyone. But then it was also unusual for one of our number to be discovered having bled out on a ten-thousand-dollar rug.

When I was young, I went to church in a small clapboard box in the North Carolina hills. Without discussion, every family sat in the same pew week after week. Nothing was different here in this conference room. I took my accustomed seat about midway down the table, next to my best friend and fellow Ray-terrorized associate, Josh Gardner.

I hadn't seen Josh all day. He ran a hand through his sandy hair and greeted me with wide eyes. There'd been a touch of heat in the way he'd looked at me the last couple of months since his divorce went through, which was new for him. As I sat, he gave me a comforting pat on the upper arm. Touching had increased lately, too. Within the last week, I'd admitted to myself that I might like it.

"Holy shit, Jane," he whispered into my ear. "What the actual hell? Amir said you found him. Seriously? Are you okay?"

He was the first—the very first—person to ask if I was all right. An unexpected tear burned in the corner of my eye.

"Yeah, I'm fine. Shhh," I said, gesturing at Greg, who was holding up a hand to silence the room. A newish associate whose name I hadn't learned stared at me from the other end of the table. I fought the urge to run.

Greg Dombrowski stood at the head of the table, his curly hair standing even taller than usual. Most of the other senior partners had taken their places in the seats closest to him. Ray normally sat immediately to his left, but the chair remained empty.

"Ladies and gentlemen, thank you all for being here. As I'm sure you're aware, we've suffered a terrible loss. Ray Corrigan died this morning from what appears to have been foul play. The police have been here most of the day securing the crime scene and will likely want to talk to those of you who knew and loved Ray."

An uncomfortable shifting rippled through the room, catching Greg's attention. He knew damn well that no one loved Ray. His error cost him a bit of momentum. "Or those of you who worked closely with him. We've advised them that we will not make any employee available unless the request comes through me. You'll be notified to come to my office should that be necessary. We all want to get to the bottom of what happened to Ray, while at the same time continuing to serve our clients. On that front . . ."

I stopped listening as Greg went on about the reassignment of Ray's cases to a partner from another department who'd agreed to come back from maternity leave early and the IT issues that had popped up for those who'd been moved away from Ray's office. He closed with a rousing call for more hard work and billable hours. His last words before dismissing us were literally, "The show must go on!"

Which, when I thought about it, was perhaps not quite the way our clients would prefer to view our work.

As everyone shuffled out, Josh touched my elbow and murmured, "Would you mind going out for a drink? I have a theory I want to float."

"About Ray?"

"Yeah."

"Um. Sure." We'd eaten lunch many times, but something about a drink felt different from anything we'd ever done before. I was probably overthinking it, though. Ray's murder was a topic that couldn't be discussed at work, and no doubt it took up all the real estate in his mind, as it did in mine.

"At Claude's? On the mall?" Charlottesville had closed off a nearby street to traffic decades before, and many of the best bars and restaurants in town hosted happy hours along it.

"Sure. Claude's it is." I wished I could say something positive about Claude's, but I'd never been there. New places were full of new people, and I never went anywhere after work other than home. I spent fourteen hours or more a day inside the offices of Blackwood, Payne & Vivant and avoided any social life at all.

I met Josh in the lobby ten minutes later. My inbox groaned with unanswered emails, but sparing an hour this once wouldn't hurt anything. Especially when this day had begun with me discovering my boss half-submerged in a pool of his own blood. A sense of disorientation overtook me. Had it been less than a day?

Josh slung a leather messenger bag over his shoulder and grinned, a clear sign that for him, the workday was over. When he'd been married, he'd been in the habit of cutting out around six or seven each night, but lately he'd been working longer. Married lawyers were given a bit more leeway, at least at Blackwood, and parents even more. Singletons like me were prized; we were perceived as having nothing better to do and were always the first to be asked to do the late-night/last-minute things.

The day Josh had seen proof that his then-wife, Miriam, was cheating on him, I found him at his desk after hours. He wept like something essential had broken. Though I normally kept to myself and tried not to get involved in other people's personal affairs, even I, with my heart of ice, couldn't ignore actual tears streaming down the cheeks of the person I spent most of my waking hours working alongside. He'd apparently hired a private investigator, who'd sent indisputable evidence that, indeed, tiny Miriam was having sex with a hulking grad student in her department. The photos were on his phone and he handed it to me without asking. I caught flashes of skin and body parts that wouldn't sort themselves into a recognizable whole—nor did I want them to. I got him a cup of water and a box of tissues and waited out his desperate grief until he could drive home safely.

The following weekend, Miriam, a psychology professor, moved alone to Ann Arbor to start a new job at the University of Michigan. Josh went on a solo vacation elsewhere. When he came back, he brought his billable hours way up. He never said another word about Miriam, even while the divorce proceeded.

We'd become friends—platonic friends, though I'd be lying if I pretended I hadn't noticed that he had nice shoulders and a head of thick, shiny hair. And kind hazel eyes behind his glasses. More than once I'd looked up from my work across a conference room table to find those eyes on me. Normally I hated eyes on me, but Josh's had no hint of recognition in them. No knowledge of what I was.

It had been a while since anyone who'd actually bothered to have conversations with me first had looked at me like that—full of ordinary desire. Most men started with attraction and never moved past it to conversation, not with me, anyway. I didn't date much—at all, really.

We were lucky enough to get a table for two without waiting. If there's anything more awkward and uncomfortable than trying to find something to talk about after sitting down at a table for two with someone you find attractive, I don't know what it is.

Our drinks arrived and I took a grateful sip, forcing myself to meet his eyes. Why did everything feel so different with a glass of wine in my hand? "So? You have a theory?"

He chuckled. "You're eager. In a hurry?"

"I'm curious. And I probably should get back to work, so, I suppose, yes. In a hurry."

"Jane. Our boss died today. Everything is going to be a complete clusterfuck for at least a week until they get all the cases reassigned to whatever-her-name-is. I think you're okay taking one evening off. Drink up."

Somehow, my glass was empty. I didn't drink often. Hangovers don't improve billable-hour totals, but if I didn't deserve to get drunk today, then I never would. Josh signaled the server, who refilled my glass as I reflexively hid my face with the fall of my hair. "Okay. I won't go back to work," I said, feeling a little spurt of unfamiliar recklessness, and disgust at myself for how cowardly I'd become.

"I'll tell you my theory if you agree to relax. You need to give yourself a break more often."

I slumped into my seat as if my spine had turned to jelly. "See? I can relax. Now spill."

Josh laughed and then turned serious. "Okay. I think it was Ray's wife."

"Felicity?"

"Yeah. Felicity. She hates him."

Felicity Kim, a woman who'd bucked the odds and managed to hang on to her first and only husband even after he got rich, had never seemed particularly warm and fuzzy toward him. Then again, Ray didn't give people a lot of reasons to act that way. Felicity had gone back to using her maiden name about five years before, but I'd always assumed that was because her interior-decorating career had taken off around that time. I knew from Irene that Ray canceled large and small plans with her, using Irene as the bearer of bad news. When Felicity did get him on the phone, he'd been known to yell at her and hang up. We all knew he drank too much, even at work, and that had to be worse at home. When he was drinking, he got red in the face, twice as profane as when he'd started, and prone to errors of judgment.

On the other hand, they still lived together. Felicity wouldn't have been without resources if she'd divorced him, so maybe he wasn't too bad. She stopped by on occasion to meet him for suppers or other personal errands. No one would describe her as enraptured with him, but not many marriages were notably romantic when they'd lasted nearly three decades.

I chose my words carefully. "Um. I mean, I don't know that she likes him that much, but what makes you think she hates him more than anyone else? She doesn't look like a killer."

Josh gave me an exaggerated side-eye. "Uh, I don't think killers ever look like killers. Anyone can shoot someone. You could do it."

My throat closed. Was he asking? Did he expect me to volunteer I'd done it?

This was the second time today someone had hinted I could be capable of it. Third, if I counted Allison outright asking me whether I'd done it.

The worst of it was that their personality assessments weren't far off. Everyone had secrets.

He continued as if he hadn't dropped that bomb. "Ray's got quite the firearm collection at home, and he's got that handgun in his desk drawer. I bet you dollars to doughnuts that when they do the ballistics, they find out he was shot with his own gun."

"Did they find the gun that killed him? I don't remember seeing one lying around, but then . . ." All I could see in my head was the saturated red rug, so it was possible it had been there and I hadn't noticed.

"No idea."

"Even if you're right, what's her motive? Looks to me like if she were going to kill him, she'd have done it long ago. I bet *you* dollars to doughnuts he's been the same old Ray for thirty years, too."

Josh raised a glass to me in appreciation of the wordplay and slid his chair a little closer for more privacy. His voice rumbled low and intimate in my ear. "True. But . . . one day last week they had a major blowup."

"How do you know?" I looked around, but both tables near us were empty. Our server had forgotten about us.

"Because I was in his office the whole time. He called me in to talk about the Avalon depositions, and she phoned and he got into it with her. Every time I tried to get up and leave to give him privacy, he waved me back into my seat like he'd only be another minute."

"How do you know it was her? And what did they fight about?"

"Oh, it was her. He was yelling—you know, the way he does, where his face turns all purple? He went on about how he was sick and tired of hearing about her interior designing, and it was damn well past time for her to pay attention to her own house rather than other people's, and on and on. Some touchy incident about how she'd bailed on a client dinner because of something to do with her work, and then he screamed that she 'knew what she did' and if things didn't change 'right the fuck now' he'd leverage some cosigns or pull financial backing or something and she'd suddenly have the time she needed to attend to what mattered."

Wow. That was both awful and totally expected. Ray was so addicted to the high he got from moneymaking that family affection couldn't compete. He handed over money to his wife and daughter and thought it substituted for love. I didn't find it hard at all to believe that he would shut his wife's business down if it wasn't convenient for him. And he bellowed *right the fuck now* so often it was nearly a catchphrase. As a motive for homicide, however, it was weak sauce.

"No way," I said, shaking my head, which felt woolly and slow. Either the wine or Josh's nearness was affecting me. "I mean, that sounds like Ray, but that's kind of the point. That's not new behavior. He's been acting ugly as long as I've known him. Felicity has stayed with him. Why would she snap and kill him?"

Josh touched my hand and lingered in a decidedly non-platonic way, changing things between us. It had been so long since anyone had touched me this way that I couldn't decide whether the increased speed of my heartbeat was good or bad. I forced myself to let it beat. "I might have thought that, too—if I hadn't seen her the next day, digging in his office desk drawer while he was in Richmond at a meeting."

"Which drawer?"

"The one where he keeps the gun."

CHAPTER FOUR

ALLISON

My email dinged as I dashed to the door of North Noble Elementary School. Dashing had become a habit and not a good one—I was always one of the last parents to pick up my child from the summer day-care program. Libby did not appreciate it and let me know about it. Having completed kindergarten had given her a bit of attitude.

Today was clearly one of the days she'd be nursing a grudge. When I waved from the sign-out area, she gathered her things extra slowly, lower lip stuck out. If she saw me looking at my phone, she'd get even more upset, so I waited until her back was turned. Jane had sent an email—a long one, it seemed—titled **List of Suspects**. Interesting, but I had no time to skim it. I stuffed the phone in my bag just in time.

"Mommy! Liam's mom picked him up *hours* ago! I hate being last!"

"You're not last," I said, gesturing at the table where three other kids with more delinquent parents than hers colored. "See? Josie Cartwright is still here."

Libby rolled her eyes like a jaded Instagram influencer. "Josie's mom is a *doctor*."

I absorbed that blow as I took Libby's backpack and herded her toward the car. "Nice, buddy," I said, mostly amused and partially annoyed. "As if doctors' jobs are so important that they can be late and I can't?"

She stared at me as if I were slow. "Doctors save lives. Lawyers don't."

She had me there. "Oh, I see where I rank. Well, unfortunately you're stuck with me. In you go. Buckle up."

She stood there, looking miserable. I opened her door and rubbed her head, gently urging her into the car.

"What else is wrong, buddy?"

"Olivia is mean. She wouldn't let me be at the front of the line. I put spit on her backpack."

Oh dear. Spit on a backpack. It had been, as always, a long day, but this was a crisis second to nothing to a six-year-old. "Okay, first of all, it might not have been your turn to be at the front of the line. And if you mean that you spit on Olivia's backpack, that was wrong and you shouldn't have done that."

Libby buckled her car seat, moving like an old woman. It never took much to feel on the outs of the social circle, and it hurt. I leaned in and hugged her. "Tomorrow you need to talk to Olivia. Friends are important, and she's been a good one. Maybe she was having a bad day."

Libby made that You'll Never Understand face I remembered well from my own youth.

"Guess what I did today, Liberina?" Because of client confidentiality, I'd never been able to tell her much about what I did, beyond the general "help people with problems." An idea had occurred to me.

"What?"

"I saw an old friend," I said, improvising and changing the details enough to get the point across. "We stopped being friends long ago because, well, because I was mean to her once."

"What did you do, Mommy?" Libby asked, her eyes wide.

"I didn't do what I should have done to make sure she knew she had friends back then," I said, trying for that teachable moment with Libby. Guilt washed over me. Teachable moment, indeed, but who for?

"Was your friend lonely? Because she didn't have friends?"

A direct hit to the solar plexus. No one ever tells you how very often parents learn more from their kids than the other way around. "Yep, buddy. I think she was lonely. She must have been. And I shouldn't have let that happen. We girls need to have each other's backs, don't you think? Like you, with Olivia."

She nodded solemnly. "Are you going to fix it? Are you going to be friends with her now?"

"Yeah, Lib. I'm going to fix it." As the words came out of my mouth, I knew what I had to do. Jane wasn't just another case. I owed her more than legal services. "Now, you ready to go to Emmett's house for dinner and your piano lesson?"

God bless six-year-olds. All the gloomy clouds of injustice lifted. Few places could put Libby in a better mood than anywhere there was a piano.

❧

I'd known Emmett Amaro exactly the same length of time I'd known Jane Knudsen—I saw them both the first day of law school, in an auditorium full of anxious first-year students clutching packets of information to our chests like security blankets. We'd started off as friends; I'd met my now ex-husband, Steve, not long after, and Emmett had met . . . a lot of women. After graduation, we eventually ended up about ninety minutes down the road from our alma mater and facing off in the county courtroom, me on defense, him at the prosecutor's table. Our last case together had been the big one we tried last fall—an attempted murder charge against my client, the PTA mom Jane remembered. I won, but by then, Emmett and I had agreed we'd prefer to kiss rather than yell "objection!" at each other from opposite counsel tables.

That was seven months ago. We'd been seeing each other ever since, but not without some bumps in the road. Libby's father had gotten remarried recently and had an overdeveloped—and unwelcome—sense of entitlement about Emmett's involvement in Libby's life. Steve's wife, Karen, had a lot of opinions about "innocent children" witnessing "inappropriate and confusing" behavior by an unmarried parent. This was an especially precious viewpoint because Steve had destroyed Libby's two-parent home by cheating on me—with Karen. Now, however, she was pregnant, had joined a church, and decided to remake herself in the image of the Mother of God, apparently.

Libby had been watching me like a CIA agent on a sting operation for any evidence she wasn't first and foremost in my life ever since she'd been a flower girl in Steve and Karen's wedding. She was needy for attention. My complete attention, to be specific. She punished me for every night I had to work at home. Every morning I woke her up in too much of a rush to cuddle her. Every stray glance toward my constantly dinging phone. Every minute with Emmett.

Given all that, I'd put my romantic life on a low boil on the back of the stove and felt guilty in every direction. Libby couldn't seem to decide from one minute to the next whether she adored Emmett or wanted to execute a permanent block. Karen smirked every time Emmett rode along when I took Libby to Steve's. The doors of the Juvenile and Domestic Relations courtroom, where custody battles played out, haunted my nightmares.

It had occurred to me I might love Emmett. There was nothing tentative about my love for Libby, though, and it had to come first. I would walk through fire for her. Sometimes, late at night when I couldn't fall asleep, I scared myself at the thought that there were no limits on what I would do if someone hurt her. Emmett would have to fit into that framework; the framework wasn't changing for him.

He greeted us at the door, and I waited for Libby to head for Emmett's huge fish tank before I let myself sink into his arms. He kissed me. "I've got fried chicken. Figured we could eat before Libby's lesson?"

"Sure," I said, dropping my bag in its spot by the door after fishing out my phone, then heading for the table, where the familiar red-and-white bucket waited. "How was your day?"

"Oh, fine," he said, rubbing a hand through his hair, released from the requirement of having to try to keep his dark waves neat for professionalism. I always pictured him at his desk, sitting on his hands for the benefit of his hair. "Three forgery and utterings. Four DUIs. One larceny of a bike."

"Anybody do anything interesting in the courtroom?"

"Nope. Just the man who wanted the judge to toss his case because his name was spelled wrong on the summons. He got kind of loud about it after you left. As if misspelling were some get-out-of-jail-free card. The cases all run together without you at the opposite table."

Libby, who'd been doing her regular fish inventory at the tank, ran over to demand a drumstick and mashed potatoes. Emmett rarely remembered to cook/buy/eat a green vegetable. It infuriated me, given his taut midsection. "Can I watch *Phineas and Ferb*?" she asked.

Emmett looked at me for permission. I shrugged, too tired to make her sit at the table and eat properly. "Sure. Use napkins. Emmett doesn't want your greasy chicken fingers all over his remote."

He winked at her. "No worries. Easy to clean."

She ran off toward the TV. Emmett and I sat at the table and selected our pieces of chicken.

I played with my food while trying to think how to ask Emmett about Jane Knudsen without breaking privilege and telling him she was my client. That fact might come out eventually if she disclosed it, or the press—God forbid—got wind of it, but I couldn't until then. I'd have to go with white lies. Lawyers tell so many. I'd stopped feeling guilty about them—mostly.

"I was looking at old law school pictures today. I'd almost forgotten Jane Knudsen. She was my first-year roommate. Did you know her?"

"Uh," said Emmett, discomfort written across his face. "Yeah. I knew her. Everyone knew Jane. Or knew *of* her, I guess. I didn't know you were roommates, though."

"Only that first year. How did you know her?"

A second ticked by. It took only one more second before the reason for his silence hit me. "No way. You dated her."

Emmett's cheeks reddened. "For a month or two, in second year." He spread his hands flat on the table. God, I loved his hands. "Look. We haven't really talked about this, because you and I were friends the whole time and I never thought we needed to, but I saw a lot of women before you." He scrutinized my face for a reaction, worry written on his. "This isn't news, is it?"

"No." I chose my words carefully. Emmett's looks were the kind that drew in women. I'd known girls in law school who'd haunted the library, hoping to "accidentally" throw themselves into his path. Midway through my first year, I'd met Steve and dated him exclusively throughout the rest of my time at UVA. I'd been taken, but not blind. Emmett had widely been considered a catch. That wasn't his fault, though, and as far as I knew, he'd never played one woman against another. He was a serial monogamist. "You were quite the player," I said finally, trying to lighten the mood.

"Hardly." He blew out a breath. This was making him uncomfortable.

I put my hand on his. "I'm just kidding. We're in our thirties. I'd be an idiot to get upset that you dated other people before me."

While that part was true, a small cavewoman in my head had trouble with the idea that he'd slept with Jane, though I supposed he must have. It was the twenty-first century. They'd been single, well into their twenties, and in a relationship for months. I squashed the cavewoman.

I had a child by someone else, for God's sake. If that bothered Emmett, he'd never said.

"Are you sure you're okay with it? Jane and I didn't last long. She was an odd duck."

I tried hard to hide how interested I was. "Well, I thought so, when she was my roommate, but why do you say so?"

"She . . ." His relaxed expression tensed up again. "Well, of course she was good-looking. All the guys talked about her when we first got to school, and I'd have had to be blind not to notice her."

"Please continue," I said in my most murderous voice, then laughed to let him know I was joking. "Yes, Emmett. Jane's beauty was always the first and most important thing about her. Even for straight women, hard to miss."

"Well, anyway, I . . ." Guilt again. "I'd gone out with other pretty women before her, and most of them are thrilled by the way they look. Their looks define them, and sometimes not in a good way. Jane, though . . ." He trailed off, searching for the words. "I mean, I won't say she didn't know she was beautiful, but she . . . tried to avoid it. Minimize it. She always changed the subject when I'd ask about her. I tried to . . . Well, I tried to get her to talk. She never did."

"Like, not at all? When we were roommates, she didn't say a lot."

"No, she talked. She was plenty smart. We weren't in classes together, but whoa, the brain on her. She understood everything, spent her free time reading biographies of women trailblazers—her apartment was full of them—and she could grind anyone into the dust in a debate about the news or politics. But she never told me anything . . . real. Barely got her hometown out of her. Kind of weird, right? Nothing about herself, or her thoughts, or her history, or her hopes or fears."

I considered that for a while. "Same. I never felt like I knew her. She seemed so . . . untouchable. Remote."

"Agreed. She was remote. I met a woman once who argued that some women are so beautiful that they're on a pedestal. That people don't treat them the same as other people. I knew guys who wouldn't even talk to the prettiest girl in the room—too much risk of humiliation. They'd zero in on her friend instead. Maybe that's what was going on with Jane. Maybe she wasn't used to anyone trying to get to know her."

"Maybe," I said, trying not to notice how often he applied the word *beautiful* to Jane. "Did she end it or did you?"

"I did." Something changed in his face.

"Because she wouldn't let you get beneath her surface?" I could have bitten off my tongue. The words, floating in the air, sounded a lot more sexual than they had in my head. I really hated the person I was right now.

"Um," said Emmett, pressing his lips together. "No. I was younger then. My reasons weren't that noble. I still feel pretty terrible about how that ended."

Great. Emmett had a One That Got Away, and she was my supermodel-like new client. "Why terrible?"

"You remember the whole Professor Graham story? That's why."

Though I would have liked to claim I'd forgotten the Professor Graham / Jane Knudsen rumor, I'd have been lying. And Emmett would have known it. Everyone at UVA Law had known that rumor. For a month or so during our second year, that was all anyone could talk about.

Jane had taken Taxation that year. First-year law students all have to take the same required classes—Property, Torts, Civil Procedure, Criminal Law. During second year, everything was fair game. Those students interested in corporate or big-firm law generally took Taxation. I didn't.

Professor Gary Graham, in only his second year teaching after some glorious outing as a tax lawyer to the rich and famous in New York City, was by some accounts totally brilliant and by all accounts devastatingly handsome and charismatic. He was also a notoriously difficult grader.

When we returned to school after the winter break and grades for the first semester were posted, Jane got an A in Taxation. It didn't take long for the entire class to discover that Jane's A was the only one. Everyone else in that class had gotten a B or worse—harsh in the friendly grade-inflated world of top law schools. More than a few people had seen Jane making regular trips to Professor Graham's office hours. One woman reported breathlessly and often that she'd seen Jane at a UVA basketball game in early December, sitting with Professor Graham. She left no doubt in the telling that they'd been "together."

An uproar ensued. At the time, I'd had trouble deciding whether those who were upset were upset because Jane had had sex for grades, or because she'd slept with a married man, or merely because they hadn't thought of it first. Competition for grades was fierce. Six-figure salaries in glittering cities hung in the balance. I could have named more than one of my classmates, women and men, who'd have been happy to swap a night with Professor Graham for an A in Taxation, if they were honest with themselves.

I knew all this because I had enjoyed the deliciousness of the scandal. I'd been in the thick of the gossip—happily spreading anything I heard as far and wide as I could. I'd shared what I knew of her, too: Jane had also been a regular at the office hours of our Crim professor, Weatherbee, and our Torts professor, Brevard, who happened to be the only male professors we'd had first year.

I'd made it harder for her. I'd been horrible. I'd gone with her to see Weatherbee, and I knew damn well nothing inappropriate had happened there.

And now here was Emmett, telling me he'd had a different kind of front-row seat to the spectacle.

"Seriously? You were dating her when all that went down? How did I not know that?"

"You and I didn't really get to be friends until later that year. After I came out of hiding. People wouldn't stop asking me if it was true, if she really did it, if that's why I broke up with her. I didn't start going out again until probably March of second year."

"Well, I'd hate to add my voice to the clamor, but I would definitely like to know whether she did it. I've been curious for eight years."

"I thought she did at the time. But now . . ."

"Did you ask her?"

"Yeah," he said, doubt written on his face. "I mean, our relationship wasn't the best anyway, what with the fact that she didn't seem to want me to get to know her, but I thought she ought to have a chance to tell her side of something so massive." He shook his head. "God, those law-school scandals were so outsized. Law school was so . . . so . . . what's the word?"

"Soap opera–ish?"

"Yeah. So insular. Like high school, in a way. Anyway, when I heard the rumor enough times to know it was everywhere, I asked her if it was true."

"What did she say?"

"She . . . she wouldn't say."

"What? You'd think if it weren't true, she'd have said so and been done with it."

"Yeah, that's what I thought at the time. That silence meant yes."

"What exactly did she say?"

"She said . . ." He stopped and gave me a penetrating stare. "Why are you so interested in Jane Knudsen all of a sudden?"

I stammered. "I-I'm curious. We got to talking about her and now I'm about to get the answer to one of UVA Law's greatest mysteries. Don't stop now." Anything he told me might be useful, and of course I'd never spread it now, but a small voice in my head reprimanded me. There was still a little too much left of the envious law student for me to be completely comfortable in this conversation.

"Okay. She said something like, 'Does it matter? You'll believe what you want to believe.' Which, you're right, I took as a confirmation at the time. But since then, I . . . I've had enough life experience to wonder if, instead, she was hurt. Hurt by the rumor, hurt by me believing it enough to ask her, hurt at the way everyone turned against her."

Until this exact moment, I would have bet a month's income that Jane had slept with Professor Graham. Word had trickled down that his wife filed for divorce that spring. Jane had never publicly denied it. She hadn't acted embarrassed or really any different. At the end of the year, someone heard she'd gotten a C for the second semester, giving her a B average for the year like most of the rest of the class. We all assumed the scandal going public had soured whatever relationship they'd had and he'd taken revenge by dropping her grade—hardly anyone in law school got a C.

But maybe she never did it at all.

"Do you think she slept with him?" I asked.

"I don't know," said Emmett. "That's all she ever said about it. Actually, she—"

My cell phone buzzed on the table, where it lay faceup. I fought with napkins to get the worst of the chicken grease off my hands. I swept the phone and myself away from the table in a single motion so Emmett couldn't hear.

"Hello?"

"Allison," said Jane, as if I hadn't spent my dinner hour talking about her like she was a long-ago memory. "Check the local news. The Charlottesville station is reporting a person of interest. And there's no way she's guilty."

"Okay," I said.

"I can't talk right now, but do you have time tomorrow? Can you come here to my office? No one knows I've hired counsel, so you might be able to talk to some people who knew Ray, get a sense of motives. There were plenty."

A jury trial I was supposed to try tomorrow had settled last week. I did have time, though I'd been looking forward to using it to catch up on hours of paperwork. "Sure. I'll come see you tomorrow. At your work, right? Ten okay?"

We agreed to the logistics and she hung up. I turned to see Emmett, his lips tight, plate pushed away, staring at me with his arms crossed over his chest like a shield. Emmett, and his whole body, had been mine to touch for seven months. I was shocked at how closed off he'd become in seconds.

"Just curious?" he asked, repeating my words in a deceptively mild tone. "You bring up Jane Knudsen after all these years—totally random, I see."

My mouth dropped open. How did he . . . ?

"Oh, don't worry," he said, allowing a satirical grin at my confusion. The grin didn't reach his eyes. "Doesn't take an investigator's badge. You'd maintain better attorney-client privilege if you didn't program your clients' names into your contacts. I saw her name on your phone when it rang."

"Emmett, you know I couldn't tell you. And I was curious to see what you remembered about her."

"Now you know. A lot more than you were expecting, I'd guess. You know, I get that we're lawyers and we have to do a certain amount of crappy things on behalf of our clients, but I'd appreciate it if you didn't go digging for gold in my dating history so you could use the things she said to me in confidence in your court case, whatever it is. You don't mind cleaning up, do you?" he asked, not waiting for me to agree. Not meeting my eyes. "Time for Libby's lesson; then I've got to make it an early night. Busy day tomorrow. And for you, too, apparently."

Shit. I had a lot more atoning to do than I'd realized.

CHAPTER FIVE

JANE

"That only supports my theory that Felicity is the one," Josh said, pointing at the article on my iPad. I sat back down on his sofa after running to the bathroom to call Allison. He handed me another glass of wine and joined me, well within my personal space.

It took me a second to hear him while I stared at the local news story. Administrative Assistant a Person of Interest in Law Firm Murder blared the sordid letters, over a picture of Irene leaving the police station. Irene didn't deserve this. She'd hated Ray, that was for sure, but she'd never risk her family to kill him.

"What? What did you say?" I glanced up, finding Josh's warm hazel gaze too close, too soon. The wine had gone to my head at Claude's and I'd agreed to come back to his apartment with him. I hadn't done that with anyone in years, and already I regretted allowing his expectations to blossom this early.

"I said I still think Felicity is the one. I agree; Irene would never have done it. She's got too much to lose and not enough to gain. If she couldn't stand Ray, she'd have quit and found another job. I think they're questioning her because Felicity pointed them that way. I wonder what she gave them."

"You don't think it might have anything to do with the fact that, of all the people who had enough access or motive to kill him, she's the only woman of color?"

"No, Jane, I don't think that. Felicity is Asian. Her daughter is Asian, too, by extension."

"By extension? What are you talking about?" I stood, scanning the room for my bag. I was too tired to straighten him out as he clearly needed to be straightened.

Josh jumped up, too, not ready for me to leave. "Aargh. I didn't mean it like that. Because Felicity is her mom."

I decided to assign the best possible intentions rather than start an argument. It had been a difficult day for both of us. It was time to leave before I let my too-long sexual dry spell and whatever emotional fallout I had yet to deal with contribute any further to bad decision-making. "I have to go. It's getting late."

"Stay. Please," said Josh in a lower voice than usual. "Jane, you are so beautiful. If you only knew how I . . ."

I turned my back so he couldn't see me close my eyes. I liked Josh, but staying didn't feel right—not yet, anyway. "That was a lovely compliment. I need to get home. I need time to process. See you tomorrow?"

Josh tried to take me into his arms. Oh dear. I dodged, spying my bag under a chair. "Tomorrow. I've got appointments, though. Going to be busier than a one-eyed cat watching two mouseholes."

"Um, that was colorful," Josh said, smiling.

I flushed, but thought better of trying to explain it.

"Tomorrow night?" He walked me to the door, untwisting my pocketbook strap on my shoulder, like a little boy hoping for a reward.

"Let's just see how it goes. Okay?" There was no avoiding him, standing there at the door. He probably felt entitled to a full-on first kiss. I had agreed to come back for a nearly literal nightcap, after all, and I had more than enough skill to give him one without emotional cost. But I didn't want to. Not yet. I leaned in and brushed his cheek, keeping my lips closed and dry, and then slipped straight out the door.

❧

I didn't go home. It was getting late, but there was still work to do. By and by, the police would be questioning me. The knot in my stomach told me they were coming, as sure as a Blackwood invoice to clients at the end of the month. In the photo on the website, Irene had been leaving the police station, which meant she wasn't under arrest. I went to her house.

Friendship had always been difficult for me, for a lot of reasons, but Irene was so warm and so unjudgmental. She knew me better than anyone ever had. Better than anyone other than my own mother.

Which wasn't saying much at all.

I texted Irene to make sure it was okay for me to come over. Though we regularly worked until ten p.m., arriving at her house at the same hour felt different. She had young children who were probably asleep. That is, if she was able to keep from them that she'd been at the police station.

She had not. Her oldest, eleven-year-old Sianne, met me at the door. Irene's husband, C. J., was right behind her. I'd met the kids only twice before, and last time, Sianne had been about nine and had stared up at me as if I were a princess. Today, her face was far more pugnacious.

"What do you want? My mom's tired."

"Sianne," C. J. said. "Time for bed. Head on up, now."

Sianne gave me a narrowed-eye warning and left. So much for hoping they hadn't been affected.

"Hi, C. J.," I said. "Is she okay?"

"She's in the den."

I whispered, "I'm so sorry."

His small smile didn't hide his worry. "Go on back."

Irene sat on a sofa in her den, both hands holding a bottle of IPA in a death grip. "Do you want one?" she said. "C. J. Get her a beer."

"No, thanks, C. J. I had wine at supper. Irene, are you okay?"

"I told you they'd pick me, didn't I?"

"You did. But you're innocent."

"I wish I believed that meant anything."

"What did they say was the reason they were talking to you?"

She let out a short yelp of totally mirthless laughter. "They said they had a tip that I was a disgruntled employee. That Ray had had trouble with me. That he'd had to discipline me for smart-mouthing him."

"Besides the fact that none of that is true, it wouldn't be a motive for murder. Do you have guesses as to who might have said that?"

"Yes, but guessing won't help much. I think it was Felicity. She and I have had . . . issues, I guess you could say, lately. Two things happened. I misplaced a message from Felicity to Ray one day last month. Three Fridays ago, I didn't send the dry cleaning home with him when she had a benefit to go to, and she had to come all the way into town to get the dress out of his office. I'll give him credit—Ray took my side both times. Said he couldn't figure why she didn't just text him directly if she wanted to talk to him, and actually said it was his fault the dry cleaning didn't go home. Can you believe that?"

Ray was awful, but he typically stopped short of evil. "Josh thinks Felicity gave them your name, too," I said. "He thinks Felicity killed Ray."

Irene leaned back into the sofa and closed her eyes. "No way she kills the golden goose. Her interior-design business is tanking. Ray's been bankrolling it all along. Turns out that having once painted a room in her own house a pretty color by accident does not equal talent enough to take on other people's houses."

"Really?"

Irene rolled her eyes. "Yes, really. You think there's anything I don't know about their finances? He makes me organize his tax stuff—you think I don't look? Half the time Ray gets me to deal with her for him. There's no love lost there, but she'd never kill him."

"Not even for the inheritance?"

Irene snorted. "What inheritance? They spend everything he earns, and then some, probably. Charity boards. Clothes. The beach house at Pawleys Island. Down payment for Brittany's condo up in Fairfax, just last week. He's worth nothing dead—only alive and billing. She'd be a fool to kill him, and Felicity is in no way a fool."

"They paid for a condo for Brittany? She couldn't rent like a normal person? Holy crap."

"Yup. Felicity was . . . um, interested in making sure Brittany moved up there. They went up to go house shopping last month. The condo should be ready right after the bar exam in July."

"Wait. Interested? In her daughter moving away? What's up with that?"

Irene suddenly looked tired. "I . . . I don't know that for sure. I don't think Brittany and Felicity had been getting along lately. Just a feeling." Her expression closed off. There'd be no more about Brittany from Irene tonight. I'd have to worry away at that knot later.

"What did the police say?"

She looked at her beer bottle, still closed up. "They said it was a homicide. No chance he did it himself from the angle of the bullet. They think someone used his own gun on him—apparently the one in his drawer was missing."

Josh had pegged that one. Maybe he was right about Felicity, too. "What did you tell them?"

"Nothing. You think I'm an idiot? I told them unless they had cause to arrest me, I'd be leaving. And then I walked out."

"Honey?" Irene's husband came in. "He's here."

Another man filled the doorway. He wore, improbably at this hour, a pristine suit and a perfectly knotted tie. He had eyes only for Irene.

"Terrell Edwards, attorney at law. Everything is going to be all right from here." He noticed me at that point. "And this is?"

I stuck my hand out to shake. "I'm Jane Knudsen. I'm a friend of Irene's. From work."

"From work?" Terrell asked, looking at Irene. "This is the one?"

She nodded.

The "one" what, exactly?

"I'm afraid I'm going to have to call a halt here, to protect my client. I'm advising her not to talk to anyone about this case, especially not coworkers. I'm a straight talker, Ms. Knudsen. The killer could be you—might well be you—and my job is to protect Irene. You don't mind leaving us to catch up now, do you?"

His advice made depressing sense. It would be a bad idea for anyone under the eye of law enforcement to share info with anyone else who might have shot Ray. And I might have shot Ray. I glanced at Irene, expecting her to give me a rueful smile, or a hug.

No smile. No hug.

It was as if Irene had morphed into a completely different person in the two seconds since I'd given my attention to her lawyer. She stood, cold and distant. I'd been jettisoned, and I couldn't even blame her. She was terrified, more for those three children upstairs than for herself, and she would follow any directions, do whatever she had to, if she thought it could lessen the pain for her family. "Jane. Thanks for stopping by."

"Um. Sure. I'll see you at work."

"Good night," Irene said, all her attention on Terrell.

"Good night," I whispered, seeing myself out. The trip to my car at the street felt chilly, even though it was June in Virginia.

As I buckled my seat belt, my phone dinged with a text.

Cherry: I saw the news. I know you done somthing. You usully do. I know you did.

Typical. Only the "elite" showed off by fixating on things like spelling and grammar, she'd say. "Regular" people knew what was what. I'd spent a lifetime trying to overcome my own bad spelling, but she was perversely proud of hers.

The accusations weren't new, either. Many a Sunday I'd spent sitting with sore butt cheeks on a wooden church pew being prayed over. Our pastor made house calls—ask me how I knew. Nothing ever helped, according to Cherry. I'd been made in the devil's image. Too tempting to be good. Too ornery to be pure. Too smart to be decent. I was the cross for her to bear.

It was nearing eleven at night. I pictured the beer cans around the sordid room where she scrolled Facebook every night. She'd be drunk by now and lashing out at anyone online she could find.

I tossed the phone into the passenger seat and started the engine.

I wouldn't be able to ignore her forever. No doubt, she wanted money. She always wanted money. She spread poison wherever she went. As much as I longed to cut her out of my life forever, I couldn't. I could change cell phone numbers again, but she'd always find me.

My mother knew how easy it would be to ruin me.

CHAPTER SIX

ALLISON

Driving the ninety minutes to Charlottesville the next day, I had plenty of time for self-loathing.

I'd been seeing Emmett for seven happy months, and we'd never disagreed like that before. In our jobs, we had to keep secrets from each other, but they were always work-related. I knew damn well I'd stepped over a line by pumping him for all that information about Jane without telling him why, but with Libby there bubbling over her newest piece of music, there'd been no opportunity to set things right. We'd parted with tight smiles and a perfunctory kiss. It had been frosty enough that Libby had demanded to know why I was being mean to Emmett.

What Emmett didn't understand was that I'd been well and truly punished for asking about Jane. My head was full of images of him and Jane together, two beautiful people who deserved each other and looked amazing—in their clothes and out of them. That last image was the karma I deserved. How could I let him see me naked again when I knew he'd seen Jane? What on earth was he doing with me?

The women Emmett had dated before me had all been stunning. I wasn't hideous, but I'd never had a lot of curves or a beauteous mane of hair worthy of a shampoo ad. My old boss, Dan, used to send me links to makeup tutorials, and even with their help, I'd never gotten the hang of eye shadow or blush.

I'd decided, when we started seeing each other, that Emmett was that rare guy who was as attracted to my brain as he was to the rest of me, and never allowed myself to worry about the girls he'd dated before me.

Jane made those girls look like backup dancers. And was brilliant besides.

Just like that, I felt small and awful, the way I had in law school watching her twirl her finger in that shining hair as she studied. Somehow, it had never seemed fair that she had brains *and* beauty in such large doses, but I knew if I'd been more confident, I wouldn't have been jealous of someone else who had everything.

I'd dealt with my jealousy by gossiping about her, which had only made it worse. Jane represented resentment during first year. She represented resentment and guilt after second year. I could not let her represent resentment, guilt, *and* relationship insecurity.

As the exit for downtown came into view, I tried to shake off the gray weight of despair. She didn't have everything right now, unless "everything" meant the need for a criminal defense lawyer. At this moment, I was doing fine.

I felt great for about ten seconds, until I realized I'd reassured myself that Jane might go to prison when I would not. Nice. So generous, Allison. So much work on myself still to do.

I decided not to mention Emmett to Jane. Even if I wanted to, I couldn't do it without giving away that my boyfriend had discovered the identity of my client in violation of attorney-client privilege. The whole thing made my head hurt. Besides, the relationship between me and Jane now was professional only; she had no need to know anything about my personal life.

In the Blackwood, Payne & Vivant office building, I was directed to a first-floor office that was decidedly dingy.

"Allison! Right on time. Thanks for coming."

Jane and I did the required small talk about traffic and had I found the office without much trouble, and I took a seat, awkward as hell because of the friendship we should have had but didn't. And because of the relationship she'd once had with Emmett that was mine now.

"So I thought we might start with coffee with Amir," said Jane.

"Amir?"

"Amir Burhan. He's a third-year associate in my work group. He worked for Ray, too."

Wait. While criminal defense always involved talking to anyone willing who might have helpful information—and Jane had been right; it would be easier now, before she was officially a suspect—it was never a good idea to do that in the presence of a client. Stories might change if Jane sat there. And I couldn't yet dismiss the possibility that Jane was guilty.

"Tell me about Amir," I said, stalling.

"He's from Charleston, South Carolina. Super smart. Went to NYU for law school. His wife is doing her master's at UVA, so that's why he's here instead of a big city. He was on law review. He probably could have taken any job he wanted. Chatty, for a guy. Very observant. He might have seen something or heard something that would be useful."

"Are you in a supervisory role over him?"

"I suppose. I was the most senior in the group, after Ray."

"Does Amir like you?"

Jane's cheeks pinked. She seemed to struggle with putting her thoughts into words. "Ah. Um. I've had to tell him to cancel plans to work late a time or two. And . . . I may have . . . contributed some thoughts to an evaluation Ray did of him last year."

Right. He didn't love her, and she knew it. Nope, we were definitely not interviewing Amir together. "Okay, Jane, here's the thing. Given that he may not be a huge fan of yours—and I promise you, if you made him cancel plans even once, he's not running the fan club—I think it would be better to interview him myself. I'll be up-front with him, but people talk better when they aren't worried their jobs are on the line."

"Fine," she said, recognizing the wisdom. What a pleasure—to have a reasonable client. "I'll introduce you and take you by the crime scene. They've got most of it roped off, but we can peek."

"Great." I took my bag and file with me. We headed down the hall and through a fire door to the stairwell.

The second-floor hallway was quiet. Unoccupied administrative workstations lined the interior wall, and doorways to offices with windows opened opposite them. Everything was white and featureless except for the extra-padded brown industrial carpeting designed not to show stains. At the fourth doorway, the yellow tape became visible.

"Where are the admins?" I asked, as much to have something to say as anything else.

"Downstairs in the conference room. They got moved right away. Here it is."

I chuckled to myself as I beheld Ray Corrigan's office. It was nicer than Jane's on about the same magnitude as my former boss's office had been than mine, before I started my own firm. Law was more than a full-time job. I couldn't blame those who'd lasted long enough to be partner for wanting to spend so many of their waking hours in a lavish environment, but male partners so predictably went for the Oval Office during the Lincoln Administration look. My office had a clean Scandinavian look with bright colors and shelves instead of cabinets. Cheaper, too—IKEA was a lot more affordable than antediluvian mahogany.

Jane and I stood in the doorway. The yellow tape marked off the room not unlike one of the velvet ropes keeping tourists out of the parlor in a historical house.

"I found him right there, behind the desk." Jane pointed to the spot. I imagined I could see the blood from the doorway, but that was ridiculous. The rug was large and patterned, and even on this side of the desk, it was apparent the dominant color had been red well before the recent soaking. "I had to walk into the room a little before I saw his foot. I keep kicking myself for not turning around as soon as I . . ."

"As soon as you what?"

"I smelled . . . something. The blood. Something different, or off, sort of, from the usual. I wish I'd had enough sense to leave."

"Did you touch him?"

"Yes," she said, looking at her hands. "I touched his face. He was lying there faceup. His eyes were open, but I thought . . . maybe if I touched him, I would feel life, or something."

"Was he cold?"

"I reckon? Maybe? I don't know. I have no idea what temperature a dead body is supposed to feel like, or how fast. He sent me an email at midnight—only six hours before I found him. He definitely didn't feel alive."

"Did you see any sign of struggle? The gun?"

"They didn't find the gun, I hear, though one was missing from his desk. His office has always been messy. So no, no struggle."

An older man passing in the hall stopped and crossed his arms over his chest. "If you need something in the office, Jane, let me know. I'll discuss it with the police," he said sternly.

I glanced at Jane. We'd been reprimanded, and it was enough to share a flicker of camaraderie. The man kept walking, but more slowly, to make sure we left the crime scene.

"Right," Jane said. "That was the managing partner, Greg. We'd better head down to Amir's office. This way."

Amir Burhan sat in an office so tiny it made Jane's look fancy. Jane walked in like she owned the place. I followed in time to see Amir look up with a certain degree of aggrieved resignation.

"Amir, this is Allison Barton. She's an old friend from law school who's helping me try to figure out what happened with Ray. Do you mind talking to her?"

Amir narrowed his eyes. No doubt he was assessing whether Jane would visit workplace misery on him if he said no. With Ray Corrigan dead, Jane might well be his boss until he was reassigned to another partner. Law-firm culture meant that he would be expecting top-down misery to be meted out. It was merely a question of from whom.

"No, whatever helps. Now?" Amir gestured at the single chair squeezed between the front edge of his desk and the wall.

"Great!" Jane said, moving to the door. "Allison—I've got a conference call soon. If I don't catch you, call me, please? Thanks, Amir. I appreciate it."

Amir was small and slight and filled with restless energy—he would have been exactly my type in high school. He likely had combed his short black hair in his bathroom this morning and hadn't looked in the mirror since. A tuft near the crown had gone askew. The rest of him was neat as a pin—carefully knotted tie, white shirtsleeves still buttoned at the wrists, suit jacket hung on a tree in a tight corner.

I sat. "Thanks for talking with me."

His body language had changed the second Jane left. He relaxed, like a drill sergeant had yelled "at ease." "I probably have more questions than you do," he said, good humor removing all the lawyerly look from his face. "First off, I wasn't aware Jane had law school friends. Or friends. What's up with that?"

"Um," I said, correcting his impression. "We were *roommates* at UVA."

"I knew she went here, but seriously, you'd never know it. This place is full of UVA grads, and she's not chummy with any of them. Ha. Jane Knudsen isn't chummy with anyone at all. Ice queen. Cold fish. Hell, Jane's so cold, she'd make a cooler full of cold fish look like they had fevers. Give me some stories about law school. Tell me something awful about her I can hug the next time she makes me read a banker's box of documents from the nineties."

I laughed despite myself. He was charming. And I knew all about the grimness of the first few years in practice. Emmett had worked for a year in a big firm in DC before becoming a prosecutor. He'd once been forced to spend a week reviewing bug-infested thirty-year-old documents inside a filthy warehouse under a single lightbulb.

"Sorry, I don't have much. We lost touch after law school."

He registered that and stowed it away. "Let me guess. She's worried she'll be arrested for the murder and she's hired you so she can snap her fingers and make you appear if it seems likely they'll want her to spend the night in lockup?"

"She hasn't been charged with anything," I said, being careful with my words.

"So yes." Amir laughed. In another life, we could be friends. I liked him. "Fine. I'll tell you the truth if you're her lawyer and not her friend. Frankly, I couldn't make the concept of 'friend' compute when it comes to Jane."

I waited, fairly certain this would be good.

"I said she was an ice queen, and upon reflection, that term has certain connotations that maybe don't apply to Jane. She's cold, but she's not a bitch. That would be misogynistic for one, and inaccurate for two. She's pleasant, so much so that she could possibly be a decent person if you chipped away about a foot of frost. Never rude. Always has a legit reason for making your life miserable. There's nothing cruel about her. She's just . . . lifeless. No connection. No commiseration at all. Damn, some commiseration would not go amiss when we're stuck here together at midnight and have to get through fourteen hundred-page documents before dawn. She honestly prefers nobody talk to her."

"Is she a good lawyer?"

"Jane? Hell yes. Bright. Incisive. Well spoken, when she speaks. She's a star. They love her here. That whole thing with walking around like a robot? They eat it up—no messy personal life distracting her from billing a million hours a year. She's up for partner next year. She's a shoo-in."

"Does she want to make partner?"

Amir stared at me as if I'd asked him if he enjoyed breathing oxygen. "Uh, well, I guess so. Don't we all? Isn't that the whole point of all this?" He gestured around his cell of an office.

"Does she have any personal life?"

Amir looked a little cagey. "Welllll. Not officially. The other guy in our group—Josh is his name—wants her bad. Kind of pathetic, actually, but then again there aren't many straight guys who wouldn't want Jane once they've laid eyes on her."

My earlier Emmett-related insecurities made me cringe.

Oblivious, Amir continued. "She's not married and she couldn't possibly be seeing anyone outside of the firm because she practically lives here."

"Outside of the firm? Amir, the way you said that, it makes me wonder . . ."

"Yeah, there's a lot of wondering. I hate to gossip, but other people love it."

"About what? Josh?"

"No, Josh would jump if she so much as turned his way, and he's single now, so who'd care? No, I mean Ray."

"Ray? The victim, Ray?"

"Yeah. Lot of people have been talking for six months or more that something was going on between them. Jane and Ray staying late, just the two of them. A janitor said he interrupted something late at night in Ray's office. Ray's wife—you know her? Felicity. Now, there's a bitch," he said, blithely abandoning all his professed concerns about misogyny.

I stared at him, an eyebrow raised.

He cleared his throat repentantly. "Ray's wife hates Jane. Like, hates her. Cuts her dead anytime she comes in, even though she's all fakey polite to me and Josh and Irene. I said Jane was a star, right? Well, that reputation has only increased since she and Ray have been working late so much. Josh should have almost the same responsibility as Jane, but he doesn't. All the good billables go to her."

Suddenly, I didn't like Amir quite as much. He had nothing to go on and was assuming a whole lot. "None of that is proof of anything."

"No," he said cheerfully. "It's not. And I'm telling you because you're her lawyer and you should know that half her workplace thinks she was sleeping with her married boss. It doesn't matter if it's true. What matters is that they all think it."

"It obviously matters if it were true—it would give her a motive to kill him if they had that kind of relationship."

He considered that. "Good point. Might also give her a motive if she finds out he's the one spreading the rumors, too. And I think he was."

"Did he actually say he was sleeping with her?"

"No, I misspoke. He didn't spread the rumors, exactly. He just let them spread. On purpose. He was a guy who liked to be thought of as a player, I guess. He liked the reputation. I'd be terrified to have anyone think something like that. Sexual harassment, #MeToo, all that. Ray—he never worried."

Men who'd risk harassment accusations rather than let their legends die were familiar to me. I had a good sense of Ray now.

"Do you think Jane could be capable of killing Ray?"

He took his time, considering the question seriously. "Yes. I think she could have done it. She had the opportunity. Probably a motive. And while her personality makes working for her tough, it would also make her excellent at hiding her guilt. No crime of passion here. Cool, calm, and collected—that's Jane."

"Anything else you wanted to tell me?" I asked, gritting my teeth. He was honest. Honest to the point of pain.

"What the hell. While I'm flinging around baseless rumors, I'll toss out one more."

"Okay," I said, bracing. Amir was a veritable font of unhelpful information.

"Before I went to law school, I was a computer science major. I'm pretty good at online research. Kind of like having a PhD in Google, you know? Anyway, one night after Jane stuck me here late, I decided to check her out. Figure out her deal, right?"

My stomach gave a lurch. I'd tried that, too, in my limited High School Diploma in Google way. "And?"

"And I couldn't find anything on her before her sophomore year of college at Duke. I traced her back that far. But nothing before that. So the next chance I got, I asked her the name of her high school. She flat-out didn't want to tell me. You know how bizarre it is to watch someone evade the question when you ask something as dumb as where they went to high school?"

I shifted in my seat uncomfortably. I hadn't the slightest idea where Jane had gone to high school. Her hometown was listed as Durham, North Carolina, home of Duke University, in the law school first-year info.

One night, though, I'd been up late when she came home from the bar, tipsy. She'd been more talkative than usual and had told me about sliding down a smooth-rock waterfall near her home as a kid. I got the distinct impression she'd grown up in the mountains somewhere, not in the urban Research Triangle. Her accent, usually clipped and careful, had softened into the cadences of Appalachia.

"She never told you where she went to high school?"

"Nope. Said it wasn't ethical to bill clients for personal chitchat. Can you believe that shit?" Amir widened his side-eye and nodded along with himself. "Weird, right?"

I almost laughed again. Ethical to an extreme I'd never heard of any lawyer meeting. Glancing at my notes, then at Amir, whose eyes kept straying to his screen—billable hours were not happening while he talked to me—I wrapped it up. "So. Jane is cold, shares nothing about herself, everyone thinks she's sleeping with her boss, and she doesn't exist before college? Any motive you can think of for her killing Ray?"

"I don't think she was sleeping with Ray. I've said that to other people, but rumors are hard to knock down. If she knew he was letting those rumors grow, it could give her a motive. While the partners might give Ray a high five for banging Jane, they'd shoot down her chance at getting partner for banging Ray. She lives for this firm. She works harder than anyone here and deserves it more than anyone else."

Okay. He was working himself back into my good graces. "Does anyone else have a motive?"

He laughed. "Ha! So many motives, so little time. Darth Vader would be more popular around here than Ray. But it's not Irene. The police are barking up the wrong tree there. I'd bet my life on it. She just got a raise and he hasn't done anything to her recently that he hasn't been doing for decades. It's not Josh. Ray did some nice—if you can believe that—shit for him when he caught his wife cheating last year. And it wasn't me—ask my wife. We had half her family in our house at the time, literally blocking my car in my driveway. My guess is Felicity the Bitch Wife or the daughter. They'd both have known he had that gun in his desk."

"Did you know he had that gun in his desk?"

Amir's jocular light went out as if I'd flipped a switch. "No," he said, obviously lying. "I heard about it since the murder. Everyone is talking about it."

I made a note to check on Amir's alibi, but he'd told me some useful things.

Now I had to decide what to tell Jane.

※

"He said what?"

"He said Ray was letting everyone think you were sleeping with him."

Jane put down her paper Starbucks cup and closed her eyes, her fists clenching. I'd taken her out for coffee so I could give her my report on what I'd learned from her associate.

"For what it's worth, Amir blamed Ray for that. He didn't believe it."

I'd never really thought about it until Amir said it, but Jane did have a robotic, not-quite-human quality about her. Like an actress portraying a role she didn't feel quite comfortable in. Her display of anger—still so controlled—when I relayed the gossip proved it. Her cheeks went red and she looked so much more . . . lifelike.

"Super. That's one on my side, but of course all the rest of them believe it. No one asks me. Or even wonders for a hot second why on earth I would want to sleep with a married workaholic two decades my senior."

I was wondering . . . and not for the first time. There'd been the Professor Graham incident, after all. It might not have been the white-hot conflagration my friends and I had savored behind our hands in law school, but usually, where there's smoke, et cetera.

"Did you sleep with Ray? Did you have a relationship with him? If you did, better for me to know now."

She glared at me with revulsion, bringing warm light to her face and making her loveliness nearly blinding. I didn't have any memory of seeing her angry before. "Easy for you to believe, too. I know you're thinking of Professor Graham. I've got a history of it, you're thinking."

I held up a hand, glancing around the coffee shop as her voice grew higher in pitch—and more accented, if I didn't miss my guess. "I'm just asking. It's better if . . ."

"Just asking, right. Please. Let's discuss law school. You were right in there with everyone else second year, whispering about me when I'd turn my head and rolling your eyes like you thought I couldn't see."

During the Graham scandal, I heard from Keegan Hurst that Lara McKinney told him that she'd personally seen the professor's hand on

Jane's thigh in section 107 at John Paul Jones Arena. Law-school life, especially after the terror of first year had worn off, was boring. Gossip was currency.

I'd always thought she didn't care, or maybe I'd told myself that to alleviate my own guilt. Before and after the scandal, Jane had appeared supremely disinterested in other people's opinions. She hadn't gone into hiding; she'd walked around with her head held high, exactly the same as before. If I'd whispered, and I was sure I had, I'd whispered at least in part my amazement at her courage.

I didn't know what to say, so I said nothing.

"It hurt, dammit," Jane said. "I know we didn't really connect that first year. You had your reasons for that, I assume, and I suppose I did, too. But I don't know—I reckon I thought some kind of former room-mate privilege would at least have kept you from openly laughing at me. I knew I was the campus joke, but it was your laughter that bothered me the most."

My breath deserted me. I heard the words she was saying, but they made no sense to me. I'd never thought of the gossiping I'd done as mockery, but now I could see how Jane made no distinction. It had never occurred to me that I was important enough to Jane Knudsen to have the ability to hurt her.

"Jane . . . I don't . . . I never thought . . ."

"You believed the rumors about Professor Graham, didn't you?"

I had, because she'd never denied them. And I was a good enough lawyer now to notice she hadn't denied sleeping with Ray Corrigan, either.

"Tell me now, then. Did you sleep with Professor Graham?"

CHAPTER SEVEN

JANE

Chilly wind blew outside John Paul Jones Arena, the home of the University of Virginia basketball team, on that long-ago night. I remembered the way it had whipped my hair in my face on my way inside. It was probably weird to go to a college basketball game alone, but I did most things alone. It was best that way.

Oh, I tried to play the role. I had coffee with other law students, debated politics late into the night or discussed books, never offering anything about myself, and dated casually, but never any one person too long. I never could rid myself of the fear of the moment of recognition, and the chance of that increased the longer I spent with people. Lately, it was becoming clearer and clearer that I'd have to dump my boyfriend, Emmett, and soon. Two months had ticked by, and he wouldn't be content with only my present for much longer. His questions about my history got harder and harder to evade.

For a wistful minute, I thought about what it would be like to have answers to those questions that didn't bring fear and shame. I wished I could be a girl who shared things with a boyfriend. Instead, I'd stand as I always did, with all my weight holding the vault door closed until my strength gave out and I had to run away before everything burst out.

Inside, I let myself breathe in the pregame buzz of excitement and the smell of the concession stands I couldn't afford. The crowd buffeted me along and I found my seat, figuring I'd read on my phone until the game started.

"Ms. Knudsen, I believe?"

My Taxation professor stopped in the aisle between sections, carrying a giant funnel cake on a plate. He appeared to be alone.

"Hi, Professor Graham." I gave him an awkward wave.

He sat down in the next seat, causing a ripple of apprehension to shiver over me. Why? Who had he come with?

"I got this for my son and his friend," he said, gesturing with the plate full of food. "They're over there, couple of sections over. It's a tradition—I don't know if he'd even come to the game without a funnel-cake promise. Would you like some?"

I'd eaten ramen for supper, and the sugary, fried mess on the plate smelled like heaven. He held it out, bending his head toward me like a coconspirator. "Come on. Won't hurt to eat a little, and my son doesn't need all of this."

"Well, okay." I reached over and broke a piece off, smiling at him even though he was definitely too close.

"Are you here alone?" he asked, looking around.

I nodded sheepishly. "None of my friends wanted to come."

"No boyfriend?"

My defense mechanisms kicked into buzzing-alarm gear. It wasn't appropriate for a professor to ask me that. Not that it hadn't happened before. Nor could I be rude. I needed a good grade in his class. "Uh, no."

His grin grew bigger. Oh shit. He thought I meant I didn't have one, not that he hadn't come. I started to explain, but too late. He put the food on his lap and stretched his now free arm around the back of my seat.

"Well, that is good news. By the way, Jane—you don't mind if I call you Jane, do you? You're easily the brightest tax student in my class. What type of law are you interested in? I'd be happy to help you make some connections."

This was blatant nonsense. Taxation, like most law classes, was taught using the Socratic method. The professor lectured a bit, then questioned the students on their reading. I'd been called on only once, and I had not acquitted myself with any particular brilliance. There were at least four tax prodigies in the class. Two had been accountants before law school. I'd considered asking one of them for help.

"Thanks, Professor. I'm looking at big-firm law."

He swallowed, drinking in my face like water. I swear he'd listened to those innocuous words and pretended I'd meant them sexually. "Jane, I've got a great thought. Please come by my office tomorrow and we'll chat."

"Um. Okay," I said, trying to think how to get out of it while keeping my grade intact. Like most law-school classes, the Taxation semester grade was determined by a single final exam—an entirely subjective essay graded at the whim of the professor. It was December. The exam was only two weeks away. Surely, I could keep him at a distance that long. By next semester, I'd have come up with a better strategy.

"If you're by yourself, I'd be happy to keep you company. I'd feel terrible going off and leaving you alone."

I'd trapped myself by admitting I was here alone. "Oh, I'm sure your son . . ."

"Eh. He's fourteen. He's got his friend with him. I'll run this food over to him and be right back. He'll have a better time without me breathing down his neck."

There was no way out. I gave him a tight smile and settled in for the game.

❧

Everyone thought they knew what was going on after that. Law-school gossip is vicious and fleet—too many people in close quarters in need of distraction. The week before the exam, Professor Graham cornered me in his office and put his hands in a place they didn't belong. I cut off a stream of disgusting talk with the word *boyfriend*. He said a few more ugly things and there was no more talk of helping me make connections for career advancement.

It was only when the grades came back after winter break that I saw how diabolical he was. I got an A. Everyone else, even the tax prodigies, got a B or lower. The whispers began. Somebody'd seen us at the basketball game. Someone else had heard I'd visited his office hours more than once, which I had, because he'd demanded it. Mrs. Graham came to campus and someone heard her hollering at him in the faculty parking lot. Even Emmett believed it. I took the opportunity to let him cut me loose, saving me the trouble. I wished he'd believed in me, even as I knew I hadn't given him enough of myself to believe in. He'd been one of the good ones, for the most part.

Now, I stared at Allison. As with Emmett, I'd been cautious with her when she was my roommate. She'd have been in a position to know too much if I'd let her, and she'd made it easy to keep her at a distance because she hadn't been the least bit interested in getting to know me. Yet it had hurt when she'd been part of the eddying flock of women on the edge of every room I entered shooting me glances and chattering behind their hands.

Even though, again, it was my fault. I hadn't tried to be her friend. She didn't owe me anything. Not really.

"No, I didn't sleep with Professor Graham," I said, telling her something true and personal for the first time ever. It felt strangely good. "I won't claim to be pure as the driven snow—far from it—but I never touched him. Graham was all over me for two weeks right before the December exam second year, and I didn't do a thing to encourage it. When I turned him down, he gave me an A. And then he told the right loudmouth that he gave me an A. That was it. That was his revenge for my rejection. Everyone believed it. Everyone."

"You never denied it," Allison said, her body language defensive. "People asked you if it was true and you didn't deny it."

Only one person had asked me outright—Emmett Amaro, my then boyfriend—but I could understand that she probably thought people had.

"Leaving aside the fact that no one would have believed me—oh, I remember law school, the way everyone grabbed on to anything at all interesting—I shouldn't have had to deny it. I never alleged it in the first place. The automatic assumption that I was a home-wrecking grade-whore was disgusting. Misogynistic. No one, not one person, assumed correctly that Graham was instead a vengeful predator."

"That's true." Allison looked stricken. "God. You're right."

"And Ray Corrigan—good lord. No. Even if I'd found him remotely attractive, which I didn't, Ray was a bitter workaholic, aged before his time. He thought of almost nothing but legal conflicts and money and the job that let him turn one into the other. Oh, I know he was attracted to me. Sometimes, working late, he'd drink too much at supper break and he'd say some gross things. A fishing line in the water, but I never bit, and he never pressed it. Once, after a client boozefest, he ran a hand down my back to my ass and raised his eyebrows when I looked at him. I said something to the effect of 'not in this lifetime,' and he took his hands off and never mentioned it again. He was far from a gentleman, but no worse than most of the others."

"Why do you think your office gave any credence to the rumor?"

"Ray never much cared about a hostile workplace, and he probably wasn't faithful to his wife." I sighed, not wanting to explain. "But the assumption wasn't about him at all. It would have been about me. It's always about me."

"What do you mean?"

I gave her a long look. "This is awkward, especially with you, but I'll try. People started staring at me when I was in elementary school.

Once, a photographer tried to follow me into school to ask my teacher for my parents' contact information. People said I was pretty, and that should have been a good thing, but for me it never has been. It's always been a bad thing."

"A bad thing?" Allison looked taken aback. "That year we lived together, I'd have given almost anything to look like you for a single day. I'd pay a lot of money, even now, for . . ."

"Well, I would trade with you. In a second. Looking like this has made every situation in my life worse."

Her mouth hung open. "That's hard to believe. All those studies they've done. About how beautiful people get hired more easily, get chosen first, have doors held . . . everything."

I laughed. Any researcher studying the advantage of so-called beauty would toss out my experiences as an outlier. The exception that ruins the narrative. "My appearance has never conveyed any advantages. Quite the opposite. At church, when I was young, a pastor used to say I was a temptation sent from Satan like the apple Eve made Adam eat. They prayed over me. The whole church. They taught me that the way I looked was evil. I know they're wrong, but at the same time, I don't *know* they're wrong."

"Whoa." Allison sat back, listening. Really listening. I'd never talked about this with anyone before. I didn't think about myself as beautiful, at least, not if *beautiful* were a good thing. The way I looked was bad. Troublesome. Evil, maybe.

"Most pretty women are attractive in a way that makes people like them. Like Donna Reed—you know, she played George Bailey's wife in *It's a Wonderful Life*. I always thought she was so pretty. My looks weren't like that. They made people want to . . . to use me. There's a . . . a dirty quality about my face. My body. Sexual. Like Marilyn Monroe, in . . . well, everything. Straight men react only two ways: the confident ones follow me around and want—expect—a piece of me, and the less confident ones are put off by me. Or too afraid to talk to me at all."

I stared at her, imagining I could see faint disgust. *Don't hate me because I'm beautiful,* the old ad went. The arrogance, she'd be thinking. *Jane Knudsen thinks she is so beautiful that it's a problem.* Allison was not the first woman to hate me for my looks. She stayed quiet, though, waiting for me to finish.

"Anyway. I have two choices—I can hide in baggy clothes and dark rooms, or I can walk around and let it be other people's problems. In law school, I tried out option two. There was a price to pay, though, which was that other people assumed the sexual part of me was the only part of me. The only purpose I served. That of course I'd sleep with a professor for a grade or with a partner for a promotion. Since then, I suppose, I've been leaning a little too hard into the dark rooms." I glanced down. Buttoned suit jacket over a blouse with a neckline that covered my collarbones. Suit pants a size too large. So the baggy clothes, too.

Allison bit her lip. She took her time choosing her words. Seconds passed. "You . . . I owe you an apology. You're right. I never thought about any of that, before. In law school . . . I . . . God, this is hard to say. I hated you, practically on sight. Moving in, that first day. You were there, and I was so insecure—I am still insecure—and I . . . I let myself assume you were awful. It made me feel better, if you were awful. I convinced myself that I was justified . . . in being a bitch."

I gave her a tight nod of thanks, but felt something inside loosen and lift.

"I can't imagine what that must be like, to have people treat you that way all the time."

Emotion thickened my throat, but I had long practice at hiding it. "Well. If you can stop doing it going forward, we'll fare a lot better."

My phone dinged. Greg Dombrowski's name appeared, and I almost tossed it aside, assuming it would be yet another firm-wide pep talk or mandatory meeting. It wasn't. The email was addressed only to me.

Jane—

The police will be interviewing you tomorrow morning concerning Ray. I've arranged for that to take place in the conference room with me present at 10:00 a.m. Thank you.

Greg

I glanced up from the phone, my stomach cramping. "The police want to interview me tomorrow at ten a.m. Can you come back again? I'm sorry."

Allison nodded, then gathered her things. "Fine. I need to go home. Lots of other stuff to get out of the way, of course, if I'm coming back tomorrow. And Jane. Thanks for telling me the truth. And for giving me another chance."

I stood and we shook hands, clasping them a little longer than necessary. She wasn't my friend, but she might be the closest thing I had right now.

⁂

Later that night, I cruised through a subdivision north of town. The houses had probably been lovely when they were built twenty or thirty years ago, but their vinyl siding was buckling and stained with red mud and their Bradford pear trees had mostly split by now. I found Professor Graham's house on a quiet circle, near the back: a yellow bungalow with clematis twisting pink and green around a lamppost. I parked in front of the house three doors down and tried to decide how much of my history I could handle confronting in one day. Not much, it turned out. Part of me must have known I'd never get out of the car to tell him how he'd hurt me.

There was relief in admitting the truth to Allison and knowing she believed me. I'd be lying to myself if I didn't acknowledge her remorse also felt good.

Professor Graham had gotten away with it. As a student, I had too many secrets to hide and not enough bravery to go to the administration about his hand on my thigh and his grading policy. I'd been planning to dump Emmett anyway, and I walked away from Taxation with the same average grade as everyone else, so I tried to tell myself no harm, no foul. Professor Graham's filthy invective was far from the worst thing to happen to me.

Now, however, it had fueled my rage. I'd carried that unearned home-wrecker reputation all this time. He'd carried on teaching Taxation every year, earning accolades and expert-witness fees in the thousands, and no doubt singled out a new "star" in his classroom every year. Didn't I owe it to those women to do something?

I did. I pulled out my phone and searched for the email address of the office of student affairs at UVA Law, and began typing.

CHAPTER EIGHT

ALLISON

Steve and Karen had picked Libby up from day care and taken her to visit her grandparents for the night. My long workday—traveling to Charlottesville involved a three-hour round trip—ended in the Noble County courthouse, so with nowhere I needed to rush off to, I walked upstairs to patch things up with Emmett. We hadn't spoken since the previous night, when he'd found out I was representing Jane.

His boss, Commonwealth's Attorney Valerie Williams, sat across from him in his office chair, more relaxed than I'd ever seen her. Valerie was a young-looking sixtysomething. Her braids were pulled into a low-slung ponytail today. Normally, Valerie scared the crap out of me simply because of her position as the popularly elected champion of law and order. Now, she looked like a tired lawyer at the end of a long workday. Like me.

"Hi," I said. "Am I interrupting something?"

Emmett stood. I loved that tiny courtesy. "No, come on in. We were just shooting the breeze."

I sat in the second office chair. Emmett sat as Valerie reached over to give my shoulder a pat. "How're things on the Dark Side?" she asked.

When I'd first started seeing Emmett after our trial ended last fall, it had been necessary for him to go to Valerie to ask permission to date me. He was a prosecutor, after all, and I was a defense attorney. Being in a relationship meant that we could not ethically be on opposite sides in the same cases. Because my office then was right across the green from this courthouse, most of my criminal clients had been charged in Noble County. Valerie employed only three assistant commonwealth's attorneys, which meant that juggling would have to happen to avoid a future conflict of interest.

To my endless surprise, Valerie had been not only willing to do the juggling but delighted. Emmett told me later that, after he'd gathered his courage to ask her and come to the end of the long, rambling explanation, Valerie's response had been only two words: "About time." She seemed truly happy for him and, by extension, me.

Within a month after that conversation, I started my new firm and began taking more of my criminal cases from Lynchburg than from Noble County, anyway, relieving her burden. None of this had changed the fact that Valerie viewed criminal defense as "the Dark Side."

"Oh, come on, Valerie. You know she does legal work other than criminal defense," Emmett said.

I couldn't tell from his expression whether he'd forgiven me for lying about my interest in Jane Knudsen. His body language was still closed off, though maybe less forbidding than last night.

Valerie didn't miss it. Her gaze flicked between me and Emmett, assessing. Good lawyers needed a nearly supernatural ability to read other people's emotions, and few lawyers were as good at their jobs as Valerie. She stood. "I do know that. What'd you have today?"

"Nothing major. Just the entry of an order. Estate case."

"Well," she said, squeezing past my chair to the door. Emmett's taxpayer-funded office was small. "I'll let you two catch up. You call me if you want a job, Allison."

I laughed. Valerie always said that to me. It had become a joke between us. She left, clacking on high heels down the hall to her much bigger office.

Before the silence could stretch too long, I leaned forward and said, "Emmett. I'm sorry."

He stretched backward in his chair, putting his hands on his head, considering me. "I know. I get why you wanted to talk about Jane, and that you couldn't tell me why. I felt played, but you didn't know I'd dated her when you brought it up."

"I'm so sorry about that." I glanced at my hands, and my next words came out in a rush, surprising me. "You don't . . . still have feelings for her, do you?"

"For Jane?" Emmett's face shifted into gratifying shock. "No, of course not. Why? You didn't mention me to her, did you?"

"No. I can't. How could I explain knowing you dated her without letting her know we talked about her? It could get awkward if she finds out we're . . ." I hated trying to find a word for what we were. *Dating* and *boyfriend* still sounded so cheesy, Sweet Valley High–ish at my age.

He grinned. I'd shared my squeamishness at these words with him before. "That we're what, exactly?"

"Together," I said, pleased to have found an alternate word. It definitely would be awkward, because Jane had brought him up. The time to be upfront about it had come and gone and I'd said nothing.

"Why would she find out? She's your client. You'd have no reason to mention your personal life to her."

Except that maybe I should find a way to do it offhandedly. Emmett was a guy and wouldn't understand the fact that, lawyer and client or not, Jane and I would always be former roommates. She would feel betrayed if she knew I was . . . seeing her ex-boyfriend, especially the one she'd lost because of a scandal she'd had no part in creating. I'd betrayed her enough back in law school, but I'd also pushed Emmett too far. I'd have to worry about it another day.

"Right. Are you ready to leave? Do you still want to . . . ?" We'd had plans to go out to a nice dinner tonight, since Libby was with her dad. I hated feeling tentative about a relationship that had been so steady and real.

"Yes," he said, getting up. I stood, too. He came around the desk. "Of course I do. Hey." He stepped close enough to tip up my chin and look into my eyes. His hand on my skin spread relief everywhere. "Let's just be honest with each other, okay? We're not on opposite sides anymore. Everything else will work itself out."

"Sure. Okay," I said, relieved he wasn't holding a grudge. I would have kissed him—his lips were so close—but we were in his office, and the end-of-the-day buzz had set his coworkers in motion toward the door. I settled for wrapping my hand around the back of his waist.

I waited while he double-checked his pockets for his phone and keys.

"So I googled Jane," he said. "I see where some guy died in her law firm yesterday morning, but nobody's been charged. I assume she's hired you in case they look her direction?" He glanced at me. I tried not to betray the stress—he was asking a question I couldn't really answer under the ethics rules. He saved me. "Wait. Don't answer that. I'll operate on that assumption, given the timing. Sorry for asking."

"Thanks."

After checking to make sure the coast was clear, he grabbed my hand just before we stepped outside his office. He ran his hand suggestively up my arm, making me shiver. "Have you asked her about the Hot for Teacher scandal? That doesn't have anything to do with dead lawyers. And I gotta know," he teased.

My stomach sank. It had cost Jane to tell me what she had. I got the distinct feeling she'd never shared it with anyone else. I couldn't attack Emmett for making a joke of it—I had done it myself only last night—but something had shifted. Jane's feelings were important to me now.

Emmett had asked me to be honest, and I'd agreed. It hadn't taken even five minutes for me to break the promise.

"It didn't come up. Shall we go?"

As a general rule, I did not recommend voluntary interviews with law enforcement to my criminal clients. Right to remain silent, and all that. In this case, however, Jane wasn't yet a suspect and still had a narrow window to keep suspicion off her by cooperating with the police.

Not that I would allow her to answer very many questions. I spent most of the drive to Charlottesville the next morning prepping her by phone. She said she'd be fine; quit worrying.

I worried anyway.

When I arrived at Blackwood, an admin swept me off to a conference room that was too large by half. I gathered the firm had chosen it to intimidate the police and remind them who was boss. Jane and the man who'd shooed us away from the crime scene yesterday sat at one end of the long, gleaming table.

"Hi, Allison, this is our managing partner, Greg Dombrowski. Greg, my lawyer and former classmate, Allison Barton."

We shook hands. Greg's expression and body language could be described only as grim. I sat next to Jane.

"Foremost, Jane," Greg said, in a near parody of pompousness, "you have to preserve client confidentiality. And the firm's reputation. Those are the paramount concerns."

I would beg to differ that those were paramount for Jane, but okay. "Greg," I said. "Do you mind going out to route the police and give me a moment alone with my client?"

Judging from his face, yes, he very much minded leaving Jane alone for even a second, but he went.

"Are you good?" I asked her when he'd closed the door. "Don't worry about that confidentiality stuff. They won't ask anything like that. I'll shut down anything too risky, or the whole interview if it goes off the rails."

"I'm good. I know how to talk to police."

I narrowed my eyes. She was a lawyer, and certainly bright, but I wanted her—needed her—to be out from under all this. What experience would she have talking to police?

The moment for asking that question passed. The door opened, admitting Greg and two men, one short and one tall, wearing the giveaway tie-and-holster combo of the law enforcement investigator. The three men chatted amiably about the heat wave we were enjoying.

Jane stood, took what looked like a second to gather herself, and lifted her chin, extending a hand and a brilliant smile to the two investigators. If beauty could ever be to her advantage, she clearly was hoping now would be a good time. "Thank you so much for coming. I'm Jane Knudsen, and I worked with Ray. I'm so hopeful we can figure out what happened and save his family the agony they must be going through."

"Nice to meet you," the taller of the two said, with an appreciative smile. We all took our seats as he gestured. "I'm Zach O'Callihan, and this is Ned Hossain. We're investigators with the CPD."

"I'm Allison Barton. Jane and I are old friends from law school, and she asked me to sit in, if you don't mind."

I caught a little side-eye from Hossain, but O'Callihan's genial expression didn't change. "Absolutely. Good to meet you. We just have a few questions for Jane."

Though Hossain was clearly wiser, enough to be more suspicious, he was younger and therefore junior to O'Callihan. O'Callihan would be doing all the questioning. They opened notebooks.

"How long did you work for Ray?"

Jane smiled. "Ray ran the insurance defense group. I started there right away, my first year. Ray bought me lunch when I got the news I'd passed the bar."

"Would you say your relationship was good?"

"Yes, he worked hard and encouraged others to do the same. Our group had excellent billables last year."

O'Callihan narrowed his eyes. "Tell me about your personal relationship."

"Personal relationship?"

"We understand that you and Ray had some kind of out-of-work relationship. You just said he bought you lunch when you passed the bar." O'Callihan cleared his throat. "No judgment, Ms. Knudsen. We only need the facts."

Jane sailed ahead without even glancing my way. "He bought me lunch when I passed the bar seven years ago because that is a tradition for partners around here to do for their newest associates. The firm frequently pays for lunch." She raised an elegant hand in Greg's direction. "Greg would know. He buys lunch for his associates on occasion."

Sitting next to her, I could detect Jane gathering her strength to answer the last part of the question. Her pause spoke of shields and armor and tiring sieges. "As for your second question," she said, "I never had any kind of relationship with Ray Corrigan other than professional."

O'Callihan and Hossain looked at each other. Hossain raised an eyebrow, not bothering to hide his skepticism. He spoke up without waiting for permission. "Ms. Knudsen, we frankly find that hard to believe. We've spoken to a number of coworkers of yours. Their understanding was quite different. Would you like to try again?"

Jane's posture sagged a bit. Hossain's tone infuriated me. As if gossipy coworkers knew more about Jane's sex life than she did. As the thought occurred to me, the realization of my hypocrisy on that exact point demanded I do something. I slashed the air in front of me. "She's answered your question. She can't help it if the truth is not convenient to your narrative."

"The answer is still no," said Jane. "Ray and I had no relationship other than as partner and associate. I don't suppose you'd like to tell me who told you otherwise."

Without thinking, both O'Callihan and Hossain glanced at Greg. Before he could erase it, Greg's face was written in guilt.

Jane bit her lip. "Greg, I don't think you'll be necessary to this interview any longer. I can finish up here."

"Are you sure that's wise?"

"We'll be fine," I said. "It was nice to meet you, Mr. Dombrowski."

After a moment, Greg stood. At first I thought he'd go and his lack of faith in Jane could be straightened out later. I was wrong.

"Take your time, Jane. You're on administrative leave as of this morning. I've granted the investigators the use of this conference room today, so when you're done here, gather your things and remain at home until further notice. Erin from HR will be emailing you later with details."

Before I could stop her, Jane asked, "What? Why?"

Dammit. He was itching to tell her why, and in front of the police, too.

"Just to protect our clients until all this . . . suspicion is removed. It does appear things were going on in Ray's department we weren't aware of."

Jane's face closed over. I would have liked to strangle Greg. Her administrative leave had been a done deal before she'd arrived in this room. And based on what? The fact that her coworkers gossiped about her? I touched her arm and leaned in. "Do you want to continue? Say the word and this ends."

"I'm fine," she said. I wondered how often she said those words. I wondered how often they were true.

Greg stood in the doorway, head bobbing between Jane and the investigators, then went, closing the door behind him.

"Please, let's continue," Jane said, having retrieved enough self-possession from somewhere to host a catered Thanksgiving dinner.

O'Callihan and Hossain pulled it back at that point, asking a lot of less charged questions about Ray's workload (heavy), the hours he typically spent in the office (most of them), who had access to his office (everyone), how responsible he was about locking the desk drawer with the gun in it (not). They asked questions about what time Jane had left the night of the murder (around ten), what time she'd received the email from Ray (midnight), and what time she'd found him dead in the morning (six something).

Because these things were all facts they could learn from other sources, I let the questioning continue as long as they stayed with Ray as a subject, and meanwhile, I made notes on what they asked so I could evaluate the direction of their investigation.

Jane admitted that Ray's wife, Felicity, openly disliked her, though she and Ray's daughter, Brittany, had gotten along fine. She told the investigators that both Felicity and Brittany had visited the office with regularity before and after Brittany had been a summer associate the previous year.

"Tell us about the rest of your work group. Josh Gardner, Amir Burhan, and Irene Robinson get along with Ray?"

I touched Jane's wrist under the table to remind her to be cautious. She didn't need my help. "All three are professionals. I heard occasional grumbling from them about the hours or the workload, but no one of them more than the other two, or more than any other associate or admin working anywhere else in the firm. Irene had worked for Ray for decades. Josh and Ray were downright friendly at times, at least as friendly as Ray got with anyone. Amir was aware that new associates must pay dues and that working for Ray could get him where he wanted to go. I can't imagine that any of them would have any animus against him. Not homicidal animus, anyway."

"We spoke to them, Jane. They'd agree with you there, but some troubling information came up about you—"

I interrupted. "She's already answered that question. No relation-ship. Move on."

The investigators exchanged glances again. "No, this was different. One of them mentioned the fact that nobody knows anything about your life."

I put my hand on Jane's before she could speak and left it there, signaling that she should stay quiet. "That's not a crime."

"No," said O'Callihan, stretching out the word. "But more than one person we interviewed said that Ms. Knudsen had concealed even the most basic information about herself. We've got a dead body in a law firm. His closest coworker has a blank for a history. Seems like something we need to check out. Help us out here, Ms. Knudsen. Where are you from?"

Under my hand, Jane's fingers were shaking. Though I sure as hell would have liked the answer to that question myself, it was way past time for me to put her desires ahead of my own need for instant information gratification. "It's entirely irrelevant. Jane's lived in Charlottesville for at least a decade—I can verify that because I went to law school with her—and she met Ray Corrigan for the first time no more than eight years ago."

As I said it, I realized I had no idea whether that was true. Maybe more had gone on between Ray and Jane than she'd told me. Damn.

I carried on anyway. "Ray turned up dead this week, not ten years ago. Her personal history before working here can be of no interest to you. You're wasting your time—and hers."

"Oh, we wouldn't be asking if we weren't interested, Ms. Barton," O'Callihan said, his brow wrinkling.

Hossain, definitely the quicker of the two, spoke up. "And she's on leave. Looks to me like she's got all the time in the world."

"Did you have any other questions about Ray Corrigan?" I glanced around, waiting. They sat there, fidgeting, like middle-school boys caught looking at porn. "No? Then we're done here."

I stood, pulling at Jane's hand. She was frozen. "Come on."

The investigators' faces lost all hint of pleasantry, even O'Callihan's.

Jane looked like she'd been hit by a train, but she stood, and as I watched, her face regained control and her professional blank mask returned, bit by bit. By the time we got back to her office, she was fully in control again.

"What was that?" I asked, closing the door. After saving her from whatever personal breakdown she'd been about to have, I figured I was entitled to know.

"What?" Jane said distractedly, heading straight to her computer. "Do you mind? If they're kicking me out, I need to send myself some documents before they stop me. I imagine Greg will be here in a few minutes. Can we talk later?"

"Well, real quick, where are you from? For some reason, back in law school, I got the idea it was in the mountains."

"I never said that." A hint of a flush climbed the smooth expanse of her neck. "Really, Allison. Call me later. I don't have time for this right now."

She wasn't going to tell me. Not even the name of her hometown.

Barely got her hometown out of her, Emmett had said.

Emmett knew the answer to that question. The real question was whether I dared ask.

CHAPTER NINE

JANE

I didn't glance up from my computer until Allison had gone. Though I hadn't been lying about needing to prepare and organize myself before Greg literally sent me packing, I couldn't look at her or she might see too much in my eyes. I was well practiced at evasion. My strategy depended on keeping people from getting a good look at my face.

What I did want to do, and right now, before another minute passed, was find out whether Josh had helped the investigators focus on me. Their questions had assumed that the rumor I was sleeping with Ray was true. Amir had told Allison he didn't believe it, and I couldn't believe Irene would. All roads, at this moment, led to Josh.

Josh had been scarce since the other night, when I had so very ill-advisedly agreed to go to his place. Maybe he'd been hoping for more than I was willing to give and was off licking his wounds.

Once all my file transfers had gone through and I'd sent all the necessary emails, I shut down the computer and gathered my things, even the cardigan on the back of my chair that warded off the air-conditioning chill. Administrative leave—holy shit. Did anyone ever come back from administrative leave? I'd have to fight it. I'd have to marshal resources and, well, the energy to marshal resources. Being sent home in disgrace didn't even feel unjust. My life history had taught me to expect that I'd get what I deserved, and then I'd get a lot worse than that.

I carried all my stuff to my car and returned, twisting through the hallways to find Josh's office. When I appeared in his doorway, he looked up. A faint furtive look crossed his face before he wiped his expression clean.

I knew it. I closed the door. "What the hell, Josh?"

He fidgeted. "What?"

"What did you tell them? The police think I was sleeping with Ray. The perfect motive. Did you tell them that?"

He blinked. I watched him trying to decide what to say. Josh worked hard. He could review documents and write briefs with the best of them, but he was terrible at thinking on his feet. He'd never be a good trial lawyer. Fortunately for him, our practice litigated mainly with avalanches of paper and not much in courtrooms.

"They asked me about the rumor—they'd already heard it—and I said I'd heard it, too. That's all, Jane. I swear." He wiped his upper lip with the side of his index finger. "I'm sorry. I was afraid of getting caught in a lie."

"Great, Josh. Just great. I found him. Right there, that makes me the prime suspect, and apparently everyone in this building was champing at the bit to tell them salacious rumors about my sexual promiscuity. Everybody loves the 'woman scorned' narrative. I expected all that. I knew I had enemies. But I didn't expect *you* to be jumping on that bandwagon. I thought you would defend me. I thought you were my friend."

"I . . . I'm sorry. I had heard the rumor." His face was stricken, and he spread his hands wide. "I admit I thought it was probably true."

"You could have *asked* me if I was sleeping with Ray, you know. Instead of just assuming. Why would I be interested in Ray? He was married! More than twenty years older. And unpleasant as hell under the best of circumstances!" In despair, I put my face in my hands, then decided to stare him down instead.

"I . . . well, up until the other day, every time I even hinted that I might be . . . you acted like I wasn't even there . . . uh. Um. I assumed you must be seeing someone—how could you not be, Jane, you're so beautiful—and then Ray was dead, and suddenly you agreed to . . . for the first time . . ."

"You never asked before! And so you naturally assumed that if I was not interested in you, I absolutely must be sleeping with Ray. And that as soon as he was dead, I would require an immediate replacement. Obviously. I see. Unassailable logic there, Josh. *For God's sake.*"

His face crumpled. "I'm sorry. I don't know why I thought that. It was wrong. Please forgive me."

"Well, that might take a bit. Thanks in part to your *Gossip Girl* tendencies, Greg put me on administrative leave and I'm the person of interest. Whatever Irene and her lawyer did apparently got the police to look elsewhere. So thanks for helping give them a reason for 'elsewhere' to be me. I've got to go."

Josh stood. "Wait, Jane. I said I was sorry."

"*Sorry* doesn't fix it. At best, I'm on indefinite administrative leave. At worst, I'm out of a job here and possibly everywhere. On the assumption that I will someday come back and we'll work together again, we're going to pretend the other night didn't happen. Is that clear?"

"Didn't happen? What? I thought . . ."

"Yes. And I thought you were someone who cared about me." I could hear the frost in my clipped tone. The ice queen. I depended on the cold to freeze out the pain. "I will concede you may not have realized all the ramifications of what you were doing, passing on that gossip. After all, sleeping with a partner wouldn't kill *your* career. It might enhance it. But it doesn't matter."

It did matter. But not to anyone in a position to do anything about it in this building.

"No," he said, horrified. "I do care about you. I want to be with you. I figured they'd already know I'd heard the rumor. I was afraid if I lied I'd become . . ."

"What? That you'd become a suspect if you expressed disbelief that I would sleep with Ray to gain a partnership inside track?" I shook my head, trying to clear it. "Don't worry, Josh. It's not that big a deal. I'll get over it. You did what anyone would do. What everyone else did do."

"What do you mean? What did I do?"

"You gave them permission to settle on the easiest, most obvious motive of them all. The oldest story in the book—literally. Blame the temptress."

I opened the door and fled.

꩜

I'd moved into a new town house six months before, after renting for most of my adult life. Somehow, the experience had not matched my expectations. Owning a house hadn't immediately transported me into cozy domestic bliss. The white walls and white kitchen and white bathrooms that had appealed so strongly to my long-held desire to be washed clean when I looked at the unit and made my offer now struck me as sterile and inhuman. Working the hours I did meant no time to paint or decorate. My sparse furniture served only to remind me that my life was incomplete and colorless.

I tossed my belongings on the pristine light-gray granite island and took a second to run my fingers along the cool, substantial expanse. The granite was the one part of the town house that made me feel rich. I'd never dreamed of possessing anything so luxurious when I was young.

There was a time, obviously, when I was young, though I didn't talk about it. I wished I could tell Allison how much I appreciated her immediate realization that I didn't want to answer the hometown question in front of the detectives. Allison was quicker than I'd thought, and

I probably should worry about how quick. She wouldn't leave me alone for long on the question of my past.

All the way home in the car, I'd pondered how much, eventually, to tell her. Like most in law school, she'd been satisfied by the new-student info, which listed my hometown as Durham, home of Duke University, where I'd lived for the four years prior to law school. Allison's mention of "mountains" had chilled me to the bone—I had no memory of telling her that much truth. But I must have.

Mountains were my reality. Every night, I visited them in my dreams. Their stony cliffs were my backbone and their green heights my escape. The hollers and waterfalls of my childhood had been the white noise that drowned out enough of what was wrong for me to keep going another day. Durham, with its urban sprawl and constant traffic and intellectual discourse, had been as foreign to me as an underwater sea cavern, but I'd adapted. I was adaptable.

I'd long since dumped all my yearbooks and school papers and even my high school diploma, but when I got in these melancholy moods, I dug out my battered copy of *Charlotte's Web*, removed the single photo I'd saved, and went to the mirror.

The girl in the picture was missing her two front teeth—a temporary flaw. She wore whatever had been on sale at Walmart in 1996. Impossibly long lashes surrounded startling eyes, and her hair cascaded, thick and shining, over both shoulders in fascinating streaks of gold and amber. Her grin stretched into near normalcy those astonishingly full lips. The photographer had captured a child who was bright, unconcerned with fashion, unafraid of life, and unaware of the curse of her own appearance. She'd left the mother who hated her at home and was safe at school, where her teacher loved her.

Clinically, I could see that this child's face was otherworldly and rare, even with the teeth missing. Even at that age.

Shrugging out of the suit jacket I wouldn't need for some time to come, I looked for that girl in the mirror, and reassured myself that she was gone for good. I checked the part in my long hair for telltale growth—I was careful about not letting the blonde grow out even a little. Though it had hardly been my focus, it turned out that the dark hair looked almost as natural with my skin as the gold had.

Many times, I'd considered plastic surgery and self-inflicted scars and acid, but I was afraid it would only draw more attention. People would stare and continue to stare. There hadn't been one minute after the day that first-grade picture was taken when the word *beautiful*, as applied to me, had brought me anything but misery.

There were a few things I needed to get done. First, the phone.

She answered the call on the first ring.

I didn't waste time. "Listen," I said, not interested in any preliminary chitchat. "I met with investigators today and I didn't point them your way. You owe me. Get a pen. Here's my lawyer's number. I need you to call her and tell her what you know."

"Oh, Jane, I don't really think . . ."

"I think."

"I can't do that to her. No way."

"You can, and you will, or I'll suggest the investigators do some checking into your job situation. I've got their card right here in my pocket."

"Please don't ask me to do this."

"I'm not asking you to rat on her to the police, though given everything, I don't know what would make you hesitate. I'm asking you to help my lawyer get a bigger picture. Either you call her or she'll call you. There's no reason to waste time."

"How do I know you didn't do this?" she asked, in a small voice.

"You don't, I suppose."

There was a long silence. "Fine."

I hung up. I wasn't the only woman who'd had a reason to kill Ray Corrigan. I didn't even have the best reason.

With that done, I glanced around. The police would be coming. Administrative leave was only the first step.

One day soon, they'd show up here with a warrant, going through everything in my pristine house; they'd take my home computer, my phone, my iPad. They'd dig through my closet for bloodstained heels or suits. They'd check my drains and toilet plumbing and my outdoor grill. They'd bag my dirty laundry and my tax returns and my bank statements.

They'd find nothing.

Or, at least, they'd find nothing after tonight.

It would kill me to lose this picture—the last memory I had of happiness—but I had no choice. It had to go. I'd take my kitchen trash to the dump tonight, and the picture would be in it.

One more thing had to go in the trash bag. From the bottom of my chest of drawers, I pulled out the soft, worn Duke University T-shirt I'd bought years ago at a basketball game. I still wore it sometimes to watch Duke play, safe on my sofa.

The royal-blue color of the shirt—Duke blue, we called it—almost, but not quite, hid the tiny stain at the left shoulder. It could have been chocolate, or the red mud of Virginia.

It could have been chocolate or mud, but it wasn't.

CHAPTER TEN
ALLISON

I made it almost to the interstate on my way home from the police interview before my phone rang.

"I don't suppose you've already left," Maureen said. "A woman named Irene Robinson called you about the Jane Knudsen matter. She's in Charlottesville and wanted to speak with you in person, if you aren't too far away."

"She called out of the blue?" I said, already looking for a place to turn around while simultaneously picturing the massive pile of non-Jane work on my desk.

"Yup. Said she's a friend of Jane's and she feels bad about things. Whatever that means."

Join the crowd, Irene. "Okay. Text me her number and I'll try to catch up with her."

I got in touch with Irene and agreed to meet her at the chain bookstore close to the highway exit. It didn't take long to find her there. Irene had described herself as Black, short, and loudly dressed, which was borne out by the sleeveless, highlighter-yellow dress she wore with matching earrings. She had the coiled energy of a woman who could still do a cartwheel past forty. Though she was much smaller than I was, her defined arm muscles made me feel wimpy.

I'd liked her on the phone. That was borne out, too, by the warm smile she gave me as she introduced herself. We found an empty table in the store's café.

She dived right in. "So Amir gave me your name after you came by. I know this is weird, but I can't publicly help Jane, because I'm afraid of getting called in by the police again. She's been a friend to me, though, and I feel like hell about the way I turned my back on her. You understand, right? They went straight for me the very first day he was dead."

"I understand."

"I've got a family. I can't let them take me from my kids." Anguish twisted her features, making me want to hug her.

"I know," I said.

"And for the record, I didn't kill Ray. He was a colossal tyrant, but he was my livelihood. The firm will shuffle me off to another partner, or if billing is down and staffing is high, they'll cut me loose. I'd have no motive to kill him. Nothing at all to gain."

"I expect the police can see that."

"So here's what I'm offering. I know they put Jane on leave. She's not going to be in the office to hear the rumors, and that will handicap her in a big way. I'll pass them on to you, as long as I'm there, of course."

"That would be amazing. Thank you." Gratitude expanded my chest.

"I'd rather do it by email from here on out. I'll create a new Gmail account and use a different VPN."

I gave her a card that included my email address. "Thank you again."

"I did have a few things I can tell you right now." She swallowed, checking her peripheral vision like a Cold War spy. "You can never trace any of this back to me."

"Okay, go ahead," I said, rummaging in my bag for my legal pad.

"The managing partner, Greg Dombrowski, has been acting weird. I worked late a couple of weeks ago and Greg and Ray had an argument in his office so loud I could hear it with the door closed."

"What was it about?"

"I don't know. Ray had just been appointed to the managing committee. Something about billing, I think."

"Was there some issue? Was Ray's billing too low?"

"No, I heard something about shares and 'if the clients discovered,' but I never got the full picture."

Associate lawyers like Jane, Josh, and Amir billed hours and got paid salaries. The partners also billed hours but were paid by dividing up the firm's earnings in "shares." In the bigger firms with multiple partners, this involved elaborate calculations and careful valuation of work brought in, non-billable time spent for the betterment of the firm, and enormous egos. The part about the clients, though, hinted that something untoward was happening with the billing. I made a note. What had Ray been up to?

"And since Ray died, Greg has been stalking around the firm, guarding the crime scene, breaking up any casual conversation even if it's not related to the murder. He's always read emails—to make sure we were working and not 'playing'—but that's why I'll use a different VPN. Anything I write at work will be read."

"Is that unusual for him? He is the managing partner."

"Yeah. It's unusual. He's never been quite that much in everyone's business before."

"Okay. I'll see what I can find out." I glanced at her. "What about Amir?"

"Amir? Amir's a clown." She looked chagrined. "That sounds bad. I meant like a class clown. The kind who is inexplicably filled with ten times the normal amount of self-confidence. I heard he had an alibi. Something about his wife's brother being in town."

"And who's the other person in the work group? Joshua Gardner?"

"Josh is a mess. Like, with his personal life. The partners don't want to know a thing about anyone's personal life. His fell apart last year when his wife left him after a brutal battle with infertility. She cheated on him. The good thing, I guess, for the firm at least, is that since that all ended, he's gotten it together and been a billing machine."

"Amir said that Josh and Ray were close. Is that true?"

She shook her head ruefully. "Dudes have a weird way of defining 'close.' Like with everyone else, Ray worked Josh into the dirt, but I guess they got along. Josh was at work when he heard Miriam had been seen with some other guy—I don't know how—and I swear his howl would have raised the dead. People on other floors heard it. Ray took Josh out to lunch—in part to get his emotional mess out of there before Greg saw him—and the next day, Ray had me give Josh the contact info for a private investigator Ray had used in a case once. The proof of the affair came in almost immediately, and I think Josh was pretty grateful. Upset about his wife, of course, but grateful to Ray. Best I can tell, they never fought."

Her phone dinged with a text. "Hey, I gotta go, but I'll be in touch. I hope that helps a little." She jumped to her feet, a ball of energy.

"Thanks, Irene. Jane will be grateful." I stood, too.

"Oh no, don't tell Jane I'm helping. I do not want anyone to know I'm helping. Nobody. Okay? I don't want the police looking at me. Promise?"

"Sure. Oh, one quick thing. Did you and Jane ever talk about her life before law school?"

Irene looked blank. "You mean like, her childhood? School?"

"Yes. Anything about that. Do you know much about her? Where she's from?"

"No, honey. She's a closed book. I don't honestly think she's got a clue how to relate to people. Not a fan of eye contact, that one. She comes to work, she works hard, she goes home, and she comes back. That's her life. Rare times we'd talk, it was about a TV show or a book or something about one of my kids. A while ago she bought a town house. Nothing else about her. No boyfriend. No friends. No hobbies. Jane's always been a nice person, but if she's got either a past or a future, I've never heard about it. She's only ever had a present."

※

Late that night, near the end of my phone call with Emmett, I dared.

"You said Jane told you the name of her hometown. God, Emmett, I hate so much that I have to ask you, but I need you to tell me. And . . . I need you not to ask why."

There was a long and unpleasant silence, long enough that I worried the phone call had dropped. Maybe it wouldn't be terrible if it had. I had plenty of time to wish I'd never heard from Jane Knudsen about her criminal case.

"I can't deny that I hate that you're asking." His voice, full of gravel from overuse, came slowly.

More silence. I didn't know what to say. "I need to know her hometown. To help her."

"And she won't tell you?"

"No. She thinks her secrets will protect her. I'm growing increasingly convinced they'll take her down. Please."

A long sigh. "All right. But don't put me in this position again. We are walking a very fine line here, Allie."

"I know." I held my breath.

It took forever before the low rumble of his voice started up again. "Okay. The year we dated, second year, she lived in a tiny hellhole of an apartment. I came to pick her up and she left me in the living room while she changed clothes in the bedroom—she'd spilled something on herself or something. I picked up a piece of mail. Can't remember whose name was on it, but it was addressed to Galt, North Carolina. Jane caught me looking at it."

"What did she say?"

"All she said was that she'd appreciate it if I didn't mention Galt to anyone else. I put the envelope down and we never spoke of it again."

"So you don't know if it's her hometown."

"No. But it upset her. I looked Galt up later. It's a pinprick on the map miles from anywhere. An hour or more south of Asheville."

Asheville was in western North Carolina.

In the mountains.

❦

"Where are we going, Mommy?" Libby looked up from the iPad I'd given her so she could watch a movie during the long drive.

"We're taking a road trip to see the mountains. I have a little bit of work to do—some people to talk to—and then we can go see a waterfall and get some ice cream. Sound fun?"

Libby's brows drew together. "Why do you have to work on a Saturday?"

"This is mostly going to be a fun day. I just need to ask a few questions and then we'll have the day to ourselves, okay?"

"How come Emmett didn't come with us?"

Her question sent a little hope flaring through me. She loved Emmett, piano teacher. She wasn't so sure about Emmett in any other capacity. And I wanted her to be sure, with a desperation that scared me.

"I thought we'd spend the day just us girls. Okay?"

She stuck her lower lip out unconsciously, an echo of the way she'd done as a baby. "Are you going to marry him?"

That was an excellent question. We'd been together only seven months. He'd once said something about what a bad idea it was to jump into marriage too soon. I'd gotten burned my first time wearing a white dress. We might be headed that way, but neither of us was in a hurry, and the ghost of Jane Knudsen didn't seem likely to speed us along.

Steve and Karen, on the other hand, cloaked now in the propriety of holy matrimony, thought I ought to marry Emmett to legitimize my relationship. That only made me resist the idea more stubbornly.

"We haven't even talked about that, Lib."

"I don't want you to get married, too." There was an edge to her voice. "I don't like Karen. Daddy never plays with me now. I only like Emmett sometimes."

Great. I opened my mouth to start the long process of adjusting her worldview, but she was over it.

"Are we almost there?"

The drive to western North Carolina's Blue Ridge Mountains had taken four hours. Libby had watched *Frozen II* one and a half times and had slept for an hour. Grumpiness was setting in by the time the GPS directed us off the interstate shy of Asheville and sent us into a national forest to the south. The tiny town of Galt made nearby Hendersonville look like a metropolis. It was, however, near to many lovely waterfalls that drew hikers from miles around. I'd dressed for that today, thinking it might raise fewer eyebrows.

Galt had, to its name, a small government-issue post office, a few older houses, a Baptist church with "Repent" on the changeable marquee in front, a run-down chain gas station with a convenience store, and a vacant building with broken windows that might once have been a Laundromat. Nothing else. The people must live spread out in the countryside in the hollows and valleys of the mountains. I decided to start with the convenience store—less intrusive than knocking at one of the houses and more likely to involve actual people than any of the other options. Besides, I could extend Libby's pre-meltdown time with a little red licorice, and I'd never been above a well-placed parenting bribe.

"Come on, Lib. Let's get a piece of candy."

Her eyes opened wide enough for me to see the whites all around her brown irises. "Okay!"

She unbuckled herself and hopped out once I unlocked the back door. Inside, Libby skipped off to dither over the candy aisle. The cashier with dead-black, dyed hair and a slightly lighter black T-shirt was likely a teenager. If Jane had a connection to this town, she'd been gone too long for this girl to have known her.

"Hi. I have a weird question. I'm trying to get in touch with an old friend's family. Are you from around here?"

Libby bounced up with Twizzlers in her hand—the king-size pack. "No, go get the smaller one. That is too much licorice." She pouted but disappeared down the aisle.

"Yup. All my life, if you can believe it. I went to Varner County High School."

"Is that the school that everyone from Galt goes to?"

She laughed, brushing a lock of dry-looking hair out of her eyes. "'Everyone'? That ain't too many people. Most of my class was from the bigger towns, but yeah. If you have a Galt address, you go there."

I handed her a ten to pay for Libby's candy and my Coke Zero. "Listen. Who do you think I should ask about my friend? She's about thirty-two. Grew up here. You know a teacher at the high school I could ask?"

The bell tied to the door jangled. "You could ask her. That's Mrs. DuPont. She teaches at Galt Elementary. Hi, Mrs. DuPont. This lady wanted help finding some other lady from Galt."

The new arrival, a woman in her late fifties, I'd estimate, fulfilled all the best characteristics of an elementary school teacher. She had a warm smile, carried just enough weight to give cuddly hugs, and wore a soft-looking T-shirt with her denim capri pants. Libby sidled up to me and stared up at her with her finger in her mouth, recognizing a kindred spirit immediately.

"Hi, Viv; how're your folks?" Mrs. DuPont asked the cashier. To me, she said, "Can I help you somehow?"

I reached into my bag to get the headshot of Jane I'd printed from her firm's website. For a beautiful woman, it was an unflattering picture. Her grin was self-conscious, as if she were trying to smile in a different way than was normal. "Sure. I'm trying to find the family of this woman—Jane Knudsen is her name. She's thirty-two. My understanding is that her family may live around here."

"Knudsen, you say? With a K?"

I nodded. "K-N-U-D-S-E-N."

"There was a Knudsen who used to teach first grade with me. Alice Knudsen. She's passed on now, but she never married or had children. And I think she was from Pennsylvania. If she had any family, they'd have lived up there. Let me take a look at your picture."

She fumbled for her glasses and peered at the picture, squinting. I watched the recognition hit her, and excitement rose. This woman knew Jane. "I . . . I think I had this girl as a student in fifth grade, if it's who I'm thinking of." She glanced at me and her eyes changed, her warm expression dissolving into a mask of pity. Pity couldn't be good.

Up until Jane's email a few days ago, if asked, I would have guessed that her life had been charmed from birth. After all, how could life be hard for someone so beautiful, brilliant, and sought after? It was only the rest of us who had to struggle for belonging and success. She was halfway there the minute she showed her face.

More recently, I'd begun to suspect that I'd been wrong. Watching this nice lady's face fall cemented it. Once again, I'd asked a question I might not want to know the answer to.

Yet the police were asking it. It would be better for me to find out before they did.

"You should go show this to Cherry Starkey. I'll warn you, she's not the type to much appreciate a stranger showing up at her door, but if you decide to, she lives in the green trailer down the road right there." Mrs. DuPont pointed out the plate glass window of the store to a narrow road that spiked off the main road on which we'd arrived. "On the left, I want to say less than a mile. Kind of a sage green. Single-wide."

"Thank you," I said, taking Libby's hand.

The green trailer wasn't hard to find. It sat in a clearing under a huge white oak tree and shared a mud-rutted driveway with a second trailer nearby, just as disheveled. Mindful of what Mrs. DuPont had said, I set Libby up in the car with her candy and her iPad and locked the doors.

I banged on the door for a while before giving up. No car sat in the driveway, and it was midday on a Saturday. No one was home. I headed back to the car.

"Are you looking for Cherry?" called a voice from the wooden porch of the other trailer. "She ain't there. Roof leaked and she took off."

A neighbor might do almost as well—this woman looked old enough to have known Jane as a child. I picked my way through the tall grass in the yard. "Do you have a quick minute?"

"I reckon," said the woman, shifting her weight off swollen ankles, one at a time. Faded light eyes blended with her papery skin and salt-and-pepper hair. She wore a worn white T-shirt with an American flag on it. There were two green plastic lawn chairs squeezed at right angles onto the splintering porch. "You want to sit?"

I waved at Libby to let her know where I was. "My daughter is in the car—I won't take up your time. I wondered if you know this woman," I said, showing her the picture.

She looked up, shock written all over her face. "Where'd you get that? That's Cherry's daughter! Lord have mercy, I haven't seen her since she graduated high school! Her hair's all dark, though," she said, stabbing a bitten fingernail at the picture. "Can't imagine why a pretty girl like that would want ol' dark hair."

Unease began to creep through my chest. I'd never once seen Jane with a different color of hair than the near-black she had in this picture. "What's her name?"

Something inside told me the next words out of her mouth weren't going to be *Jane Knudsen*.

"What? Why, that's Renee! Renee Starkey. Prettiest girl in Varner County, though she was prettier when she was blonde. That hair she had. Lord. Like gold. No one on TV had any better. I always wondered where she went off to. Cherry never would say. All's she said was they had words and Renee went off to the city and she ain't never heard nothing more."

"Do you know when Cherry might be home?"

"Naw. When the roof leaked couple weeks ago, she and . . . what's his name? Good for nothing, that's for sure. I can't keep 'em straight, all these boyfriends Cherry's got. You'd think at her age she'd've quit by now, good glory." She shook her head as she muttered, and I suppressed a wild urge to laugh. "Anyways, she went off with him somewheres he knew 'til the landlord fixes it. Could be a while. He ain't in no hurry."

"Do you have a phone number for her?"

"Oh sure. Let me get it."

She left me sitting there absorbing this bombshell until she returned a minute later with a slip of paper. "Here 'tis. Well, honey, if you see Renee, you tell her hey from Paula Lockaby. Sweet girl. She and Cherry didn't get along too good; Cherry's not a natural mama."

"'Not a natural mama'? What does that mean?"

Mrs. Lockaby looked around like she was going to share a state secret. "Well, I don't pay no mind when a mama needs to do a little correction, and if you ask me, girl with those looks was probably born asking for trouble. 'Tween you and me, though, Cherry was right mean about it. I used to hear screaming and yelling over there all the time. I thought about calling the po-lice a few times, but then I figgered it was Cherry's business and none of mine."

None of mine. My heart broke for Jane.

"Thank you so much for . . . for the phone number," I said, as if I cared about the phone number. I'd never call it.

"You're right welcome. It's nice to have a chat. Lonely out here, sometimes."

In a daze, I walked back to the car, buckling my seat belt on autopilot. Jane—*not Jane, Renee, dear God*—had been abused by her mother, and her neighbor had never lifted a finger to help her. Good glory, indeed.

"Can you stop asking questions now, Mommy? I want to see a waterfall."

"Yeah, buddy. I am absolutely done asking questions."

Until I could absorb the magnitude of what I'd learned, I had no need to ask another one.

PART TWO

PAYNE

CHAPTER ELEVEN

JANE

Monday morning I woke up as usual—two minutes before my 4:45 a.m. alarm went off—then slumped back onto my pillow. I hadn't set an alarm, because I was on administrative leave. Barred from my clients, barred from my work, barred from doing anything at all to fix this mess.

At the moment, however, the most pressing problem was how on earth I would fill another whole day with nowhere to go and nothing to do. I was a workaholic for a reason: I didn't enjoy being alone with my thoughts. My stomach twisted with anxiety, but I forced the bad thoughts back into the lockbox.

Find something to do. Now.

I got up to make coffee, the same as I did every other day. Maybe I could fill the time. I could scrub things some more. Catch up on the news. Read that biography that had been half-finished on my nightstand for weeks. Organize my closet. Go to the paint store and think about painting my white walls a color. Go buck wild and replace all my plastic food storage containers.

By seven thirty, I'd showered and eaten and scoured nonexistent dirt from every surface in my kitchen. Before the familiar terror of idleness that had already begun buffeting me from the sides could take hold, I grabbed my cell and called Allison. I didn't really need to talk to her, but I'd think of a reason any second.

"Hello?" she answered, sounding far more harried than I'd ever seen signs of before. "No."

"What?"

"Jane. Hi. No, that was not to you. I'm sorry. Hang on a sec."

In the background, I could hear her arguing and the high-pitched sound of a child. Allison had a child? How had I missed that? I hadn't spared a second to wonder about her personal life.

"No," she said, her voice muffled but unmistakable. "You can't wear those. It's too hot for tights. Take them off."

"Is this a bad time?" I asked.

"Hang on one more second," she said to me. "Libby. Go put on something that you can wear on a day when it's going to be ninety-three degrees. You'll get all sweaty and your face will turn red like Rudolph's nose. Hurry up. Go."

I tried not to chuckle, imagining the little girl dressed for winter in a Virginia summer.

"Okay," said Allison, with palpable relief. "She went to change. Sorry about that."

Just in time, I thought of a reason. How pathetic. I paid Allison to take my calls—a lot of money. And I'd happily pay more to keep the aloneness at bay for another couple of minutes. "I have a witness who agreed to call you, if she hasn't already."

"Oh, right." There was a pause. "I was going to call you about this later, but I guess now is as good a time as any. I . . . I need you to tell me your real name."

My knees buckled and I sat down hard on the sofa. My thighs began shaking. "My . . . my real . . ." How? How had she done it? Maybe she was only guessing. "My real name is Jane Elizabeth Knudsen."

"Not that one."

Only one person in all these years had figured it out, and that person would never tell. "I'll be happy to show you my papers. I know you don't think the bar would have granted me a license if I were using a fake name."

She sighed. Her daughter yelled something unintelligible from another room. "Okay," she said. "Sure. As an attorney, I am aware that names can be legally changed. I've even helped people with the paperwork before. I'm assuming you changed yours before law school. Before I met you. I know it wasn't Jane when you were in high school." The little girl yelled, louder. "Coming, Lib. Just a second."

She knew. Holy shit, she knew. "How?" I whispered. Somehow my lungs hadn't taken in enough air to speak properly.

"That's too long a story for this second, because I have to get my daughter out the door. Real quick, though: the police think you're hiding something, and they're apparently right. May well not be relevant, but they think it is. The longer they go without knowing, the bigger a deal it's going to blow up to be."

"I don't . . . I still don't know . . ."

"Fine. I get it. You don't want to talk about this, but we're going to have to, and soon. Pretend I'm only your lawyer and not your former roommate, if that makes it easier, Jane." She took a breath. "I probably brought it up the wrong way. I shouldn't have asked when I already know." She pulled the phone away. "Yes, go get in the car. Yes! Now."

"You had no right," I said, reaching for anger like a life preserver I knew I'd never be able to hold on to. How? How had she done it?

"I had every right the second I heard the police were investigating your background. It's my job to stay ahead of them. To know what they know before they do. It's easier to throw up roadblocks that way, and as hard as you've worked to keep it hidden, I'd think you'd be glad to have some help. Take the help. Trust me."

"I can't." I'd never trusted anyone. Not a single person; not since first grade in Mrs. Knudsen's class. I could feel the familiar terror knocking me off my feet and carrying me out to sea—none of my usual islands in sight, nothing at all to cling to.

"I have to go before my daughter drives away in my car. You can start by telling me whether I'm right. It's Renee, isn't it? Renee Starkey?"

Somehow I must have hung up, or she did, because I knew nothing more until I came back to myself, still on the sofa, still clutching the dying phone, after I'd missed lunch.

☙

By suppertime—I assumed for most people six p.m. was suppertime; eating the last meal of the day at a regular, pre-dark hour in my own kitchen was foreign to me—I'd regained control. I'd spent the afternoon cleaning the grout in all three bathrooms. It had, of course, been spotless to begin with, but cleaning was a positive way to pass the time. I went to the kitchen to locate a Lean Cuisine to heat. The doorbell rang.

The sound made me freeze in place. I felt bruised and vulnerable, and no one ever came to my house. On tiptoe, I crept to the door and looked through the peephole.

Josh.

Josh, who hadn't learned in five years what Allison had figured out inside a week. Josh, who'd cried over losing his wife. Josh, who'd helped make me the primary suspect.

I opened the door, unsure whether I planned to yell at him or hug him, but grateful he was here nonetheless. A day of being alone with myself, punctuated by the shock of what Allison had said to me, had put things firmly into perspective.

"Are you okay?" he said, brushing a strand of hair off his forehead with one nervous hand. "I brought an apology." He held up bags that smelled delicious. "You haven't eaten, have you?"

"No." I caught myself. "I mean, no, I haven't eaten. I'm fine."

"Jane. I want to apologize. You were totally right. I passed along that gossip to the police because I was protecting myself, and I neglected to add that I had never seen any evidence that you were sleeping with Ray. I could have said that, because it was true. I should have said that. I screwed up all around, and if you want me to leave the dinner for you and go, I'd understand. I'm an asshole, and I'm so sorry."

There was honesty in his voice. Or maybe I was hearing what I wanted to because I couldn't stand to be alone here with my thoughts any longer. No, his face was written in misery. I relented.

"I accept your apology. Stay. We'll eat together."

Relief brightened his face, and we moved to the kitchen island to unpack the bags.

"What did Greg say was the reason I was on leave? Did he say anything at all?"

"Nothing. He did that thing where he stomps around looking like he's going to taser anyone who asks an invasive question, but no official word. The gossip is, unfortunately, that you're the main suspect and you're on leave because they have to protect the clients from any illegal or retaliatory action you might take."

"Wonderful," I said, though none of that was surprising in the least. No lawyer at a firm like Blackwood, Payne & Vivant labored under any impression that we weren't expendable at the slightest provocation.

"Greg sat in on my interview with the police today and didn't say anything about putting me on leave. And the motive the police wanted to talk to me about was the shitty evaluation Ray gave me in March."

"Really?" I asked, as if I hadn't been aware. Ray had made me tell him about Josh's work ethic, because he couldn't be bothered to keep track of it himself. He'd been prepared to give Josh a two out of a possible five, based solely on his billable hours, which were low at that time because Josh and his ex had been working out the separation agreement and finalizing the divorce. I talked him up to a three, explaining that Josh's quality of work made up for it.

"Yeah. Here's a fun fact I learned from Greg during the interview: associates with lower than a four out of five on any one of the quarterlies in a given year are disqualified from a bonus at year-end. The police asked if I killed Ray because he kept me from getting that massive thousand-dollar check next Christmas. As if."

Many of the huge firms in the big cities gave bonuses to associates as well as partners—a reward for sacrificing their lives in the name of the billable hour. Blackwood, Payne & Vivant gave bonuses largely so they could *say* they gave bonuses, but Charlottesville was not Washington or New York City. The bonuses were yanked away for the flimsiest of reasons and hardly huge when you got them at all. No rational person could believe that sabotage of such a bonus would constitute motive for a cold-blooded murder.

"Thanks for bringing supper. I was about to eat a frozen meal."

I opened the first Styrofoam container, and savory-smelling steam burst out. Josh had been to the dumpling place on the Corner near the university. On rare occasions, I busted out of work for the dumplings there. My heart swelled. He'd noticed.

He leaned a hip against my beloved granite island as I pulled silverware out of a drawer, taking in the surroundings. It hit me that he was my very first guest here.

"This has to be the cleanest residential dwelling I have ever seen," he said, with a teasing smile.

"I cleaned today. I'm not usually home to do it."

He stepped a little closer, one side of his mouth grinning more than the other. "Uh, I've seen your office. There isn't a speck of dust on your desk. I'd bet you dessert that this place looks like this all the time."

I could feel the heat in my cheeks. He was here, in my space. Inside the walls. I'd forgotten how to flirt, how to respond to flirting. I spent too much time hiding. I didn't know what to say, so I handed him a fork. We sat at the island stools and ate in silence for a while.

"Do you think they're really looking at you for this crime?" I asked. I couldn't imagine it.

"I don't know," he said slowly, after swallowing. "The interview was kind of like a formality for the first part. I was more afraid of Greg, to be honest. Uh, he's not usually a fan of hearing about low spots in average weekly billables. But then they asked me about an alibi. Sounds like they're looking at a window of about midnight to, like, two or three in the morning."

"And?"

"And I don't have one. I was home. Alone. Not using my phone or streaming Netflix or even shopping online. I crashed early."

"Me, too. Exactly the same."

He laughed, a short, wry huff. "Want to pretend we started up a little earlier?"

"Funny." My insecurity reared its head—was he only here to persuade me to give him an alibi? I shoved it down. Get a grip.

"I'm only half joking." He chewed another bite. "I really don't want to go to prison. I've lived a pretty soft life. It would easily be the worst thing ever to happen to me."

"You would survive," I said. I didn't want to go to prison either, but it probably wouldn't be the worst thing to happen to me. And people could survive a lot more than they knew.

"Have you ever known anyone who was in prison? Convicted of something really bad?"

I glanced at him. His stared down at his plate, his expression young and scared. "Yes," I said. "I have. I think the world outside prison is a lot scarier."

"Who was it?"

"Someone I knew when I was a kid. Nobody, really."

"How did you know him?"

"I didn't say it was a man." I stood up, gathering the empty plates and turning away to rinse them in the sink. To hide my face.

"Just telling me you knew someone who went to prison is more than you've ever said about your childhood." Josh stood, gently nudging me aside to take over putting the plates in the dishwasher. "You've never told me anything about it, and we've known each other for years."

"There's not much to say."

He considered me. "Okay. You don't want to talk about yourself. I get it. Can I try to guess?"

Alarm looped through me in panicked spirals. I should send him home. End this—whatever this was—now. I'd never been able to have a relationship for long. The truth of me was sealed up like a vault with motion sensors: every attempt even to touch them caused the systems to flash red and deploy the bunker lockdown.

With difficulty, I ignored all the internal disquiet. I didn't have to tell him anything. All I had to do was remain outwardly calm and lie if he guessed right, not that he would. It should be easy. I'd been lying and pretending almost all my life.

I was so tired of being alone.

"Sure. You're welcome to try."

"You won a Miss America pageant when you were eighteen and then atoned for it by majoring in women's studies?"

I laughed. His guess was far off the mark, but yet not totally inconsistent with my personality—and made it possible to give him something tiny. "Umm, no. I hate tiaras with a passion. But you're almost there—I majored in history. So close!"

His face split into a grin. "Close? Uh, yeah, like, 'Eureka!' I guessed you majored in *something*. Almost as if you needed a degree to get into law school."

"Amazing deductions. Try again," I said, a little lightness beginning to ease the choking feeling to my throat.

"All right. Hmmm. Let's see. You're the princess of a small and impoverished principality and your parents were going to sell you into marriage to a rich but ugly king of a more powerful country, but you decided that reviewing documents and drafting briefs about insurance would be more exciting."

I grabbed a dishcloth and my spray bottle of disinfectant to clean the counter where the plates had been. This guess had been both ludicrously off the mark and far too close at the same time. My hand shook, so I scrubbed harder.

"Easy there," Josh said, coming closer. "Don't tell me I guessed right. Your Highness." He bent before me in an elaborate bow.

I got control again and put up the spray bottle, avoiding his gaze. "No, unfortunately I'm not royal. Wrong again."

"Jane." He moved closer and took me by the elbow, forcing me to stop moving and look at him. With concentrated effort, I met his eyes. "Look. I can see you're uncomfortable, and we can stop. I'm okay taking this slow." His thumb rubbed lazy circles on my upper arm. "You tell me what you want to tell me. Okay?"

I nodded. He gave me a smile so kind that I grew dizzy enough to forget to wonder why he was bothering. I leaned in and touched my lips to his in exchange for that kindness. His lips were soft and gave me a safe landing. Kissing, I was good at. Kissing didn't require me to turn over any part of my past or my soul. Kissing was an action, a skill, a thing I could do with my mouth to keep it from spilling things that should never be said.

I remembered another man, the only other one who'd noticed that I was holding things back. In college and law school, I'd had occasional boyfriends; if I'd ever believed sexual intimacy was something special that had to be paired with love, I'd long since forgotten. Nearly from our first date, Emmett had understood that he didn't know the real me. He was the first person who gave me the impression he'd like to. I'd wished, at times, that I could let him.

Josh was handsome and smart and more than kind enough. I remembered handing him tissues while he cried over his wife. I could try again at trust. I was thirty-two years old. What was the alternative?

To spend my life alone? My mind flashed forward to the day when my octogenarian heart would give out. I'd collapse onto my ammonia-scented floor and lie unnoticed until the smell of decomposition wafted into the next town house. They'd take me to the morgue and my body would spend a couple of weeks on ice while they fruitlessly looked for next of kin to arrange a funeral. They would find no one willing, and I'd be buried without mourners by whatever funeral home gave the lowest bid to the city government.

On that depressing thought, I pulled back to look at him. "Okay. Let's take it slow. Thanks for coming to check on me. And supper. Dumplings are my favorite."

"I know," he said, smoothing the hair behind my ear. His eyes were such a nice hazel. I could do a lot worse.

"I move slow," I said again, to make clear nothing more would happen tonight. "Do you want to watch a movie?" I paid for every available streaming service—there's not much else to do when you have no friends.

"Sure," he said, smiling. "Let's do that."

CHAPTER TWELVE

ALLISON

On Tuesday morning, while I was in the middle of answering a set of interrogatories for a personal injury client, my cell phone rang with an unfamiliar number.

"Allison Barton."

"Um, hi. This is Brittany Corrigan."

The daughter of Jane's victim. I meant, the daughter of the victim in Jane's case. Ahem. I'd been trying to figure out how to approach her and her mother, but here she was on a silver platter. "Hi, Ms. Corrigan. How can I help you?"

"I, um, hear you're representing Jane Knudsen. Is that right?"

"Yes. I'm helping her out while the police are investigating the murder of . . . I believe it's your father?"

"Yes." There was a hitch in her voice. This was the daughter who'd made Jane's short list of people who might actually miss the dead man. "He was my dad. His funeral is tomorrow."

"I'm sorry for your loss. I assume you have a reason for calling?"

There was a small sob. "I . . . Yes. But . . . I don't . . . I don't know if I can say it."

"Okay. Why don't we start with something easier? Were you and your dad close?"

Long pause. I used the time clicking around my screen to pull up Brittany Corrigan's Instagram page.

"We used to be. When I was little, he used to bring me a present every Friday night. Something small, you know. He used to say I was a born lawyer—never quit arguing." She laughed, a sad little chuckle.

"And after you were little?" I asked. Brittany's social media profile photo showed a pretty young woman with skillful makeup and dark brown hair in long, stylish waves. She had a lot of followers and posted mostly pictures of an adorable French bulldog, alternating with some political slogans and celebrity GIFs. Most of the pictures of people were either selfies or various girls' nights at bars.

"Well, you know, he was busy," she said. "By the time I was in middle school, we hardly ever saw him."

This didn't match what people had told me about how she hung around the law firm, calling him Daddy. "You're about to take the bar exam, right?"

"Yeah. Only thirty-five days from now."

My turn to chuckle—I remembered the bar exam summer. It wasn't at all unusual that she knew down to the day how far away it was. "Hang in there. You're almost done. You've got a job in DC, Jane says?"

She made a noise. She didn't like that I knew that much. "Yes. Well, not DC. Northern Virginia."

"You did your summer-associate stint at Blackwood, right? Can't blame you for not wanting to work in the same firm where your dad was a partner."

"I . . . Well . . . Yeah. It would have been awkward. Anyway. I have to tell you the thing I called about. It's my mother."

"Your mother?"

"Yes. You should check into her design firm. Daddy didn't like it. She wanted to merge her business, go in with another designer, you know, make it much bigger, and he put a stop to it. I don't know what he did, but she'd already found the rental space and had talked to this lady who had been competing with her. Corrine Peterson. They'd gotten pretty far into the planning. And now . . . not."

I'd assumed from the second she said her name that she was calling to give me a lead, but of all the people I thought she might throw under the bus, I never imagined it would be her own mother. She'd knocked me for a loop. I had enough presence of mind to write *Corrine Peterson* in my notes.

"How . . . how did your father have the power to do that to your mother?"

Brittany laughed, bitter as sugarless lemonade. "Oh, let me count the ways. He made the money. She's not very successful as a designer. He kept her on a short leash. She slipped it last winter to cheat on him. Is that enough reasons?"

"Ugh. I'm sorry about that. Are you sure she cheated?"

"Yeah. She went to some conference for interior design in Charlotte and met someone. She and Daddy got in a fight, and she threw it in his face. I overheard them arguing."

"Can I ask you a question? Right now, the police are looking at Jane for this crime, or one of her coworkers. You're the wealthy daughter of the victim and you're calling me to give up your own mother as a suspect. Why?"

There was a long silence. "You asked me if I was close with Daddy. We had our issues, but I was still a thousand times closer with him than with my mother. She and I . . . don't get along. She . . . is disappointed in me. Not the perfect daughter she envisioned."

"Still."

"I know. I'm not saying she did it. I don't even think she did, really. But, you know, reasonable doubt."

Okay. I would take it for what it was worth.

"I assume you're aware that your mother is telling the police she thinks Jane killed your father," I said.

"Oh yeah. I know about that. I'd be surprised if Jane did it. Mummy has a lot more reason. Not that those are the only people who had a reason."

Something about the way she said that made me blurt out my next question: "Did you have a reason?"

She gasped, once, and hung up.

಼

I didn't waste any time. I arrived at Interiors by Felicity, located in a not-very-upscale strip mall along the state highway north of Charlottesville, thirty minutes before closing time.

Inside, no customers browsed the offerings of mass-produced wall art, bolts of fabric, lamps, candles, or decorative housewares my mother called "sit-around stuff" notable only for needing to be dusted regularly. I ran a finger along the back of a leaping wooden gazelle as high as my waist and rolled my eyes at a shelf full of fake books. Books as color-coordinated, nonfunctional decor was a pet peeve. I waited, but no one appeared to be in the store, though the door had been unlocked.

"Hello?" I called.

"Oh, hi, hi!" A woman who must be Felicity Kim came from the back. She was about fifty but had lovely unlined skin and silky black hair that fell to her shoulder blades. She wore a red poplin sheath dress with oddly utilitarian brown heels. She gave me a practiced smile. "Can I help you? We've got all throw pillows on sale today, twenty percent off."

She didn't look like a widow. Though I knew everyone processed grief differently, there was no sign of red eyes or sleeplessness about her. Her dress blared confidence and joie de vivre.

I stuck out my hand the professional way. She took it the social way, graceful and limpid. "I'm Allison Barton. I heard an exciting rumor that you're going to be working with Corrine Peterson. Is it true?" For effect, I picked up the nearest object—a baroque brass candlestick—and examined it as if in a million years I might buy such a thing.

Her voice dropped from sunny and welcoming to funereal. She moved a throw pillow to better position it, and I caught the white knuckles as she gripped it a touch too hard. "Well, I was hoping to, but for the time being I'll be staying here. Expansion . . . uh, it's not the best time."

Brittany had been correct. The plan to expand Felicity's business through a merger had existed and had been scuttled. I had no intention of asking Felicity any more about that; I'd come here for other information. I'd already called the well-known Charlottesville designer Corrine Peterson. She'd readily confirmed that she and Felicity had made big plans and a down payment on a nicer office space, but that Felicity had backed out, cursing her husband's name most foully, about two weeks ago. Corrine had already joined forces with another designer and was going ahead with the lease.

"Oh, I'm so sorry to hear that." I put down the candlestick. "Actually, I'm an attorney for Jane Knudsen. I'm investigating the matter of your husband's death." Then I stood back and watched the bombs go off.

The emotions that crossed her face in quick succession were almost as good as a play. Confusion, then rage, then superiority, and finally, a bland mask of upper-class pity. This kind, I knew well.

"I doubt very much you want to hear what I would have to say about your client," she said, adjusting a display of picture frames to line up neatly.

"On the contrary. I would very much like to hear what you have to say about my client." I glanced around at the emptiness of the store. "It looks like you have a few minutes before closing."

"A very few. You probably don't know my husband is being buried tomorrow. I have company coming in from everywhere this evening."

"Why didn't you take the day off? I'm sure everyone would have understood a grieving widow closing the store for a few days."

"Nonsense," she said, crossing her arms over her middle. "I have a client whose project . . . never mind that. My work helps me. Distracts me." She sniffed, her nostrils somehow contributing to her overall impression of extreme thinness. "You want to know about Jane? Jane is a secretive, home-wrecking bitch." She punctuated all the words in the sentence with a downward-slashing index finger. "She was sleeping with Ray all over that firm: on her desk, on his desk, in the law library, in the elevator. He told me himself."

Bluffing, I took a stab in the dark. "That was after he found out you were cheating on him, wasn't it?"

Shock froze her features in a weird attitude of superciliousness and horror. "How . . . who told you that?"

The answer to that question was, of course, her own daughter, but also Corrine. Corrine, it seemed, had not much appreciated being left in the lurch with a lease in hand and was happy to tell me about Felicity's away-from-home indiscretion. She'd been at the same conference and had bubbled away with all the torrid details.

"I can't answer that, I'm afraid."

"It never happened. It's a lie."

"All right. I believe you." I didn't, as a matter of fact. Corrine had been far more credible, but if Felicity wanted to continue pretending, I didn't need to argue. I picked up a picture frame to give myself a reason to stop staring her down. "Tell me about Ray and Jane."

"Why should I help you?"

I thought about my next words, and about what I'd gleaned about her as a person in the last five minutes. "Because I seriously doubt anything you say will help Jane, and because I imagine it will feel good to let it out to someone who has no reason to pity you."

She pressed her lips into a line. When she headed to the back of the store near the cash register, I followed.

"Fine," she said. "I'll tell you this much: I suspected Jane was interested in Ray for a long time before he admitted to it. She called him at home. She stayed at work when he did. Once she found out he was an early riser, she started going to work early. They literally spent fourteen, fifteen hours together every day. He'd never have been able to resist a woman like that throwing herself at him."

I put a pin in "a woman like that." "They worked together. Lawyers work long hours. How do you know she wasn't interested in someone else at work?"

"Ha. Not likely. None of them had his money. I could tell she was trash. You hear her accent sometimes? Straight-up hillbilly. And the way she looks—like one of those Halloween costumes. Slutty Lawyer. Must be ten tons of collagen in those lips. I swear, every time I went by his office, she was literally feet away from him at all times."

"He told you he was sleeping with her?"

"Yes. He bragged about it."

"Did he suggest he was going to leave you for her?"

Felicity's face shuttered over. He had. I no longer had any doubt that Ray had indeed told his wife he was having an affair with Jane. Whether he'd said that because it was true or because Felicity's infidelity had hurt him and he wanted to get back at her, Felicity would never know.

"I know she killed him."

"Why? If he was going to leave you for her, what motive would she have?"

"He wasn't going to leave me. We reconciled. I imagine that was her motive. I have proof she did it."

"What?"

"That email, you know the one he supposedly sent her at midnight? The night he died?"

"Yes. What about it?"

"I saw it. He didn't write it."

"How do you know?"

"Because it had two spelling errors in it. Ray was a stickler—ask anyone. He never spelled anything wrong. He was obsessive about it. When our daughter was in school, he used to quiz her whenever he happened to be in the car with her, which wasn't often, quite frankly. She never was good enough for Ray, oh no. Poor Brittany. She tried so hard to please her daddy, following him to Blackwood and everything, but she always did everything wrong. Nothing was ever enough."

One track at a time. I'd understood Brittany did fine at Blackwood, and she described her relationship with her father as better than that with her mother. Irene might know more. For now, I'd focus on Felicity. "What spelling errors? And he sent the email at midnight. He had to have been tired. Couldn't they have been simple typos?"

"No. Not these. They weren't mistyping or autocorrect things. He spelled *there* wrong. The sentence started 'There's a reference to' some document. He spelled it T-H-E-I-R. Almost impossible once. But then another sentence began with *there* and he spelled it wrong a second time."

Despite myself, I had to think there was something to it. I'd known people—educated and intelligent ones—who had trouble with *there*, *their*, and *they're*. The error tended to trip them up every time. I tried to think whether Jane had that issue, or if I'd seen enough of her written communications to know.

"What makes you think it was Jane and not whoever killed him?"

"Because she wrote a thank-you note to Ray and me after Christmas two years ago. It had that same mistake in it."

Something uncomfortable formed in my stomach. "Can I see it?"

She smiled, a cat's smile. "I already gave it to the police."

CHAPTER THIRTEEN
JANE

I watched some movie about a serial killer once, and the police caught him by going to the funerals of his victims, where he sat in the back rubbing his hands with glee. Or something like that. Apparently killers can't resist going to funerals to . . . what? Gloat? Make sure they've been successful? Siphon the life force of the grieving family members who've been left behind?

I was going to Ray's funeral.

The parking lot outside the funeral home wasn't full. A few stragglers made their way in for the service. Even Felicity must have realized there'd never be enough mourners of Raymond Corrigan to fill a church.

Although I was the last person currently in a position to provide comfort to his family, I had a right to be at this funeral—maybe even a duty. I waved off a funeral home employee trying to offer me a tissue. They'd have plenty left over after the service. Few would sob for Ray.

Oh, I had no intention of trying to unmask Ray's killer among the small crowd of mourners. No, I had another objective. After days of being stuck at home away from my job, I'd had about all I could take of leisure and being alone with my own thoughts. About all I *would* take. This was my chance to put an end to that.

As I made my way to a seat, I adopted the posture I'd long ago started thinking of as the Take No Prisoners one: head high, shoulders back, no shame. I'd chosen three-inch heels to add to my height. The dark dress looked like it had been made for me. Strangers moved aside to let me pass. Something most people don't know: there can be anonymity in attention.

Near the front of the room, Felicity and Brittany greeted friends in a sort of impromptu receiving line at the casket. They both bowed their heads and smiled bravely in similar black suits. From the doorway, the age difference wasn't apparent—Brittany was the image of her mother. I dropped my posture, skipped the receiving line, and took a seat at the aisle end of a row in the first third of the room, right in front of Greg Dombrowski. No one would sit by me. They never did.

Greg was the real reason I had come today. He sat alone, having divorced his second wife three years before. The high-billable practice of law was hard on marriages. I knew few partners whose home life ran smoothly.

I turned in my seat and gave him my best shark's grin. He acknowledged me with a nod and an efficient lift of the corners of his mouth.

"Jane. Hello."

"Greg. Hello to you, too."

He glanced at the tiny funeral program in his hand as if, suddenly, the identity of the pallbearers was of vital importance. I waited.

"So, Greg," I said, in my friendliest manner, while not caring at all whether I was actually coming across as friendly. "I'd like to return to work."

"I'm afraid that's not possible at this time."

"Oh please. You need me. I can name at least four of Ray's cases where the client contact calls me first every time. I did half the research. I did all the brief writing. I know those cases like the back of my hand, and you know the clients aren't going to pay Helen Reeves to get up to speed," I said, naming the partner who'd been chosen to take over Ray's section.

"I wish I could do something, Jane. Really, I do."

"You have no basis for sending me home. I've done nothing wrong and I am the top biller in my associate year."

"Yes, dear, but the funeral is about to start. Call me next week and we'll talk."

I glanced at the front of the room. Felicity and Brittany were accepting the hugs of an older woman. The casket was still open. They were not close to starting. I twisted back in Greg's direction. "Hmmm. No, I'm afraid now is convenient for me."

He started to speak, but I held up a hand. "So, Greg, I want to give you an example of exactly *how* closely involved in Ray's work I am. See, Ray preferred to have me and my team do everything. He'd come along behind us and bill a second time for the work we'd already done. According to him, you knew about that because you did it, too. All the partners do, Ray said. You and Ray were overheard arguing. The argument was quite . . . vociferous, I think. I'm guessing that once he joined the management team, Ray found out you were giving yourself more partner share of all that extra billing than you deserved. He had me crunch enough of his management team numbers for that guess to be an educated one. Is any of this sounding familiar to you, Greg?"

Greg turned ashy pale. "Ray wasn't authorized to share any of that partnership data with you."

"Nevertheless, he did. I sure hope you didn't kill him to keep that quiet. Since, you know, you'd have to kill me, too."

His eyes bored into me. Greg did not enjoy being outwitted. "I'm going to let that remarkable effrontery pass, given your . . . difficult circumstances right now. If Ray did bring you into confidence about that information, you're subject to being disbarred if you violate that confidentiality."

"Oh, absolutely. As a working lawyer of the firm who is *not* home on administrative leave, I would absolutely feel constrained to keep secret the discrepancies between the hours you and Ray worked and the bills you sent to your clients. Absolutely."

He coughed delicately. "Fine. Report tomorrow. Are we clear?"

"Clear, but while we're talking about boundaries and confidentiality, I'll point out that Ray wasn't authorized to look down my blouse in his office, either. Nor to grab my ass. Neither, I might add, is Adam or Rich." I named two other partners whose attitudes in my presence veered quickly from flattering to offensive on a regular basis. "The culture of the firm isn't kind to women. Not women lawyers, and not admins, either. I think it might be time for sensitivity training. A mandatory one, on office time, with no penalty for failure to bill during it. I'll be happy to prepare and lead that."

"Fine," Greg hissed, going quite red in the face. "Anything else?"

Well, sure, Greg, while I'm at it. Amir had been the only one to express disbelief about the rumor Ray and I were having an affair, so why not?

"Yes, as a matter of fact. Amir Burhan's wife is pregnant. She's due next month. When she delivers, you're going to let him take his leave to be with her and their little boy. You will not hint that although he's entitled to that leave under federal law, he should really consider not taking it. None of this nonsense about how he's a lawyer who needs to bill time and doesn't need to breastfeed. Try, for once, not to be a fugitive from 1952. Sound good?"

Greg gritted his teeth, but nodded his assent. The organ music swelled and I faced front, tamping down the grin that would be, at a minimum, less than appropriate at the funeral of a man I was supposed to have killed.

The service was lovely, although at times I wondered whether I had wandered by accident into the funeral for a loving family man instead of Ray. The pastor described him as kind, honorable, and so deeply religious he was likely smiling down on us now from a seat at the table of our Lord. I couldn't help but remember that when Irene had asked to leave last Christmas Eve in time to go to her family's six p.m. church service, he'd bellowed, "I don't give a shit if it's little baby Jesus's fucking bar mitzvah, I need you to get that motion edited right the fuck now!"

After the pallbearers, only two of whom worked at our firm, carried out the casket, I stood at my seat, waiting for the crowd to disperse.

Josh had been sitting with another lawyer who worked in the trusts-and-estates section of our firm. As they filed out the center aisle, they greeted me. Josh could communicate nothing more to me than casual greetings in this room full of the partners who controlled our lives. Irene, C. J. at her side, touched my hand briefly, but said nothing. She was still following her lawyer's directions. They kept moving and were swept out with the crowd, such as it was. Amir hadn't come at all.

Once an older couple three rows behind me slipped out, the two detectives from the interview became visible in the back, heads together and conferring. Hossain stood impassive, a steely-nerved professional. O'Callihan was avidly swiveling his head like a puppy, whispering in Hossain's ear. Seriously? That thing from the movies where the police come to the funeral of a homicide victim was for real. They were here to watch for the killer to make some suspicious move.

No one made any suspicious moves. I wended my way to the reception area, where the guest book had been, and where, now, Felicity and Brittany stood in two groups of mourners. A somber funeral director waited to usher them into the vehicle that would carry them to the grave site.

I took on my Take No Prisoners posture and strolled slowly by them, making sure they saw me. It worked. Though Felicity stuck her nose in the air, Brittany scurried after me.

Up close, Brittany didn't really look much like her mother. She was less brittle—less perfect, somehow. More like a real human being. She weighed a touch more, but on her it was athleticism. I knew she was—or had been, before law school—a competitive swimmer.

We'd gotten to know each other the previous year, when she'd worked at Blackwood as a summer associate. Ray had no doubt made sure she got that opportunity, and told me once that he'd expected from a young age she'd follow in his footsteps and join him in law. To avoid any outcry of nepotism, however, the firm had assigned her to the trusts-and-estates department, and she'd done well there. Despite being raised a rich girl, Brittany had a good work ethic. Her intelligence was clear. She'd have had to have been an excellent student to get into and then through UVA's law school.

Ray started that summer pleased as punch Brittany was working at the firm. They took lunch together. He smiled on at least two occasions when no clients were present to witness it. But then about two months in, he turned downright mean, ignored Brittany, and made his associates' lives a living hell. No one had the guts to ask why. When August came, Brittany was the only summer associate not offered a permanent job.

After Brittany went back to school, an almost visible weight lifted off him.

"You," Brittany said. "I talked to your lawyer. I can't believe I did that, but I did."

"Thank you." I felt a little swell of pity. She had just watched her father's casket carried out.

"I thought we were friends, you know," she said. "Your lawyer went straight for me. Then she talked to my mother yesterday, and now my mother blames me—even more—for ruining her life. She somehow thought her affair would never come to light."

Oh no. "Allison would never have told your mother who gave her that info."

"Doesn't matter. Mummy said I was the only person who could have known it. I wasn't, but she doesn't know that. My fault, I guess. I'm a bad daughter—all around, survey says. Anyway, everything is awful. You being here has made it worse."

"Brittany, I'm sorry. About your mom, and your dad."

"Just . . . just leave me alone."

A tear rolled down her face.

⸙

I bought myself a bottle of excellent-quality wine on the way home. Which was fortunate, given that Allison was standing on my steps when I got there.

"I'm sorry to show up unannounced, but I thought you might be home, given that you're on leave."

"Actually, I go back tomorrow, but come on in. Would you like a glass of wine? I know it's early, but I thought maybe . . ."

"Sure. Listen. I'm not charging you for this visit. I wanted you to know that. And all I can think about is how much work I have to do and how much I hate owing my ex-husband and his wife for keeping my daughter so I can come here, but—"

I interrupted. I was not ready for her to ask me about my other life yet, though I knew that had to be the reason she'd come. A glass of wine in my hand would help when that moment arrived. "I appreciate that. Let's treat this as an opportunity to catch up, then," I said, as coolly as I could manage.

Inside, I headed for the kitchen to deposit the wine on the island and sneak in a quick caress of the countertop stone to calm me. Allison followed me, turning her head as Josh had.

"God, you were always so neat. Some things haven't changed at all."

"I like things neat." I opened the wine and poured. "I meant to ask you—how many children do you have? I feel bad that I didn't know."

"Only the one," Allison said, accepting a glass. "She's six. I don't know if you remember the guy I dated in law school—Steve Barton? I married him after graduation and we had Libby and then divorced not long after that."

I only vaguely remembered she'd had a boyfriend in law school. So much for the self-pity that Allison hadn't wanted to be friends then— she'd had a whole marriage, child, and divorce I hadn't thought about, or asked about, until now. I hadn't done any better a job finding out about her life than she'd done with mine. She was definitely winning right now. I led the way into my living room and gestured at a sofa. "I'm sorry. About the divorce."

She laughed. "I'm not. Steve cheated. He's a high school teacher. He got caught with another teacher in flagrante delicto, as the lawbooks say, on the top of a chemistry lab table. A sophomore forgot her notebook and walked right in on them making out. Fortunately, they were still dressed, but they were both fired." She gave me a mischievous side-eye that I envied. How I wished I could manage that kind of casualness about things that must have hurt so much. "He's married to her now. The teacher, not the sophomore. Guess what her name is."

"What?"

"Karen. For real."

A sound bubbled out of my mouth that I almost didn't recognize: a giggle. "How can you be so . . . so okay with it all?"

"Many, many containers of ice cream. And shouting sessions in my car alone. It helps that Karen is the most Karen of Karens and I don't have to struggle with liking her. She even has the haircut." She stopped, her smile fading. "I'm not really okay with it. I never pictured being thirty-two and already divorced, or a single mother. I've learned to project that I'm okay with it."

She turned her glass by the stem in her hand. "You think, when you're young, that your life will look a certain way. Happy ever after, with someone to love, and children, and a job that fulfills you, and everything your heart desires. And then it doesn't. People cheat, and lie, and we make mistakes and more mistakes. And then we just . . . keep going, changing the story as we go. If I hadn't met Steve and moved to his hometown, I wouldn't have Libby or my job or . . . anything else I care about. And for now, they're enough."

She looked away, off into the distance. I took that last sentence, and her expression, to mean she didn't have anyone else in her life now. I wanted to ask, but it might be a sore subject. If she had a significant other, surely she'd have mentioned him in that short list of blessings.

At this point, every question I asked about Allison's life put off my own moment of truth for a little longer. I scrambled to think of another, but I was too slow.

"Speaking of life looking a certain way, obviously yours has taken a few turns," Allison said, focusing her attention back on me. "I know you don't want to talk about it, but I really do need to know what's going on with your name change."

I said nothing, trying to gather myself.

"You don't trust me, and with good reason, given the way I acted in law school. But that was then, and now, I need to know. If the police are narrowing in on you, and they are, they'll find it. We need the time to figure out how to handle it. Please, Jane. Take a sip if it helps, and tell me the truth."

I took her advice about the sip, while thinking about how best to say what I had to say. And how much. The truth. I could tell it, while not telling the whole truth. Maybe Allison could use the piece I could give to talk to O'Callihan and Hossain and keep them away from the rest of it.

"Okay. Here's the truth. I grew up in Galt, North Carolina, which is not much more than a crossroads with a post office. It's not far from Hendersonville, but I'm guessing you already know that."

She nodded. She was thorough, I'd give her that much.

"And yes, my name used to be Renee Starkey. I changed it when I was a freshman in college."

"A woman in Galt told me she knew a teacher named Knudsen. Is that where you got the name?"

I smiled, remembering Miss Knudsen and her kindness. "Yes. She was my first-grade teacher, though I couldn't quite get behind Alice. I picked Jane because I loved Jane Austen, and how, in her books, characters named Jane were secondary most of the time. Jane Bennet. Jane Fairfax. I wanted that for myself."

Allison's brow wrinkled. "You wanted to be a secondary character? In your own life?"

"I know it sounds dumb. It really does sound dumb, now that I'm saying it. I've never told anyone this before. But yes. I never wanted to be the star of the show. I only wanted not . . . to be noticed so much."

She considered me. "Did it work?"

"Better than you might think, maybe. I mean, people still notice me, but that's not . . ." I shut up before I said too much.

"I don't buy that, Jane. Try again. People who look like you never get to be the secondary character, no matter what you might wish for. Why did you change your name? And dye your hair? Who were you hiding from?"

A piece of the truth. A piece of the truth. Give her something.

"My mother." I looked at her sharply. "Have you met her? Cherry?"

"No," she said. "I . . . uh . . . did enough research to find out about Galt. I went there on Saturday and showed your picture. Someone at the convenience store directed me to Cherry's trailer. She wasn't there, but the neighbor identified you. She says hi, by the way. Paula Lockaby."

I rolled my eyes. "Mrs. Lockaby prided herself on being nice. So nice that she never once tried to interfere in what she had to know was going on." I girded my loins to say the hard part. "My mom was abusive. Pretty horrifically abusive, in all the ways you can imagine and some you probably can't. I studied hard in school to get the grades to get away. I got into Duke—straight As, good test scores, state-ranked cross-country runner, lots of scholarships—and left Galt."

"But why not just walk away? Why change your name?"

"Because after I turned eighteen, my mom stole my identity to open up credit cards. To cosign loans. To steal money, basically, and leave me holding the bag. Once I got it all straightened out, I changed my name."

There. All that was true, but the identity theft had been an easily corrected trifle. I'd left off the primary reason I'd changed my name. I'd told a subplot but left out the main story.

"I appreciate you telling me."

"Please. Go ahead and tell the police all that, but only if you think it will keep them from digging any further. I've got the identity theft receipts. But I don't want to relive my life before. It has nothing to do with Ray and his death. Nothing at all. Get them to stay out of my business."

"Okay. I'll try."

"And Allison. I don't know if we qualify as friends, or if we ever did. But I'm asking you, too. Please don't investigate any more about Renee Starkey. She had a shit life and she's dead and gone. I really need her to be gone. I can't revisit that and still function. It's a thing I'm not okay about and will never be okay about."

"I'm sorry, Jane. So sorry. I was wrong about so many things about you in law school. I never had a clue you were dealing with that. I was always so . . . so jealous. Back then, I imagined you had this glamorous life—brains, looks, all the hottest guys panting around. I'm sorry."

"Don't be. I kept—keep—everyone at a distance. It's hard to be close to anyone when you can't talk about your childhood. There was only one guy I dated back then who was worth anything at all."

Allison's posture underwent some weird little change.

"Are you okay?" I asked her.

"Fine. Fine. I . . . um . . . thought I was going to drop this wine-glass. Who was that?"

"Do you remember Emmett Amaro? We were together a couple months—that was a long time, for me—in second year, but then the whole Professor Graham thing happened. He's the only guy I ever regretted losing. He was different from the others. Better."

"Oh. Right. Emmett Amaro," said Allison, finishing her wine in a deep gulp and jumping up. "Can I pour you another glass?"

"No, but you go ahead." God, it had been so long since I'd talked about something as normal as dating. "I probably should tell you, since you're my lawyer. I've kind of been . . . I don't know, not dating exactly, but started seeing . . . someone. I don't know where we're going, but anyway."

Allison sat on the sofa with her refilled glass—water this time. She started speaking, as if to comment on my romantic life, and stopped. God. We'd gotten so close to friendship. She couldn't say, "I'm happy for you" or even ask me if he was cute? I sighed.

Allison was all business, though. "Jane. I understand you got an email from Ray at about midnight on the night of his death. There's some question as to whether he wrote it, and of course, it matters because if he didn't, whoever did would likely have been the killer. Do you still have it?"

"Yes, I think so." I went to find my phone. Everything in my work inbox synced to my phone. I pulled up the one she wanted easily—the date was hard to forget—and handed her the phone. "Here it is. It wasn't anything out of the ordinary."

She peered at it, frowning. "*There* is spelled wrong twice. Was Ray normally a bad speller?"

"Really? I didn't notice that. I'm not a good speller myself. Let me see." I took the phone back. She was right.

"This is really important," Allison said, leaning forward. "You're bad at it, fine. Was Ray?"

Oh no. Someone had . . . Oh *damn*. "No," I said, knowing I was screwed. "He was a perfect speller. He was a total asshole about other people's spelling errors. But I struggle with spelling, and it's worse when I'm tired. Like at midnight."

"How many people know that?"

I let out a long breath. "Everyone who's ever received an email from me. So everyone."

Allison sighed, her exhale the twin of mine. "Did you write this email?"

"No. I didn't."

"Okay, then. We'll just have to figure out who did."

CHAPTER FOURTEEN

ALLISON

Driving home from Jane's gleaming white operating room of a home, I had time to dwell on what a hypocrite I was. I'd demanded Jane tell me the truth about her past, even though she'd made clear she didn't want to, even though it was painful, even though it likely had nothing to do with any accusation that might be forthcoming now, and she had.

And then I'd kept quiet. Twice—once when I'd listed my blessings and once when she'd actually said Emmett's name. What a mess. Where was the line between professional and friend? Was it fair of me to ask her to tell me her most personal secrets and then lie about mine by omission? It might be correct professionally—her secrets might matter for her case and mine did not—but it felt all wrong.

During that conversation, Jane would have found it extremely relevant that a toothbrush belonging to the same Emmett Amaro she'd been reminiscing about reposed even at this moment in my bathroom medicine cabinet. Yet the opportunity to tell her now was well and truly missed.

When Jane had said Emmett was better than other guys with that wistful expression on her face, I'd nearly thrown up. He was, she was right, and I'd wasted too much time not telling him so.

As the summer twilight fell and the lights of Lynchburg came into view, I drove faster. Steve had Libby for the night. I didn't need to pick her up until tomorrow.

I needed Emmett. Right now. My gas tank was near empty, but I didn't stop until I'd pulled into his driveway.

When he opened the door, I fell into his arms like a drowning person. God, the warm laundry smell of his clothes combined with the heat of his skin dropped my blood pressure ten notches. I was an addict.

"Allie. What's going on?" He wore ratty shorts and his favorite *Game of Thrones* T-shirt, and his unruly dark hair had slipped the control of whatever product he'd used this morning to rein it in. I'd never, ever been more attracted to him.

Without even thinking about it, I blurted everything out. "I haven't said anything about you to Jane, but she talks about you. You're her 'one that got away,' and it's killing me."

I couldn't sort out the emotions that had gone into the stew of misery I'd been swimming in since Jane had mentioned his name. Jealousy—that was the first ingredient, but there was also guilt that I hadn't told her he was my boyfriend, sorrow at the inevitability of that fact ruining whatever repair Jane and I could do to our own relationship, and worst, the shame of feeling that tiny flicker of . . . triumph. That last bit made me feel about two inches tall.

"I'm her what?" He hauled me over the threshold and onto his sofa. Emmett lived in an old house near downtown that he'd slowly been restoring. It had original tile fireplaces and curving crown molding—and the grand piano my daughter loved so much. Just looking at the gleaming piano made me wince. I had not figured out how—or whether—to tell Emmett that Libby desired us never to marry and preferred to see him only "sometimes."

He sat beside me and pulled me onto his lap, tipping up my chin before kissing me.

It was getting so much harder to keep the things I loved in neatly fenced pens, separate from each other and never mixed up and messy. "Jane told me this afternoon that you were the only guy she ever regretted dumping."

"She didn't dump me. I dumped her, though she did make it very clear she wouldn't mind if I did."

This level of specificity to Emmett's memory did not make me feel better. I scooted off his lap.

"Where are you going?" he asked. "That was years ago. What about any of that bothers you, Allie?"

"Well . . . I . . . when I think about Jane with . . ."

"What?"

"I . . . dammit. I can't help feeling inadequate. Inadequate and . . . and unpretty."

He pulled my hands away from my face and dropped a kiss on them. "Whoa. Wait a minute. You are not inadequate. Or whatever the hell 'unpretty' is. Is that even a word? If it is, it has nothing to do with you." He ran a hand up my arm, rubbing circles of warmth into it and pulling me back closer until I could feel his breath as he spoke. "You are the most beautiful woman in the world to me. You are amazing. You. Everything that you are. You've arranged your life to be what you want it to be, and Allie, I'm so impressed with that, every day. You've moved to a new town and shucked off a cheating husband and ditched a bad boss and gone down your own path. You are a terrific mother. A brilliant, gifted lawyer. And, most importantly, you don't keep everything important about yourself hidden. Jane is not you. You are not Jane, and thank God for it."

I let myself bathe in that remarkable speech for ten seconds while I kissed him in thanks. "But Emmett. I didn't tell her about me and you. When she talked about you, I changed the subject. I didn't say anything, and now I've definitely missed the bus."

"She's your client. There's no reason in a professional relationship for her to know who you're seeing."

I was quiet a minute. "I kind of want to be her friend."

"Wait a second. What? Why?"

"Because she needs one." I couldn't tell him about her childhood, of course, but that much was obvious to anyone who'd ever spoken to her. "And because I should have been one, back in law school, and I feel like I owe it to her to make it right now."

"But you can't be friends with your clients."

"I think you can. Or I can. This time. And Emmett—she's not guilty. I know she isn't. She can't be." I snuggled up against his side and he pulled me close, breathing in at the top of my head.

"You don't know that." He searched my face, apparently finding determination there. "But okay. If you want to try it, I'm with you. You'll have to tell her about us at some point, then."

"I know." I basked in the immense joy of having someone who would back me up anywhere I wanted to go. It's so rare, that kind of support. I knew that, now.

"Allie. It's been a while since we talked about this," he began, his muscles tensing slightly.

I sat up. Oh no. "Do you want a glass of wine?"

"No. Stay. We need to talk about this. I want you and Libby to move in here. I want to be together every night. I want to paint the extra bedroom whatever color Libby likes now. Every night I come home and you're not here, I hate it."

"Emmett, I . . . I'm not ready. With Libby, it's complicated. You know that." We had never talked about getting married. No proposal was on the table, and given Libby's mulishness and Steve's self-righteousness, I wasn't sure I was ready for one. And I couldn't move in with Emmett before being married. Not with Karen already making noise about immorality and innocent children. I'd seen judges deny visitation, much less custody, to unwed parents who had overnight romantic guests.

"I do know that, and I respect that if you're not comfortable yet. If it's moving in together that's the issue. But is it the issue? Is there a bigger problem than Libby? Do you . . . do you not feel . . . ?" He closed his eyes and swallowed. Gently, and with my heart squeezing, I put my index finger on his lips.

"No. *No!* It's not that. Steve and Karen got married so fast, and they sprang it on Libby with no notice, and she's so . . . so watchful all the time. She can't handle my divided attention and she's . . . she's not happy like she was. She used to dance around, and now . . . but oh, Emmett. If I knew it wouldn't hurt Libby, if I could . . ." I swallowed and took a breath. "I love you. More than you know. I was thinking how much, on the way here. It's not that. It's never that."

The look on his face tore me into pieces. I tried to erase it the only way I knew how—by climbing into his lap, kissing him, and then putting my hands under that nerdy T-shirt, until his muscles tightened to a different degree.

And in this time-honored way, I put the question off for another day.

⁊ʂ

The next morning, I called Zach O'Callihan, the chief investigator of the murder of Ray Corrigan. I didn't exactly know what to make of an investigator who was so pleasant and eager to talk to a defense attorney, but he took my call and greeted me as if he'd been hoping all day to hear my voice.

"Ms. Barton! It was great to meet you the other day. Thanks so much for calling. What can I do for you?"

This would be a careful dance. I wanted to preserve whatever buddy-cop-movie vibe we had flickering, direct his investigations elsewhere by throwing a lot of dirt around, and keep my own client from moving any closer to the front of the line as a suspect. Somehow, what Jane had told me about her abusive mother felt too raw for me to toss out there. I'd give it up if I had to, but only if I had to.

In the meantime, I had other red meat to throw out.

"Have you arrested anyone for the murder of Ray Corrigan yet?"

"Ha! No, not yet. Though we're getting closer every hour. Won't be long, I don't think."

"I came by some information you may be interested in. Can I count on your discretion?"

"Well, that depends on what you mean by 'discretion,' now, doesn't it?" He chuckled, his laugh a "rat-a-tat" that in small doses was cute but would annoy in under twenty minutes.

"Fine. Do with it what you will. I spoke to Felicity Kim."

"I've spoken many times to Felicity Kim. Felicity Kim calls me every day, sometimes three times. Felicity Kim is the voice I hear in my dreams," he said, trying to charm me.

I had to admit, he was kind of charming, and disarming. I wasn't used to talking to law enforcement in my criminal cases who didn't treat me like I was myself a suspect at best, or a hardened criminal psychopath at worst.

"Did she tell you she cheated on Ray? And that he found out about it?"

There was silence. I pressed my advantage.

"I'm guessing that's a no."

"Uh, yeah. That's a no. She calls every day, demanding an arrest—your client's arrest, to be specific—and somehow has failed to mention anything about marital difficulties. To hear her tell it, she and Ray were skipping through the tulips, holding hands and singing. How did you hear she cheated?"

"I spoke to two sources, one anonymous but with good reason to know, and one a woman named Corrine Peterson. She's an interior designer in Charlottesville. She can tell you about the design convention where it happened. She saw them together. Not that Felicity's adultery would be a motive by itself, but Felicity was planning to expand her interior design business with Corrine as a partner. Ray shut it down. I did some checking. Corrine is a bigger-name designer. Felicity would have done well with her. Without her, she has to compete with Corrine. When I went in Felicity's store, it was empty. Lots of stuff on sale."

"And you say Ray had something to do with that falling apart?" Despite himself, he sounded interested.

"According to the anonymous source, he hated his wife's business and put a stop to the expansion. Apparently he was the bankroll."

Over the phone, I could hear his long, frustrated sigh. "I'm gonna be completely candid with you. I don't like Felicity. She calls so often I'm afraid to take my cell phone to the bathroom. Right now, she's all about your client: her certainty that Jane and Ray had a thing, her description of your client as a 'slutty, trashy redneck,' which to me, at least, seems crazy. I mean, your client . . . Great day in the morning. The looks on her." He coughed. "I mean, I can see why the wife would hate her hubby working with somebody who looks like that." He coughed again. "But . . ."

"But?"

"But Felicity's cried wolf a time or two. She blamed Irene Robinson first, you know, the secretary?"

Most people preferred *admin*, but sure. "Right."

"Started off with her, same insults, except she left off *slutty*. She claimed Irene's motive was that Ray was also a 'little bit' racist and insulted Irene."

Um, sure.

"But then we checked out Irene. She's got a family, and one of the kids had a nightmare and got in bed with Mommy that night, and a neighbor verified that her car was in the driveway when he came home from a night shift. Doesn't look like she had the opportunity, so we're still looking at Irene's husband. You know anything about him?"

"C. J.?"

"You know him?"

"No, but I—" I stopped myself before I jumped in with too much enthusiasm over the possibility of another suspect who might knock Jane off her primary perch. I didn't know C. J., but I knew Irene. She'd called me, out of the blue, to help Jane. Irene had taken the risk, despite her terror of the police hurting her family, which included C. J. I'd been ready to throw someone into the investigative jaws of the police on Jane's behalf, with no clue whether there were any grounds. *Back up, Allison.*

"No. I don't know him, but I'd think he was unlikely."

"That's kind of where we are."

"Did you tell Felicity that Irene had an alibi?"

"Oh, sure, sure. She's the family, you know, of the victim. We have to keep her updated as to how the investigation is coming along. Best we can, anyway. That's when she got on Jane."

"Of course she did." Here was my chance to blanket-discredit Felicity. "I bet Felicity hasn't said a word about the two male associates who worked the same hours for Ray."

"Well, no, she hasn't mentioned them. They seem clean, though. Little bit of a history of bad evaluations, but that's nothing without more."

"You don't have any more about Jane, either."

"That's not exactly true, unfortunately."

"What do you mean?"

"Ms. Barton, you seem like a nice lady. If it helps, I think Felicity is either batshit crazy or a vindictive bitch, or both. She sure as hell isn't grieving like she actually misses the guy. But we've got some other evidence I can't talk about that creates a real problem for your lady."

The email misspellings, I'd guess. They were a real problem, indeed. Jane had told me herself she had no alibi, but maybe there was something. A traffic camera that caught her going home. A cell phone ping she forgot about far away. I could begin hard-core investigating. "What's the time of death for Ray Corrigan? Do you have a window?"

"Oh, now, you know I can't share that kind of stuff."

"Come on, Zach," I said, in my sweetest voice. "It's not going to change any of the facts. You telling me that won't make her not guilty if she's guilty."

"Fair, fair. Medical examiner says sometime between midnight and two a.m. Or thereabouts."

The email with the misspellings sent from Ray's computer to Jane had a time stamp of 12:09 a.m. It was possible that he'd sent it tired, hadn't noticed the misspellings, and had then been shot by someone who walked into his office, but it was more likely that someone else had sent it for him—his computer screen would have been open and easy to access—to mess with the timeline after killing him.

The fact that Jane regularly misspelled *there* did not help her.

Then again, if Jane was widely known to misspell *there*, the killer might have done it on purpose to mess with not only the timeline but the list of suspects. How many people knew that about her?

"I appreciate your help, Zach. Really."

"You're most welcome." He cleared his throat. "And I'll, uh, check out that stuff about Felicity's business."

You will never know the answer to a question you don't ask: "Do you have an estimate for when you're going to pick up someone for this?"

He laughed, that machine-gun sound already beginning to grate. "Ha, wouldn't you like to know? I expect we clear C. J. in the next day or so, so soon," he said. "Real soon."

CHAPTER FIFTEEN
JANE

Five days after telling Allison about my mother, if not about the rest of it, I stood at the Keurig coffee maker in the break room at work. My return to the office had gone largely unnoticed, since I hadn't been absent all that long in the first place. Josh, Amir, and I had been assigned to work with Helen Reeves, who'd taken over Ray's cases after returning from maternity leave—a rarity among partners in our firm. The maternity part, at least.

So far, Helen was a dream. I hadn't known her well before her leave, though what I had known was that the reason the partnership hadn't shuffled her off the main track despite the egregiously billable-incompatible decision to have a child was that she was brilliant and had one of the most prestigious law degrees in the place. She'd gone to Columbia Law School, and few here could touch her. No firm in a small city like Charlottesville could afford to alienate a star like that.

I'd almost cried the previous night when she caught me at my desk at six and told me to get the hell out of here.

Amir charged into the break room with wide eyes, mug in hand.

"Almost done," I said, gesturing at the Keurig. "It had to heat up."

"No, Jane. Those police dudes are in your office with Dombrowski." He glanced at my coffee cup, now full and steaming. "If you want to drink that, you might want to stay here."

For a second, our eyes met. In his, there was pity but also a little bracing outrage. Amir was occasionally a goofball, but he was a decent goofball. I picked up the mug and downed a few swallows, then put it aside to toss away the coffee pod and clean up the area. "Thanks, Amir. Your turn."

"You're not going to stay here?"

"No. Best to get it over with."

"I guess? Just tell them you have nothing to hide. That's what they always do in the movies."

I gave him a wry grin. If only that were true. I typed a quick text to Allison and retrieved my mug of coffee.

The more suspicious of the two investigators, Hossain, stood in my office doorway, leaning against the frame but clearly keeping an eye on the hallway. I held my head high and walked straight toward him. Inside, Greg sat bolt upright in my chair, and O'Callihan lounged in the guest chair, shiny wingtip on the top of the desk. Make yourselves comfortable, gentlemen.

"Hello, this is a surprise."

"Is it, really," said Hossain, all pretense at pleasantry gone.

O'Callihan stood up. "I'm awful sorry, Ms. Knudsen, but you're under arrest for the murder of Raymond Corrigan Jr. You have the right to remain silent. Anything you say can and will be used against you in a court of law. You have the right to an attorney, and to have that attorney present during questioning. Do you understand these rights as I've read them to you?"

"I do." I took one last sip and put the mostly full mug down. I wondered who would empty it or wash it. Probably no one. Hossain pulled handcuffs out of his pocket.

Greg started forward, his primly pleased expression melting into alarm. "Is that really necessary? I'm sure she'll cooperate. This is a law firm."

"Yeah, it's necessary. This woman is charged with murder."

"May I alert my attorney before you handcuff me?" I asked.

Hossain shook his head while O'Callihan waved magnanimously in my direction. "Sure, sure."

I decided O'Callihan was in charge and texted Allison again. She hadn't read the first one yet, but she would. Then I held out my wrists for the cuffs like a good girl.

The shame didn't start until they paraded me out, taking their time and raising their voices in the hallways so as many heads would turn as possible. I hadn't felt shame like that for a long, long time, but the feel of it was coded into my muscle memory, and by the time O'Callihan placed his hand on the top of my head to mash me into their nondescript sedan, I'd lost track of what I was being arrested for.

⁊ₛ

Jail wasn't as bad as most people thought. One night there wasn't a big deal, and the overpowering smell of disinfectant comforted me, somehow. The other inmates—I'd never been as afraid of any woman as I was of all men—left me mostly alone, except for one old lady who told me to avoid the potato salad at supper.

The worst part was the holding cell in the courthouse. It was small and windowless and made me feel trapped and guilty. They'd brought me over early in the morning for my bond hearing, but I'd been waiting alone for forty-five minutes while my fellow prisoner had her preliminary hearing for grand larceny. She'd taken her ex-boyfriend's brand-new TV when he kicked her out.

Doors buzzed and unlocked. A man wearing a deputy's uniform brought in Allison, loaded down with files and yellow legal pads.

It was so bizarre to be the client and not the lawyer.

"Hi. I'm so sorry, Jane. I think it's going to be okay, though. I located a couple of witnesses that I think will help. They dropped everything to get here. You're not without friends."

"What am I charged with?"

"Murder in the first degree."

"I knew the penalty for that when I took the bar, but it doesn't come up a lot in insurance law. Remind me?" I glanced at the walls of the cell, bracing.

"Twenty to life," she said bluntly. "Even with that, I think there's a decent chance you'll get bond."

"You've got to be kidding. How often do murder defendants get bond?"

Allison dropped her gaze. Yup. That's what I thought. "Not often, but don't give up. Like I said—"

"What do they have on me?" I cut off her cheerleading. No need. I knew the odds. "Besides hatred?"

"They're going to say that you and Ray were romantically involved. He told his wife about it. She's going to say she put her foot down, and when he dumped you, you killed him with his own gun from his drawer. Then you sent yourself an email to cover your tracks and left to dump the murder weapon, which they have not found. Your fingerprints are all over Ray's office and his computer. Most of their evidence comes from Felicity, and frankly, I think she's making a lot of it up."

"Great."

"She really hates you and has maybe a better motive than you do."

"What evidence is there that I was romantically involved with Ray other than Felicity's imagination?"

"I'm not sure of all of it, but apparently a custodian saw you and Ray in some sort of compromising position at work one night. Look, Jane, I don't care if you and Ray had a thing. It happens. It's not a motive. Seriously. You can tell me the truth."

"The truth," I bit off, with my teeth gritted, "is that Ray put his hand on my ass if he drank too much and once grabbed me and tried to kiss me. I reckon the custodian must have seen that, because I swear there's nothing else."

"Did you report it to the partnership?"

As if there were any scenario in which a woman associate reported a partner for sexual harassment and still had a viable route to partnership afterward. "You've worked in law firms, right? What do you think?"

She grimaced, then nodded once. "Okay. Had to ask. We'll deal with it." She glanced at her notes. "Oh, one more thing. Because you and Ray are both members of the Charlottesville Bar Association, the local judge and commonwealth's attorney recused themselves immediately. Today our judge is from Parnell County, and the commonwealth's attorney is from Devonshire County. A woman named Nina Hilcko. Which is a bit of a stroke of luck. She went to UVA Law, too, and—"

Allison broke off when the deputy returned, this time to take us both out to the courtroom. The judge's nameplate read EVAN GARCIA. I'd never seen him before, though honestly, bar association or no bar association, I wouldn't likely have known the local judge. Our practice group mainly litigated, when we went to court at all, in the federal courts. I glanced at the gallery. To my surprise, Josh, Amir, and Helen Reeves sat in the front row. Good God. Helen had known me all of three days. Josh winked.

I really hated appearing before Helen Reeves—and Josh—in an orange jumpsuit and shackles, but I went to the mantra I repeated in my head when things were bad: *I have been through worse.*

Judge Garcia greeted me with a friendly manner. He called the case and a woman unfolded long legs from where she'd been chatting with a bailiff. With a jolt, the pieces fell into place. I knew her, though she wouldn't know me. Nina Hilcko, Devonshire County commonwealth's attorney, was famous and handling my bond hearing. Damn. Damn. Damn.

We'd never met, but once, in law school, I'd attended a lecture she'd given as an adjunct professor. I hadn't taken her class, but I'd had to stand in the back to hear her talk about breaking the glass ceiling of law. She'd been in her late forties then, the child of Russian and Peruvian immigrants, and had been the youngest woman ever elected commonwealth's attorney in Virginia. She was tough, scrappy, and had gained her fame prosecuting a man who'd coached girls to the Olympics in swimming—and molested dozens of them over the years. She had wild dyed-platinum hair that she wore barely restrained at the back of her neck. I'd hero-worshipped her from that long-ago lecture. I even recalled the random fact that she'd once followed Phish around the country when she was young.

Commonwealth's attorneys employed junior prosecutors who tried most of the cases. It was rare for one to step into the courtroom themselves, even in a recusal situation like this. It happened only in high-profile cases. Knowing that I rated that honor was not welcome news.

The judge started things right away and Allison called the first witness. In bond hearings for charges this serious, the presumption is that bond will not be granted. It would all be on Allison: prove I wasn't a flight risk or enough of a danger to the community that I'd have to stay in jail until the trial.

The first witness was Amir, to my surprise. He took his position and was sworn in.

"Can you tell us your name and position, please?" asked Allison.

"Amir Burhan. I'm an associate at Blackwood, Payne & Vivant. I've worked with Jane Knudsen for three years, since I graduated from law school."

"Would you describe Jane as unreliable?"

He laughed, a contagious sound from deep in his belly. "Get out of here! No way. She is the opposite of unreliable. She shows up for work every single morning exactly three hours early. She hasn't taken a single vacation or sick day in the entire three years I've been there."

"Do you have any reason to believe she would fail to show up for court if she were released on bond?"

"No. No reason at all."

"Do you feel safe at a workplace with her?"

"Yes. The only thing she'd ever do to me is make me read a box of documents and bore me to death."

"Thank you, Mr. Burhan."

Nina stood. "Mr. Burhan, Ms. Knudsen has a large family, does she?"

"No," he said, thrown by the way she'd phrased it. "Not that I know of."

"And a wealth of activities that keep her tied to this community?"

"She spends all her time at work, best I can figure."

"You weren't in the office of Ray Corrigan the night of June fourteenth, were you?"

"No."

"Thank you."

Allison waited for Amir to head out and called Helen Reeves. She got Helen's name and position in quickly, and even that she was a graduate of Columbia Law. Allison didn't waste time.

"As a senior partner at Blackwood, Payne & Vivant, will you have any issues if Jane is incarcerated prior to trial?"

"Many. Frankly, client expectations will not be met. It could cause us to lose business or even commit malpractice."

"Can you explain that?"

"Yes. I've taken over Ray Corrigan's four-attorney practice group after his death. Other than Ray, and now myself, Jane is the most senior attorney. It took less than no time for me to figure out that she's the linchpin. Without her, nothing happens. She receives assignments from the partner and doles out the work to the other two associates." She raised an elegant hand and gestured to Josh and Amir. "There they are sitting there, to show their support."

Odd little butterflies took wing inside me. I had never really thought about other people supporting me. Finding me attractive, yes. Flattering me in the hopes I would sleep with them, sure. But plain old support? I'd never known I had it.

Helen continued. "I think both would agree that Jane does far more than one-quarter of the group's work. I think it's fair to say that when Ray was in charge, she was doing probably fifty percent of it. I mean to adjust that ratio more in her favor going forward, but for the time being, while I get up to speed, I simply can't get along without her. To do otherwise would mean committing legal malpractice."

She smiled graciously at Nina Hilcko. "You know how it is, I'm sure."

Nina smiled a tight smile back at her. There was a bit of enjoyment in it. Part of me felt like I was watching this whole discussion from somewhere far outside my body. There's no way to prepare yourself to listen to other people talk about you this way. It was like listening to your own funeral eulogy.

Nina asked her the same questions—no, I had no family or life to keep me from heading to the nearest non-extraditing tropical paradise, and no, Helen hadn't been present to be assured I hadn't killed Ray. She was excused. Before she moved, she leaned forward conspiratorially. "You don't mind if I say one more thing before I go, do you?"

Nina clearly minded very much but knew perfectly well that if she didn't allow it, Allison would recall Helen and she'd say it anyway. "Go ahead."

"Jane is one of the finest lawyers—and women—I've ever met. She works hard, she's kind, she has a true moral compass, and I would bet my firstborn she didn't do this. And you should know I returned from maternity leave this week—my firstborn. Thank you."

I tried not to cry. I failed. A tear rolled down my face. While I struggled for control, I looked around. Josh was the only one left who'd come here for me. He must be next.

I almost fell over when Allison called Professor Elijah Weatherbee. When we were first-year law students, Allison and I had been in the same nine a.m. section of Criminal Law. Professor Weatherbee was old, vengeful against any student who showed up late or unprepared, and notoriously grumpy.

I'd had trouble with his class right from the start—funny, right?—and had been left with no choice but to brave his office hours to talk through the particularly difficult concepts. Underneath that curmudgeonly exterior, he turned out to be a sweetheart. Allison went with me on the second visit, after I reported back that the crotchety persona was a facade. He told us that we'd passed a test more important than any exam: any student who put knowledge ahead of fear enough to ask questions had learned half of what we needed to know.

When I was looking for a job later, he personally wrote me a recommendation. I assume he did the same for Allison.

Now, he limped up the courtroom aisle to the witness stand, stone-faced.

I glanced at Nina Hilcko. Her mouth hung open. I'd forgotten: she'd gone to UVA Law, too, and Professor Weatherbee had taught there since forever.

He stood straight and tall to be sworn. Even Judge Garcia looked impressed. The professor didn't wait for Allison to finish asking the first question. His voice rang out in the tones that had struck fear into my heart the first few weeks of school.

"I am Professor Elijah H. Weatherbee, professor of criminal law at the University of Virginia School of Law. I've taught first-year students there for thirty-odd years. I taught the defendant nine or ten years ago. I taught the defendant's counsel in the same class."

The judge turned interested eyes to Allison.

Professor Weatherbee knew his audience. "Quite the Virginia alumni reunion we have here. I believe I also taught you, Ms. Hilcko, and you, too, Your Honor. Criminal law, all of you."

Holy shit. How had Allison gotten him here? Nina's mouth was closed now.

Allison consulted her notes. "Professor, you don't employ Ms. Knudsen, do you?"

"I do not, but I wish I could. Ms. Knudsen is one of the most intelligent and hardworking students I ever had, and that includes all of you. She is also one of the most honest people I've come across. During her first year of law school, she picked up her final exam—a twenty-four-hour take-home exam—and brought it back an hour later. She advised that she had seen the first question the previous week during a visit to my office hours. She didn't think it would be fair to take the exam after she'd had a chance to consider the question, however subliminally, for a longer period of time than the rest of the section. We arranged for her to take the makeup exam the following day."

"Is that unusual?" Allison asked, knowing damn well it was. The judge's eyes were wide.

"Yes." Professor Weatherbee harrumphed. "Ask yourselves if you'd do the same, any of you. Ms. Knudsen doesn't say much, but what she does say is honorable and true. If she says she didn't do this, she didn't. If she says she'll be here for the trial of this matter, she will. I will vouch for her, and I will post her bond."

"Thank you, sir."

He harrumphed again. "Are we done here? Ms. Hilcko? I assume you have no questions. This young lady has no criminal record of any kind, standing in the community, gainful employment where she is badly needed, has been vouched for by three separate upstanding members of this bar, humbly including myself, and is presumed innocent until proven guilty."

Nina Hilcko looked ready to argue, but hesitated. I didn't envy her in this position.

Professor Weatherbee wasn't done. "Yes, Ms. Hilcko, we are all aware there is no presumption of bond in a case of this seriousness, but it is hardly unheard of when it is justified. Three defendants charged with murder in the first degree have gotten bond in the last two months in this commonwealth, one of them in your home county, Your Honor. It is certainly justified here."

"Ms. Hilcko?" Judge Garcia asked, looking for all the world like he wanted Nina to take the decision out of his hands. "Cross?"

She bit her lip. "No, sir. Commonwealth will agree to bond. We'd ask five hundred thousand dollars."

Allison spoke up, brazen as hell. "Two hundred thousand dollars."

"Thank you, Counsel," Judge Garcia said, with palpable relief. "Court will grant bond in the amount of three hundred thousand dollars. Defendant to have no contact with the victim's family. Defendant must remain in good standing at her place of employment, stay in Virginia, and surrender her passport. Ms. Knudsen, please don't give Professor Weatherbee any reason to change that exalted opinion of you. I weep for all of us if that should happen. Professor, it was good to see you again."

"Always glad to spread a little more light of rationality in a dark world. Life's work, you know." The professor tipped an imaginary hat at me and limped out the way he'd come.

"Anything else, Counsel?" the judge asked, making clear by peering at us over the tops of his glasses that the answer had better be no. Both lawyers shook their heads. "Fine. Schedule your preliminary. Ms. Barton, you may speak to your client over there before she's taken back to the jail to be processed out."

I didn't even know what to say. In twenty-four hours, Allison had rounded up possibly the perfect witness to help me get bond. One she'd known would stymie any argument the commonwealth might have made that I needed to stay in jail. One I had no idea had felt that strongly about me.

"Good God," I said to her. She was flushed with success. "That was a hell of a bond hearing. Obviously, I will pay whatever retainer you ask for my defense. I should say that first off. But how in the world did you think of Professor Weatherbee? How did you know?"

Allison smiled, still pleased. I'd forgotten: me getting bond was her victory, too. No doubt she was also pleased that she could now expect a fairly sizable payday. "At first I thought of calling Professor Graham. I figured he owed you, but thinking about law professors made me remember Weatherbee. I followed your lead that year, you know, going to the office hours and cultivating a relationship with him, though I'm ashamed to admit I did it mainly because I thought it might help my grade. You, on the other hand, did it because you were actually interested in him as a legal scholar and as a person, and he never forgot it. He told me once what a gem you were. I called him; figured it couldn't hurt. He dropped everything to be here today. You've got more friends than you know."

I didn't trust my voice to speak. I nodded instead, my throat thick with the tears I was fighting. "Thank you. More than *you* know."

"Professor Graham isn't the only one who owes you." She swallowed. "I do, too. I hope I've paid off a little of the balance. I should have been a better friend."

I was unable to speak. I had a choice between silence and sobbing, and I made the same choice I always had before.

CHAPTER SIXTEEN

ALLISON

I watched as a jailer walked Jane away through the metal door that led to the holding cell to be processed out on bond, feeling both thrilled at that epic bond hearing and already vaguely worried I'd never be able to top it again. I sincerely doubted I'd ever have another client Professor Elijah Weatherbee would vouch for.

"Well done, Counsel." Nina Hilcko leaned against the doorframe, her tailored suit unrumpled. "It isn't often I've found myself weighing whether it would be unpardonably rude to suggest a person charged with first-degree murder not be offered bond during a hearing, but you managed it. Good lord—Weatherbee. I never, not in my worst first-year nightmares, in a million years imagined I'd have to cross-examine Elijah Weatherbee after he schooled me in the law of criminal bond. He used to terrify me."

"Me, too, if it helps." I smiled. I kind of liked her.

"It's Allison, right? You practice in Lynchburg?"

"Yes. And in Noble County."

"Well. I'm far from my usual office, too. Let's go get coffee or something."

I wavered, always worried about breaking an ethical rule.

She laughed. "Come on. We'll talk plea bargains and settlement, if it helps."

"All right."

Charlottesville's courthouse sat a block away from their popular downtown mall—a street closed to vehicle traffic and lined by cafés and restaurants with outdoor seating, bookshops, theaters, and a juice bar. We walked to the juice bar, exchanging small talk about how the mall had changed since we went to school in town, then sat, Nina with a green smoothie and me with plain juice.

"So. It's not often I am so totally crushed in a simple bond hearing, and frankly, I want to hear about you. While you were conferring with your client afterwards, I googled you. You were the one with that case last fall—you represented that lady who dumped the . . . the . . . what was it? Some kind of poisonous flower in a drink at a damn fifth-grade graduation party? And you got her off. Amazing."

"She wasn't guilty," I said, using three words that were true but hardly encapsulated the actual truth. The poisoned drink in question had been a smoothie. I glanced at the cup in Nina's hand and decided not to add that detail.

"I don't think her guilt or innocence was why Google has info on you. I think it was the way you litigated it. You mean business."

I had done well in that case. The notoriety and influx of clients afterward had allowed me to open my own firm. Sometimes the case itself, however, still gave me nightmares. Nina Hilcko seemed like the kind of person who'd understand why, if I told her. Then again, this whole "let's have a fun chat and get to know each other" thing might be intended to entice me into making a mistake. Congeniality among attorneys was expected, but it could slip over the line into exploitation on a dime. Nina might well think I was green enough to fall for the camaraderie routine and spill things she could use against me—and Jane. "I'd like to think so."

"Whatever happened to your client? The PTA lady? She still owning the elementary school?"

She was not. She'd been forced to give up custody of her children and existed, I heard, as a ball of explosive nitroglycerine in a state of constant rage.

"She . . . uh. She and her husband are divorcing, last I heard. I didn't take the divorce case." A vague feeling of nausea overcame me at even the thought of that former client. "So were you serious about plea bargaining?"

"Not really, not yet. I don't know enough about this case, and neither do you."

"She didn't do it."

"So you say, and apparently Weatherbee agrees, but we both know that's not enough to get me to drop the case. The wife is breathing down my neck already. I spoke to her for forty-five minutes in the car on the way here. She would contradict you, emphatically, and will, I expect."

"She wants someone to blame. Ask yourself why. Then check out why her planned business expansion didn't happen. And her behavior at the interior-design conference she went to in Charlotte."

Nina narrowed her gaze.

"Your investigators know all this. I told them. You might want to check it out, too."

"Oh, I will. I'm just getting up to speed. I only got the case yesterday. I'm always going to check out every loose end, but as of right now, your client looks good for it. I hear she's hiding some major shit of some kind. The investigators are working on that. Could be a real problem for her at trial if she's got a big secret but is asking us to believe she's as open and honest as Weatherbee said."

"What would you say if I told you that it was childhood shit and nothing that has anything to do with the murder of Ray Corrigan?"

She considered me. "Then I'd be interested in hearing it all. Letting the jury decide whether it's relevant or not."

Oh crap. "Jury?"

"Of course a jury. This is first-degree murder. I always ask for a jury in a murder case. Are you serious?" She took a long slurp from her smoothie. "So what's the childhood shit?"

"She was abused as a child."

Nina stared at me, as if waiting for me to finish a sentence. "And? If this were a trial for child abuse and she were the victim, that might matter. I need more than that."

I had liked her, but that blasé attitude made me doubt whether to trust her with any more. "I can talk to my client about whether to share more, but her past has nothing to do with the case." I understood the score now: Nina might be moved if I could convey spectacular trauma, but not otherwise. Jane would balk at providing trauma porn to a person who had every motivation not to care. I'd have to beg her. Harrowing abuse was painful to discuss and relive, but surely Jane would rather disclose it than go to prison to avoid talking about it.

At least I hoped so.

"You know as well as I do that your client's secretiveness can and will be an issue with the jury. You know these things have a way of coming out in the media. You're welcome to try to make a motion to keep it out of the courtroom, but the damage will be done. And I'll be better prepared next time." She smiled. I couldn't tell from the grin whether she was trying to be kind or threatening me. Or both.

"Sure. Well. This was great, but I've got to be heading back down the road."

"It was nice to meet you. I enjoyed this morning. It's always fun to have a worthy adversary."

Fun. My stomach gave a decisive roil, then settled back into baseline stressed resignation.

As I walked back to my car for the trip home, my phone rang. Libby, in day care, had a fever of 100.2, tripping the pickup requirement. Could I come?

Almost nothing made me feel worse about myself and my life choices than getting these calls—away from home, in a courtroom, having to decide the priorities of my child versus my job based on the degree of her temperature or the amount of blood she'd spilled on the recess pavement. Libby hadn't been sick when I dropped her off this morning. In this case, though, I had no choice. I was ninety minutes away. I would have to ask for help. I texted Steve, knowing he'd likely ignore my phone call for longer.

Me: Libby has a fever and has to be picked up. I'm in Cville. Can you go?

The "typing" dots appeared, then disappeared. He'd seen it. I bit my lip, trying to imagine him—a high school teacher on summer vacation—coming up with an excuse.

Steve: OK but I can't keep her long. Come get her ASAP.

Relief and annoyance mixed: crisis averted, yet Steve, who generally spent his summers helping his buddy with a landscape business on his own schedule, still expected me to drop everything for Libby. And I would. Knowing how unhappy Libby had been as the third wheel in his passionate romance, I didn't even try to think how to demand he be a better father.

When Libby was born and we were still together, Steve did his share. We both worked and we divided the diaper-changing and the spit-up baby-clothes laundering and the middle of the night soothing—or at least he helped me with that last one. Once things went south, however, and he moved out, he and Libby lost a lot of their closeness.

I spent the entire drive thinking of all the tiny things Steve did that hurt Libby—dropping her off without hugging her, refusing to let her pick up what she'd forgotten at my house when it was his weekend, letting Karen select the Saturday night restaurant because "Karen always chooses the best restaurants," missing Libby's school concerts, never once asking to hear her play piano, not even when they visited his parents, who owned one. By the time I pulled into his driveway, I was shaking with anger.

The fact that Karen answered the door did not bode well.

"She's feeling better now, thank goodness," Karen said, opening the door wider for me to pass. Karen, also still a teacher, spent her summers by their pool or on girls' weekends to Myrtle Beach.

That ever-present sense of relief and annoyance that I associated with both Steve and Karen heated, filling my head with the fumes. I needed them as backup, but I also wished I could eradicate them from my life, if not from Libby's. Since I could not be free of them while my daughter still drew breath, I forced my lips into a smile.

"That's great. Thanks, Karen." My phone dinged: Emmett, checking on how the bond hearing had gone. I shoved the phone into a pocket.

Karen watched me, hands on her pregnant belly and mouth full of judgment. "Was that work or Emmett? Libby says one or the other takes all your time."

"I'm in the middle of a workday," I said, gritting my teeth. "It's not unusual to have emails during a workday." *Not that you would know, Summer Fun Karen.* I pushed past her to the living room sofa, where Libby sat, playing a game on Karen's phone. It had to be Karen's, because it was in an animal-print case. "Hey, buddy. How're you feeling?"

"Mommy!" Libby said, tossing aside the phone and running to my legs, where she clung like a koala. "I don't feel good!"

I reached around to find her forehead—warm, but not too warm. No stuffy breathing or congestion in her voice. "Does your stomach feel bad?" I asked, looking around for Steve. Surely he could fill me in. No sign of him. I picked up her backpack, the only item in sight. She insisted on taking it, even in the summer, when it contained nothing more than her stuffed lion and two pieces of homemade art she'd done right after school got out.

"No, my head hurts."

I squeezed her tight and kissed the top of her head. Yes, I'd likely get sick if she was, but the comforting came first. "Where's Steve?" I asked Karen.

"He had a job he had to do. He left about half an hour ago."

Of course he did. "Great. Thanks for keeping her. You ready, Lib?" She skipped out to the car.

Karen pursed her lips in the way she did right before she said something that would piss me off. She did not disappoint. "You know, Allison, you sent a sick child to day care and put other kids at risk. And then you were too far away to pick her up. You really need to do something about that job. I told Steve; it's just so sad for Libby."

Libby hadn't been remotely sick this morning. Not only that, she had two parents, not one and an alternate. *That job* of mine kept Steve from having to pay child support. But somehow, none of those excellent arguments came out of my mouth. Sometimes, the shame at not being there when my child needed me was too great.

"Thanks again for taking care of her. She said she had a great time at Steve's parents', too."

"Oh, we loved having her. We're happy to keep her for you and Emmett to have some alone time. I remember how that is!" she said, bumping my arm like we were gal pals. *Nudge nudge wink wink.*

Still in BFF mode, she leaned close. "So? Has he popped the question yet?"

"Not yet, Karen. We're taking it slow."

"You'll want to throw a lasso around that one quick. Those shoulders! He's a catch, all right."

"He sure is," I gritted out. The smile this time was so tight it nearly pulled a muscle.

"Must be hot and heavy with someone that gorgeous. Go, you! Of course, Libby tells us how much it grosses her out when Mommy and Emmett kiss. So confusing, for the little ones, when single parents are having sex lives. Best not to see it, don't you think?"

"I so agree, Karen," I said fervently. "Sometime you'll have to tell me how you and Steve handled talking to Libby about *your* single sex lives! You know, after he broke up her parents' marriage for you. But right now, gotta run." I gave her my best shark smile, full of teeth and devoid of goodwill, and made my getaway. I'd regret that later, but unlike Karen, I didn't aspire to sainthood.

At home, I got Libby settled down on the sofa the way my mom used to do for me: a quilt under her, a light blanket over her, a pillow from her bed at one end, PJs on, TV tuned to whatever she thought would cheer her up. She drifted off a few minutes later and I decamped to the kitchen to keep up with my workday as best I could.

I started with the first call—Irene, who'd left me a voice message.

Once I got her on the phone, and she found an excuse to go outside for a walk to talk freely, she sounded like a new person: happier, lower stress, less of a pinched sound to her voice.

"New boss," she said, when I commented about it. "Helen is way better than Ray. Kind of amazing, really, how much better a job I want to do when I'm not going to be yelled at ten times a day. So I can't talk long. You know how Ray's daughter Brittany's starting a job up in Northern Virginia after the bar? She—and Felicity, too—are trying to pretend like they're thrilled, like she chose that job. She didn't. I saw a document, and don't ask me where I saw it; I can't say. Ray scuttled her. He's the reason Blackwood didn't offer her a job."

"What?" I said, blinking at the horizon. "His own daughter?"

"Yes. Each summer we have three, sometimes four, law students work here as summer associates. They offer jobs to all of them as a rule, unless they're total idiots."

"To all of them? How do they find enough work for that many new lawyers every year?"

Irene cackled. "Please. They get paid a fraction of what they bring into the firm. All the extra goes to the partnership. Lots of them move on when they realize how miserable they are. The ones who stay try to make partner and those who fail move on then. Associates earn most of the money for the firm. There are never enough of them."

"So what happened with Brittany?"

"Each August, they send around an evaluation sheet to every partner who worked with one of the summer associates. Brittany got good reviews from all the partners who filled hers out, except for Ray. He wrote 'DO NOT HIRE' in shouty-caps Sharpie, and that was that."

"Why? Do you know?"

"You'd have to ask someone from HR, though it's definitely possible that no one cared enough to ask him. Summer associates—even daughters of partners—are only valuable while they're billing."

"That was last August, though. Almost a year ago. Why would that be a motive for murder now?"

"Brittany came in a few weeks ago. Asked for her employee file. That evaluation would be in it and she would have seen it. For the first time."

"Are you sure about that timing?"

"Yeah. She came in and asked me for it. Said she wanted it for her new job. I directed her to HR."

I thanked her and got right on the phone to O'Callihan. I told him everything Irene had told me.

Investigator Zach O'Callihan had dropped all the friendly banter and was no longer interested in solving Ray's murder.

"Ms. Barton, I appreciate all your 'help,' but there's no point to this. We know who did it. It's your client—and I get it, I get it—you've got to defend her. Calling us up and telling us about other suspects is wasting all of our time. This case is solved."

"How many of the people you looked at had alibis?"

"Guy was murdered at midnight. Nobody out that late. Not many online or using their phones. Not many alibis, except for Irene and C. J. Robinson and the Burhan dude. He had a houseful of guests. Looks like everyone else lives a lonely life."

"Your case is crap. A misspelled email? Give me a break."

"We have more than that. Her fingerprints on the desk. Footprints in the office in blood. Fraud, probably, on diplomas, job applications, even the bar exam background check, maybe. Your client could be going by an alias. It would make things a lot clearer if she'd talk to us about why."

They were bumbling it. If they only knew she'd legally changed her name, she'd be cleared of this much at least. Name changes were usually public records, though not the reasons why. I'd have thought they'd have found it by now. Surely they hadn't arrested her simply on dead-body-adjacent fingerprints and a suspicious email.

Oh damn. They probably hadn't.

"What else? What else do you have? You arrested her for some reason. What?"

"Murder weapon, that's what. Your girl lives in a new development. Her town house is finished, but we found the gun that's missing from Ray Corrigan's desk drawer in a pit they dug across the street for more houses. No more than a hundred feet from her garage."

Oh.

Shit.

CHAPTER SEVENTEEN

JANE

After Professor Weatherbee—God bless him—paid my bond and I'd had a chance to go home to shower and change, I went back to work. I really had nowhere else to go. This was both a relief and probably something I should be concerned about, but I'd worry about that another day.

To my surprise, Helen greeted me like I'd just won a big case for a client instead of avoiding months of incarceration for a brutal, bloody crime she had no idea whether I'd committed. She gave me a time-intensive assignment, and within minutes I was back to billing clients for the partnership.

Right when my stomach started grumbling near suppertime, Allison called. She didn't mince words.

"They found what is likely the murder weapon in a construction pit, feet from your house."

"They what?"

"That's why they arrested you. It's not only the email. They apparently also have your fingerprints all over Ray's desk."

A certain resigned inevitability settled over me, the kind you feel when bad news stops scaring you as the anxiety is replaced by certainty. Certain misery is somehow better than possible misery. They were building a case. "Well, the fingerprints part wouldn't be a shocker. Ray loved making me search through all his stuff to find things. He got off on the power of it all. Irene, too, and probably Josh and Amir as well; we all had to spend half our time plowing through the crap on or in his desk."

"Did you know the gun was there?"

"We all did. You couldn't miss it—he kept it in the bottom drawer under his hanging files. That's the drawer we had to dig in the most."

"Let me ask you this," Allison said. "He was killed, presumably with his own gun, inches from the drawer where it was kept. I'd imagine the killer must have retrieved it when he wasn't at his desk. How possible would that be?"

"Very. He never locked his office or any of his drawers, even with the gun in there. He wasn't fastidious about his belongings. Anyone could have taken it when he was in a meeting or in the bathroom."

"Great," she said, though it clearly wasn't great.

"Whoever it was must have done it fairly close to the murder, though. He would probably have noticed it was missing more than a day. He was a slob, but one of those slobs who knew where everything was."

"Would your fingerprints also be on his keyboard?"

I thought a minute. "Yeeees, probably. Sometimes the things he wanted found were emails. Like I said, he enjoyed watching us jump when he said jump."

"Great," she said, again. "I got that stuff about the murder weapon from O'Callihan. He also said they think there's this huge untold story about you and that you're using an alias and lying about who you are. Nina Hilcko seemed to think that secret past is likely to make you look very guilty in front of the jury she intends to ask for, and I don't think she's wrong. Why haven't they figured out what's going on? I need to know why they haven't found your change of name."

"I did it under seal. The judge agreed when he heard the reasons." I gripped the armrests of my office chair, feeling faint at the memory of telling the judge the reasons.

"What are the reasons, Jane? Is it more than the credit card theft? Is your mom dangerous? I promise I won't share what you don't authorize me to share, and I definitely won't judge you—that would be crazy; an abused child, my God—but I don't like lurching around in the dark."

I wanted to tell her. I did, but something in my throat swelled and expanded, stopping my air. I shook my head, knowing she couldn't see me. For a time, I had to concentrate on bringing air in and out through my nose.

Enough time passed while she waited and I struggled that she gave up. "Okay. I'll let you go for now, but I really don't want to find out the answer to that question from O'Callihan on the stand when I can't do anything to blunt it."

"I . . . I have to do something, first. I'll tell you. I will. But I need . . . some time."

There was a pause. I pictured that judgmental look she used to wear while she sat on her bed, surrounded by books.

"All right." A sigh whistled down the line. "I can't help you, unless you let me."

"I'm working on it."

❧

Some years ago, they built a bypass around Danville, Virginia, to speed up the trip between Washington, DC, and the growing city centers of North Carolina. Danville, already struggling from textile factory closures, no longer had much through traffic to populate its roadside restaurants and shops. It had been years since I'd even slowed down there, but today, I'd located a home-cooking restaurant downtown, the closest

I could get to North Carolina without breaking the terms of my bond. It was the kind of restaurant where my mother would feel comfortable. I didn't doubt she'd come. I'd offered her money. Like a yellow jacket to an open can of Coke at an August picnic, she'd be sitting down to a meat-and-three supper no later than ten minutes after my arrival.

Part of me, the small, young, defenseless part, wanted her to come for me. I had spent years reading psychology books and magazines to figure out why, when they've hurt us worse than anyone else can, we still so desperately crave love and approval from our parents. There were days I wished she would call, tell me she was sorry, ask to have a real relationship, even though the rational part of my brain knew she wasn't capable of that kind of growth. Only pain lay down that path. Hope opens flesh and causes bleeding in relationships like the one I had with Cherry.

Knowing all that had never yet stopped me from hoping.

She got there even before I'd ordered. And she looked bad.

I hadn't seen Cherry in at least four years. She usually did her extortion via text, changing phone numbers every six months as one cell company after another disconnected her for unpaid bills. She'd lost at least ten pounds, and she hadn't had it to lose. She'd be fifty-two now, but she looked at least sixty in the ropy strings of her neck and the thinning of her lusterless hair. Her skin sagged at her cheeks, chest, and upper arms, the color of congealed oatmeal. As she slid into the booth, the stench of cigarettes and the Walgreens perfume she favored nearly made me choke. I envied women whose mothers smelled like bread or watermelon shampoo or comfort. Mine smelled like fear.

A server approached. He stared at me a little too long. My throat dried up with the familiar terror, but I managed to order a side salad, the only fresh-vegetable option the place had. Cherry ordered barbecued chicken, mac and cheese, and green beans that would arrive so overcooked they might be mistaken for slime. I'd eaten in many a restaurant like this before.

"How much you got?" she said, in her rusty voice. I'd always thought maybe it had once had the same smoky quality as mine.

After the server left, I was able to make myself lift my head and look her in the eyes. There was nothing to see there. "That's beautiful, Ma. So heartwarming a greeting. Good to see you, too."

"Leave it. How much?"

"Enough," I said. "Why? You out of booze?"

"Ricky got fired. Roof needs fixing and that asshole says I gotta pay part. Things is tight. You owe me, anyway."

I'd never met Ricky; her boyfriends came and went, mostly went, so I didn't care much about his job prospects. I'd come here to say a few things. Those things had choked off my speech and kept me up walking the floors too many nights, and the price of getting to say them was giving her the money she constantly demanded. I'd known that all along.

"I don't owe you a single dime," I said neutrally. "It's the other way around, and you know it."

"Quit your crying. You didn't lose nothing in the end. You won. Look at them fancy clothes. You got everything, and I got nothing."

Everything was doing a lot of heavy lifting in that sentence. I took a sip of my water, composing myself. "At the end of this meal, which I hope will be mercifully brief, I will give you this envelope of cash. It will be the last."

She started to protest. I held up a hand in front of her face.

"The last. I didn't win anything. Nothing. You got pregnant from a proverbial teenage roll in the hay and got saddled with me, and then blamed me for everything bad that happened in your life after that. You made me go to church, God knows why—"

"Don't you blaspheme his name, missy."

"*You* blasphemed his name. You let Pastor Stan tell me I was Satan's spawn and backed him up every chance you got. 'An unholy temptation to men.' My face was my fault, my looks a test of faith no man could pass. You know how much that messes a kid up? How bad it still feels, even now? There's no way to feel good about yourself when you get told—by your mother—in *first grade* that you're a tool of the devil. The same devil you're still young enough to be afraid is hiding under your bed. Pastor Stan told me I was evil. Too impure to speak to decent people."

"He never did nothing like that. I don't know nothing about that."

"You live in a fantasy world. It's absolute bullshit and you know it. You knew, because you said the same things. You took me to his house for 'special prayers' that started when I was six. Six years old. He didn't only lecture, Ma. He explained in detail exactly which of my parts were the source of my impurity. He forced me to look at them in the mirror. He told me what helpless men would have no *choice* but to do to me because of them. By the time I was seven, I had a better understanding of sexual mechanics than I did the multiplication table."

"That ain't none of mine. I didn't know nothing about that."

"You did. You made it possible. You helped him do it. And then you punished *me* for it. How many times did you beat me? 'Go cut a switch,' you said, like it was some time-honored parenting move. Didn't matter what I'd done. Pee my pants. Spill a drink. Made no difference. Half the time you didn't want to give me the chance to escape in the yard. We had hairbrushes, spatulas, your belt, wet pillowcases, the cord of the venetian blinds. Even a hammer, once. I never said a word. I should have, because it didn't take long for it to get so much worse."

"You got quite the imagination. I don't know what you're talking about."

I stared at her, trying not for the first time to see inside her mind. She was a weak person, given to impulsive behavior and without a maternal bone in her body, but she was a person. There must be something human in there—regret, a capacity for joy, occasional reflection—surely? She'd always had boyfriends. They must have been attracted to something. What was the spark they saw, if only at the first meeting? It was nothing I'd ever seen.

"You do know what I'm talking about, but I know better than to think you'd ever admit it. So listen. This is the last time we're going to talk. First off, inside the envelope is five thousand dollars. In cash. It's yours, but make it last. I'll never give you another penny after this."

Her glazed eyes grew clever, darting like crows who've spotted a cornfield. "Ha! That's what you think. I can make you famous, *Renee*, if you don't answer my calls. More famous than you ever even thought of."

I glanced around instinctively at the mention of that name, but all the booths were empty and the server was nowhere in sight. The first customer other than ourselves, a man in the polo shirt and khakis of a big-box retail worker, entered after she finished talking. Just in case, I hid the side of my face with my hair.

"That's the second thing I'm here to tell you," I said, lowering my voice. "I've hired a lawyer, and I'm fixing to tell her about you and Len and what you did."

She smirked, so sure of herself, so sure I was still the cowed daughter she'd raised me to be. I might still be, if I hadn't been forced to take matters into my own hands. "No, you ain't," she scoffed. "You know what that means."

"I'm aware of the possibilities. My lawyer and I are going to talk about how best to handle the things that happened to me. I reckon . . . I reckon this is a warning to you. If you're smart enough to see the handwriting on the wall. I'm tired of running."

"You tell her, then everyone knows. I promise you that. Don't get smart now, missy."

"I tell her and it's confidential. If everyone knows after that, I'll know it came from you. If it comes from you, I'll see what I have to do to prosecute you for what you did."

"You can't touch me. I didn't do nothing. Everyone who did is dead now."

"Except you. You're still alive." I caught her faded gray eyes and held her gaze, channeling Allison in court. "If you 'make me famous' like you say, I'll make you incarcerated. It's only been recently that I think I might have the guts to do what I'd have to do to get you convicted, but it's becoming clearer and clearer every day. You talk, it's jail. Understand? You say nothing, you keep this five thousand dollars and I'll leave you alone. Are we clear?"

The food arrived. We dug in and didn't say another word to each other until it was gone. I stood, tossed bills on the table for the meal, and slid the envelope of cash across to her. "Remember. I don't want to be famous. You don't want to go to jail. Don't call me again."

She grabbed the envelope and gave me a glare so full of loathing something inside me broke. I walked out with my chin raised, hoping gravity would hold back the tears until I could hide myself again in my car.

৯৫

I got back to Charlottesville around nine thirty that night. I texted Josh from the side of the road about halfway home and asked him to meet me at The Virginian restaurant on the UVA Corner. They stayed open late and I needed that kind of hearty food to erase the misery of the desiccated salad I'd picked at in Danville. A restaurant would also make clear to Josh that I was more in the mood for talking than anything else tonight.

When I finally found parking and rushed through the door, he'd already taken a booth. He handed me a menu with a smile. I waved it off.

"I need mac and cheese. This place has my favorite."

"Are you okay? I mean, I get liking mac and cheese, but *needing* it?"

We put our orders in before I answered. I did not want to delay that mac and cheese even another minute.

"So what are we doing here, Josh?" I asked, almost as surprised by the words as he was when he registered them.

"Eating?" He tried a wry grin but knew it wouldn't work. "I don't know, Jane. I don't think it's any secret I'm interested in more than that. Hell, the whole firm and probably most of Charlottesville knows. I can't stop thinking about you. Full disclosure: I'd love to take you home 'right the fuck now,' as Ray would say. I guess a lot depends on what you're doing here."

"I don't know the answer, either." I played with my paper napkin, folding and unfolding one corner. "I'll be blunt. I haven't dated in a while, haven't had a relationship for a long while, and I . . . I need someone to talk to." I watched his face. He was disappointed. Had he really thought we'd just go off somewhere and have sex?

He recovered himself and looked more like the Josh who'd cared about me for years. "Is it about the bond hearing? Because, Jane, you know I was there to pay it, but your professor got there first. Put up his house! But I wanted to. That's why—"

I smiled, though I could feel how it didn't make it to my eyes. "I'm a mess, Josh."

"A what?"

"A mess. I invited you here because, in case you really were interested, I thought you ought to know. I just came from a diner in Danville, where I paid my mother five thousand dollars to stay the hell out of my life."

He blinked. To the best of my knowledge, Josh had grown up happy with two parents and a younger sister in a middle-class subdivision in the suburbs of Richmond. I watched him try, and fail, to understand such a scenario.

I took pity on him. "My mom is a drunk and an occasional drug addict who lives off disability and whatever she can sponge from boyfriends. And from me. She hits me up from time to time."

"I'm so sorry." He reached across the table for my hand. I took his, enjoying the feel of his warm skin.

"It is what it is. Or, was, I hope. I've let her hang on too long. You asked me about this case. It's going to make me a star, in ways I doubt you can imagine."

"Oh, I have a pretty good imagination." The server brought our food. The mac and cheese made my mouth water. "Listen. You're a mess. Okay. I'm a mess, too. Kind of a relief to admit it, really. Everyone is a mess, I think, in ways you can't always see. Let's be messes together."

"Do you think?" I said, feeling a cool breeze inside my heart for the first time in ages.

"Let's see how it goes," he said. "We've got time to fix all the world's problems. Right now, let's eat mac and cheese."

The mac and cheese tasted like hope that night.

CHAPTER EIGHTEEN
ALLISON

My assistant, Maureen, had taken to gently reminding me that I had other clients besides Jane Knudsen, usually by placing files on my chair or keyboard on the theory that if I touched them with my hands, I might remember they existed. Things were getting a bit desperate in the workload area, but I couldn't let go of this case. I'd become obsessed with the mystery of Jane. So far, I'd been keeping my head above water with vats of coffee and late-night catch-up sessions.

Even though I had ten more pages of a brief to write, cite-check, and edit before morning, I agreed to see Jane at four p.m. when Maureen mentioned at lunch that she'd called. Jane had told Maureen she'd like to come in to tell me "what I wanted to know." My curiosity rose up, drew a blade, and sacrificed any plans for pre-midnight sleep tonight without mercy.

When Jane arrived, she plucked two tissues from the box on the corner of my desk. She clutched them as if grateful for something to hold. I gave her time to settle in and compose herself.

It didn't take long.

"You know my mother was abusive. I'm going to tell you the extent of it, and then I think you'll probably understand why I changed my name, and why the judge allowed it to happen under seal."

She took a huge breath and let it out, shuddering. I watched her chest rise and fall and held very still.

"I don't know who my father was. I only ever lived with my mother. Her parents died when she was young, so I never had any other family. She got pregnant with me at nineteen. She had lots of boyfriends—they changed about every other year or so, and they always lived with us. She liked it that way, because then they'd pay her expenses, and mine, I suppose, with whatever job they had. They never made a lot of money, and I ate free lunch at school and wore Goodwill clothes. You know. The usual.

"Most of the boyfriends were a lot nicer than she was. She was jealous and territorial and she used to accuse me of 'hitting on' whoever it was at the time. This started up in first grade."

"First grade? That's nuts."

Jane laughed bitterly. "She said I was too pretty. Pretty 'in a dirty way' and I needed Jesus."

"What the hell does that mean? In a *dirty* way? A kid?"

Jane let out a tiny sigh. "In a sexual way, I reckon. Different from cute. The lips, I think."

I glanced at her pillowy lips and let out a sigh of my own.

"Anyway, she took me to find Jesus. I don't even remember the name of the church—one of the Bible-thumping kind—I only remember the portrait of Jesus that hung in the vestibule, and the way the light came in through the transom over the door. The pastor there was named Stanley something, though we were supposed to call him 'Pastor Stan,' like he was a buddy.

"My mom was blunt. I was too pretty. I was tempting her boyfriend. I was a tool of the devil. Pastor Stan wholeheartedly agreed and told her he would like me to come in once a week for 'special prayer sessions' to pray away the temptation."

Oh, that was a whole different kind of abuse. I held my breath.

Jane glanced up, expressionless. "He never touched me inappropriately, but he told me I was impure, sexually evil. He stripped me naked and forced me to stare in the mirror at myself. At the tool of Satan that would ruin good men by forcing them to rape me. He explained in great detail what rape was and how it would feel painful yet cleansing. These sessions lasted hours, sometimes. I was six. I remember the feeling of terror. Of being evil without my consent."

"Oh, Jane. Oh no." My daughter was six. She weighed forty pounds and still needed several inches to reach four feet tall. She believed in the tooth fairy and slept with a stuffed lion and wrote painstaking letters to Santa asking after Rudolph.

"At home, my mother beat me every time her boyfriend even looked my way—nice guy, that one was, Mike was his name. He felt bad for me, I think. He left her not long after I turned seven. He bought me a bag of gummi worms as a parting gift. I remember saving the last one for years. I didn't get many presents."

"He didn't . . . touch you, did he?"

"No. No one had touched me, but what Pastor Stan said was almost as bad. Well, other than the beatings from my mom. It was her next boyfriend that started the problem. His name was Len."

I started to write down his name, like I had the pastor's. Jane held up a hand.

"No need. He's dead now." She swallowed. "She moved him in right after Mike moved out. I can't recall in all my life ever living more than a week or two without 'a man of the house.' That's what she called them. Len lasted four years—the longest time she dated anyone while I lived at home."

I watched her square herself, straightening her legs in the chair, lowering her shoulders as she took in another long, fortifying breath. This was going to be bad. I didn't know how it could be worse than mental abuse and beatings, but it was. I planted my own feet flat on the floor, bracing.

"Len was a mechanic by trade, at least that's what he said. He was probably, judging from my mother's more recent boyfriends, also a small-time drug dealer, but it was the mechanic job that paid our bills. My mother didn't have a job. Len got fired and brought nothing in. There were a lot of days in there—second grade by this time—where all I ate all day was the free lunch I got at school. Then Len got his bright idea."

"What?" I said, full of dread, a tiny inkling of where this was going beginning to glimmer.

"He said I was beautiful." She pronounced the word as if it tasted like long-sour milk. "Thick blonde hair almost to my waist. Big eyes with long lashes. The lips. Len said I should be a model."

Oh no. Oh no, no, no. An image flashed of Libby and her kindergarten report card that described her as "so cooperative!" Libby happily followed instructions of grown-ups, any grown-ups. She trusted them. She had no other choice. And she dearly loved having her picture taken. I fought back a desperate urge to go and collect her from day care right now.

"He and my mother sold something—I think it was the clothes dryer—and bought a camera. At first, I was excited. My mother switched from calling me a tool of the devil to calling me pretty and a good girl. I thought she'd started to love me. She pulled out her best bedspread and put it on the bed in her room—blue for my eyes, she said, and used it as a backdrop. The first pictures were of me in my school clothes. A cheap sundress from Walmart. I remember it. It was yellow, with tiny pink flowers on it. Straps at the shoulders. Len said it would look adorable if I let one of the straps fall. And pulled up the hem a little bit."

My heart was breaking. Libby had a skinned knee right now. Her little leg was so skinny I could wrap a single hand around it. There were things that no mother could hear without crying. These were things that no one with any human emotion could hear without crying. "Oh, Jane. Stop. You don't need to tell me any more."

Her voice drained of all emotion, making it possible for her to dissociate from pain and continue. Brisk—a lawyer's voice. She still clutched those tissues in her hands, but her eyes were dry: blue chips of cold flint. "You can figure out the rest. Len knew people. Who knew people, I suppose. It was the late nineties. The internet was taking off. Suddenly everyone had a shiny new email address: Yahoo, AltaVista, AOL. At first, it was a secret. I posed for pictures, partially naked, completely naked except for a tiara, alone, sometimes with Len or one of his buddies. I didn't tell anyone, of course. I knew better than to do that: first, my mother would beat me if I did, and second, Pastor Stan had taught me what my parts were for. What they would force men to do. I'd been expecting it. I know now it's called grooming, but then, all I knew is they let me have a chocolate sundae after."

I wrote words—I don't know what words—on my legal pad to force myself to stay in the room instead of running. "Did it stop?"

"Eventually. Len had sex with me, of course, whenever he got a chance, which enraged my mother when she found out. She hadn't cared when it was one of his buddies, but she was territorial. She found a picture of me with him on his computer. She kicked him out and started right up with another guy with a good job at the post office. I was eleven."

"Jane," I said, unable to bear it. "He didn't have sex with you. He raped you. You know that, as an adult, right?"

A faint indentation appeared between her eyebrows. She might have been told, but she didn't *know*. These memories were primitive and childlike. The dent between her brows stayed, like a hint at the mutilation beneath. My God, the desolation she was covering. I bit my lip, unable to fathom damage like Jane's.

"Huh. I suppose. It's hard to think about it rationally." She swallowed. "The federal government caught Len not long after that—I doubt he was a criminal mastermind—and convicted him of manufacture and distribution of child pornography. He went to prison for ten years for it. When he went on trial, the whole county found out about all of it. I became a bigger star than anyone in Hollywood, at least in my corner of North Carolina. I was twelve."

Oh, holy crap. Being twelve was hard enough as it was.

"And your mother? Was she charged?"

"My mother claimed she hadn't known any of it was going on and played on the my-poor-little-girl-needs-her-mommy heartstrings of the prosecutors. She somehow never got charged; I suppose because I didn't turn her in. Len must not have, either. They asked me if she'd been there, and I lied. She was the only mother I had. I didn't have anywhere else to go."

I could barely speak through my thickened throat. "Where is he now?"

"Len died within a year of coming out of prison. During our first year of law school. A bar fight, they said."

My brain scanned all my memories of Jane that year. His death must have been a huge event for her, yet she hadn't betrayed a thing. She'd been going through all that and getting As in Criminal Law and Property and Torts. I never saw a sign.

"The pictures, on the other hand, are still out there. They'll always be out there. Every time the government finds someone with a collection, they destroy them and prosecute the guy, but there's no way to scrub them all. They're out there, proliferating like those magic marching buckets in the Mickey Mouse short. He published them all with my real name on them. You can still search 'Little Renee Star' and find me. Easy enough to shorten the last name. Good porn star name, I'll give him that." Gallows humor had always been Jane's go-to. Now I knew why.

"Oh, Jane. No wonder. You changed your name. You dyed your hair. You hide your face. No wonder. It's a miracle you're still alive."

"The occasional person still recognizes me, unfortunately. I was apparently quite popular there for a few years among perverts who like little girls. My face is mostly the same, but the dark hair throws off people. The dark eyeliner helps, too. I know how to look unlike myself in photos when I have to have one taken, like for work."

"I never knew your hair was dyed. How did you do it? I never saw even a hint of it when we were roommates."

"It was drugstore dye, then. I did it in public restrooms—usually at the gym. Being a brunette wouldn't help much if everyone knew it was fake. Now, I tell my colorist I want to look like early Katy Perry. She dyed blonde hair dark, too." A faint smile ghosted across her face.

"How did you know how to change your name? You must have been young."

"Yeah. I changed my name my freshman year at Duke—I was eighteen. My mother did steal my identity, but I asked a professor for help after I saw a group of guys whispering and glancing between me and their phones. It was clear they'd recognized my name and found the pictures. The porn name was so close to my real name. You know, with all that was done to me, you'd think it wouldn't have meant anything that they also used my name, but it did. It does. It's nice to choose your own name, but I resent that I couldn't keep my old one. It was one more thing they took from me."

"Jane, I don't even know what to say. This obviously has nothing at all to do with Ray's murder or any possible motivation you might have had."

"Unless they find it."

"Even if they find it, they're not inhuman. You were a victim." There'd be no way, once they knew the reason for her secret past, they'd link it to Ray. How could they? "I could tell them the reason for your name change and they'd have to let that part drop. I mean, seriously. We'd still have to deal with the murder weapon and the email and the fingerprints, but no one would think . . ."

This time her laugh was bitter. "Right. And then they decide that, in fact, this *is* the motive. Ray found out about my deep dark secret and was fixing to out me, they'll say. I must have killed him to silence him. You've given them a motive if you tell them. Motive is what they're missing."

"That's a bit far-fetched. I don't think . . ."

"Ray did find out, Allison."

Oh damn. "What?"

"He could be a jerk as a boss, but he was very far from stupid. It came up somehow, months ago, that I had some secret past. Some offhand question I evaded that caught his attention. He figured it out. I don't even remember how. Like you did, I reckon. Somehow, he kept it secret. I truly believe he didn't tell anyone. He said he wouldn't. He . . . he was kind to me about that."

"Would anyone be able to prove that he knew?" My brain ran through simulations, one after another, trying to think how they might be able to show that he'd known.

"I don't know. His computer search history, maybe. What did he google? He might even have pulled up a picture. They have ways of tracking that. Even if they can't prove it, I don't doubt Felicity would suddenly 'remember' that he'd told her."

"Okay," I said, writing all that down while sweat began to dampen my underarms. She was right. Silencing a boss who'd found out about her secret could have been a motive for her to kill him. Her tragedy might lighten her sentence, but if she was convicted of killing someone unrelated to that tragedy to hide it, her sentence wouldn't start out low. "Let's think about this. There might be a way . . ."

She held up a hand. "I've read about your big case last year, Allison. You ought to know better than anyone that all you have to do is dangle an explanation. I took a lot of psychology classes in college—people need to understand why something bad happened. They'll grab any reason that's even suggested to them to make it make sense in their minds. All they need is enough to hang their hats on when they find me guilty. And . . ."

"And?"

"And I don't want you to tell the police. They'd never keep it secret. I'd have to live with the knowledge of the whole Charlottesville police force looking at my pictures online and either pitying me or, God forbid, getting turned on. This is where I live. Those police are the ones who patrol my community. I have a job here. A life. At least, sort of a life." Another bitter laugh. "Right now, I can go for months and years at a time without encountering anyone who's seen me naked, at least not anyone who'd admit it. Imagine what it would be like, every time I see a police car. I don't want to . . ."

"What don't you want?"

"I don't want to be a freak show. A victim. An object of pity. I don't want to be famous like that again. I've spent too many years hiding every trace of Renee Starkey and I can't . . . I will not go back there."

"If we tell them, it will blunt any argument that you were hiding anything. It might even give them sympathy for you. If we don't tell them, they'll find it anyway, and they'll view you as suspicious for hiding it. They've only been looking a few days. It might really be used as your motive for killing Ray."

"I'm aware of that."

I tried another tack. "Jane, you know that right now, those same police are viewing you as a cold-blooded killer. Surely you'd prefer they—and the world—see you as a victim of predators rather than as a cold-blooded killer? One of those options means certain incarceration."

She stayed silent, then chose her words carefully. "You're saying my choices are to announce to the world that I am Renee Star and hope that makes people feel bad enough to either not convict me or give me a light sentence, or keep it hidden and let it become my motive to kill Ray, thus ensuring my conviction and maximum sentence. That's a hell of a choice, Allison."

"It is. Don't decide now. Take some time to think about it."

She stood. "Fine. And maybe, while I'm doing that, you could start building a defense that focuses not on pity for my victimhood and more on the fact that I. Did. Not. Do it."

CHAPTER NINETEEN

JANE

I managed to make it out to the car and into the rush-hour traffic leaving Lynchburg before my anger gave way to tears. I got almost twenty minutes farther before I had to pull over to the side of the highway.

Allison wanted me to be a victim again.

To hell with victimhood.

I would not go back there.

I knew victimhood. Victimhood was a frenemy. It was like a heaping helping of onion rings—delicious for five minutes going down, a painful lump in your stomach for hours afterward. Being a victim meant people absolved you of all blame, even for things that clearly had little to do with whatever had created that status, but it also meant that people perpetually viewed you as broken. Not whole. Less than. People felt sorry for victims, but they didn't want to taint their own lives by getting too close.

The only thing worse than pity was blame. More than once, I'd been blamed for what had happened to me, and not just by my mother. I should have known better, gotten help, done something to stop it. Even a child, they said, should know right from wrong. Even at seven. For most of my life, I'd thought they were right. My failures. My fault.

The police were investigating, and unless they were totally incompetent, they'd find a name-change petition under seal in the courthouse near Duke University.

There were only two real choices: give them my past as a motive, or hope they wouldn't find it. No choice could be easier.

A small chance at not having to revisit the past was better than nothing.

When I was twelve, they'd arrested Len in a car down in Georgia, heading for what he was probably dumb enough to assume was "the border" and safety, but was more likely just Florida.

That year I was in seventh grade at the county middle school. Girls had begun whispering about sex in groups in the hallways and in the changing room after gym. For them, it was the romantic future. For me, it was my sordid reality. There was nothing hopeful or idealized about sex for me. Sex meant being used and discarded like a Kleenex. Sex represented pain and shame. I felt a thousand years old and had only recently stopped throwing up when any grown man came too close.

I was old enough by then to know that what Len had done to me was wrong.

I might even have eventually arrived at the conclusion that what happened to me was rape, was not my fault, but then the local paper published a news story about Len's arrest and described his crime in vivid detail worthy of the grabbiest of supermarket tabloids. It referred to me as "a minor," of course, but it was a small town. Everyone knew everyone, and everyone knew exactly which minor Len had lived with and had access to during the relevant time.

Seventh-grade boys are not known for their grace and tact. They are, however, known for both their supernatural ability to overhear all their parents' gossip and their remarkable skill at finding things on the internet they should never, ever see. The photos had stopped only eight months before. In the later ones, I was very close to the same age as my classmates.

It started with whispering. Tyler Knight led it. He was the popular boy, the one who'd somehow bucked the odds and added some height early when the rest of the boys were still dwarfed by the girls. He had the Jonathan Taylor Thomas haircut and all the swagger. For the first few days, whispering was the worst of it. No one said anything to my face, but I could hear the hissing as I passed in the halls or took my seat in class.

"Porno."

"Slut."

"Nympho."

"Ho."

Once he'd seen the success of his whisper campaign, Tyler got braver. He started confronting me at the front of a pack of smaller boys, all grinning nervously. Middle schools are full of isolated places: The stairwell. The bus departure area. The aisles of the student assemblies.

"Did you get rich, Renee? Is there good money in being in pornos?"

"Settle a bet, Renee. Chris says your tits are A cup. I said B. Can we check your bra?"

"I need some advice, Renee, since you're the expert. Do girls like it on top or underneath best?"

I never responded to him, to any of them. Emboldened by Tyler, soon half the school was asking me for sex advice or calling me a slut. The teachers did nothing about it, though they must have known. On the rare occasions I got called on in class, hisses of "slut!" filled the air. No one got in trouble for it.

Never one to have a lot of friends—it had been hard to be friends with anyone when I hadn't been able to share anything about myself—I retreated. I walked through school holding my books like a pathetic shield and said nothing to anyone. I tried to let the words bounce off me. My voice went dormant, my face expressionless. I wore too-large granny clothes to cover myself. I wore my coat all the time, even when it was hot. There were never enough clothes.

I made it through middle school that way—in total silence. To my intense dismay, as I aged, the misery that came from the way I looked only got worse. All I wanted in the entire world was to disappear, and instead, by fifteen, I had long, slim legs worthy of a runway model, breasts too big to be hidden by my year-round winter coat, a tiny waist, and a face that turned heads everywhere I went. I fingered razor blades in the drugstore and fantasized about trails of blood and disfigurement and scarring. I bought dark eyeliner and practiced empty grins to thin my lips instead. If I couldn't be ugly, I could look different from the exploited little girl I had been.

By my junior year, the student body had tired of me. I'd succeeded in becoming invisible. No one expected me to speak at all. I got perfect grades and ran cross-country and studied hard in the school library for the fee-waived SAT. The day the score came was the first time a real smile came naturally in years—the SAT results were my ticket out of Galt. I could leave Varner County and never return. Colleges would admit me. I could be gone. I only had to make it until then.

Tyler Knight also grew. His early height gave way to a hulking six feet four by the time he was a senior. He played football and baseball and was homecoming king and stayed immensely popular in that fear-tinged way that high school boys with no empathy sometimes do.

Things had been quiet for so long that I wasn't expecting it when it happened.

One beautiful Saturday morning in the fall of my senior year, I walked in the tall weeds alongside the country road from the convenience store toward my house, carrying a paper cup of coffee and a packaged blueberry muffin. My mother had gone off somewhere with that year's boyfriend a couple of days before—I had no idea where she was, and no real interest in learning. A jacked-up pickup slowed to a roll beside me. Tyler leaned out the driver's side window.

I glanced around instinctively. I was still half a mile from home. There were no other houses nearby—only woods on either side of the road. Cell phones were still years away from usefulness in that part of the country.

"Hold up, Renee."

I kept walking, praying that a car would come along.

"I want to apologize. Stop. Please."

The word *please* slowed my footsteps—enough for him to throw the truck into park, jump out, and dart after me. I was a fast runner, but couldn't outpace a six-foot-four football star. He caught me by one elbow and spun me around. "I'm sorry I was a dick to you in middle school."

The fact that he'd chased me down kind of made the sincerity of that apology ring hollow. Fear licked up my spine. "Let me go."

"No, wait, you have to hear me out."

I didn't have to do jack shit. Not anymore. I yanked my arm free, turned my back on him, and kept walking.

"Bitch! I'm trying to apologize!"

"I don't accept your apology. I'm not interested in talking to you," I called over my shoulder.

He stood still, hands in his pockets. "You'd be interested in my dick. I've seen the proof. You love dick. Come back here and we'll jump in my truck and have a good time. These other girls in our class are amateurs. I've never been with a pro. God, those hot lips around me. Come on. You know you want it."

I walked and prayed, and my prayer was answered, for the first time I could remember. A car—my neighbor's antiquated Ford Taurus— came into view from the opposite direction. I flagged it down. Tyler stood beside the road, his mouth hanging open, honestly shocked that this move had gone so wrong.

Mrs. Lockaby waved at me and stopped. Her car was full of smelly crap, but I swung open her passenger door with a metallic creak. Before getting in, I caught Tyler's gaze over the roof. "Don't ever speak to me again. If you do, I'll call the police. Understood?"

That was the first time I ever invoked the power of the law. It was long overdue.

I could not, would not, go through all that again. There was that small chance that if I didn't disclose my past, the police wouldn't find it. Even if the choice came down to admitting it and getting acquitted or being convicted and incarcerated because I'd hidden it, I would choose incarceration. Jail wouldn't be so bad. I was more than tough enough to handle what prison life could throw at me, and looking at things honestly, I was already incarcerated in every way that meant anything. I had no life. No friends. No hobbies. I'd be swapping my sterile white town house for a sterile gray cell.

I'd miss my shiny granite countertop, but not much else would change.

⁂

When I got home to that sterile white town house, I called Allison's cell. I didn't want her to go on any longer thinking that she was going to talk the police and the prosecutor into treating me with kid gloves because I'd been a child-pornography victim.

The phone rang and rang and I'd almost hung up when a male voice said, "Hello?"

There was something familiar about it, but Allison was divorced. If she had a boyfriend who'd answer her phone, she hadn't mentioned him to me, much less introduced him. Why would his voice be familiar?

"Is Allison there? This is her client, Jane Knudsen."

A long silence stretched over the phone line.

"Uh. Jane. She . . . she's putting Libby to bed." More silence. "This is Emmett. Emmett Amaro."

What?

"Em-Emmett. What . . . what are you . . . ?"

The answer to that question was obvious. I'd called Allison's cell phone at eight p.m. She was putting Libby to bed, which meant she was home. He'd answered her cell, which meant he wasn't a casual visitor in her house.

"Allie and I are seeing each other," he said bluntly. "It's good to hear your voice again."

"How long have you been together?" I asked, trying to remember his face as it had been in law school. Emmett had been kind. I'd thought of him many times since we broke up. And now he and Allison . . . the cosmic perfection of that was almost too much to absorb.

"We've been friends since the second half of law school, and we both moved to the Lynchburg area after that. We started seeing each other last fall." Good boy, Emmett. Still so straightforward and honest.

Unlike Allison, who'd neglected to mention her boyfriend of six months or more, even when I'd said his name.

"That's great. I didn't know."

"Listen, Jane, I'm sorry about that. I told her not to tell you. I thought you might do better as lawyer and client if I didn't come up."

"So you know about my case?"

Another short silence. He should not have known I was Allison's client, and he knew it. "I saw your name on her phone when it rang once. Later I saw you were arrested. I don't know anything about your case except what I've read online."

"Didn't you see my name this time?"

"No. She took my advice and deprogrammed her clients' names for privacy when I pointed it out." He cleared his throat. "Are you doing okay?"

Something burned at the backs of my eyes. "Yes. As well as can be expected. You?"

"I'm doing fine. Things are . . . good. Listen, I'll tell her you called. Sometimes it takes a while to get Libby to give up for the day."

"Great. Thanks. And . . . Emmett. It was a surprise and . . . a pleasure to hear your voice, too—and . . ."

"Wait a second. Here she is."

Emmett and Allison held a mumbled conversation I couldn't decipher.

"Hey," Allison said, a note of guilt threading her voice. Good. "Have you thought any more about what—"

"Yes," I said briskly. "You are not authorized to share that information. You have it, and you can use it as you choose to anticipate the prosecution's case, but you may not share it with them in any way without specific authorization from me. Are we clear?" I heard the anger and the bitterness in my voice but was powerless to stop it. Hell hath no fury and all that. God, I was so weak. I should have learned by now that people hurt you. I should have figured out how to prevent myself from being hurt. Allison dating Emmett shouldn't have hurt.

"Jane . . . what . . . ? What's going on? Are you okay?"

"I'm fine. I thought we were inching back toward friendship. You said we were, anyway. I shouldn't have fallen for it. If you were my friend, you would have mentioned to me that you were seeing the guy I told you was the one I regretted the most. But not a word. You didn't say anything. You've made me feel stupid."

"I didn't mean to make you feel stupid. I didn't mention him because I didn't think it was relevant."

"*Relevant.* There's a nice legal word. And an interesting one, coming from the woman who spent the afternoon trying to persuade me that I should share my totally nonrelevant pain with the prosecution so that you can parade a victim in front of a jury instead of just a woman who isn't guilty."

"That's not the reason at all. I don't want to see you convicted! I'm prepared to do anything I can to keep that from happening."

"Well, I'm not. I'm not willing to become a victim and a celebrity again. You'll never understand what that was like. How it followed me everywhere. How it ruined my life, then, now, and forever. I should never have told you."

"Don't say that. You need to tell people. You'll never put it behind you if you . . . swallow it, like some kind of bag of drugs that will poison you if it gets the smallest hole in it. You need to talk to a therapist about it, at a minimum. I spent all afternoon thinking about who could help you, and . . ."

"Well, you can stop. I saw a therapist in college. He didn't help at all. Let me guess. Emmett is standing either there in the room with you or close enough that he can hear your half of the conversation."

She stammered a bit. I knew it.

"Fine. You tell Emmett. Honestly, it would be better for me if I *knew* he knew about it rather than just *suspecting* he knew about it. He's a smart guy, and a lawyer. You confer with him and then I'll give you one more chance to tell me how disclosing any of this to anyone—prosecutor or otherwise—will help me not wake up every day hating myself and wishing myself invisible or dead. You have my permission. But that's it. One person, and I benefit from it."

"I won't, if you don't want me to," Allison said in a small voice. "Jane, I'm so sorry. I'm sorry I didn't tell you about Emmett. I'm also sorry about what you went through. My God, there aren't enough words to express how sorry. I . . . I'm . . . I can't even . . ."

"Tell him if you want to. You don't have to be sorry. There's nothing you can do to erase it. You just have to be my lawyer."

I hung up and stared for a while at my blank white walls.

It was amazing how many ways, small and large, there were to be humiliated and betrayed, and how the little ones hurt almost as much as the big ones.

PART THREE

VIVANT

CHAPTER TWENTY

ALLISON

The phone went dead.

I'd had some unpleasant conversations with clients before, but not like that. I was bordering on malpractice. I'd allowed my boyfriend to discover the identity of my client. I'd lied by omission to my client about something I knew would matter to her. And then I'd admitted to having this whole cringeworthy conversation within Emmett's hearing. I put the phone down like a toxic thing on the corner of the kitchen counter where I kept my charger.

"That didn't sound good," Emmett said, loading the dishwasher from dinner. "Is she okay?"

"She's upset I didn't tell her I was seeing you," I said, thinking. Did she seriously want me to tell him about Renee Starkey? Maybe Emmett would have some ideas about how to best defend her. Before I opened my own firm, I'd worked for Dan MacDonald, an older, more experienced lawyer. Though he'd been a terrible misogynist and a massive ethical corner-cutter, he had, on occasion, helped me see a case from an angle I hadn't considered. Sometimes a second set of eyes made all the difference.

"I'm sorry. You did tell me she would be." He upturned the last glass into the dishwasher and started it. Even after seven months, our relationship was new enough that I still wanted to cry with gratitude at his help with the day-to-day household chores.

"I think she'll get over it," I said. "But . . ."

"But?"

"But there's something else. She gave me permission to tell you about her case on the condition that you'd share your thoughts and help."

"That's weird, but okay. What about her case?"

"The commonwealth arrested her because they found the murder weapon dumped in a construction site feet from Jane's house."

"Ugh. That's bad. And?"

"They also have some evidence that whoever killed Ray wrote his last email on his computer and sent it. It's misspelled in a way that implicates Jane. And fingerprints of hers on his desk, computer, et cetera. All that's bad and would be enough for probable cause. I can address all that, I think. But here's the deal. The commonwealth thinks she's hiding a secret past, and that the past may have motivated her to kill Ray. She finally told me about the past, and yes, she's hiding one, and yes, Ray found out about it, and yes, it would absolutely be a motive to kill him to keep it hidden."

"What is it?"

"You'd better sit down."

Fifteen minutes later, Emmett wiped his hand over his face and said, "Jesus Christ on the cross." Emmett was Catholic and fairly observant. I'd never heard him say a thing like that before. It sounded more like a prayer than a curse.

"Do you want a beer?"

"Yes," he said, leaning back on the sofa like his neck wouldn't support his head. "Please."

I got us both beers. Merely telling the story had been hard. *Then, now, and forever,* Jane repeated in my head.

"Okay. I guess I have my answer as to why she was so hard to get to know. No wonder. Holy shit. Okay," he said again, taking a huge gulp. "So the commonwealth hasn't discovered Renee yet. There's a small chance that they won't, and she doesn't want them to, right?"

"Right, but I'd guess there's at least a seventy-five percent chance they'll get there. And they'll think it's even more suspicious that she hid it and an even more likely motive. I don't want to make things worse for her." I jumped up and started pacing the room.

"Wait a second," Emmett said. "Seventy-five percent chance they'll find it and think it's the reason she killed Ray. If you tell them, looks to me like there'd be a one hundred percent chance they'll think it's the reason she killed Ray. It's a small chance, but Jane is right. Why give it to them and make her relive it if they're only going to use it to blame her?"

"You don't think it would help if they knew this thing had happened to her? You work for the commonwealth. Are they all heartless? Jane has suffered terribly. You don't think they would care?"

Emmett covered his face again. A groan issued from behind his hands. "What happened to Jane is appalling, and yes, people who work for the commonwealth would care on a personal level, and no, of course they're not all heartless. Their job is to convict someone for the murder of Ray Corrigan. If she hid this stuff and Ray found out about it, it looks a lot like a motive. They already think she did it. This will make them think she did it for a damn good reason. The commonwealth convicts murderers, sweetheart. Even the ones who had logical motivations."

I laughed, though nothing was funny. "So I'm on the *Titanic* and the iceberg is in the rearview mirror."

"No. You're not. But whatever moral dilemma you're struggling with needs to end now. Your client wants this to stay quiet. In my opinion, she has excellent reasons for that that don't conflict with your legal strategy."

"Do you know Nina Hilcko?" I asked, still wishing I could make life easier for Jane.

"Nina? Is that who's handling it? She's not in Charlottesville, is she?"

"No. Devonshire County. But because the victim and defendant were members of the local bar, we've got guest stars."

"Right. Yeah, I know Nina. I met her at a conference a year or so ago. She's tough. She would care about Jane."

Some expression changed his face. I couldn't identify it. "What?"

"I don't want you to think what I'm about to say changes any of my other advice. At the conference, she was on a panel. About . . . prosecuting child pornography."

Despite myself, despite knowing he was right, hope rose. Jane was being prosecuted by a woman with enough expertise in the field of bringing child pornographers to justice that she'd been asked to speak to a statewide conference of prosecutors. For a blissful second, I let myself entertain the notion that Nina would draw the line at publicly outing one of those victims.

Then sanity returned: she wouldn't hesitate, if she thought Jane had committed the worse crime of murder. It was her job. The legal system wasn't supposed to be some game of moral relativism. Its goal was to deal justice on a case-by-case basis, not on a lifetime quota system.

I had trouble with that, sometimes.

"I wish that would make a difference, but I know you're right."

"I'm still processing, I guess. I'm looking back at that time in second year and now everything looks different about her. Why she wouldn't talk. Why she paid so little attention to the internet or the newest smartphone. She had almost an aversion to technology. No wonder. Damn, she used to wear her coat all the time. Covered up from neck to toes. She said she was cold. Holy . . ."

"Are you sure you don't regret her? She regrets you," I said, hating my insecurity and need for reassurance.

"I regret that she was in pain and didn't feel like she could tell anyone. I regret that she let me break up with her rather than sharing enough about herself to keep it from happening."

Something sour turned over in my stomach. He stood to toss his beer bottle in the recycling, then pulled on my hands to tug me out of the armchair I'd been perched on. I stood in the circle of his arms. "But I don't regret that those things ultimately led me to you. I want to be with you, not Jane, not any other woman I've ever seen or spoken to. You."

I melted a little into his chest. I loved his chest. I loved breathing his air. There was nowhere else I felt more content than right here.

Contentment heated and changed to urgency. We fitted ourselves closer, and soon our lips were seeking and our hands roving. How was it possible for every time I kissed him to be as good as the last time I'd kissed him? He tipped my chin up and pulled away, our noses an inch apart.

"Move in with me. Please, Allie."

Upstairs, on cue, a bedspring squeaked. Libby was not asleep yet. Lately she'd been fighting harder and harder to stay awake.

"I can't, Emmett."

"Can't? That's some new decisiveness." He dropped his arm and suddenly became interested in staring at my family room bookcase. "Last time we discussed this, you were acting like you were thinking about it. Like you wanted to. Now you've decided? Were you going to tell me?"

"I haven't . . . I have Libby. I can't just move in with you. I have a child that would affect."

"I love Libby."

"I know you do, but it's not that easy. Karen's been going on about immorality lately. Steve and Karen might file for custody if we moved in together. And they could get a judge to agree with them. You know they could."

He paused, refusing to look at me. The lines of his body were rigid. "Fine, then. Maybe we should get married. Would that help?"

It felt like a punch in the gut. He wasn't asking, and even if he were, it wasn't supposed to be this way. Not with him angry and faced with ultimatums and staring at my ragged line of Liane Moriarty novels. Maybe I shouldn't care—Steve had proposed with flowers and champagne and dinner and a ring and look how that turned out—but I did care.

As emotionlessly as I could manage, I said, "It would make all the difference to a court if we were married. No judge would have issues with a minor child in the house if we were married. Steve couldn't protest at all. All very logical and practical. But dammit, Emmett, I'm going to pretend you didn't suggest that."

"What?" He turned. Oh my God. I'd hurt him. Badly.

"I might be open to a marriage proposal, but that wasn't one. Or at least I hope not. You've never mentioned marriage before, and I damn sure don't want you proposing because you're angry and hurt. I don't want to marry you to . . . to tie up loose ends, or because it's the logical thing to do. If you want to marry me, I want it to be because you want to be with me, forever and under God and the law, and not as . . . as some life coach–type mumbo jumbo to organize your life all tidy."

"But it is the logi—" Emmett practically yelled, his eyes wide and his mouth hanging open.

I threw up a hand. "Nope. Stop right there. Don't do that. If you say what you're about to say, I'll never unhear it." I knew I was raising my voice, and I couldn't stop myself. "Maybe men don't need romance. Maybe you all think of marriage as a way of organizing your lives. Making things more convenient. Cutting down on your commute, or something. I don't want to hear it if that's where your head is. If you propose, I need you to make me feel like you can't live another day without me. I need there to be nothing remotely practical about it. I need . . . I need more."

He fisted his hands in his hair in frustration. "Allie, I swear to God! I don't know how—"

"I'm calling Daddy!" Libby stood at the bottom of the stairs, dressed for bed in an oversize T-shirt with skinned knees on display below, one hand on her hip like a warrior. Her other hand held my cell phone. The screen lit up with the connecting call. "Stop yelling! You need to go home, Emmett! You're making my mommy mad!"

Oh crap. I dashed over to her to collect her in a hug and to get the phone. Too late. Steve was already saying hello by the time I got it to my ear.

"Steve. Hi. Libby dialed you by accident. Sorry."

"Daddy! Mommy and Emmett are yelling at each other!" Libby shouted at the phone.

"What's going on, Al?" Steve's voice grew sharper, concerned.

"Nothing. Everything's fine."

"It's obviously not fine. Libby's upset. Do I need to come over there?"

Damn, damn, damn. Emmett came over and held out his hand for the phone. With misgivings, I handed it over.

"Steve. Hi. This is Emmett," he said, all business. "Everything is fine. Allie and I were arguing. No, nothing important." I met Emmett's impassive eyes as he said that, and pain sluiced through me. "Yeah. Libby heard us and got worried . . . Right. Yes. No, we're good. Thanks. Right. Goodbye."

He hit the red button on the screen and put the phone on the counter with the kind of slow movements he might use if it had been a live grenade. Which, in a manner of speaking, it was.

We were left in an angry tableau of three, all with our hands on our hips like actors in a melodrama. Emmett glanced at me—it was my job to break the impasse with some kind of soothing parental wisdom. Absolutely nothing came to my mind.

"Libby," I said, crouching down to her level. "You know that adults argue sometimes. Emmett and I were just discussing things and our voices got loud."

"You were yelling! You said 'don't do that'! Emmett said 'swear to God.'"

I pulled her onto my thigh, which required me to put the other knee on the bare hardwood floor. Ouch. "I'm sure it sounded scary, but it wasn't. Everything was fine. You are safe when I'm in the house, Libby. Always."

I thought of Jane at this age. Never safe ever, not with anyone. Though I was irritated with Libby for calling Steve and involving him in something that was none of his business, I hugged her until she squirmed.

"What were you talking about? What, Mommy?"

"That, Liberty Bell, is none of your beeswax." She spluttered in protest—Libby believed that everything under the sun was her beeswax—but I needed to talk to Emmett, who'd stayed silent when usually, in a situation like this, he'd lighten the mood with a silly joke to make her giggle. "Off to bed with you. I will come up to tuck you in—again—in five minutes. Go on now."

She went, stomping up the stairs to make clear her thoughts on beeswax, or lack of it.

I turned to Emmett, praying the right thing would come out of my mouth. "I . . . I don't . . . I had no idea she . . ."

Not the right words. His face closed over, but he touched my cheek with a cool fingertip. "I'd probably better get going. We're tired. We'll say things—more things, I should say—that we'll regret. Let's talk tomorrow." He turned to look for his messenger bag and hung his discarded tie around his neck.

"Emmett. Stay. I . . . I'm so sorry about Steve. And what Libby said."

"Steve and Libby aren't the reason I'm upset. They're the reasons you would prefer to think I'm upset." He rubbed a tired hand through his disheveled hair. "I wanted to . . . I asked . . . dammit, Allie. I can't do this right now. I need to think."

He opened the door and paused on the threshold. "Good night," he said, pulling the front door shut. I waited until I heard the car door slam and then went to the plate-glass window at the front of my house to watch his taillights go dark in the distance.

Damn.

As I climbed the stairs to Libby's room, my legs felt weighted. Had Emmett proposed? Did he want to marry me? I'd well and truly rejected him, if he had indeed proposed. And Steve would be watching Emmett like a hawk from now on. The concerned-father show was far more for Karen's benefit than Libby's, I suspected. What a nightmare the whole scene had been.

I leaned against Libby's doorframe. She was already asleep, face-down on top of her comforter as if she'd run up the stairs, taken a dive onto the bed, and passed out cold. I switched off her bedside lamp, flicked on the tiny night-light in the shape of Tinker Bell, and went downstairs to work late into the night.

I wanted to marry Emmett.

If it was okay with Libby.

And if he ever asked a second time.

CHAPTER
TWENTY-ONE
JANE

Two days later the offices of Blackwood, Payne & Vivant closed for the Fourth of July. Josh took me to that tried-and-true Charlottesville date-night restaurant, the C&O. I'd never once eaten there, though it had been around forever and was the sort of place that my still-impoverished-but-dreaming-of-better law school classmates went with dates on Valentine's Day. I ordered the trout. Josh got the filet mignon.

Josh and I exchanged looks and shy smiles, like kids from a sitcom whose moms had driven them to Applebee's. I'd never felt this vulnerable on a date before, and I suspected it had to do with Allison's advice that it might be healthier to talk about this. Josh was the perfect person to start with, but I had no clue how to begin.

You couldn't exactly dump "I was a child porn star" into a conversation over a nice supper at the C&O. Maybe it was crazy even to consider the idea.

"You look stressed out. Is it the trial?" Josh asked, neatly slicing his beef.

"Yes. They found the murder weapon right near my house, apparently. I . . . I think they'll likely convict me." I glanced around at the other diners. Most were couples out on a date night, even the married ones. One older woman at the next table over caught my eye and smiled approvingly, like I was any ordinary person at a romantic meal with a handsome man. She said something to her husband, and he looked over and winked. "I mean, it's nice to be out with you tonight, but honestly, Josh, I don't think this relationship—or whatever this is—has much future. I'll be in jail."

"I think you're wrong. How could they think you did something like that? You didn't do it." He reached out and squeezed my hand.

I flattened my napkin on my lap and tried to smile. I was ruining this. "Maybe you're right. I think my lawyer is good."

"Of course she is. And besides, I'm feeling a little awkward, too, if it helps. The last time I was at this restaurant, it was my anniversary. I thought everything with Miriam was going great."

He looked down at his plate, his silverware forgotten in his hand.

"Would it help to talk about her? You haven't, much, since you found out . . ."

Josh's eyes, when he lifted his head, sent an echo of his pain through me. "Since I saw those pictures, yeah. Of her with another guy."

"What happened? You two always seemed so happy together."

"We were. Miriam and I met in college. She lived in my freshman dorm. I didn't think I'd ever seen such a beautiful woman, Jane. Not as beautiful as you, maybe, in the regular way, but the look in her eye. Her dark, thick hair. Satiny skin. She was so tiny but so smart. She was in psychology, and that's actually why I took the job at Blackwood—so she could get her PhD at UVA."

"She was very beautiful," I said, remembering the childlike woman who'd made her Lebanese immigrant parents so proud by getting her doctorate. "And kind. It's hard for me to believe she cheated. I can't picture it."

Josh took a gulp of water. I watched his Adam's apple bob in his throat. "I saw the proof, but I . . . I remember even while I was staring at those pictures, thinking maybe she had a good reason."

"What? No way. What reason?"

"We tried for years to have kids. Years. Eventually, we went and got tested. When I think of all the pain she went through, all those tests, all the poking and prodding, and it was me the whole time. Just me."

"You?"

"The odds of me fathering a child are remote, at best." Longing twisted his lips into a grimace of pain. My heart squeezed.

"Josh, you're not saying . . ." Oh crap, no, that was not a reason to cheat. Surely he didn't think Miriam would have gone out to find other seed like a farmer with rotten corn.

"I didn't know, but I wondered. She denied cheating at all, even with the pictures, but yeah, I thought she was trying for a baby with someone else since I . . . She wanted a baby so badly."

I stared at him wordlessly. It didn't seem possible.

"Maybe you don't know what it's like, wanting a child like that. Infertility is devastating. It gets right at the core of who you are, all your dreams, what you thought you were . . . *for*, or something. I'd catch her standing at a window, staring out but not seeing anything. She'd be so hopeful, every month, and then . . . not. She used to cry."

"No, Josh. No. She wouldn't have done that. She wasn't the kind . . ."

"She was the kind who wanted a baby more than anything. I hired a private investigator and everything. He followed her. Told me he caught her at a hotel by the interstate. The one across from Wegmans. You know. Sent me the pictures to prove it. Maybe it made me feel better to think there was a reason. Some reason, anyway. God, it killed me. When I found out, I thought about suicide. I literally didn't think I could live from minute to minute."

I remembered. The day Josh got the pictures that nailed the lid on the coffin of his marriage to Miriam, I'd sat silently beside him in his keening grief. I'd never seen a man cry like that. I didn't know they could. After she moved to Michigan, he missed work for a week, even though Ray had been right in his face about how if he didn't get his ass back to billing, he'd never be a partner.

"What made you think to hire a PI? What in the world made you think she might be cheating?" I couldn't remember if I'd heard this before. I remembered the arrival of the PI's report, but I didn't think I'd heard this part.

"Ray, actually. Ray said he went over to the UVA grounds to have lunch with Brittany—she was still in law school then—and saw Miriam on a bench with a guy who wasn't me. He said she was all over him. Left no room for doubt."

"Typical of Ray to drop something like that into a watercooler conversation. Well, then, yeah. I'm sorry, Josh. I know it had to hurt."

"I had a bad time, for sure." Something shuttered in his face. He hadn't purged all the pain, but he was done talking. "But I'm here with you, now. Life turned out not to be so bad." He raised his glass and I clinked it, feeling a little silly.

"You've been so honest, I feel like I owe you a little honesty, too. I told you I'm a mess, right?"

"Yeah." He cleared his throat, making an effort to follow along as I changed the subject. "Do you want to tell me? You don't have to."

"I don't think I'm capable of telling you all of it, not yet, but when I was a kid, I . . ." My tongue grew thick and my throat dry. I tried again. "I was abused. Pretty badly."

Josh put down his fork and grabbed both my hands. "Oh, Jane. Oh no. Your parents?"

"My mother. I never knew my dad. I told you she was an addict. She and her boyfriend. It was . . . it was . . ." I swallowed and whispered, "Sexual abuse."

Saying those two words alone left me limp with exhaustion and panting like I'd run up a mountain. It was as far as I could go tonight and remain upright. As much as I could give him. Nothing about the name change, nothing about my stardom, nothing about the loneliness and the shame and the ostracism. Even so, a weight had been lifted with the small amount I'd shared. I felt a little lighter, a little taller; my smile muscles seemed looser. Maybe someday, with someone, I could . . . let go of this. But not today.

Josh tightened his grip on my hands. It felt like a lifeline. "Death is too good for some people. I'm so sorry."

The fervent support in his voice made my eyes burn. To fight the tears, I glanced at the older couple at the table next to ours. Something had changed. They were less relaxed now. They'd pulled their chairs closer together and were whispering, interrupting each other with the angry buzz of wasps trapped against glass. I could have sworn I caught more glances at me, and not the smiling kind. I knew this feeling. A sick-feeling cold passed over me.

It was unlikely the woman had ever seen the Renee Star pictures. She was the high-class sort who spent her time arranging flowers and shopping for boiled-wool jackets at Talbots and had perhaps owned a small antique shop if she'd worked at all. She wore a string of real pearls around her neck.

Her husband looked like a well-off small businessman or a retired economics professor. He wore pressed khakis with a needlepoint belt and a pristine plaid button-down shirt tucked in with military precision. None of that meant anything, however: men of all kinds looked at child pornography. Rich, poor, old, young—all of them were possible perverts. I'd learned that early. If he recognized me, he'd be making a story up to tell his wife to explain why. He'd seen me in a "slutty" photo calendar on the wall of the auto shop where he took his BMW, maybe, or perhaps I was the woman someone he knew had cheated on his wife with. He'd lie to make me unsavory to cover up how unsavory he was for knowing me. At first, I'd been surprised that men like this didn't just stay silent, but no one could resist knowing a celebrity.

Josh followed my eyes and his lips pressed together, which made no sense. He couldn't possibly understand why our fellow diners had pulled their chairs to the side of the table farthest from me. The man signaled for assistance. The C&O was known for its service, and it took no more than ten seconds for the server to appear at their side.

Josh and I fell silent, no longer even attempting to ignore it.

"Yes, sir," said the server.

Like many men of his age, Mr. Button-Down didn't modulate his voice. "I believe that woman sitting there is Jane Knudsen. Shot her boss in cold blood at his desk. I must admit, my wife and I don't feel comfortable sitting this close. Is there anything you can do?"

Oh.

A bubble of laughter started in my chest and rose so light and free I almost had to clap a hand over my mouth to keep it from bursting loose. The older couple didn't know me as Renee Star. They only thought I was a murderess! I didn't even know how to name all the emotions that flitted through me, except one: relief. Relief followed immediately by hilarity—I lived such a pathetic life that I was glad, delighted even, that two upper-class C&O patrons were horrified by me only because I supposedly murdered someone and not because I'd been turned into a juvenile sex object by my own mother.

The server, a young man in his early twenties, glanced at me with wide eyes, then remembered his job. He bent down and began whispering to the couple. No doubt tonight's prime rib would be discounted.

"Excuse me," said Josh, standing up. The couple and the server pulled their heads out of their impromptu huddle. "The last I checked, people are presumed innocent until proven guilty. We were enjoying a nice dinner. Please apologize to my date."

I cringed. Oh lordy. "Josh. Stop. Sit down."

"No. This isn't right."

"Josh, I'm begging you. Let's go." I swept my napkin off my lap and tossed it onto my plate, standing.

"No. They're going to apologize."

The server, looking desperate, glanced around at the other tables. All had fallen silent. Every other diner watched every move of this little dance. "Uh, sir," he said to the man in the button-down. "I can reseat you over there."

"That won't be necessary," said Josh, looking thunderous and handing his credit card to our own hovering server. She dashed away with it like it was a hot potato. "We are leaving. We will accept an apology for having our dinner cut short."

The pearl-wearing wife clutched her husband's arm. "Bill. Please. Just apologize. It's the fastest way for this to end."

The man scowled and moved his body between his wife and me as if prepared to take a bullet for her. "Sir, if you took offense, I regret it." His gaze strayed to Josh's clenching fists—that wouldn't be enough. "Ma'am. Apologies."

Though Josh appeared ready to demand a far more flowery expression of remorse, I grabbed his arm, caught the server bringing back the credit card, and tossed it at him. He signed the receipt and we walked out.

The air outside felt fresh and clean, despite the July humidity.

"Jane. What the hell? I got a weird vibe. Why didn't you care whether he apologized? You looked like you thought it was *funny*, or something."

The champagne bubbles of relief at being recognized as something other than a porn star still popped and fizzed in my veins. What a messed-up world we lived in, where I'd get more respect as a cold-blooded slayer of bosses than as a vulnerable girl, naked on camera. We used the word *killer* as a compliment, for God's sake. A murderer held power. A murderer wasn't pathetic, weak, a victim. A murderer controlled events and never cowered in shame or fear. This country loved its sex and violence, but only violence earned awe and admiration.

I had not had nearly enough therapy.

Or maybe it was America who needed therapy.

"I . . . I did think it was funny. The idea that that poor man, who only wanted to take his wife out for a nice supper, was forced to sit next to a stone-cold lawyer killer at the C&O. I kept thinking he was going to say *riffraff*. He was totally the type to say it. Wouldn't it have been hilarious if he'd said *riffraff*?"

We reached the car and Josh's mouth still hung slack. "I don't understand this reaction. Good lord, Jane. Why are you so calm? Those people thought you were a murderer."

"They're not the first, are they? And they won't be the last, either."

"But you didn't do it!" Josh burst out, frustrated at my clear lack of grounding in reality.

The giggles wouldn't go away. "How would you know?"

"What?"

"Maybe I did." To Josh's horror, I doubled over in helpless laughter.

❦

The date ended soon after that, even though originally we'd planned to go see the fireworks at the nearby park. Josh never recovered from how upset he'd gotten in the restaurant, and like a child who hears someone pass gas in church, I couldn't stop giggling. The combination wasn't a good one. Josh, struggling to control his irritation, dropped me off at home early and I went inside alone.

I had a bottle of wine in my fridge that was mostly full, but as I passed the kitchen, I realized I didn't need it. I was already drunk. Something had happened in that restaurant, and though I had long years of experience taking most of my emotions, folding them neatly, and putting them away in the dark cupboards of my mind, where I wouldn't have to deal with them, this time, I wanted to look.

I was drunk with power.

If people were going to keep their distance from me anyway, it would be so much more satisfying if it were because they thought I was dangerous to them.

From somewhere nearby, a neighbor fired off a rocket. There was a bang and the sound of sparks. A dog set up howling in the distance.

A life raft had been bobbing alongside me in the ocean all this time. Maybe it was time to grab it and climb aboard.

CHAPTER
TWENTY-TWO

ALLISON

After my fight with Emmett, things calmed down. I called him the next morning and apologized, stiffly. He apologized, also stiffly, and suggested we go out on a real date outside of our houses the following weekend. The topic of marriage did not come up.

I called Steve and explained the situation to him somehow. He repeated everything I said to Karen, as if it were her business, while I gripped the chair arms to keep myself from swearing at him.

I hugged Libby extra tight before dropping her off at day care.

It took me three days to do the bare minimum on my other cases before I had a chance to head to Charlottesville once again, though I'd pretty well perfected the art of calling clients to update them on their cases as I drove north through the rolling fields and hills of Central Virginia.

Today would be a day to take stock. Talk to Jane, talk to her coworkers once more, meet with Nina Hilcko at the end of it to see where the commonwealth was. We were three weeks out from the murder, and almost two weeks after Jane's arrest. Most of the pieces would be in place by now, and I could begin designing a defense to address those pieces, one by one.

Jane was still stuck on a conference call when I arrived, so I went out to the hallway to Irene's station to say hello.

"Good morning, Allison. Hey, Jane said you were coming today, and I wondered if you'd have time to meet with me and Amir and Helen for a few."

Perfect. All Jane's allies in one place.

Within minutes, Irene and Amir had taken their places at the table in the nearest empty conference room. Helen, apparently, had been held up in a meeting with Greg Dombrowski and would join us in a few minutes.

They exchanged glances, each offering the other the chance to start. Amir tugged at the knot of his tie and gave a hand flourish to Irene. "You go."

"Fine. Amir was working late a couple of nights ago, and Felicity came in. Greg had gone home long before, so his usual prowling around the police tape at Ray's office had ended for the day. Felicity ducked under the tape, right?"

Amir jumped in. "Right. I asked her how she got in and she acted like I was some extra-gross gum she'd gotten on her shoe. 'Keys,' she said, and went straight to going through Ray's desk. She started stuffing things in her bag. She had one of those L.L.Bean tote bags, you know, the kind with the colored straps?"

"I know the kind. Go on."

"Anyway, I figure I don't have to take Felicity's shit now, because Ray is dead and can't cancel Thanksgiving for me in retaliation anymore. I asked her why the hell she still had a key when she was no longer related to anyone who worked here."

"Did you actually say that to a grieving widow, Amir?" asked Irene.

"Yeah, and Felicity is about as much of a grieving widow as I am," said Amir.

I leaned on my hand to cover my smile. "Still, Felicity digging in Ray's desk doesn't mean anything by itself. She'd own whatever personal effects were in there, and maybe the police gave consent to release them."

"Maybe," Irene said, "but don't you think it's odd she'd do it that late? How late was it, again?"

"Like nine at night." Amir nodded, like he'd cracked the case.

"Felicity works a day job, though," I said, wishing any of this would help Jane, though it was nice to see she had friends who wanted to help. I'd give anything for a legitimate alternate suspect, but I'd have to defend Jane the usual way—discrediting the commonwealth's evidence and arguing reasonable doubt. "She might have come by after dinner."

"I think Felicity and Brittany are working together," Amir said. "Ray kept Brittany from getting this job, here in her hometown. She saw her HR file, so she'd know. He also ruined Felicity's business expansion and found out about her cheating. I'm not sure which of them actually did it, but I bet it was one of them, and now they're covering for each other."

"Um, Amir," Irene said. "That doesn't make sense. Felicity and Brittany have been at each other's throats for months."

They had nothing. This was a waste of time, but I didn't want to make them feel bad. I appreciated what they were trying to do. "Thanks, y'all. It's a theory, anyway."

They were chattering about how Felicity could have dropped the gun in the ditch when Helen came in. She greeted me with a warm smile, then asked politely if the others would mind giving her a chance to talk to me alone. They went.

Helen closed the door and shed a lot of her boss demeanor when she sat casually in the chair closest to mine. She wore a camel pantsuit and kicked off a shoe to tuck her foot under herself. "Were they telling you how they think Felicity and/or Brittany sneaked in here like ninjas in the middle of the night to shoot Ray?"

I let out a bark of surprised laughter. "Um, yes, as a matter of fact they were. Why? I take it you don't share that theory?"

"No. But I was the HR-partner liaison before I went on maternity leave. Had been for three years."

"HR? Are you familiar with the reason Brittany didn't get an offer here?"

"Yes. It's an unfortunate story. Brittany was talented. Ray was thrilled with her as a potential hire until his wife put an end to it. I asked Ray why he'd vetoed her when she'd been so well received. He admitted it was to keep his wife happy while they worked out some issues. Apparently, Brittany told her mother she was a lesbian during her summer here at Blackwood, and Felicity didn't handle it well. She thought Brittany would be 'happier' in a big city."

Holy crap. No wonder Brittany had been willing to talk to me about Felicity. Poor girl. I spared a second to hope she would indeed be happier away from her mother. "Well. I heard Amir and Irene tell me their theories. Do you think there's anything to them?"

"No. I think Brittany understands how her family dynamics worked against her. She's more upset with her mother than her father, and not homicidal in any case. I've heard all about the supposedly suspicious behavior of Felicity rummaging through the desk, but honestly, that seems normal to me. Like most partners, Ray kept personal documents at work, and she'd need them to settle the estate."

Helen hesitated, as if deciding whether to say more. I waited. She'd come to see me for a reason.

She opened her mouth, closed it, and then shifted in her seat, starting again. "But I do have to point out that there is one person who hasn't really been on anyone's radar, and that person is Josh Gardner. He took a leave of absence last summer for a mental health break, he has an unhealthy obsession with Jane, he worked for Ray, and I hear he has no alibi."

I paused a moment, a little taken aback. It was true; I hadn't really considered Josh, but something in that sentence bothered me. "I understand his wife left him for another man around that time," I said, bristling slightly. Divorcing a cheating spouse was no joke—I should know. "We'll have to agree to disagree that unrelated mental health issues make someone a more likely murder suspect."

"Oh, please don't be offended. I'm sharing what I knew to be the case from my time with HR, and what I've observed since Josh has come under my supervision after Ray's death."

"What? Tell me the rest."

"When Josh went on leave last year, he went to a suicide crisis center. I believe he was briefly held on a temporary detention order for his own safety. HR considered asking him to take a longer leave, but we let him come back. We required him to come in for regular checks with HR, however, and I sat in on all those meetings. I'll be honest. He is a hard worker and a smart lawyer, but he is very, very fragile."

She shouldn't have told me any of that. It all violated federal privacy laws if she'd come into that knowledge while in her official supervisory capacity. She was a lawyer and a partner who'd been assigned some of the HR duties at the firm. She would know all about federal law. To take the chance I wouldn't report her, she had to be worried.

"Almost anything could set him off," Helen continued. "Since his ex-wife moved to Michigan for her job, he's lived entirely alone. I've seen no sign of dating, friends, any life outside of work. It disturbs me. No support network that I know of."

"What do you mean by an obsession with Jane?"

"Firm gossip says that when he had his mental break over his wife last summer—at his desk, apparently—Jane sat with him for a long time while he cried. After that, he . . . he talks about Jane a lot. Ray mentioned it. While we were keeping a lookout on how Josh was coping after the thing with his wife, we occasionally asked Ray how he was doing. Ray reported in February or March that he'd come into Josh's office and seen pictures of Jane on his screen before Josh clicked away. He said it was like a collage—her official firm picture from our website, and some others he couldn't identify that quickly."

I wrote all that down.

"What else? Since you've been supervising him, have you noticed anything odd about Josh?"

"Yes," Helen said, hardly waiting for me to finish the question. She wouldn't have broken all that confidentiality if she didn't think there was a damn good reason. "He's moody, a bit whiny, and his work product is crap. Too much time away from his desk. Mistakes. Poorly supported conclusions. Misreadings of statutes and case law. I've read his evaluations and spoken to Jane about him. There's no hint that other than during the immediate fallout from his separation last year, he's been in any way inadequate as a lawyer before. This is new, since Ray died. You'd expect that of Jane, given the accusation and the disruptions, but she is producing at or slightly above her prior levels. Josh is the one who seems most affected by this—and my assumption is that it's because of his obsession with Jane."

"Have you seen signs of an obsession?"

"Nothing you could take to court, but yes. The way he watches her in meetings. He mentions her a lot. Finds ways to do so. You know. I give him an assignment and he'll say, 'I'll ask Jane about that.' It wouldn't be odd for him to refer to her, but the frequency is remarkable. I've caught him passing her office with a cup of coffee more than once, and her office is not on the way between his desk and the coffee maker. That kind of thing."

That didn't sound like much. Jane was beautiful on a scale where that sort of thing happened. Guys had found reasons to pass our dorm suite all the time.

"Okay, Helen, I'll keep it in mind, but I'm not sure . . ."

Her lips turned up in a brief half smile. "I'm not sure, either. I wish I had something better than worries and feelings to tell you, but I'll leave it at this: Josh gives me the creeps."

ॐ

Jane was still on the phone, eyes wild and desperate for escape, when I finished talking to Helen. We exchanged ludicrous hand gestures and increasingly illegible messages via Post-it note. I walked out of Blackwood, figuring I'd make some calls while I waited for her.

I caught Nina Hilcko in her daily break between her morning cases and lunch. She gave me five minutes. I dived right in and asked her straight out if she'd looked at Josh as a suspect.

"Allison. I thought you were calling to ask about a deal. I'd consider one, by the way, but your client has to serve a sentence."

Taken aback, I stammered. I was accustomed to working with Emmett's boss and the other commonwealth attorney's offices around my area, where deals were scarce even for misdemeanors and downright nonexistent in murder cases. "Um. Right. Well, it's a bit early for that, but I'll keep it in mind."

"In answer to your question, yes, I believe O'Callihan and Hossain looked at the Gardner man as a suspect but dismissed him early on. No motive. Nothing but a bad evaluation and the potential loss of a small bonus. No record. No evidence that points to him, nothing suspicious about his behavior, and no one else seems to think he did it. Does your client know you're asking me about this?"

"My client? She knows I'm investigating her case, yes. Why?"

Nina laughed, a suggestive chuckle to her voice. "Well, because it strikes me as odd that she'd give you permission to try to throw her boyfriend under the bus. Trouble in paradise?"

Boyfriend? Thank God I was on the phone and not in Nina's presence so I could cover my shock. What the actual . . . ? Jane and Josh were a thing? Josh was the "someone" in Jane's life? That made no sense. Even to me, Josh seemed very different from the type of guy she'd dated in law school.

Very different from Emmett, said a voice in my head.

"This isn't *The Bachelorette*," I said, trying to regain the offensive. Damn Nina. "I don't care if we get to the rose ceremony. I have an innocent client charged with murder. It's my job to overturn every stone." I rolled my eyes at my own self-righteous priggishness.

Nina laughed again. "Sure, sure. Well, keep flipping them, then, but I'm pretty sure we've got the right defendant."

I held my tongue, sensing she was about to tell me something I definitely would be happier not knowing.

"In addition to the murder weapon, we've found some interesting searches on Ray Corrigan's work account. Your girl had something to hide."

"Like what kind of searches?"

"He was looking for her high school. For her birth record. He'd actually hired a skip tracer—or, well, he hired the skip tracer the firm usually used and billed the partnership for the search."

Skip tracers came in handy to find missing persons. Most law firms kept one handy—they helped locate long-lost heirs, deadbeat parents who owed back child support, last known addresses of defendants so they could be served with lawsuits. They were good at their work and likely had found the name-change record. Ray had found out about Renee Star from a skip tracer.

"Did any interesting information come of that?" I asked, closing my eyes in something like prayer.

"Hard to say. They're still combing through. I'll let you know, but all that secrecy, and the fact that Ray was onto it, means she might have had quite the motive to stop him from looking. And then there's her trip down to Danville."

"Danville?" Oh crap, I really hated when the commonwealth knew more about my client than I did.

"Yeah, a week or so ago she got in her car and drove south. We knew she had connections to North Carolina and she'd break the terms of her pretrial release if she crossed the border, so the police tailed her in an unmarked vehicle."

I held my breath, waiting for her to tell me my client had broken bond.

"She stayed in Virginia but met a woman in a diner. They weren't in there long, but Jane handed the woman an envelope. Our officer overheard her indicate it was five thousand dollars, in cash. He didn't catch everything, but he heard enough. Something about 'you talk, you go to jail' and 'I'm tired of running.' The woman refused to say a word to him after Jane left, but none of it sounds good, Allison."

What the hell was Jane doing?

"Great, Nina. Thanks for your time."

"You let me know if your client is interested in an admission of guilt in exchange for a plea bargain. She's a smart girl. Odds are not in her favor. I'd be willing to shave a few years off her sentence to save myself the prep work. You tell her, now, hear?"

The line went dead.

I had to tell Jane—I was ethically bound to. My biggest worry was that she'd accept a sentence of decades or more in order to keep Renee Star from seeing the light of day.

When I went back to Jane's office to touch base, there was another Post-it note on the door:

A—Had meeting. Too swamped today. I'll call you Monday.

—J

I dashed off a text to her.

Me: Just discovered—from Nina, no less—that you are seeing Josh. Not a good idea when this case is going on. My official lawyer advice is to put that on hold.

I'd driven all the way to Charlottesville to meet with my client, and she'd blown me off. Try as I might, I couldn't think of a good reason for it, which left me plenty of drive time to think about hidden office romances and five-thousand-dollar cash envelopes to strange women in Danville diners.

Jane did have a major secret.

Ray had searched for the secret and learned it.

Jane had told me herself she'd rather go to jail than reveal that secret.

Maybe when I'd heard murder hoofbeats, I'd looked for a zebra when all along it had been a horse. An obvious, homicidal horse named Jane without a single stripe of unpredictability.

Maybe my client was exactly the killer everyone thought she was— and I'd been the only one dumb enough not to see it.

CHAPTER
TWENTY-THREE
JANE

Sports that involved fancy equipment had never been an option for me—there'd never been money for more than a sports bra and a cheap pair of tennis shoes. I started running and hiking early. I relished the ability to get away from everyone into the woods where no one would follow, and the idea that in theory I could literally outrun most of the middle-aged men in western North Carolina even if I couldn't escape them online. It was a small comfort, but an important one.

Though I still went for the occasional run, I hadn't been hiking in years and I missed it. When Josh suggested we do a day hike at nearby White Rock Falls, I jumped at the chance, even though my lawyer had impersonally told me to quit dating him. The terseness of her text had annoyed me. Who did she think she was, telling me who I could date? Even if Josh and I weren't meant to be soul mates—and I didn't think we were, most likely—he was willing to spend time with me, and I wasn't exactly drowning in company.

With Helen not constantly checking to see if our butts were in our chairs billing clients, I'd dared to take a Saturday to spend outside with Josh. He'd picked me up just after dawn so we could avoid the worst of the summer heat. The trail had been a pleasant surprise—mostly downhill for more than a mile from the parking lot on the Blue Ridge Parkway. We'd reach the base of the falls that gave the trail its name in less than half a mile. I needed this. Out here, in the woods, I could breathe.

"Have you been hiking much?" I asked.

"Miriam was the hiker. I'd never done it before I met her, but she was really into it. She said it would be a shame to live somewhere as beautiful as Virginia and not hike."

He talked about Miriam a lot—still. Or, more precisely, *again*. After the worst of the divorce disruption, like most people, he'd gone quiet about his ex. Recently, though, she'd begun popping up in conversation regularly. He was comparison shopping. It had to be.

I was silent.

"I guess she hikes in Ann Arbor, now."

I'd never been to Michigan, but I'd seen pictures of the Midwest. "Do people hike over flat cornfields?"

He laughed. "Well, maybe they hike along lakeshores."

"Josh, I don't know how to say this other than bluntly, but you don't seem to be over Miriam." As I said it, my toe caught on a root and I went stumbling forward. Josh, who'd been right behind me, rushed up to catch my elbow. I'd already regained my balance, but the thought was nice. The trail widened a bit and we stayed side by side.

"Miriam was my wife. She's perfect. Was, I mean. I loved her more than life itself. Seeing those pictures is the worst thing that's ever happened to me."

His voice wobbled. I glanced at him. He stared straight ahead and blinked determinedly. Oh no. *Please don't cry again.* The night I'd handed him tissues, he'd been unhinged. I'd been worried for his sanity. "I know."

"I have an enormous capacity for love, though. That should be good news, right?" He nudged my arm to get me to look at him.

At the look on his face, unease curled in my stomach. He'd just been talking about Miriam. He'd said he loved her more than life. And here he was two seconds later, staring at me with a smoldering expression I'd never seen before. Capacity for love? We'd just started dating. We'd only kissed a few times.

A stream bubbled to our left, and the sound of rushing water got louder. The trail widened and turned to cross the creek. Before, the trees had hemmed us in on both sides, but this looked like a spot where giants had abandoned their toys—huge boulders and broken trees left behind by long-ago floods made easy, dry footholds across the narrow water. Smaller, newer trees grew in between the ancient debris: nature, that eternal optimist, replacing in increments what a wall of water had wiped out in a second.

On the other side of the creek, Josh swung in front of me, stopping my forward progress. "Hey," he said, grasping my upper arms lightly and rubbing his thumbs up and down my bare skin. "That is good news, isn't it?"

Something prickled along my spine. I glanced around, but everything was silent except for the bubble of the water. No one was around. An older couple and their dog had passed us a mile back, near the trailhead, but we hadn't seen another person out here since. The woods were beautiful, until you let yourself remember how vast and empty they were. Josh's hands tightened.

I'd forgotten that the woods had been where I'd gone to hide my face from other people.

Because there weren't people in the woods.

"Josh, let go of me."

I had no idea what made me say that. There wasn't anything harsh or concerning about the way he was holding me. I wasn't used to being so . . . alone with him. That must be it.

He dropped his hands like I'd slapped him. "I was trying to tell you I want you." He cleared his throat. "Because I love you, and you . . . You react like . . ."

Now it was my turn for a slack mouth. Wrongness made me blink. "What? You *love* me? Josh, I . . . um. It's . . . we only . . . You don't love me. You couldn't. You're missing Miriam, for some reason, and mistaking loneliness for something it isn't."

"What are you saying?" Josh's Adam's apple bobbed in his throat. His lips tightened and a fist clenched around a backpack strap. His face was written in wounded adoration. Rationality had disappeared. The hair rose on the back of my neck.

"I . . ." A twig snapped nearby. My head turned that way, desperate for other people, but a squirrel ran up a tree. "Josh . . . we've been having fun, and obviously I have a lot going on in my life right now, and I . . . I was glad for your support. For your companionship."

"My companionship?" he said, his knuckles going white as the stiff strap curled in his grip. Bitterness and something else I couldn't identify turned the words ugly and worthless. "I thought this was going somewhere. That we could be together. Have you been wasting my time? When were you going to tell me?"

"Tell you what? I hadn't ruled out that it might go somewhere, if I don't go to jail, that is. But Josh, it's too early. Too soon. What . . . why are you . . . ?"

I couldn't make sense of his transactional attitude. I'd thought we were moving slow. He'd said we were. Deep down, I knew already he wasn't The One, but where was it written I couldn't date someone casually? I'd never promised him anything.

He set off walking, right quick. The trail headed sharply up from the stream, the slope steep enough that the pebbles under our feet could easily face-plant an incautious hiker. I tried to keep up, but I was puffing hard in seconds. I'd let my billable-hour quest rob me of too much fitness. Did he mean to leave me here? "Josh! Wait, Josh."

He said nothing, climbing upward with furious strides that ate the ground. Josh wasn't much taller than I was, but he could hike.

"Tell me what's in your head," I panted, maintaining the pace. "You were telling me how much you loved Miriam, more than life, and then you tell me you love me, and . . . will you stop? I have whiplash, Josh."

He stopped above me on the trail, giving him a height advantage he didn't normally have. His eyes—that indeterminate color between brown and green—were intense in a way that reminded me uncomfortably of that night handing him tissues at his desk. Unable to stop myself, I checked the trail again for other people to no avail. I found myself staying at least six feet from him.

"I thought we had something, Jane. You act like this is early, too soon, blah blah blah, but you have to know I've wanted you for a long time. I imagine it, all the time. You're so different from Miriam, the way you're built, but I think about you, about your body, in my bed. I dream about it."

"You never said a word until after Ray died. I thought we were friends. You talk about Miriam all the time."

"That's because I haven't wanted anyone since Miriam. I thought that would be obvious." He stepped closer and raised a hand. My blood pressure spiked, but he only reached for the slim branch of a nearby tree to steady himself on the incline. "I want you. We're adults. We've been out on dates. I want to strip you naked. You know you want it, too. God," he said thickly, "you were made for it, I know you'll be amazing, I want to . . ."

Without warning, my gorge rose. It had happened all the time in the first years after Len when a man looked at me a certain way. As time passed, the automatic response slowed and disappeared. Its return meant something. I had to pay attention. "Stop." His eyes. They weren't right. Fear slid between my ribs, wrapping tendrils around my lungs. There was nothing of my gentle friend and coworker here. The woods stood silent and vacant of anything that would help me. "No, Josh. It's too soon for that. I'm not ready. This . . . we haven't even been going out for three weeks yet. This is all too . . . too intense. Too . . . much."

He stood there a beat, completely motionless but for the blinking of his burning, feverish eyes. Then all his muscles tensed, his white lips pressed into a tight line, his fists clenched, and there was a sharp crack. The tree branch—several inches in diameter—came away in his hand. As it came loose, he lost his footing and came running down the slope at me, still gripping the branch like a jagged, leafy spear. After that, I was pure instinct.

Go cut a switch.

My mother's muscles used to tense like that—by the time I was in kindergarten, I knew it was the signal to run and hide. Sometimes, like Josh, she broke whatever she was holding, or threw it at me reflexively. No matter how fast or far I ran, she always caught me, or waited out my hungry stomach. I could never hide for long. When Len or another of her boyfriends was around, she'd postpone the punishment until they'd gone out, but the muscle-tensing was a foolproof forecast.

Without even consciously making the decision, the five-year-old inside me did an about-face and raced back down and across the stream the way I'd come, praying I'd find help in the parking lot, where a number of other cars meant other hikers. I would not get into a car with Josh. I would go nowhere with Josh. Not ever again. I would wait all day for someone trustworthy-looking if I had to, or walk to where my phone had a signal and call an Uber.

"Where are you going? Jane!" Footfalls pounded behind me. A splash sounded as he missed a step and went into the creek. "Dammit!"

I kept going. The gentle downhill I'd loved so much on the way from the parking lot now seemed a lot steeper going up. Josh caught up to me and grabbed for my arms.

I shook him off. "Whatever this is, it's over now. Allison told me this wasn't a good idea. That you weren't a good idea. You're scaring me, Josh. Keep back."

"She said what? This is crazy. Don't be stupid! You can't find your way out, and you rode with me."

"We hiked here on a blazed trail. I grew up hiking and I can find my way back. You go on and complete the hike. I don't want to spend any more time with you."

"You're ruining it! This was going to be . . . You need me to drive you home. You need me."

"I don't need you. I mean it. I'll find a ride. Do not follow me, Josh."

He didn't. I walked back alone, full of a terrible certainty I'd dodged a bullet.

Or maybe I hadn't exactly dodged one.

❧

In the parking lot, my cell had no service, but I found a man and his two teenage sons who were loading a pickup truck camper shell with what appeared to be overnight gear. I hesitated only a few seconds before telling them my problem. They looked well scrubbed and friendly—the father wore a UVA hat. One of the sons had on a T-shirt from a ski race at a nearby resort. I swallowed my terror of strange men and took the chance.

They were in fact delightful. I told them only that my boyfriend and I had had an argument and asked if they could drive me to where I had a cell signal and could call an Uber. They insisted on driving me all the way back to Charlottesville and dropped me off at Barnes & Noble. We had a nice chat about UVA's prospects for the coming football season.

Once I was safely bolted into my town house later that afternoon, the shaking began. I found a fleece blanket to wrap around myself. It wasn't warm enough. I got another.

My stupidity was as boundless as the starry sky. I'd worked along-side Josh Gardner all these years and I'd never had a clue he was . . . not quite right. *I want to strip you naked.* There was something wrong about him—the odd juxtaposition of coarse and lovey-dovey, which was off-putting enough, but the entitlement was worse. He thought he was entitled to me. Like Tyler. Like Len. Like so many others.

I'd thought he saw me as pretty Mrs. George Bailey. Instead, I was still sex-crazed Marilyn Monroe.

My frozen hands refused to warm, so I stood, blankets hanging around my shoulders like a superhero cape I definitely hadn't earned, to pace in frustration. How had I missed that Josh had begun thinking of me as a possession, a sexual trophy to claim? Dammit. I threw a sofa pillow at my front door. I'd never understand men well enough to have a normal relationship.

My mind began playing back all my interactions with Josh—something was still off. He said he loved me. If that was the case, why had he waited until the day Ray died to ask me out for a drink? He'd claimed it was to discuss his theory that Felicity was the killer. I had assumed that Josh used the excuse of discussing suspects to get me to go out with him, but maybe it was the other way around.

He'd been so intent on throwing suspicion on Felicity, within hours of Ray's death. In retrospect, that night at Claude's, he'd been far more interested in focusing on Felicity than on beginning any kind of romance with me.

Why? Why so determined to get me to think about Felicity? And it made no sense for him to try to convert a long-simmering crush into a romance on the day I found our boss bled out from a gunshot wound.

Unless all of it was intended to distract me from the game everyone else at work was playing. The Who Killed Ray Corrigan game.

Unless he was worried I might, without his input, settle on a dif-ferent possibility.

I pulled the blankets tighter around myself and bit down hard to stop my teeth from chattering.

I'd never really considered the idea that Josh might be a legitimate suspect, but the uncontrolled rage that broke a tree—a tree!—this morning had removed any ability to see him as innocuous. I knew that kind of rage and what it could do. Not for a second did I think he would have shot Ray over a bad work evaluation, but what if it had something to do with what he really cared about? I had proof—a night of desperation-soaked tissues—that he cared greatly about something.

He cared greatly about someone.

I'd met Josh's ex, Miriam, one time, almost exactly a year ago at the annual summer office gathering where everyone's family was invited to a park for a cookout. The partners hated the picnics because billable hours had to be sacrificed for this afternoon nod to work-life balance. The associates hated it because they knew the partners did. Usually, only a few of the admins and interns got anything like enjoyment out of the free food and booze.

Last summer, Miriam had been finishing up her PhD and interviewing at different universities for associate professor positions. Josh brought her to the office picnic. We hadn't talked long, but I remembered a shy woman with birdlike, expressive hands who'd spoken with excitement about her teaching and the research opportunities available in her field. At my interest, she'd shared an article she'd written on women in leadership positions. She'd had a second interview scheduled at the University of Michigan. Josh had been excited, too, and I distinctly remembered that I'd asked him the next week what he would do if Miriam got the job.

"Go with her," he'd said, without a second of hesitation. "I can take the bar exam anywhere."

"Does Ray know that?" I asked, kind of shocked and a little envious. I'd never dared imagine an escape from Ray's authoritarian regime.

Ray didn't like to train new associates and had no patience for learning curves. Amir's life had only recently begun to be less than horrendous.

"I think so," Josh had said. "I haven't been quiet about it."

Without warning, a wave of nausea bent me double. Josh told me that Ray was the one who'd seen Miriam on the UVA Lawn with some other guy. Ray had told Josh about it. Ray had given Josh the idea to hire a private investigator. Ray had "hooked him up" with the PI he knew.

Miriam had indeed been offered the job at Michigan she'd interviewed for in June last year. I'd handed Josh tissues as he cried over the photographic proof she'd cheated only a few weeks later.

I stumbled blindly to where I'd dropped my bag and phone.

I had her number because she'd texted me the link to her article. Her cell rang only once before Miriam's sweet voice said hello.

"Miriam?"

"Yes? Can I help you?"

"This is Jane Knudsen. I work at Blackwood, Payne & Vivant with your ex-husband, Josh. We met last summer, at the picnic? Some things have happened, and . . . I had a few questions. Do you have a minute?"

The sweetness in her tone evaporated, replaced by another note I couldn't identify. "I remember you. I can't promise I'll answer all of them."

"That's fair. Josh told me once, before you separated, that he was planning to move with you to wherever you got a professorship."

"That's true. He was going to move to Ann Arbor with me. Detroit's got lots of law firms and it's only forty-five minutes away. We were going to work everything out, but then those pictures."

Wait. They'd had issues before the pictures? This was news. Josh talked about her as perfection.

"What all did you have to work out?"

There was a silence. "Josh had . . . some things I thought he needed to see a psychiatrist about. At first, he refused to go. We'd been seeing an infertility doctor, but I said we'd have to pause that until he got some therapy. We'd made some progress, but then he came home with those pictures."

"I hate to be intrusive, Miriam, I really do, but I need to know what things. What was wrong with him?"

"I . . . they were addiction issues. I don't feel comfortable saying any more," she said, flatly. There'd be no more information on that topic.

If Josh had a substance-abuse problem, I'd never seen the first sign of it. I'd have to find out about that another way. Moving on.

"Did Josh's boss know about Ann Arbor? Ray Corrigan? Did he know you were planning to move? That Josh was going, too?"

"Yes. Josh came home in a foul mood after I got the job offer here. We'd celebrated the night before—went out for a nice dinner on the mall. When we got home, Josh checked the internet to see what the requirements were to be admitted to the Michigan bar, and then we looked at real estate websites and everything. We talked about a new start and it was one of the best nights of my life. I felt hopeful for the first time in a while. Then he went to work and mentioned it to Ray, and Ray apparently went ballistic. About all the time he'd put into training Josh, and how ungrateful he was, and everything. Josh was still excited about going—maybe more so after that—but Ray had made clear he'd make Josh's life miserable until he left."

"And did he?"

"Well, I'm sure to you it won't sound unusual, but yeah, Josh stayed at work until past eleven for the next week or so. I barely saw him. Then there were two days when he actually ate dinner with me, and on the third day, everything went to hell."

"What happened?"

"He came home and said someone had seen me kissing some guy. I told him it was ridiculous—it was ridiculous, I hadn't done anything of the kind—and I thought we were done with that."

"I take it you weren't?"

"Well, obviously not. We argued the next morning, over . . . over some old issues, and it was like a switch flipped. He didn't speak to me the rest of the morning, and nothing but short sentences when absolutely necessary the rest of that week."

"I'm sorry about the divorce. More than I can say."

"Well," Miriam said, in a tone that left no doubt she was not entirely sorry. "You know what they say about silver linings. I met someone. We're engaged, and I just found out I'm pregnant. About twelve weeks along."

"That's wonderful," I said, thinking about Josh telling me he couldn't have children. "When did the pictures come into it?"

"It was fast. A few days, a week later, at most. Things were tense like that, and then, Josh was home with one of those post office cardboard mailers full of pictures. He had them on his phone, too. Oh my gosh, they were gross. And . . . and it looked like me in the pictures. Most of them were body parts, backs of heads. But there were one or two, same lighting, same positions, where my face was visible. I don't know how they did it, but it wasn't me."

"It wasn't? Josh was so sure."

"It wasn't. We had our problems, but I never cheated on Josh. I told him that. Over and over and over. He kept pointing to the pictures. I said Photoshop was a thing, but he scoffed. 'Why would anyone do that?' He said he knew I wanted a baby and I'd gone out to get one. It was so wrong. He was so different from who I thought he was. He . . . went down the spiral and he never came back."

"And you separated."

"He told me to get out. I had the job offer, so I went. I stayed with a college friend here in Ann Arbor until I could find a place. The divorce went through. Most of it was done by mail. We didn't own much, had no kids. It was an easy divorce, as divorces go."

"Throughout the whole thing, did he keep believing you'd cheated?"

"Yes. I never could make him see reason. And then I stopped caring whether he did." She halted and I could hear an intake of breath. "Until a few weeks ago. He called me out of the blue and for some reason I didn't hang up."

"What did he say?"

Her voice was careful. "He said he'd heard about 'deep fakes.' About the technology they were developing to make convincing videos of politicians saying something they never actually said. You know, for political ads. The technology's advanced from 'simple Photoshop' to take photos and video to something truly frightening that could ruin lives and obliterate truth."

I knew a few things about how photos and video—especially sexual ones—could ruin lives and obliterate truth.

"He . . . he asked me if I'd been telling the truth. If the photos had been faked. I told him the same thing I'd told him all along—they had. I hadn't cheated. I knew he'd hired a private investigator and that's who'd sent him the pictures, but for the first time I asked him where he got the name of the PI in the first place."

"And?"

"Ray Corrigan gave him the name."

"Did he believe you this time? About the cheating?"

"I think he did. No, I know he did. He started crying. He asked if I'd give him a chance to prove how sorry he was. He wanted me back. I . . . I had to tell him about Yusef, and about the baby. I mean, my heart broke for him a little bit, but he had so many chances and he never believed me. And we did have other problems, so . . ."

Oh dear. He would not have taken that well. "When did this phone call take place? Do you remember the date?"

"Um, it was June 14. I remember, because it was my sister's birthday. In the evening. Josh said he was on the way home from work."

Holy crap. Oh dear God. Ray Corrigan—who'd told Josh he'd seen Miriam with another man, who'd given him the name of a PI, who'd exterminated Josh's marriage to make his own life a touch more convenient—had died a few hours later.

"Thanks, Miriam. You've been a big help."

A terrifyingly big help.

"Can I ask you a question?" she said politely, surprising me.

"Sure."

"You said things have happened. Can I ask what you were talking about?"

I owed her that much. And in Michigan, out of contact with Josh, she might not know. "Ray Corrigan is dead. Shot through the chest at close range in his office sometime after midnight in the early morning hours of June 15 with his own gun. I'm charged with his murder."

There was a silence. "You didn't do it, or you wouldn't . . . Oh no. Oh my God. Josh must have. The same night . . . oh no . . . Josh must have done it."

"I'm beginning to think it's possible, yes."

"Yusef!" she yelled to someone out of range. Her voice had grown hysterical. Maybe I shouldn't have told her. She was pregnant. "Yusef! I have to go. I'm sorry."

"No, I'm sorry. Thank you for talking to me."

I hung up and called Allison. No answer on her cell phone. No answer at her home landline. No answer at her office, either. I texted. No response.

That was odd.

CHAPTER
TWENTY-FOUR
ALLISON

Saturdays when Steve had Libby were good times to get work done, especially when Emmett was spending the day playing in some charity basketball tournament. Sometimes I went to watch, but I'd gotten behind on all my cases because of the time I'd put in on Jane's. Jane, who had most likely shot Ray Corrigan deader than a doornail. I didn't look up from my pile until a punctuation-optional text came in from Steve at four that afternoon.

Steve: I know you were going to pick up Libby at six but can you come at five Karen wants to go out to dinner

Of course she did, and not to the kind of restaurant that would have crayons and a kids' menu. Sometimes I wondered how divorced women with kids managed to keep their eyeballs in their heads from all the rolling.

Me: Fine. See you at five.

I tossed my phone onto the coffee table and glanced at the piles of work still undone. I'd been banking on having more time, but at least this way I could take Libby for burritos on the way home. I got up to get another Coke Zero and stretch. Maybe Emmett would be done in time to meet us at the burrito place. Before I could text him, my doorbell rang.

The doorbell rang so infrequently I forgot what it sounded like for months at a time. Like a responsible adult, I peered through the peephole before opening it. Josh Gardner.

Odd. I hadn't called him or contacted him after I'd learned that he and Jane had a thing. Maybe she'd sent him to shore up her case somehow. Or maybe he had information about Jane that he didn't want her to know he'd shared with me.

As my hand closed around the cool metal of the door lock, Helen saying Josh gave her "the creeps" flashed before me, and an odd shiver held me still. I shook it off. Ridiculous. No male lawyer would hesitate at the chance to interview a friendly witness just because he was home alone.

The flash of caution persisted, though. I glanced out the front window. My neighbor buzzed by on his lawn mower and waved as he caught sight of me from twenty yards away. With that safety precaution taken, I unbolted the door and stepped out onto the porch with Josh.

"It's Allison, right?" He smiled and stuck his hand out to shake, waiting to be invited in. "I hope it's okay I stopped by. My mom lives in Lynchburg and Jane asked if I could bring you something she found in the ditch by her house, you know, near where they recovered the gun, while I was down here." He rooted through several pockets in his cargo shorts, his movements jerky and panicked, like he'd lost whatever the item was.

I decided he was harmless. "Come on in." I held the door open for him.

My open laptop and the piles of files on the coffee table caught his attention. "Oh, you're busy. I'm sorry. I ought to know better what lawyer Saturdays look like."

"No, no, come on in. I was about done." To pick up Libby at five, I'd have to leave in about thirty minutes anyway. "Can I get you a glass of water? Or a Coke Zero? Have a seat," I said, closing the door behind him to keep the air-conditioning in and gesturing at the armchair at one end of the coffee table.

"Sure," he said, standing awkwardly inside the door, not moving toward the chair. "A Coke Zero would be great."

I headed for the adjacent kitchen to get it and came back to find him turning the bolt on my front door.

The metallic click as the bolt slid home sounded like a gunshot. Some undigested lump in my stomach did a backflip. He darted to the coffee table, hesitance gone now, and closed my laptop.

"Hey, what are you . . . ?" I didn't have time to finish the statement before it became very clear what he was doing. He tossed the laptop onto the chair where I'd invited him to sit, swept my phone off the table, and pocketed it, swapping it out for the dull gray barrel of a handgun.

He had a gun.

Sweet lord in heaven. I should have listened to my intuition. What was happening?

As casually as if he were sitting down for a staff meeting, he perched on top of my computer and gestured at me with the gun. "Put the drink down. Sit. Please. We're going to chat."

"My boyfriend is going to be here in a few minutes," I said, cursing the babbling note of panic in my voice. A silent scream of gratitude that Libby wasn't home roared in my ears. Emmett was not going to be here. We'd left it that we were going to get in touch after his tournament to decide whether to see each other tonight, given that I'd have Libby. No one was coming and I was armed with a glass full of ice and soda.

"I doubt that, but he'll head out when he gets here if you don't answer the door. It is locked, you know." He patted his pocket where my phone reposed. "He won't get an answer if he texts you for a while."

"Jane didn't send anything with you, did she?"

"No. Nothing in that ditch but the gun."

"What do you want, Josh?" I asked, trying to remain calm. "What can I possibly do for you?" I moved toward the kitchen as if to put down the more-ludicrous-by-the-second glass of Coke Zero. My one landline phone gathered dust in there. Maybe there was a chance.

He gave the gun a sharp jerk. "Sit. Don't make me ask you again. I had an unpleasant morning this morning. I started a hike with the hottest woman I have ever seen in my life and ended it alone. All that time I put in, dinner at the C&O, not a damn thing to show for it. I think you've had a lot to do with that. Sit."

I put the drink on an end table and sat. "Wh-what do you mean? I didn't have anything to do with that."

"Jane is sex on a stick. She gives off pheromones from the next zip code. Somehow it's even hotter when she wears all that prude, up-to-the-neck clothing. She says she's cold but she's hot. A woman like that going to bed alone is a crime against nature. I had a chance. I was in. I was willing to overlook things. Turn lemons into lemonade. And then she met you, and now everything is all screwed up. She listens to you. *You* told her not to see me and she called it off before I could close the deal."

"I . . . Josh, you've got it all wrong. That . . ."

"I need you to call her and tell her you've changed your mind. She owes me."

A thousand police procedurals ran through my head. Though none of his long rant about Jane's hotness made any sense, I knew enough to keep him talking. He'd gone too far to turn back now. He'd already committed the crime of abduction—with a firearm—by trapping me in my own living room. If I lived, he'd be going to jail, and he must know that. Or if he didn't know, he was delusional, which was worse. I needed him to keep me alive long enough to think of a way out. "I'm not sure I understand, Josh. What do you mean by 'overlook things'? Or the lemons. What does that mean? Are you talking about Ray's murder? Because she . . ."

"That's not what I'm talking about. Don't pretend to be stupid!" As if these unhinged things he was saying were perfectly clear.

"Then what do you mean?"

"I mean she was a porn star! Didn't you know? For years! I'm willing to overlook the fact that she's a porn star."

I sat silent, stunned.

"Not many men would, you know. Sure, they'd all want to do her—everyone wants to do Jane, all the guys at work, probably some of the women, too. In private. But no one but me would be willing to be seen with her in public. I was going to be with her. To get her the upstanding way, by paying for dates first. I was going to look past it."

"To look past it," I repeated dumbly.

"I mean, seriously. I'm, like, the only guy who could handle it. This isn't a movie. This isn't *Pretty Woman*. You know that movie script originally ended with Julia Roberts going back to her whore life and Richard Gere saying sayonara? Did you know that?"

"I did know that. But the studio hated it."

"Right," he said, jumping up to pace. I glanced at my computer—it was no help to me now. "Right! So, to make the audience happy, they had to change Richard Gere from a normal, realistic guy who'd never want to be with a whore to some fairy-tale prince who climbs up a damn fire escape to get to her. Don't you see? I was willing to do the whole fairy-tale-prince routine!" He cackled, his eyes glazed and wild. "I'm the prince!"

Oh dear God. "Right. The prince."

"Jane doesn't even know I know about her slut years. I know she doesn't do that anymore, but the damage is done. But now she's in reach, see? Affordable, like a fancy car after a hailstorm!" He chuckled as if he were the cleverest man alive. "If she were normal, she'd never be with me. This is my chance. To be with someone that fucking beautiful. Because I am the prince. A prince among men. Ha! That's funny, right?"

He couldn't seem to stop his unhinged ranting, which was fine. Keep him talking. "How did you find out?"

"About her superstardom? That was easy. You probably don't know this because you're a girl, but there aren't many online porn stars as famous as Renee Star. Here, let me show you," he said, pulling out his phone. It was one of the extra-large iPhones.

"No, please don't," I said, turning away. "I don't want to see."

He was undeterred, scrolling through his phone. It didn't take long. He must have had the photos saved. He shoved the screen in my face, and I saw a hazy image of lots of skin and blonde hair and a skimpy pink dress and princess tiara before I closed my eyes.

"Fine," he said. "Don't look. Doesn't change the fact that she was a legend, right at the beginning, when the internet was going nuts. There was a window there, when the feds had to switch from finding stuff in print to finding it online. Renee Star was the queen of that window. I didn't even know all this shit was out there until Miriam left me and my ordinary . . . avenues didn't do it for me anymore. I recognized her, that's all. Couldn't believe my luck when I realized my ice-queen coworker was a queen of a whole different kind."

My mind whirled with revulsion. He hadn't done any kind of sleuthing through public records like Amir and the commonwealth had tried. He hadn't found Jane's past through targeted searching, like Ray. He'd found it the disgusting, pedestrian way—by being a lonely, perverted aficionado of child porn. And here he was, bragging about it.

"She was a child, Josh, in those pictures."

"There's video, too, in her later career. She's not much of a child in those. You should see the expressions on her face. She freaking loved it. *Fuck*." He shivered in a twisted kind of ecstasy. "And you ruined my chance with her!"

I could tackle him. I could try to use the element of surprise. Already the gun was drooping down toward the floor as he relived his sick fantasies involving a prepubescent Jane. My muscles tensed as I calculated the distance I'd have to spring.

His eyes caught the tiny movement and the gun snapped back into place.

Another idea occurred to me. "You said you wanted me to call her, right? To talk her into getting back together with you?"

"I took her to the C&O—the C&O!—and hiking, and . . . and she said you told her not to see me!" Josh's face sagged, like a child who'd been told his only options were to go to bed now or go to bed in ten minutes. "But if I let you talk to her, you'll tell her I'm here with a gun."

Yup, that was the plan.

"I won't, Josh. You'll shoot me if I do, right?"

He stood, his emotions swinging wildly to rage. "You think I'm that dumb? Why would you ask me to let you talk to her?"

"Well, Josh, I need to pick up my daughter soon." I glanced at the clock on the microwave in the kitchen and tried to keep my voice as calm and rational as possible. "I'm already late leaving. You said the reason you were here is to get me to talk to Jane on your behalf. I'd like to get that done so my daughter doesn't worry about me."

"Forget that! You're going to write another text to Jane. Or I will, on your phone."

"And then what, Josh? I assume after that you're going to kill me?"

"What? No. No, I'm not a killer." There was hesitation there—just enough.

"Did you kill Ray?" I asked, suddenly certain he must have.

"No! What? No! It was Felicity."

I couldn't tell if he was lying. All his body language was agitated, but then it had been before. Without warning, he darted to my front window and, in a single motion, ripped the roman shade clean out of the frame. He dragged the whole thing over to me.

"Get on the floor. Hold your hands out."

"Josh, I'll sit here on the sofa. I won't move. I promise."

"I don't like asking twice! Get on the floor!" With an open hand, he smashed his palm into my cheek, hard enough to snap my head back. He was deteriorating. I got on the floor as the pain sparked and burst in shock waves from my smarting face.

Awkwardly, balancing the gun, he used the shade pull to tie my wrists to the bar that separated the top surface and the lower shelf of my coffee table. The tether forced me to kneel uncomfortably on the rug next to the table. Josh left the room. From the bathroom off the kitchen, I could hear the sounds of retching.

Retching meant there was still some humanity there. Humanity meant hope.

As the worst of the pain of the blow eased, I tested the coffee table leg. Sturdy, and the table itself was massive and too heavy to overturn and drag behind me. I scanned under the sofa, under the table, under the chairs. Surely Libby had dropped something I'd missed that I could use. A pair of kids' safety scissors, or even a colored pencil. Nothing. Dammit.

Josh stayed in the bathroom—whether strategizing or panicking, I had no idea. Time passed. If I twisted into a pretzel, I could still see the microwave clock. Ten after five. Quarter after five. My upper arms began to ache from the angle they were tied.

Josh came storming back into the room, holding my ringing phone out like an accusation.

"Did you want me to write Jane a text?" I asked, using my bound hands to pray he'd let me have the phone.

"It won't stop ringing, and now it's Jane calling. On a Saturday night. You two are as thick as thieves. You bitch! I'm not into rape. I put in the work. Hard work to get her naked and then you told her to dump me!"

"If the phone is upsetting you, put it on silent. It's the switch on the side."

"I know where the switch is. Shut up."

He switched off the sound and the ringing stopped. He held it, staring at its face, waiting for the call to go to voice mail so he could start typing a text to Jane. The kitchen landline started its shrill ringing, causing Josh's fists to clench and the veins in his neck to tighten and throb. His agitation was rising. He had not thought this through. Whatever plan had formed in his mind when he'd driven up to my house had not had an ending. That fact made my stomach feel like it was turning inside out. He would have to kill me, eventually. I took a second to send up a prayer that Libby wouldn't be the one to find me, and that Steve and Karen would take good care of her. And remember to love her.

A perfunctory knock sounded at the front door. The handle turned and the deadbolt caught and held. Josh's gaze snapped to the door. Within a second the doorbell rang and rang alongside simultaneous pounding on the door. "Allie!"

Emmett. Blood roared relief in my ears. Thank God. My crappy Toyota was parked in the driveway, along with Josh's car. He'd know I hadn't gone far. He knew I was supposed to pick up Libby, though he didn't know the time had changed. He was here.

"Who's in there?" Emmett yelled from the porch.

Josh threw himself onto the floor next to me, slapped a hand over my mouth, and stuck the hard metal of the gun barrel at the back of my head. "Don't make a sound."

"Allie!" The doorbell rang again and again, then stopped.

"Stay quiet," Josh hissed, the gun forcing my forehead into the rug. "Where is he going? Is he climbing into the bushes? Dammit!"

I couldn't see anything except the blurry pattern of the threadbare rug, but Josh had ripped down the shade that normally blocked the view of my living room from the street. I bit my lip and stayed quiet. Seconds ticked by. Josh cursed and prayed under his breath in a long stream of gibberish.

Emmett's voice was back on the other side of the door. "Allie! I've called the police. Something is wrong. I'm waiting right here. They're on their way."

I didn't know whether I would survive the five minutes it would take for the deputies to arrive. Josh had very little to lose at this point.

He must have decided that as well. He pulled at his own hair, then ripped the shade cord tying my hands loose. A fair bit of skin came off with it, and blood from my wrist dripped onto the rug. Grabbing my aching arm, he yanked me to my feet and dragged me upstairs, out of sight of the front window. His breathing rasped hard and panicked.

"Where are we going?" I said, breathless.

"I don't know!" He pushed me inside the first door he saw—my bedroom—and closed it behind us, leaning against it. He shut his eyes but continued to wave the gun. I sat carefully on the bed, hands palm-up on my thighs. Angry red marks slashed my wrists, but they didn't hurt yet.

"Listen to me, Josh," I begged. "I don't lie. When they get here, I'll tell them the truth. You were upset. You lost your head. You did things you normally would never do. I know it. They'll have to consider that. You need to let me go now, and it will be easier for you. Really."

"I don't have any choices! I . . . You can't . . . Dammit! Everything keeps getting worse. I'm going to jail. It's gone too far!" He waved the gun as if all this were the gun's fault. "I might as well kill us both right now."

In the distance, sirens grew louder. Emmett yelled my name below. Josh pointed the gun at my head and curled his finger around the trigger.

A vision flashed—Libby, in a cheap polyester Santa hat, twirling outside in a December twilight, a string of lit Christmas lights wrapped like a stole around her narrow shoulders. Emmett laughed nearby, waiting to hang the lights on the porch rail.

"No, Josh, don't," I said, unable to entirely suppress the sob. "Please. You've got a great job. A . . . a mother who loves you. You said you were in town visiting her, right? I'm a mom, too. I have a daughter who needs me. She's only six. Please don't!" Rationality failed me at the thought of Libby growing up without me. Of Emmett, outside on my porch, hearing the gunshot. My eyes burned. I didn't want to die.

The sirens stopped close by, and the sound of doors slamming replaced them. Everything stopped. Josh froze, gun pointed at me, hazel eyes dilated and blinking in terror. A minute passed or an hour—I'd never know which. From downstairs there was a crash—the front door-frame breaking. Unintelligible shouting drifted up the stairs.

"Allie!" Emmett shouted again, this time from the living room.

Josh swallowed. His thin throat moved in slow motion. Even more slowly, the gun barrel began to arc up, up, up—until it stopped.

The muzzle rested against his own temple.

CHAPTER
TWENTY-FIVE

JANE

As I dug in my fridge for take-out leftovers for supper and waited for
Allison to call me back, I made one more call, to Irene, who remembered the name of the private investigator off the top of her head.

"Ken Pentecost. How do you forget rhyming and religion all rolled
into one name?"

"Right. You don't know the number, do you?"

"No, but he's online. Not under private investigators. If he has a
business, it's so under the radar that it's invisible. I think he's just a guy
Ray knew."

I thanked her, hung up, and found his number.

"Hello?"

"Is this Mr. Pentecost?"

"Yeah. Who's asking?" Ken Pentecost had a thick country accent.

"My name is Jane Knudsen, and I—"

"Wait a second. Jane Knudsen. Name is familiar. Give me a minute."

"I got your name from—"

"Hang on. I'll get it. Never forget a name." He hummed. It sounded
like the *Jeopardy!* theme song. Good lord.

"I got your name from Ray Corrigan," I said in a rush, unwilling to spare enough time for this little game.

"Aha!" he said, like he, and he alone, had solved the puzzle. "Now I remember. You're the pretty girl, worked for him. He talked about you."

"How did you know Ray?"

"Went to high school with him. Of course, Ray, he was always a brain, went off to school and become a lawyer. Me, I didn't do nothing after school but be a security guard, retired from that a few years back, but I know people. I was always good at finding stuff. Ray used to give me a call now and then, get me to help out."

"Do you remember a time he referred you to Josh Gardner? An attorney in his firm? To do a private investigation of his wife cheating?"

The garrulous Mr. Pentecost fell silent. Already I knew him well enough to tell that he did remember, and he didn't want to tell me about it. "Mr. Pentecost?"

"Uh, right. Sorry. Dropped the phone. What was you saying?"

On a dime, I changed tactics. I wanted to see his face for this interview. Ken Pentecost had some interesting stories to tell. I glanced at the unappetizing leftover fried chicken that was all I had in the house for supper. "Hey. I don't know if you're doing anything right now, but would you be willing to let me buy you supper? I could meet you at Chipotle, on Pantops. I have a . . . a job I need you to do. Good money in it, potentially."

"Chipot-el? That the place with the tofu tacos?" he asked doubtfully.

"Would you prefer the TipTop?" I asked, naming a diner close to my town house where more old-fashioned food was on the menu.

"Yeah! See you there in thirty minutes or so?"

"Sure." I glanced down at myself. "I'm wearing a pink . . ."

"Oh, I'll recognize you. Don't you worry about that."

There was no scenario in which that could be good.

The TipTop Restaurant was one of those Charlottesville institutions that never seemed to change. I liked their Greek food, and it was close enough to my house that I could get there in five minutes. I glanced around, but the place was full of men who could be former security guards with a penchant for excavating skeletons in closets. I asked for a booth and was in the process of being seated when someone tapped me on the shoulder.

"You've gotta be Jane," said a burly man several inches shorter than I was. "Prettier than advertised. I'm Ken Pentecost."

"I don't believe I advertised anything of the kind," I said, hackles rising.

"Oh, you didn't. Ray did. And he didn't come close to getting it right." He grinned appreciatively, showing off what had to be at least twice the normal number of even white teeth. That smile put me in mind of a jack-o'-lantern. Or a shark.

"Uh-huh. I wanted to ask you about Josh Gardner. He hired you, on Ray's recommendation, to check out whether his wife was cheating. You sent him pictures. In a cardboard mailer, and by email, too. Ringing any bells?"

"Yes," he said, in the manner of a man who'd practiced this speech in the car on the way over. "I did take that case. Pretty lady, the wife. Dark-headed. I went to a hotel at the I-64 exit by the fancy grocery store. Saw her and some guy. Took the pictures, got paid, and that was that."

"The pictures showed them in the act, right? Naked, I understand."

"Yep. Got right on down to business."

"I'm impressed."

His brows drew together, making him look like a caveman.

"How on earth did you manage it?"

He licked his lips and blinked. "Well, you know, I'm pretty good, and I . . ."

"No. You misunderstand me. I saw the pictures," I bluffed. "They were soft-core porn. You'd have had to be in the room with them to get photos like that. It's impossible. They were faked."

"Naw, honey, I have a telephoto lens and I set up the room and everything. You don't know much about my line of work, that's why you don't—"

"Bullshit," I said, enunciating clearly. The server brought us tall glasses of water. Pentecost gulped his. "You'd have had to know which hotel they were going to go to far enough ahead to have the desk clerks and at least two housekeepers on payroll to pull that off. Might be possible with an unlimited budget and a presidential candidate, but for a regular marital infidelity in Charlottesville? No way." Pentecost tried to bluster, but I raised a hand and he shut up. "You took Josh Gardner's money, but the setup was with Ray Corrigan, not the hotel clerk. There was no hotel. No naked bodies. Your skill isn't private investigation. It's Photoshop. My guess is you stuck Mrs. Gardner's head on a porn star's body. You took Ray's money, too, and I'd bet he paid you a lot more."

"Well, now, I don't hardly know . . ."

"Ray is dead, Ken. I think this job of yours might have been part of the reason he was killed."

"You . . . what? A few faked pictures? No way."

"So, yes, they were faked?"

He goggled at me, caught. "You gotta understand, I owed Ray. Ray and I . . . we go way back. I ran wild in my youth, got in some trouble. Ray helped me out. He tells me he's going to send me a client—kind of a sissy boy, that one was, but Ray said he needed to get rid of the wife, so I . . ."

"Who needed to get rid of the wife? Your client, or Ray?"

"Ray," said Ken, fully aware now how screwed he was. "He said the boy was going to move away for the wife's job and he needed him not to quit or some shit. Something about some bonus he'd get the more the kid worked, something like that."

Something like that.

If Ray hadn't already been dead, I'd have wanted to kill him myself.

"So you Photoshopped the pictures."

"Yeah, I never saw the girl in real life. All I had to do was use some tech to alter photos from the web. That girl had a million selfies." He rubbed his hands together, as if we could have a fun little crime-solving session now that we'd gotten the unpleasantness out of the way. "You think she killed Ray?"

"You know what, Mr. Pentecost? I'm not really interested in talking to you any longer. Buy yourself a meal." I threw a twenty onto the table. "I don't eat with people who hurt other people for money."

"Cold bitch," he said, pocketing the money.

"When you're asked—and you will be asked—you'll tell the commonwealth's attorney what you just told me. Ray's ruined enough lives. He's not going to ruin mine."

§

I tried Allison again. Still no answer.

Drunk on my own power, I drove to the address of Ray and Felicity Corrigan. It was still early evening. I might be able to catch Felicity or Brittany, or both, at home.

The Corrigan house was in the tony Rugby Road area of town, where the driveways were long and the brick on the mansions was Monticello red. I'd been once before, when Ray had been sick at home with the flu but had demanded I bring him files anyway.

An in-ground sprinkler watered an impossibly green lawn as I got out of my car on the stamped concrete driveway and stared up at what Felicity no doubt called a portico. Maybe this was a bad idea. I steeled my courage, skipped up the steps, and rang the doorbell. I was to be feared, I told myself. Felicity believed I was a murderer. *Stop hiding and use your damn power, for once.*

Brittany answered. Her eyes widened, but she stepped out onto the porch and pulled the front door mostly closed behind her. "What do you want? My mother will freak if she sees you."

"It's actually your mother I'm here to see. I think she needs to learn a few things."

"Uh, Jane, I don't think this is a good idea. She's not your biggest fan."

"The feeling is mutual. I have a few things to say to her. This won't take long."

She glanced at me appraisingly, then shrugged. "Okay. Come on in."

Inside, the space opened up immediately to a foyer so large it had a round table centered under a curving, ebony-railed staircase. I remembered the table. I'd left the files on it before the germ-ridden Ray could come downstairs and breathe on me. Brittany disappeared through a doorway opposite the front door.

I hadn't been invited to sit, so I wandered into the museum-like living room to my left. Good God, they paid Ray too much. A fireplace was flanked by matching antique chests—I'd estimate at least two hundred years old. Even though I rarely bought anything, I loved antiques shops, and hardly ever missed an episode of *Antiques Roadshow*. Those chests cost five figures. Each.

"This is a level of effrontery I'd scarcely imagined, Jane," said Felicity from behind me. "You couldn't have called? You kill my husband and you saunter in here to . . . what? Survey the damage?"

I turned. Both Corrigan women stood in opposite corners of the foyer, the table between them. "I didn't kill your husband. I have a pretty good idea that Josh Gardner did."

Felicity opened her mouth in surprise. She hadn't expected that.

"I'm sure the conventional thinking is that there's never a good reason to shoot your boss dead at his desk, but if there were, Josh had one."

Felicity said nothing, apparently robbed of speech. Brittany's brows drew together. "What are you talking about?"

"Josh told Ray he and his wife were moving out of state. Ray didn't like that—you know how much he hates training people." I directed that to Brittany, who certainly knew it after her summer at Blackwood if she hadn't before. "Josh's ex-wife confirmed it. So Ray told Josh his wife was cheating on him, and manufactured evidence of it to get Josh to leave her. The evidence was persuasive and it worked. I spoke to the person who faked it. When Josh's wife moved away without him, he fell apart afterwards. His ex, Miriam, told me that she spoke to him hours before Ray died and finally got him to believe that the pictures were fake. He asked if she'd take him back, but she's engaged to another man now."

"Oh shit," Brittany said, wringing her hands.

"Ridiculous," Felicity said. "You were sleeping with Ray. They found the gun at your home."

"I was never sleeping with him. And they didn't find the gun in my home. It was in a ditch outside my house—Josh must have put it there to confuse people."

"And the email?" demanded Felicity. Brittany believed me. She looked gut-punched.

"I imagine Josh wrote that, too, right after he shot Ray. He knew about my spelling thing. Everyone I worked with did."

"But . . . it all seems a bit unbelievable, Jane." Brittany was processing the stages of grief faster than her mother. She'd swooped through denial and was headed for bargaining. "Word is you and Josh are seeing each other. Why would he be interested in you while he was supposedly framing you for murder? That makes no sense."

It didn't, unless he'd only been interested in sex without needing to commit to a long relationship. He'd likely considered the idea he wouldn't have had a lot of competition while I was out on bond for murder. He'd killed Ray, and then he'd sent an email that would implicate me and dumped the gun at my house—when? That first time he came by; it must have been. God, how could I be so stupid over and over again?

"He's not really interested in me." Not for *me*, anyway. Just my outward appearance. To Felicity, I said, "I came here because I know you think I was sleeping with Ray, and it occurred to me that you'd never asked me if it was true. I'm here to tell you the truth. I wasn't sleeping with Ray. Ray was a demanding boss, but he never demanded that."

Not exactly, anyway. He'd made clear he'd have been happy to partake, but he never demanded it. I'd have left if he had. "I never have. I wouldn't sleep with anyone married."

Felicity closed her mouth, her expression going less hostile.

"I'd never voluntarily do that to another woman, and I wouldn't settle for less than the whole myself. I wanted you to know. That, and what I think happened to Ray. If you take some time, you'll recognize it's consistent with his character. He played with people's lives for his own convenience. He did it to Josh. You both must realize, deep down, that he did it to you, too. Your job at Blackwood, Brittany." I glanced at her, but she was glaring at her mother. "And your new firm expansion, Felicity. Neither of those things was convenient for Ray, and he was accustomed to bending the universe to his will."

Both women stood silent, like ghosts. Nobody moved for almost a minute. Felicity's face softened a touch—maybe I'd gotten through to her.

"I'll go. I'm sorry to tell you the things I had to say, but you would find out anyway, and maybe, just maybe, it might make you feel better to know that he manipulated everyone, not only you."

Brittany opened her mouth to speak, then shut it. Felicity picked up her phone and punched it a few times with a manicured index finger. Languidly, she raised it to her ear.

"Mummy. No. Don't—" Brittany tried to get to the phone, but she was too far across the room. Felicity held her off with a glance so full of disdain I sucked in a breath.

"Yes, hello, this is Felicity Kim. Felicity Kim Corrigan. I'm going to need police here. Jane Knudsen has demanded entry to my home. Yes, that is the correct address. She is out of jail on bond, and the conditions require that she not have contact with me. She's charged with the murder of my husband. Yes. She's standing here violating her bond. Thank you."

My feet stayed frozen as I reeled in dumb shock.

Felicity hit "End" and smiled at me. Brittany blinked, her mouth slack.

I turned and, for the second time in my life, fled the scene of a crime I'd committed.

Outside, twilight had fallen. My phone rang and I scrabbled in my bag for it, expecting it to be O'Callihan or Hossain but hoping Allison was finally returning my call. Not Allison. The number was unfamiliar, but I answered it anyway.

"Jane? This is Emmett Amaro. Can you come down to Lynchburg? There's been an incident."

I shouldn't, of course. I was officially on the lam. I had completely forgotten I wasn't supposed to have contact with Felicity and Brittany. I should turn myself in, but seriously. This, by contrast to a murder charge, was small freaking potatoes. And if I went to Lynchburg, it would take them a while to find me.

He rattled off an address and I repeated it to myself, hanging up so I could type it into my GPS app before I forgot it.

A house in Lynchburg, but whose?

I'd driven all the way out to the highway before I realized I'd forgotten to ask whether Allison was okay.

CHAPTER
TWENTY-SIX
ALLISON

The cacophony of shouted commands, crashes, and sirens from downstairs solidified into an unintelligible wall of anxious sound as every ounce of my attention went to Josh's face, bloodless like death. Whatever was happening in my living room was too far away by miles to make any difference now. Josh pressed the gun to his temple and adjusted his grip. He would do it. He had nothing to lose and very, very little to gain.

"Allie!" came Emmett's anguished howl.

I had so much—oh please, everything—to gain. I didn't think beyond that, just sprang at Josh, no idea where I'd fall, my target the arm that held the gun. I needed to knock it loose before he could get that index finger in place.

I didn't know what, exactly, happened after that. I couldn't form coherent thoughts. Everything was grappling and muscles struggling and wordless grunts and exclamations. And naked, shaking terror.

A concussion exploded near my ear. Was it the gun? I hit the floor on top of Josh. If I'd been shot, I couldn't feel it yet. The boom had deafened me and left me robbed of all my wits. Nothing made sense.

The door burst open and two Kevlar-clad sheriff's deputies filled the room with life, not death. They set me gently aside, murmuring comforting things I'd never remember, and lugged an uninjured Josh to his feet and out the door so fast it was as if he hadn't been there. A bullet had buried itself in the drywall near the head of my bed—so little time had passed that the dust motes still filled the air near the spot. I managed to get to my knees and let loose a few sobs before Emmett, who must have had to wait to let the deputies perp walk Josh past him on my stairway, dropped to the floor beside me and hauled me roughly into his familiar-smelling arms.

Sense returned.

"Are you all right?" He ran hands over my head, my hair, my neck and collarbones, frantic and breathing hard. Nothing burned or stung or hurt. Whatever bullet had made the hole in my wall hadn't passed through me first. "Oh God, Allie! Are you okay?"

"I'm okay." I ran my hands over his cheeks, trying to bring myself back to reality, to soothe him in return. "He was going to shoot himself. He put the gun up . . . I . . . I stopped him, I think."

Satisfied that his touch wouldn't hurt me, Emmett fitted himself closer and threaded his fingers into my hair. We kissed, fierce, desperate for proof that we were unharmed, until I had to gasp for breath. He was so warm and I lost track of where I ended and he began and didn't want to find it again.

"Of course you did," he said, laughing a little hysterically and hugging me to him. "What was I thinking, that you needed help?"

"How did you know?" I asked, mumbling in a daze of relief under his jawline. "How did you happen to come by?"

"After the last game, I texted you, but no response. And then Steve called me. He was annoyed you hadn't picked up Libby. I gather you were five minutes late. He said he'd just arranged it with you and couldn't understand why you weren't answering texts or calls."

"Oh, Emmett, I thought he was going to kill me. He was so . . . so . . . desperate and unbalanced and . . . off. So far off. He knew about Jane's past. About the pictures. I got the distinct sense he . . . he'd enjoyed himself with them. They'd been dating—Jane probably thought he was really interested—but he was trying to make a fantasy happen for real. A disgusting fantasy. She dumped him, and he kept going on about how he paid for fancy restaurants and she owed him, but it was so confusing."

"What was confusing?"

"He showed up at my door and took me hostage almost immediately. He blamed me for losing Jane. Because I told her seeing him wasn't a good idea while the case was going on. He kept ranting about how I'd ruined things, and he was so out of it, and just committing one felony after another like he didn't care about anything . . . that I asked him if he killed Ray."

"And? What did he say?"

"He denied it, but there was something there. Too long a pause, or something. I don't know. Nothing feels real."

"Enough about that," Emmett said, kissing my hair. "I've never been more terrified in my life than when I looked in that window and saw a strange man holding a gun. I can't imagine what you were feeling, but Allie, I swear I saw my life pass before my eyes."

"I'm okay. It's okay." I nuzzled my head closer. There was no close that was close enough. Maybe if I merged with him I could stop shaking.

Abruptly he slid me off his lap, setting me on the floor. He rose to his knees to face me and extended his hands for mine. Unsure what he was doing, I gave him my hands and got to my knees, too.

"You were right," he said, feverish spots burning on his cheeks, his dark eyes wide and glittering. "I did it all wrong before, but I'm going to do it right now." Our gazes met and held. "Allison Quinlan Barton. I love you. When I heard that gunshot just now, I thought . . . ." He swallowed. "I don't even know how to describe the . . . the wreckage, the utter devastation I felt. I never want to feel that again. You . . . you make me a different person. A better one. I don't think I can live without you." A half smile acknowledged the melodrama in his words. "I mean, I know I can stay alive without you, but it wouldn't be living. Not any kind of life I would want. I need you."

He gripped my hands tighter. My mouth went dry and my heart expanded inside my rib cage until the bones felt inadequate to hold everything in.

"Will you marry me?" He grinned, his face open like the sun. "And keep me alive?"

For a few seconds, all motion stopped. I occupied the space between before and after. The last time I said yes to a proposal of marriage, it had been so scripted and planned. The nice restaurant. The special date. The fact that Steve had ordered champagne when he normally upgraded from regular beer to craft beer in a fancy restaurant. By the time the server made his way over with dessert and a big bunch of flowers, I'd have been surprised if Steve had *not* been on his knees.

I'd never expected Emmett to propose on the dusty floor of my bedroom, next to a fresh bullet hole in my wall, with an unhinged psychopath being read his rights in my living room. I swallowed and the world—brighter now—began turning again.

"Yes. Of course I'll marry you," I said, and then to my horror, a huge sob escaped me.

After that, there weren't any words for a while. He pulled me to him and our lips met again, as urgent as if we hadn't kissed in weeks. "But," I said, when the crying and the laughing and the gasping eased enough so I could draw breath.

"But?"

"You've only gotten past the first obstacle. That was the easy yes. You'll have to ask again to get the more difficult one, and you'd better study up."

He rubbed a thumb over my tearstained cheekbone. "Right. Of course."

Together, we chorused, "Libby."

⁂

After I gave my statement to the sheriff's deputies and let an EMT examine me, I was free to go with Emmett, after no fewer than three deputies moved their squad cars to let him out of my driveway. Steve agreed to keep Libby for the night, and actually sounded relieved that I was okay. If he hadn't been so impatient for me to pick up Libby and called Emmett, things could have turned out differently.

On the way there, Emmett called Jane and asked her to meet us at his house. Some difficult conversations needed to happen. We stared mindlessly at old episodes of *Parks and Recreation* while Emmett force-fed me soup and toast as if I were sick.

Night had fallen by the time Jane's Subaru pulled up in Emmett's driveway. She got out in a worn T-shirt and yoga pants. I barely recognized her. Saturday Jane looked ten years younger.

At the doorway, Emmett greeted her with a warm handclasp. "Jane. It's good to see you."

"And you," she said. I turned to lead the way to the sofa. If there was hurt or loss in her eyes at the sight of Emmett after all these years, I was still not quite secure enough to want to see it, even engaged.

Inside, we poured wine and sat to compare notes of our eventful days. The conversation flowed without too many hiccups for three people with as much history as we had. Jane cast one glance at Emmett's arm, firm around my shoulders, but said nothing.

"Are you all right? Truly? He didn't hurt you?" she asked.

I shook my head. "I should ask you the same."

She took her time. "He didn't hurt me physically, though I was pretty scared for a second out there, alone in the woods." She glanced again at Emmett. "Allison told you about what happened to me, as a kid?"

"Yes." That one word, giving her the gift of grave and unwavering sympathy, made my heart squeeze. "I'm so sorry, Jane."

"Well," she said. "I won't lie: it does hurt to know that he's been looking at my pictures and coming up with sick fantasies for that long. At work, when we ate lunch together, at the coffee maker. It makes the office feel dirty and tainted, now. It makes me feel unclean. More unclean, I mean."

She bit her lip.

"And sad, of course. At my own naivete at thinking there would be a guy who'd never know that stuff about me. Who would want me for anything other than that. I fell for it again."

Emmett shifted beside me on the sofa. "There will be guys. I didn't know any of that when we dated. Now that I do, the most important thing I know is that you were abused—and that's what it was, terrible abuse—and I would never look at those pictures. There are guys who won't, Jane. Lots of them. They'll care about you too much."

"And you didn't fall for anything," I said. "You balked. He was off, and you saw it, even if you didn't know what you'd seen. You never slept with him, did you? There was a reason it didn't really progress. Some part of you read him correctly. You knew, deep down, that he wasn't okay."

"That's a nice theory. Let's go with that." She sipped her wine. "So now what?"

"Well," I said, "Josh never admitted even once while he was pointing a gun at me that he killed Ray, but he's clearly lost his grip, and if he blamed Ray for destroying his marriage, he has the motive to end all motives. He's in jail and won't be out until Monday morning, if he gets bond. You look as innocent as a kid on Christmas compared to him at this point."

"We need Miriam and the private investigator to talk to Nina."

"Yep," Emmett said. "No way Nina hears the sleazeball faked those pictures at Ray's request and Josh found out they were faked hours before the murder and doesn't jump the track right away."

"I'll email her what we've learned and ask for an appointment on Monday morning," I said. "You could be out from under this mess by lunchtime. She has to throw it out. What will you do to celebrate?"

"Oh God, don't say that," Jane said, making the sign of the cross like she was warding off a vampire. "You'll jinx it. We don't know he killed Ray."

We took a few minutes with my laptop to write up everything we'd learned from Miriam, Ken Pentecost, and Josh himself during his gun-toting break with reality, included all the contact information for Miriam, Ken, the Noble County jail where Josh could be found, the local sheriff, and Emmett's boss, Valerie Williams, the Noble County commonwealth's attorney, for good measure. I was proud of it. There was no way she could hear what we'd heard and not agree that Josh was, if not guilty as sin, at least a far more likely suspect. I hit "Send," closed the laptop, poured more wine, and settled in for the unexpected pleasure of reliving law school with my old roommate and my brand-new fiancé.

And I spared a moment of sadness for Jane: as bad as this day—the most frightening of my life—had been, it didn't touch what she'd been through as a child, day after day after day.

🦅

I still hadn't heard anything from Nina Hilcko by lunchtime Monday. It did not bode well. I gave up and called her. Maybe she hadn't gotten the email. Maybe she'd been in court all morning.

She answered on the second ring. "Nina Hilcko."

"Hi, Nina, this is Allison Barton. I was calling to make sure you got the email I sent Saturday night."

"Ah, yes." An uncomfortable silence stretched. "Yes, I did. Did you have a question about it?"

Did I have a question about it? Uh, yes. "I was curious to know if you'd considered dropping the charges against Jane Knudsen."

More silence. "You know, Allison, after your performance at the bond hearing, I thought, well, I'm up against a tough opponent. I'm really going to have to stay on my toes. But you've surprised me again, and not in a good way."

"Pardon me?"

"Last I checked the rule book, you defend your client by preventing me from proving her guilty. That is what they teach at UVA, no? Instead, you keep tossing a new suspect-of-the-week in my lap. It's Felicity! No, wait, now it's Josh! The girl-who-cried-wolf thing is getting old. You don't win a case by distracting me with shiny objects. I'm not a toddler."

Flabbergast, if that is a noun, cleared my mind of any snappy response. "Wh-what are you saying? You didn't even read the email? You didn't call the witnesses?"

"Oh, I called them. I'm not a monster or even incurious. Miriam Gardner said what you said she would: she didn't cheat on Josh and that she thought he might have finally believed her the day or so before the victim was killed. I'm not sure, though, what you thought the private investigator was going to say. He told me he took pictures of a man with Miriam Gardner and sent them to Josh Gardner. He said he knew Ray Corrigan—went to high school with him, I think—but when I asked him if Ray had anything to do with the job he did in the Gardner divorce, he said no. Josh hired him. Josh found his name, and Josh paid him. He never spoke to Ray about the Gardners in any way, shape, or form."

"He . . . he was lying." Oh no.

"I honestly don't give a damn one way or another. My job is to put witnesses on a stand who have stories that are relevant to a murder case. This one is not. I'm sorry the Gardners divorced, and I'm more sorry than I can say that Josh Gardner turned out to be a nutball and held you hostage. That's terrible, and I hope the folks down there in Noble County throw the book at him for that. But you said in your email yourself that he talked only about his obsession with Jane. When you asked him if he killed Ray, he flat-out denied it. There's nothing here, Allison, at least nothing that has anything to do with the murder of Ray Corrigan."

It had never occurred to me that Ken Pentecost would tell Jane the truth and then lie to Nina. And that was my rookie error—of course he would. He was afraid of being arrested for fraud and who knew how many other crimes.

"Do me a favor, Allison. Prep your case. Stop calling me and the law enforcement folks to change our minds. I'm sure it seems friendlier or more genteel to do it that way, but that's not how it works, and I'd think you'd know that."

I did, though the justice system might function better, maybe, if the two sides cared more about solving things and less about winning them. Court proceedings that started with scorching the earth and ended by salting the ashes too often missed the point entirely.

"There's nothing friendly about a murder trial," Nina continued. "We're going to court. To try Jane Knudsen for murder."

I swallowed. Dammit.

"Oh, and for violation of bond conditions. She must not have told you she paid a visit to Felicity Kim."

"She what?"

"Yup. I need to send a deputy out to arrest her, but if you can get her to turn herself in by the end of the day, say, tomorrow, I'll save them the trouble."

Holy crap. "Yes. I'll bring her myself by tomorrow afternoon at five if she doesn't come before. Thanks for giving me the heads-up. I assume Felicity is fine?"

"Oh, physically fine. She says she was greatly 'mentally distressed,' of course. Bond conditions are bond conditions. Looks like your girl will be waiting for trial in jail. Advise her to wrap stuff up at work today."

"Thank you, Nina," I said, aware she was doing Jane a favor to give her that long. A big one.

"I'm tiring of this case, Counsel. Fair warning."

Right.

☙

I had an afternoon divorce hearing anyway, so I pulled into the courthouse parking lot thirty minutes early, made a beeline to the Commonwealth's Attorney's Office, and asked the receptionist if Emmett had a second. He did. I caught him eating a ginormous hamburger so shiny with grease it would make a cardiologist faint.

"It would be nice if you could make it all the way to the wedding without a triple bypass," I joked. Emmett had a BMI better than most Olympic swimmers' and could run five miles without breaking a sweat.

"Eh. Who needs functional arteries?" he said, taking another disgusting bite and winking.

"If I were ever going to have an end-it-all-in-two-seconds stroke, it would have been very convenient during the call I just had with Nina Hilcko," I said conversationally, though the memory in combination with the sight of that hamburger roiled my stomach.

"Why? What happened? Is she not ready to drop the charges?"

"She's not dropping them at all. The private investigator lied to her. Says Ray had nothing to do with those pictures, and that they were real. She believed him."

"What?"

"The worst of it was she pitied me. Called me the girl who cried wolf and patted my head and reminded me that trying to distract her with 'shiny objects' wasn't criminal defense. It was humiliating as hell. Oh, and Jane violated her bond conditions. Spoke to the victim's wife."

"That's not good. Did she forget?"

"I have no idea, but she's got to turn herself in by tomorrow afternoon. Dammit. I can't keep her out of jail this time."

Emmett didn't think so either, judging from his expression. Lawyers couldn't save their clients from every stupid thing they did. "About the murder case, though. Nina's dismissed Josh Gardner as a suspect and she's going ahead against Jane?"

"Yup. That's it. He's probably already out on bond, isn't he? Today's Monday. I assume you did bond hearings this morning?"

"I did, but not that one. You'll love this. Guess who Josh hired for his defense?"

"Who?"

"Dan MacDonald. He wasn't available for a bond hearing this morning, so Josh is hanging out in jail until tomorrow."

Dan MacDonald was my old boss. He was a renowned criminal defense attorney and a horrific misogynist with a movie-star face, which created a weird synergy that caused him to appear in every "Hottest Lawyers in Town" list and collected him all the most lurid of criminal defendants. He was a formidable opponent.

"Oh no. That's just great. Dan will probably get him bond, and then get him acquitted, and Jane and I will have to move to a remote island off Newfoundland to keep him from appearing randomly at our doors. Oh wait, that'll just be me. Jane'll be in the state pen by then, busy filing motions for ineffective assistance of counsel. If you're coming to the Canadian island with me, you might want to invest in a sturdy winter parka."

"Okay, Eeyore," Emmett said, grinning. "You don't know Dan will get him acquitted. He's guilty as hell of abduction at least, and Valerie herself is handling his case. I expect she's going to want to hear from you soon—every single thing Josh said."

My mind started whirring. Every single thing Josh said.

"Wait a second. I just thought of something. Something he said. Maybe we can pin him down another way."

"Valerie's down the hall. Did you want to talk to her now?"

"Yes. Right now."

CHAPTER TWENTY-SEVEN

JANE

I took the whole day off. If I'd be going back to jail this afternoon, I damned well didn't want to spend my last day of freedom at work.

Valerie Williams had called the previous afternoon to see if I might be willing to testify in the bond hearing of Josh Gardner, and though I didn't want to be anywhere near him, I agreed. There'd be plenty of time afterward to return to Charlottesville and turn myself in. Allison would be testifying, too. To feel a little safer, I wore a pantsuit with a blouse that buttoned up to the neck. Every inch was covered, even in the heat of a Virginia summer.

Inside the Noble County courthouse, Allison and Emmett met me at the metal detectors, in the clear belief that I'd be the one needing comfort. I hated that they were right. It should have been the other way around: Allison was the victim of Josh's crime today.

We sat in the front row of the gallery inside the general district court, watching four prisoners be advised of their right to counsel via video feed. The judge, whose nameplate read Georgia Pearson, dealt with all those cases in a matter of minutes.

"*Commonwealth versus Joshua Gardner*, bond hearing," the judge said to her papers, then peered around. "Mr. MacDonald?" The bailiff, who'd been talking with the commonwealth's attorney like old friends, headed to a side door to get Josh out of what I assumed must be the holding cell, while an extremely dapper man with a slim file stood, smoothing and buttoning a suit coat tailored so closely to his body that he wouldn't be able to eat three extra bites at any meal while wearing it. An anxious-looking woman trailed him with the more conventional leather briefcase. She was very young, but she followed him past "the bar" separating the gallery from the counsel tables in the well, so she must be a lawyer.

The bailiff led in Josh. I'd expected the orange jumpsuit, but I hadn't expected him to look so . . . the phrase "rode hard and put up wet" from my North Carolina childhood came to mind. His sandy hair hadn't seen a comb in days and purple rings circled his eyes.

Valerie and Josh's lawyer took their places before the judge.

"All right. Mr. Gardner is charged with statutory burglary, abduction, and use of a firearm in the commission of a felony. You know perfectly well I'm not inclined to grant bond for an array of charges like that. Call your witnesses, Mr. MacDonald."

"I'll start with Greg Dombrowski."

Holy shit. I turned to see our managing partner walk up the aisle, his head thrown back like everyone in the courtroom was lucky to share air with him. He was sworn in and took his position. From behind, I watched Josh's head swivel, eyes on Greg as he passed.

"Mr. Dombrowski, how do you know the defendant?"

"I am the managing partner of Blackwood, Payne, and Vivant. Mr. Gardner is a valued employee there. His billable hours are in the top ten percent of our associates. He's a graduate of the University of Richmond Law School and has an exemplary record at our firm."

Everyone at Blackwood had to know that Josh's output had fallen since Ray died. What hogwash was this?

"Have there been any issues with him at all?"

"No. None at all."

Valerie raised her eyebrows and made a note.

"You're aware that he is charged with entering the home of Allison Barton, holding her at gunpoint, tying her to furniture, and preventing her from leaving his presence?"

"I am aware he's charged with that, but innocent until proven guilty. The actions you describe sound completely out of character for Josh. He is a very mild-mannered sort. I've never even heard him raise his voice. Like I say, an exemplary lawyer and member of my community."

"Would you have any concerns about releasing him to the community?"

"None whatsoever. In fact, I would invite him to stay with me until trial. I've made a call to an excellent mental health professional. I plan to take him there straightaway. That ought to alleviate any concerns. Oh, I should say. I'll personally post his bond."

"What about that, Ms. Williams?" Judge Pearson looked far more open to the idea of bond than she had before. "Any objections to that plan?"

"Yes, Your Honor. Though we have no objections to the defendant going to live with Mr. Dombrowski should he get bond, and we're all in favor of any attempt to improve mental health, we do have serious objections to him getting bond at all. This man entered the house of a woman alone under false pretenses and held a gun on her."

"All right, Counsel. Any more questions, Mr. MacDonald?"

"No, ma'am."

Valerie stood up. "You are prepared to offer a home to a man charged with all these offenses?"

"Yes. Innocent until proven guilty."

I wanted her to ask him why he was so eager to go to bat for Josh when he'd practically delivered me to law enforcement with a bow on top, but I suspected I wouldn't like the answer.

Valerie must have agreed. She asked a few more questions, mostly hammering home for the judge the magnitude of the offenses Josh had committed, but nothing seemed to blunt the effect of this upstanding member of the bar vouching for the defendant and offering him a home. The judge looked at Josh a whole new way now. I made despairing fists—these same tactics had worked for me, too. Wealthy white professional defendants got a lot more leeway than the impoverished kind I'd seen on the video feed accepting court-appointed counsel.

Allison leaned over to me. "Why on earth would Dombrowski make that kind of offer?"

I hissed back, "I assume because he's lost my billable hours now and can't abide losing Josh's as well. Before he got so enthusiastic about holding people at gunpoint, Josh was a pretty good biller. Or maybe it's just because he has a penis. Greg's not the most . . . evolved."

Allison didn't look convinced.

The next witness was a Charlottesville City police officer, out of uniform. Dammit. If there was anyone who got more automatic credibility than a law firm partner, it was a Cop Friend. He testified that he and Josh played golf on the weekends and that he knew him well, knew him to be law abiding and definitely not a flight risk, and offered not only to check in with him regularly but to set Josh up with a counselor to make sure he had someone to talk to about any "issues."

Valerie was wise enough to ask only one question of this witness: Was he aware that Josh had been charged with what amounted to a home invasion—statutory burglary, abduction, and use of a firearm in the commission of a felony? The officer said, adroitly, that he was aware of those charges, but that Josh was innocent of them until after his trial.

"Any more witnesses, Mr. MacDonald?" Judge Pearson asked, slipping a strand of hair back into her ponytail.

"No, Your Honor."

"All right. Ms. Williams, do you have witnesses?"

"Yes, ma'am. Two."

Judge Pearson checked the time on one of those desktop digital displays. "I'm behind here, Ms. Williams. I'm going to allow you to proffer their testimony, if Mr. MacDonald doesn't object."

Judging from their expressions, Mr. MacDonald definitely didn't object, and Valerie knew she'd been outfoxed. She'd be able to tell the court what we'd say without cross-examination, but she'd lose the opportunity to put a victim's face and emotions before a judge who'd already been impressed by the witnesses in favor of bond. Dan MacDonald tried hard to hide his glee. He wouldn't have to cross-examine Allison, a fellow member of the practicing bar of Noble County, before the judge who heard both their cases on a regular basis. "No objections."

"Very well," Valerie said. She asked Allison and me to stand in turn as she described what Allison had witnessed in her house, and the rage I'd witnessed hours before that during the hike. In turn, we each got the chance to verify that the descriptions of our testimony were accurate.

Dan MacDonald cleared his throat and said, "If I may, Your Honor."

"Yes?" Judge Pearson said, peering over her reading glasses at him. She clearly viewed this as a faux pas. He had agreed to the proffer, which had been intended to shorten the proceedings by eliminating cross-examination. He was asking for it anyway.

"I believe, if the court were to review the Virginia Criminal Information Network, you'd find that Ms. Knudsen is currently on bond, awaiting trial for murder. We'd like to point out that she may not be the most credible of witnesses, lovely though she certainly is. Ahem." He glanced at the judge, oozing charisma and magnanimousness. "Ms. Barton, however, we don't object to."

How dare he?

"Your Honor, Mr. MacDonald agreed to the proffer and is now attempting to have his cake and eat it, too," Valerie said, enunciating crisply. "We'd ask that the court not consider any of his uninvited proffers and find that Mr. Gardner should not be granted bail as he is a danger to the community."

"Yes, yes," the judge said, paying no attention to Valerie as she clicked away on her computer, no doubt to confirm me as a defendant in the state system. "The court will grant bond in the amount of one hundred thousand dollars with all of the usual conditions. Mr. Gardner, as soon as that bond is taken care of, you are free to go."

I looked at Allison and Emmett, who didn't seem either surprised or upset. Why?

Dan MacDonald flashed a brilliant smile in our direction, exactly as if he hadn't called me a lying murderer, and put his head together with Greg Dombrowski, sitting ten feet away. Presumably, he was giving instructions as to where to go to pay the bail. The bailiff removed Josh, shackles clanking, to the holding cell. Judge Pearson dived into a pile of paperwork on her desk, signaling for a clerk to bring her another pile. The courtroom was mostly empty by now.

Valerie nodded at Emmett, who beckoned at another deputy sitting in the back of the courtroom. I'd thought he was there waiting for another case or to take over as bailiff. He came forward with a sheaf of papers; then he and Valerie approached Dan MacDonald, whose brows drew together in baffled confusion.

Allison said into my ear, "This part will be better."

"What part?"

"Dan," Valerie said, glancing my way. It was an unmistakable invitation to listen in. "I hope you have a minute. And that you got a sizable retainer from Mr. Gardner. Well, I'm sure you did. You always do. It seems that Josh has been a bad boy. Much worse than we realized when he was first arrested."

"Oh?" Dan asked, wary at the prospect of an ambush. Greg's nostrils narrowed, ready for whatever show this would turn out to be.

"Deputy Morinelli here has a few search warrants for your client's electronics. Well, more than a few, actually."

"Do tell," gritted Dan. He shot his cuffs in a way that was clearly a nervous tic.

"While he had Ms. Barton imprisoned on Saturday at gunpoint, he attempted to show her some pictures on his phone. Ms. Barton saw enough on the screen to raise substantial concerns. Of course, the phone was in his pocket when he was arrested and is even now in a box of his belongings that will be returned to him should he be bonded out. We will be searching that phone, as well as his home computer, any additional devices registered in his name, and—oh, wonderful, Mr. Dombrowski, you're still here—his work computer."

"For what?"

"Child pornography," Valerie said coolly.

Oh my God.

Dan scoffed. Greg gasped, a touch too theatrically. Always on guard, I stared at him. Did he know? Had he seen my pictures?

"Possession of, at a minimum," Valerie continued, "and it's a rare porn aficionado who doesn't share with friends—you always get distribution alongside. It seems he had a fetish for a particular subject. And he told Ms. Barton all about it. She saw a picture of a very young girl in a princess tiara on his phone. Probable cause, you know."

Oh, holy shit. They were going to search all Josh's devices for pictures of me, and he was in jail and wouldn't have the opportunity to scrub them. Over the years, I'd known of other people arrested for viewing pictures of me. Child pornography was a crime that racked up massive numbers of felony charges—one charge of possession for each picture on a device. One charge of distribution for any forwarding or sending of it to another person. If he had even five pictures, he was looking at years in prison, and there were thousands of pictures of me out there somewhere.

Greg grimaced and stood, pulling his suit jacket straight and smoothing it over his stomach. He looked less comfortable than he had only seconds before. It never failed to surprise me how even lawyers could find some crimes understandable and others far beyond the pale, regardless of their codified legal penalties.

Dan glared at Allison. "Dammit. You. Of course it's you. I'm beginning to think you have a personal vendetta against me."

"No, Dan, only against guys who turn women—and girls—into objects." They locked eyes.

"Far be it from me to tell you what to do, Mr. Dombrowski," Valerie said, "but if I were you, I'd leave Mr. Gardner in jail so he'll begin his inevitable sentence now. In any case, Dan, I'm prepared to discuss this matter, say, Thursday morning? We can consider what . . . sentence your client might agree to for all of these matters, considered together, should we find what I expect to find on his phone." She turned to the deputy holding the warrants. "Go on and get started. Oh, and Dan. Ms. Knudsen and her lawyer, Ms. Barton, are invited to be part of that discussion."

"Why on earth should I allow that? What the hell does Ms. Knudsen have to do with anything?"

"I don't have to tell you that," Valerie said. "She'll be my guest."

"You damn well . . ."

I held up a hand. "You can tell him, Valerie. It's okay."

"Why does she come to the meeting?" Dan asked again.

"Because," Valerie said, kindness emanating from every pore, "she's the girl in the photos."

Despite everything, the sight of Dan's sculpted, spray-tanned face sagging into slackened shock was a little bit funny. Greg, on the other hand, betrayed no shock at all. Either he was a better lawyer than I'd thought, or he'd already known about my past. The unclean feeling crawled out over my skin again.

"Hey," Allison said, watching me. "Some good news, Jane. Nina got tired of listening to me, but she was willing to take Valerie's call. With her on the phone, Nina was willing to give you until Friday to turn yourself in for the bond condition."

"Why? Why would she change her mind?"

"Nina isn't a fan of child pornography, and she's been an advocate for its victims for years. Though she's not quite willing to drop the charges, she'd like to hear what Josh has to say on Thursday."

"Are you serious?" I asked, flabbergasted.

"As the grave. Enjoy the rest of your day off."

CHAPTER TWENTY-EIGHT

ALLISON

Some kind of elaborate negotiations took place before Thursday morning, because we ended up meeting in the conference room on Dan MacDonald's home turf. My old law firm. Dan's office and the conference room next door were designed to intimidate with opulence. My desk in the same building had come from the consignment store.

Josh had been freed on bond and sat, quiet but better groomed, in the chair next to Dan's at the head of the gleaming mahogany. A pad of yellow legal paper sat in front of him. The page was blank: a prop.

Valerie sat at the midpoint of the table. Her posture was so confident that her lack of a "power seat" didn't matter at all. Jane and I took seats at the other end of the table.

"Are we ready?" Dan asked, checking his watch in a show of annoyance.

"We're waiting for one more person," Valerie said calmly. "I hope she didn't have trouble finding us."

"One more? Dammit, this isn't a garden party. Who else have you invited as spectators here?"

The door opened and Patty, one of Dan's several administrative assistants, ducked deferentially into the room to whisper in his ear. "What?" he boomed, and then followed that up with a few choice curses. "No! She can damn well sit out in the waiting room. Nina Hilcko is not a party to this."

Patty and I had been friendly when I worked here. She looked at me, unsure.

Valerie didn't even raise her voice. "I think, in the name of efficiency, your client would prefer to address all possible areas of criminal liability at once."

"Nina is handling a murder case, and Josh Gardner had nothing to do with that murder. Your girl—" Dan made a rude gesture in Jane's direction. "She's the one."

Josh said nothing, but looked downright green.

"Fine," Valerie said to Patty. "Thank you. Do you mind telling Ms. Hilcko we'll be with her shortly?"

A vein jumped in Dan's temple. He hated it when other people gave orders on his turf. "You're here to discuss a deal. Let's hear it. You can go, Patty."

Valerie smiled, completely at ease. God, I wished I had her poise for even a second. Maybe it would come with time. Maybe—a blasphemous thought occurred to me—maybe she actually felt terrified on the inside, too.

"Very well. Your client is already awaiting trial on the home-invasion charges. Additionally, as expected, we found fourteen pictures of a sexualized minor saved on his phone, five in the deleted files on his work computer, and thirty-one on his home computer. He had, in fact, shared these photos with more than one person, so he'll be looking at distribution charges as well. Here is a list of all the charges he is facing so far." Valerie reached into a leather messenger bag in the empty chair next to her, pulled out two copies of a stapled document, and slid them down the highly polished table to Dan and Josh. "You'll note that these charges span three jurisdictions: Noble County, the City of Charlottesville for the work computer, and Mr. Gardner's county of residence for the laptop at his house."

Dan scowled at the paper. Josh's hands, clasped on the table, trembled. He never, not once, glanced Jane's way. Did he even feel an iota of concern for her? Hadn't they at least been friends before he swirled down the porn drain and came up with whatever horrendous fantasies he thought he'd paid for with expensive dates?

"I think you'll agree, Dan," I added, feeling a surge of nerves at jumping in on Valerie's show but unwilling to let him see me as a passive participant, "that it makes sense for your client to do a deal to avoid trials in all these different places with all these different juries. Every trial but the first will involve him having a criminal record, and there's enough child porn here for ten defendants."

"Get on with it," bit off Dan, ignoring me and focusing on Valerie. The vein pulsed in his forehead.

"We have the photos—far more than we need to put him away—and we arrested your client in the house of Ms. Barton with a literal smoking gun in his hand. Your defense will be . . . difficult," Valerie said, unperturbed by my interruption. "We will allow him to plead guilty to the fourteen counts of possession for the images on his phone here in Noble, and he will plead guilty to abduction and use of a firearm in the commission of a felony. We'll drop the statutory burglary."

"Oh, very generous of you," said Dan sourly. He realized how very far south everything had gone, even if Josh didn't yet understand. "Why are we wasting time meeting? Every photo carries five years. Plus the home invasion. That's not an offer. That's a threat. What you just listed is enough to stick him in prison for two lifetimes, at least."

Josh's head snapped up. His eyes were wide. If he hadn't understood before, he did now. He was going to die in prison, and it was the porn that would keep him there, not the home invasion.

"Nevertheless, it is an offer. An offer in exchange for a guilty plea to bring matters to a close. Is that a yes, or will we be going to trial on all charges?"

Dan was a smart guy. Further, he was a businessman. Dan took criminal cases on retainer—for a home invasion, he'd have asked for a starting payment of twenty thousand dollars or more. He'd get paid more for less work if the case ended here. "We'll confer."

"What!" Josh squawked. Like most criminal defendants who could afford a fancy lawyer, he no doubt hadn't considered the idea that justice might catch up with him anyway. "You're not going to do anything?"

Dan shushed him.

"There's one more thing," I said, holding up a finger. "My client would very much appreciate it if Mr. Gardner helped us solve a murder case in Charlottesville."

Valerie followed up as we'd agreed. "We'd like to know what might have happened to Ray Corrigan on June 15. That's why we invited Nina Hilcko here."

Josh opened his mouth as if to speak.

Dan, watching him, slashed a hand at him. "Don't say a word, Josh. What does he get out of that? Even if you've got him dead to rights for the porn and the invasion, why would he also admit to a murder? You're hardly going to *suspend* any of his time for an additional crime."

"It would be a small way to repay what he's done to Jane. It would provide closure to the family of the victim," I said. "He'd be unburdening himself, and doing the right thing at the same time."

"Dan," Josh said. "Let's discuss this. In private."

"Fine," Dan said, suddenly over all this and ready to move on. Dan was an excellent lawyer because he never wasted time dithering over the clients he couldn't save. Josh could not be saved. "But get out so I can speak to my client."

Jane and I stood to follow Valerie, who'd already disappeared into the hallway. When Jane stopped short of the door, opposite Josh, I did an about-face to see what she was up to.

"Please, Josh, tell the truth," Jane said, quietly, her face white. "You know I didn't kill Ray. I might have, though, if he'd done to me what he did to you. I might well have done it. You loved Miriam, and Ray destroyed your marriage. There's nothing Mr. MacDonald can do for you about the charges you already have. You know you're going to prison."

Josh started to shake his head.

"No. Talk to your lawyer first. Just do the right thing. Please."

A tear trickled down Josh's face and he broke the eye contact, looking down at the table.

"Out!" Dan yelled.

᳄

Forty minutes later, we returned to the conference room, Nina Hilcko with us. She took the seat next to Valerie and directly across from Josh. Valerie and Nina had conferred with Dan for the last few minutes of the break time. Valerie was unreadable. Nina looked annoyed. I had no idea what to make of either expression.

Dan cleared his throat. "As we discussed, Mr. Gardner has information relevant to the murder of Raymond Corrigan. In exchange for that information, he will plead guilty to ten counts of possession of child pornography and abduction only. Use of a firearm gets dropped."

What? Valerie had agreed to reduce Josh's charges. How in the world had Dan managed that? What the hell had Josh said?

Valerie nodded. "The commonwealth's attorney who has jurisdiction over the computer at Josh's house has agreed to these terms. No sentence recommendation will be made. At sentencing, the defense will have the right to make all arguments for leniency. The prosecution will stipulate for purposes of sentencing that the defendant was cooperative in this unrelated murder investigation."

Unrelated? What did that mean? I glanced at Jane. Her brows were drawn together. Something unexpected had happened here.

"Do you accept that offer, Mr. Gardner?" Valerie asked.

"I do," whispered Josh, all life drained out of him.

Nina spoke up. "I would like him to describe his knowledge of the events that ended in the death of Ray Corrigan. We will, as discussed, record this."

"I would like that, too," I said. Next to me, Jane murmured something prayerlike.

Dan nodded at him. Josh drew a breath.

"Everything went so wrong," Josh said. His voice was almost too quiet to hear until he cleared his throat. "But it all starts with Miriam. That's where everything fell apart."

Miriam? The ex-wife?

"I made the mistake of telling Ray I was going to be moving with my wife to Michigan. We had a huge environmental case at the time. Ray told me he didn't know where the hell he'd find a new associate who knew anything about groundwater or percolation. I have a science undergrad degree, which is rare among lawyers. Next thing I know, he tells me he saw Miriam twisted up with some guy on a park bench. I went straight home and demanded answers and she told me I was imagining things."

He bit his lip, his face awash with despair. Under normal circumstances, I might have felt pity. Instead, the memory of the picture of that beautiful abused child on his phone reminded me that he deserved every second of the despair he felt now, and the misery he would feel for the rest of his life.

"I should have believed her," he continued. "It's hard to imagine now why I believed him instead, but it didn't occur to me that he'd have a reason to lie. Sure, he was a dick of a boss, but I'd never known him to lie. Not like that. Not to me. He lied to his wife all the time. He lied to his daughter, but I guess I never thought he'd lie to me."

What a breathtaking description of arrogance.

"The next day Ray said if I was worried, I should hire a private investigator to get to the bottom of it. He offered me the name of one he knew, and I took it. Things at home had been tense. We'd been having a rough time anyway because of infertility . . . and . . . and some other things . . ."

"What other things?" I asked.

Josh sat there for a minute. No one moved. "Porn, okay? The legal stuff, but she didn't like it. Anyway, I hired the guy, and bam, within days, almost, I've got Miriam porn of my own—digital and physical— with some guy I didn't recognize. It was her face. It was right there for me to see. She still denied it, and that was that for our marriage. She moved to Michigan, and I went out of my head, but I stayed where Ray wanted me."

He uncapped one of the bottles of water the administrative assistant had handed around and sipped it. It irritated me. How dare someone who'd done the things he'd done drink water like a normal person? It was a good thing I wasn't sitting close enough, or I'd have knocked that bottle over.

"Miriam and I talked again for the first time since the divorce went through on June 14. I'd listened to a podcast on the way home about deep fakes. It's terrifying, what they can do. They can make a Republican endorse a Democrat, or vice versa. It occurred to me that maybe Miriam had been telling the truth when she said there was no park bench, no pictures of her. I called her. She'd found a new guy, was pregnant—I lost . . ."

Josh suppressed a sob but continued. "But she still said the pictures were fake. Even with nothing more to gain, she said she never cheated on me, and I . . . I believed her. I couldn't go to sleep that night. Ray had said he planned to work very late. I got back in the car and drove to the office past eleven thirty. I wanted to . . . I don't know. Yell at him, hit him, something. Get the truth from his lying mouth, at least. It was all him. The park bench. The PI referral. I had no plan. When I let myself in, I got to the end of the hallway leading to Ray's office, and I heard it."

"What?" Nina asked.

"A gunshot. Just one. I froze, and was, like, trying to decide whether to run or be a hero, when I saw him come out of Ray's office door."

"Who?" Jane gasped.

"Greg. Greg Dombrowski."

Greg? Managing partner Greg? Greg, who'd sat in on Jane's police interview and vouched for Josh at a bond hearing?

"Why, Josh? Why would Greg kill Ray?" Jane asked, eyes wide.

Josh wouldn't look at her. "Money. Greg was billing clients double. For each hour of associate work, he billed the client for two, and assigned half to the partners' column. Ray probably wouldn't have minded that much, but he really hated it when he found out about how Greg was assigning himself more credit for the firm's billing, to make his pro rata share larger than the rest of the partners'. Greg told me Ray was going to bust him at the partnership meeting."

"I actually accused him of that, at the funeral," Jane said, dazed. "I . . . never really thought . . ."

"Did he see you? In the hallway?" Nina asked Josh.

"Yes. He looked all crazy and waved the gun at me. I thought I was dead for a second, but then he kind of . . . recognized me or something. He smiled. Like I wasn't a threat. Told me IT had found stuff on my computer that shouldn't have been there, and if I said a word, he'd turn the proof over to the police. He reminded me that porn carries a longer sentence than murder, if you've got enough of it. He made clear he had enough of it. Said I'd be quiet and cooperate or I'd . . . find myself in a bad position." He smiled a terrible smile, full of self-pity. "This position."

"And the email? With the misspellings? Did he write that?"

"No," Josh said, looking miserable. "I did. We had this surreal conversation practically right over the top of Ray's dead body about who the police might look at other than us, and how to point them that way. Greg said it had to be Jane, and that if Jane had done it, she would cover her tracks. He waved the gun some more and made me write that email so his fingerprints wouldn't be on the keyboard. Since mine were, I put in the misspellings to make it look like Jane."

"Why Jane?"

Josh took a deep breath. The room was silent. "He gave me a lot of reasons. Jane was probably the last one to leave work that day and would be the first one to get there in the morning. Ray had said some sexual stuff about her to other partners, which could give her a motive. And Greg wanted to get rid of her anyway because he'd recognized her in the pictures on my computer. If that came to light, he said, it would damage the firm's reputation."

There was a gasp of outrage from someone—Nina, I thought. I glanced at Jane. She sat there, impassive. Greg had judged Jane—despite her star performance as a senior associate and *because* of the abuse done to her—the most expendable employee in the firm, even more than the employee who'd downloaded the pictures of her. The breathtaking awfulness of that made my stomach heave.

"The day after Ray was found, Greg told me to get rid of the gun," he said, unaware of my indignation. "Walked into my office like it was normal and handed me a red expandable folder with the gun and two handy rubber gloves hidden in office paper. Said to put it somewhere near Jane's house."

"It never occurred to you to turn in the gun? Even anonymously?" Jane asked, in anguish. "Rather than frame me with it?"

"He would have known. At that point, he had more on me than I had on him. I couldn't let suspicion fall on either him or me. Framing you kept me out of prison. I dropped the gun in the ditch, or whatever that was. That first time I came to your house. When I brought dinner. If it had to be you or me who went down, I picked you."

There was a long silence. Rage boiled and simmered. I held it in as best I could.

"Well, Ms. Knudsen, I pick you, too, to have charges dropped," Nina said, looking chagrined and sick. "We'll dismiss the matter today. Consider yourself free of bond conditions, and any violation of them. I'll make a call to Charlottesville right now, to pick up Mr. Dombrowski." She turned to me. "And Allison. You clearly had no clue who did this, but at least you were right that your client didn't. I apologize sincerely, for disregarding the email you sent me last weekend."

Jane wasn't done. She stared at Josh as if she hadn't even heard Nina. "I should know better than to ask this, but I will anyway. It was all a lie, right? You never really cared about me."

Josh took a long time to answer, never meeting her eyes. "You were a means to an end and hot besides. I figured I might as well give it a shot."

"Come on," I said, pulling at her arm. "He's disgusting."

"Were we ever even friends?" Jane asked. Her voice was nearly inaudible.

"Sure, friends, I guess." Josh's eyes, furtive and guilty, took in the ceiling and the wall sconces with avid interest. "You were nice to me when Miriam left. But it was a bad time for me, and eventually, I found your pictures. I'd always looked at regular porn before. After that, every time I saw you or heard you speak, they were all I could think about."

"How could you do that?" Jane's voice crackled and broke. "You'd known me for years."

At last, his eyes stopped moving and focused on her face. "*You* disappeared. The women in those photos aren't people. They're . . . just sex."

His last word, weighted and amplified with all its loathsome ramifications, seemed to ricochet off the paneled walls and pound in my head. I had to blink to clear it.

"That's it. Not another word," I said. The knowledge that I would one day have to release a child into a world with Josh in it—and all those like him, so many like him—made me want to smash him and this room and maybe the entire planet into bits of dust. I put my arm around Jane. For the first time, understanding began to glimmer. Since she was seven, Jane hadn't had a single moment of peace. She had to walk out of her house every day, wondering whether every person she met was thinking those things. It was impossible to imagine. It was monstrous.

"Thank you, Valerie," I said, "for letting us get this closure, but we're done here. We have no more interest in sharing another minute of our lives with this putrid excuse for a human."

I dragged Jane out.

CHAPTER
TWENTY-NINE
JANE

Allison towed me straight out the door and into the parking lot.

"I don't have words," she ranted. "That guy showed up for work and drank coffee and visited his mom and all the time . . . well. I fantasized about killing him today . . . right there, strangling him until he died or I did. And I still think I'm a better person than he is."

We'd reached the end of the road, Allison and I. They'd dropped the charges. I was no longer under criminal suspicion. I could go back to my quiet, drudge-like life and hide in my immaculate town house. I wouldn't have to spend much time worrying that people had seen the pictures or knew who I was if I never came into contact with new people.

Irene and Amir and Helen would support me. Irene had been there all along, Amir had shown surprising growth, and Helen might well be a powerful ally who would advocate for me to become a partner next year when the time came. I wasn't alone.

But were they enough?

I glanced at Allison, wrestling her stuff into her car, suddenly unwilling to let her go. We hadn't been friends in law school, and both of us had been at fault for that. I hadn't trusted her. She'd assumed things about me without facts. Suddenly, with a longing so intense I could almost taste it, I wanted a friend. Imagine the greed: I wanted a fourth friend, one who'd known me when I wasn't a billable-hour machine, when I'd drunk too much or stayed out too late. One who remembered a girl who hadn't yet outlived hope. I wanted to see whether it was possible to show myself as I really was to another person. Allison had seen some bad stuff and hadn't charged away screaming yet. There was still more, though.

"Do you have a few minutes?" I asked. "I . . . I think I need to stop running."

She put the last file in her car's back seat and turned slowly around, a slight wrinkle appearing between her eyebrows. "Sure. Do you want to go for a ride?"

"Sure." I opened the passenger door of her ancient Toyota. It gave off a metallic groan. The seat springs had seen better days, too. Allison started the engine and we drove off, out toward the country roads near the courthouse. It was a beautiful day with unusually low humidity, making the sharp outlines of the Blue Ridge Mountains visible to the west.

"So you were saying you wanted to stop running? From?" asked Allison, keeping her eyes on the road, almost like she knew it would be easier for me to talk if she wasn't looking at me.

"From my past, I suppose. I hate it that Josh had been looking at those pictures, and Greg, and IT, even . . . oh God. I can't tell you how much it bothers me. But those pictures are out there, aren't they? They'll always be out there. It happened to me and I can't erase it. I'm so tired of watching everyone I meet, trying to decide if there's recognition in their eyes, if they go home at night and get off to pictures of me. I'm so tired of believing the worst about other people. I'm tired of living like this—alone, and nervous, and secretive. I'm thirty-two. Do you know I've had consensual adult sex fewer times than I was raped in elementary school?"

Allison was quiet. She let me talk and didn't try to tell me what to do. "What do you want to do about it?"

"I want to get help. I want to be open about it, at least to Irene and Helen and Amir. I want to make partner and get the credit and reward for my hard work. I'm so tired of worrying that everyone around me will recognize me . . . that they'll see me instantly at my most vulnerable and exploit it to hurt me." I stared at my hands. "A couple recognized me at the C&O. I thought they recognized me for being a porn star. Turned out it was my arrest for murder they'd seen. I felt relieved . . . and . . . and powerful. To be known as a murderer instead of a child-porn victim. I realized that I liked it. That feeling of the absence of . . . shame. That's kind of sick, right?"

"Well," said Allison, mildly. "I wouldn't recommend pursuit of fame that way. It might be better to find another kind of power."

"Probably," I said. "But I don't want to feel like the victim anymore. I want to accept what has happened to me and feel like I have the control. Like I'm the powerful one."

"I know a counselor," Allison said, eyes on the horizon. "You're not alone, you know. There are probably millions of pictures out there, and you're not in all of them. There are other girls—and boys, too—this happened to, lots of them. People's reactions might surprise you; this isn't middle school anymore. I found a counselor in Richmond who specializes in this specific kind of sexual abuse. It would be a bit of a drive, but you—"

"Oh, Allison, yes. That would be great. Thank you." An emotion filled my throat, and I had no idea if it was relief, delayed grief, or . . . love.

"And I'll be there for you, anytime you need me. I screwed up before, but it won't happen again."

I couldn't speak. The road rolled under the tires in silence until I got control of myself.

"Will you keep your name, or reclaim the old one?" asked Allison.

"This one, I think. I'm angry I had to change, but most of the better parts of my life have happened to Jane, not Renee." A tear splashed onto my lap—I hadn't even noticed that I'd started crying. "I can recognize that emotion now—anger—where before I thought it was shame. I think it was shame before. And maybe it's good that it's changing."

"What about your mother? Will you call the police?"

That was a good question. I sagged back into my seat and stared out the window as we passed a herd of Black Angus cows. "I don't know. I'm damn sure I'm not giving her any more money. She's poor and unhealthy and . . . guilty as hell. I don't know. Maybe she's been punished enough. I don't know."

"For what it's worth, Jane, I think she could be punished a lot more. You know I have a daughter. She's the same age as you were when you met Pastor Stan, and only a year younger than you were when you met Len. There is no power on earth that would stop me, no distance too far for me to pursue him, if a man hurt my daughter the way you were hurt. She was your mother. Maybe she couldn't love you, maybe she was too broken and lost to care about you the way you deserved, but she was all you had. If it were me, my child, I . . . I might have killed him where he stood for that. I can't even imagine . . ." Allison swallowed and gripped the wheel tighter. "Anyway. You do what you think is best. No one would fault you for having her arrested."

For a moment there was no sound but the engine and the tires on the asphalt. Allison was a good listener and far more open to bloody revenge than I'd expected. In this silent car, on this lovely day, with my old roommate, who knew almost all the worst of me, I felt safe. Maybe she might . . . Maybe I should . . .

I would feel a lot better if I did.

"Jane, I—"

"Allison, I—"

We giggled. "You first," I said.

"Okay," Allison said. "I want to apologize again. About law school. I was so jealous, thinking that because of your looks you had a charmed life. I'm so sorry. I'm sorry I assumed it, and I'm so much sorrier than I can say that I was wrong. I never suspected. Not once. I jumped right in, assuming the worst about you at every turn. A true friend would never have done that. A decent person wouldn't have done it. Emmett didn't believe that Graham stuff—he only thought you wanted him to break up with you."

"I did want him to break up with me," I said. The truth was that I hadn't been sure I would be able to do it, but the scandal showed up at the right time. Emmett and I could never have worked. He was kind enough, but I wasn't brave enough. Not then. "I could never allow anyone to get close to me. They'd want all the stories—all the fun things I loved as a kid, what my parents were like, all the things I did with my high school friends. I've never been good at fiction. But I hope now . . . I hope, after this case, we can maybe . . ."

"Be friends at last? I'd like that."

We smiled at each other. Relief flooded me. Peace hovered just out of reach. There was one more thing I had to tell her before we could be friends. Real friends.

"About that, though. You're still my official lawyer until the papers dropping the case come through, right?"

Allison laughed. "Sure. I don't think you have to worry that Nina won't drop it. She'd have a hard time convicting you with an accessory testifying that he helped frame you for it."

"So, if you're still my lawyer, then everything I say is still privileged, right?"

Allison jerked the steering wheel over and pulled without a signal into an empty country church parking lot.

CHAPTER THIRTY

ALLISON

Oh, Christ on a cracker. "Um, Jane, I really hate it when people ask that."

Last year, a client had asked me about attorney-client privilege, and I'd told her it meant that I had to keep every word she said to me confidential for the rest of my life unless she told me she planned to kill someone. Seconds later, she'd told me enough to ruin my sleep for three months and much of my faith in humanity for all eternity. That was another story, though.

"Is it privileged?" Jane persisted.

"Yes, dammit, all except for plans to kill someone or commit bodily harm. Please tell me you have no plans to kill anyone."

"Noooo," she said, looking far too thoughtful for my taste. "But it has to do with what I was saying about power."

Oh God. Oh God.

"I'm getting the sense you'd rather I didn't say, but if I'm going to go to counseling, I want to be honest enough to get the help I need. I need legal advice to know what I can tell a counselor."

A car drove by and slowed. An elderly couple—most likely members of the church where I'd parked—rubbernecked at us to make sure we had no nefarious graffiti-type intentions toward their unoccupied building.

I sighed, one of the big, gusty ones. There was no escape. I was her lawyer and she needed legal advice. If it was as bad as what I'd heard last year, I could revoke my offer of friendship, drive away from her forever this afternoon, and never see her again. I braced my hands on the seat, gripping the sides. "Go ahead. Ask away."

"The porn empire was Len's idea. My mother was an enthusiastic part of it, but it was Len's thing."

A fine shiver started in my thighs. I put the car in park and flattened my palms over them.

"Of course, when he got caught, my mother pleaded ignorance and I didn't contradict her. I was afraid of being an orphan, so I helped her blame it all on Len. Online porn as a crime was only in its infancy then, and I don't know how it went down, but he only got ten years. Ten years for what he did to me. What he is still doing to me, every day, over and over and over. Someone is downloading one of my pictures somewhere in the world right this second."

Nausea rose. They probably were. The world was full of people. They all had computers. Far too many of them were deviants. "It was a travesty of justice. No question."

"I was almost thirteen when he went to prison. If the justice system worked, he'd still be there, but it didn't. That's why I wanted to go to law school, by the way. To figure out how a system that was supposed to protect me failed so miserably."

"Did you ever get an answer to that?" I asked, knowing full well how non-idealistic most law graduates ended up being.

She snorted. "No, but let me finish telling you."

"Okay," I said.

"Do you remember Thanksgiving break our first year of law school?"

That was out of the blue. What? "I . . . not really. I must have gone home to Northern Virginia. My parents hadn't moved to Florida then. What did you do?"

"I thought you might remember I left a day early. Blew off Civ Pro and Con Law and took off for North Carolina on Tuesday night."

"Yeah, I do remember that. You never skipped classes, and then you didn't go home at all for Christmas or spring break. Now I know why, of course, but . . ." In midsentence, a horrible thought went through my head. "That Thanksgiving was ten years after you were twelve, wasn't it?"

Jane held my gaze, her huge blue eyes sober. "Yes. Len had just gotten out of prison."

I pushed away all my thoughts, my concerns, my fears, all the rules and the rights and the wrongs. I owed it to her to listen. "And?"

"Len was the one," Jane said, something bitter and ruined and mountainous in her usually cultivated voice. "Len took those pictures. He started with suggestive ones, then a little touching, but the pastor had . . . taught me my function, promised me rape, so it didn't take long for Len to move on. The pictures got more graphic. His language got more explicit. There are probably prostitutes on the Vegas Strip who know less . . ." She swallowed. For a second, before she blinked, she looked as ancient as those mountains she loved.

I shuddered.

"Well, you get the idea," she continued. "And he did that to me. Len. You don't know what it was like. Even once I got away from him, there was middle school. Imagine middle school, only all the bullies have seen pictures of you naked and having sex. Imagine figuring out where to sit in the cafeteria or whether to answer a teacher's question when it might call attention to yourself. Imagine dating. Guys thought I was theirs for the cornering. Imagine begging a judge to change your name and help you hide your entire life, knowing he'd probably looked at the pictures before walking into your hearing just to make sure."

"Jane . . ." Dear God. I could imagine.

"That fall the prosecutor's office mailed Renee Starkey a letter. The usual one, to let the victim know about a prisoner release. My mother opened it and called me to tell me. She thought it was funny. At the time he got the sentence, I thought what happened to me was mostly my fault, and you know not a single person ever tried to tell me it wasn't. The first week of law school, I skipped ahead in the Criminal Law casebook to get to the part about child pornography. I looked it up. He should have gotten life with thousands of pictures and the distribution. They cut him a break, the judge, the prosecutor, whoever. I don't know who. He didn't simply download my pictures to look at, like Josh. He created them. He sold them. He took the most private parts of me and . . . and handed them out to perverts all over the world, forever. I can never get them back."

She looked at her hands in her lap. I held my breath.

"I went home to Galt that Thanksgiving and slept in my car on a logging road up in the mountains where nobody ever comes. I had to hide in the woods because people notice my face. It took me two days to find Len, but I found him. He had a home-cooking restaurant he liked, and I hung out in the parking lot and watched for him. From there, I followed him to a bar and waited until he'd had enough time inside to get good and drunk. I put on rubber gloves, grabbed an empty beer bottle in the alley, and called his name when he came out. He wasn't sorry. He was angry when he saw me. Blamed me for prison and what had happened to him there, even for that short little time. Violent, probably, if he'd been less incapacitated. I hit him with the bottle."

"Did you plan to kill him?"

"I don't know. I think I'd meant to . . . I don't know, tell him how much I hated him, but instead, I . . . I smashed that bottle into his temple as hard as I could."

I laughed, though nothing was funny. "If this were your trial, we'd have to work on that answer. You told me you put on rubber gloves first. I'm sure you know how that detail would play."

She looked abashed. "Yes. You're right. I did want to kill him, but until I actually did it, I didn't know if I would. Or could. He was a small man, smaller than I am now, and the bottle shattered into bits, I hit him so hard. He dropped and never moved. I let go of what little bit of glass was left in my hand and took off into the night."

"Did they ever arrest anyone for it?"

"No." She took a huge breath. "They never solved it. Wrote it off as a bar fight gone wrong. I doubt the sheriff's office tried hard—they knew what he'd been in prison for. I felt better, after I'd done it. Alive, sort of. Better enough so that most of that year, I almost had a life. Then the next year, there was Professor Graham."

She looked at her hands. "The power didn't last. It didn't erase what happened. It didn't even the score. I still need help with that, but I'm not sorry I did what I did. I don't think I'll ever be sorry."

I blinked and tried to sort out my reaction. Jane watched me closely, waiting for it.

It wasn't what I expected.

It wasn't what it should have been.

Maybe it had happened at last. Some criminal defense attorneys lost the distance with their clients. The clients' crimes became the defense attorney's crimes to hide or normalize. The attorney's moral judgment was eroded and washed away like a sand dune in a hurricane, until she looked at the world the way her client did: in terms of what was justified instead of what was legal or illegal. Or right or wrong.

Len had destroyed Jane. He'd taken what was left of her childhood and degraded it on film, out there forever for the most perverted among us to see for the rest of Jane's life and beyond, probably. He'd locked Jane away from any true human interaction for going on twenty-four years. She might emerge, but her therapy would be intense and expensive.

Most people would say killing someone was the most terrible crime of all. Even young children knew that. It wasn't true. Josh would go to prison for far longer than Greg. The system got it right, sometimes. There were worse crimes than murder.

I had lost my distance, because I wasn't horrified that Jane had killed Len. No morality in the world would convince me that she hadn't earned the right to do exactly what she'd done.

I was glad he was dead.

Glad, relieved, even proud of her. I could never say that out loud, though. Never admit it to anyone. Never again allow that thought to occupy the same brain that loved Libby and Emmett. There were ways to keep things separate, to block out what I knew about the vilest of us, so I could still smile and chat and walk joyfully where strangers were. So I could let Libby do those things, too.

"Well?" Jane asked. "Aren't you going to say anything?"

I checked the digital clock on my dashboard. "Sure. I'm going to say it's after noon. Let's go get a drink."

࿇

That night I stood in my kitchen, cleaning up the remnants of a frozen pizza Libby and I had eaten for dinner. She never ate the crusts—crusts were "pizza handles." She bounced alongside me in the kitchen, "helping."

This time, when the doorbell rang, I didn't freak out. Josh and Greg were in custody and Emmett had said he'd be coming by tonight. To be on the safe side, though, I didn't let Libby get the door until I was standing right next to her. When I opened it, Emmett gave me one quick wink and all the rest of his attention to Libby.

"May I come in?" he asked her in a grand, royal-retainer sort of way.

She caught on immediately, lifting her chin and straightening her back. "You may."

Once inside far enough for me to close the door, he dropped to his knee and held out a small box to her. Libby tried to grab it, but I commandeered her from behind, my hands on the fronts of her skinny little shoulders.

"Miss Elizabeth Barton, I would like to ask formal permission for you to become my stepdaughter."

"What?" she said, swiveling her head to look at me and scrunching up her nose. I held my breath. Slowly her nose unscrunched. "Oh no. Is this some weird way of asking Mommy to marry you?"

I doubled over giggling, but Emmett, God bless him, stayed on his knee and maintained a solemn face. "I'll try not to be offended at the 'weird' part, but yes, I am asking your mommy to marry me. That would mean you'd be my stepdaughter."

"Oh." Suddenly shy, she curled in on me.

"And," continued Emmett, "if I searched the world over for a little girl and her mommy to be my family from now on, I don't think I'd ever find any two people I could love more. So what do you say?"

"Have you asked Mommy about this?" asked Libby suspiciously. "Because I don't think she will let me decide. She won't even let me decide about piercing my ears."

Emmett gave in and laughed, sitting back on both heels. Knees hurt after age thirty. "I have."

"I said yes, if it was okay with you, Liberina," I said, my heart pounding.

Libby took her time with such a momentous decision and was not about to lose a chance to extract some conditions. "Okay, but I get to pick my dress for the wedding. And it's going to be pink, not that stupid green Daddy made me wear."

"Done," I said, but she wasn't. Done, that is.

"Aaaaaand," she said, managing an imperious eyebrow arch that would serve her well when she was trying a case someday, "I get ten dollars every time I have to watch you kiss."

"No way," I said, at the same time as Emmett said, "Two dollars." We glanced at each other, suppressing grins. I nodded.

"Two dollars for your college fund. Take it or leave it," he said.

"I'll take it!" Libby yelled. Emmett handed her the box, which contained a birthstone necklace. He handed me another one, with a different stone inside.

We paid Libby the first two dollars.

Later, as Emmett was leaving for the night, he said, "I never asked you about how it felt to get those charges dropped. Must have been amazing. Did Jane say anything interesting?"

"Nope, nothing much," I said lightly. I couldn't tell him, and he didn't need to know. "She's going to stop trying to hide what happened to her. She's a good person. I think it's time for her to have the life she deserves."

And then I paid Libby another two dollars.

ACKNOWLEDGMENTS

Writing acknowledgments never gets easier. I'm constantly worried I'll forget someone, just like an Academy Award winner who loses her tiny piece of paper somewhere down her bra and then forgets she has a spouse and children.

So, on that note, let me start with them, just to make sure! I couldn't write books without my husband, Frank, and my sons, Austin and Matthew. They encourage me when I worry I'm only a writer impostor, they cheer every little success, and when things get truly desperate, they decamp to the woods to give me the peace and quiet to make sense of my thoughts. I love you.

I wouldn't have the knowledge necessary to write this book if it hadn't been for the professors and friends I had at the University of Michigan Law School, and current and former judges Ellen White, Samuel Johnston, John Cook, Stephanie Maddox, and Brooke Gaddy. Special thanks to prosecutors Paul McAndrews and Sally Steel—and again, my husband, Frank, a talented defense attorney and UVA Law graduate—for answering specific questions. Despite access to all that genius, however, I take full responsibility if there are any legal errors here.

Thank you a million billion times to my crowd of writer friends, without whom I would have quit writing after the first thirty, forty, or one hundred rejections. Elly Blake, Jennifer Hawkins, Mary Ann

Marlowe, Kelly Siskind, Summer Spence, and Ron Walters—if I didn't have you, I would have a very large cache of Word documents, possibly in Courier New. You are the oxygen.

Thank you also to the many readers, encouragers, and hand-holders who helped me reach this point: Margarita Montimore; Michelle Hazen; Cara Reinard; Megan Collins; Cathy Moore; Brooke Wright; Sherry Harding; Dawn Osal; Meghan Crowther; Pat Davis; Mary Louise and Frank Wright; Geoff, Kari, and Audrey Button; Judy Oswood; and the rest of my coworkers and extended family.

Thank you to my irreplaceable team at Thomas & Mercer: Liz Pearsons, Caitlin Alexander, Grace Doyle, Lauren Grange, Sarah Shaw, Tara Whitaker, and Kellie Osborne. You are the ones who turn those Word documents into real books that people can read, and I'm well aware of how hard that job is.

I don't know where I'd be without my wonderful agent, Sharon Pelletier, who sends me calming emails in response to ones with subject lines like "A Small Bit of Neuroticism." Thanks for being just a click away.

My parents, Bob and Nancy Button, made books, reading, and words central to my life, and without them, you wouldn't be holding this book. I love you, Mom and Dad.

One final word. Jane is fictional. Unfortunately, her secret life is a reality to far too many children out there. There are hundreds and thousands—and sadly, hundreds *of* thousands—of grown-up Janes out there, trying to find peace one day at a time while hiding in plain sight. This book is for them.

ABOUT THE AUTHOR

Photo © 2018 Lindsey Hinkley Photography

Kristin Wright is a graduate of the University of Michigan Law School and has simultaneously been a small-town general-practice lawyer handling criminal defense and the vice president of the elementary school PTA. She is the author of *The Darkest Web* and *The Darkest Flower* in her acclaimed Allison Barton series. She lives in Virginia with her husband; sons; and beagle, Indiana Jones. For more information about the author, visit www.kristinbwright.com.